# THE ROYAL HANDMAID

# BOOKS BY GILBERT MORRIS

## THE HOUSE OF WINSLOW SERIES

1. *The Honorable Imposter*
2. *The Captive Bride*
3. *The Indentured Heart*
4. *The Gentle Rebel*
5. *The Saintly Buccaneer*
6. *The Holy Warrior*
7. *The Reluctant Bridegroom*
8. *The Last Confederate*
9. *The Dixie Widow*
10. *The Wounded Yankee*
11. *The Union Belle*
12. *The Final Adversary*
13. *The Crossed Sabres*
14. *The Valiant Gunman*
15. *The Gallant Outlaw*
16. *The Jeweled Spur*
17. *The Yukon Queen*
18. *The Rough Rider*
19. *The Iron Lady*
20. *The Silver Star*
21. *The Shadow Portrait*
22. *The White Hunter*
23. *The Flying Cavalier*
24. *The Glorious Prodigal*
25. *The Amazon Quest*
26. *The Golden Angel*
27. *The Heavenly Fugitive*
28. *The Fiery Ring*
29. *The Pilgrim Song*
30. *The Beloved Enemy*
31. *The Shining Badge*
32. *The Royal Handmaid*

## CHENEY DUVALL, M.D.[1]

1. *The Stars for a Light*
2. *Shadow of the Mountains*
3. *A City Not Forsaken*
4. *Toward the Sunrising*
5. *Secret Place of Thunder*
6. *In the Twilight, in the Evening*
7. *Island of the Innocent*
8. *Driven With the Wind*

## CHENEY AND SHILOH: THE INHERITANCE[1]

1. *Where Two Seas Met*
2. *The Moon by Night*

## THE SPIRIT OF APPALACHIA[2]

1. *Over the Misty Mountains*
2. *Beyond the Quiet Hills*
3. *Among the King's Soldiers*
4. *Beneath the Mockingbird's Wings*
5. *Around the River's Bend*

## LIONS OF JUDAH

1. *Heart of a Lion*
2. *No Woman So Fair*
3. *The Gate of Heaven*

[1]with Lynn Morris    [2]with Aaron McCarver

GILBERT MORRIS

# *the* ROYAL HANDMAID

Minneapolis, Minnesota

*The Royal Handmaid*
Copyright © 2004
Gilbert Morris

Cover illustration by William Graff
Cover design by Danielle White

Published by Bethany House Publishers
11400 Hampshire Avenue South
Bloomington, Minnesota 55438
www.bethanyhouse.com

Bethany House Publishers is a Division of
Baker Book House Company, Grand Rapids, Michigan.

Printed in the United States of America

**Library of Congress Cataloging-in-Publication Data**

Morris, Gilbert.
   The royal handmaid / by Gilbert Morris.
     p.   cm. — (The House of Winslow)
   ISBN 0-7642-2856-0 (pbk.)
    1. Survival after airplane accidents, shipwrecks, etc.—Fiction.
2. Winslow family (Fictitious characters)—Fiction.  3. Women
missionaries—Fiction.  4. Rich people—Fiction.  5. Oceania—Fiction.
6. Islands—Fiction.  I. Title  II. Series: Morris, Gilbert. House of Winslow.
  PS3563.O8742R695    2004
  813'.54—dc22                                     2004002031

GILBERT MORRIS spent ten years as a pastor before becoming Professor of English at Ouachita Baptist University in Arkansas and earning a Ph.D. at the University of Arkansas. A prolific writer, he has had over 25 scholarly articles and 200 poems published in various periodicals, and over the past years has had more than 180 novels published. His family includes three grown children, and he and his wife live in Gulf Shores, Alabama.

# Contents

PART FOUR
**March–September 1936**

# THE HOUSE OF WINSLOW

★ ★ ★ ★

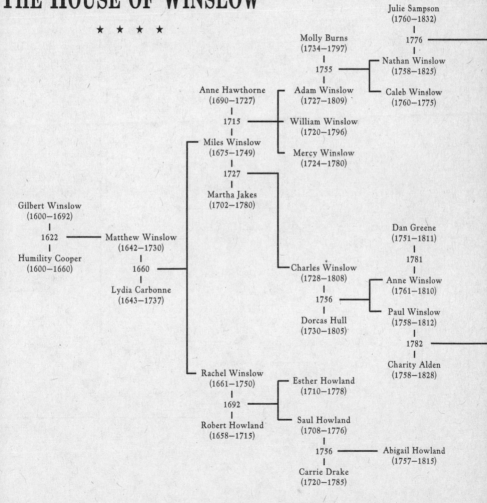

Gilbert Winslow
(1600–1692)
|
1622 ———— Matthew Winslow
(1642–1730)
|
Humility Cooper
(1600–1660)
1660
|
Lydia Carbonne
(1643–1737)

Miles Winslow
(1675–1749)
|
1727
|
Martha Jakes
(1702–1780)

Anne Hawthorne
(1690–1727)
|
1715
|
William Winslow
(1720–1796)

Adam Winslow
(1727–1809)

Mercy Winslow
(1724–1780)

Molly Burns
(1734–1797)
|
1755
|

Nathan Winslow
(1758–1825)

Caleb Winslow
(1760–1775)

Julie Sampson
(1760–1832)
|
1776 ————

Charles Winslow
(1728–1808)
|
1756 ————
|
Dorcas Hull
(1730–1805)

Anne Winslow
(1761–1810)

Paul Winslow
(1758–1812)
|
1782 ————
|
Charity Alden
(1758–1828)

Dan Greene
(1751–1811)
|
1781

Rachel Winslow
(1661–1750)
|
1692
|
Robert Howland
(1658–1715)

Esther Howland
(1710–1778)

Saul Howland
(1708–1776)
|
1756 ———— Abigail Howland
(1757–1815)
|
Carrie Drake
(1720–1785)

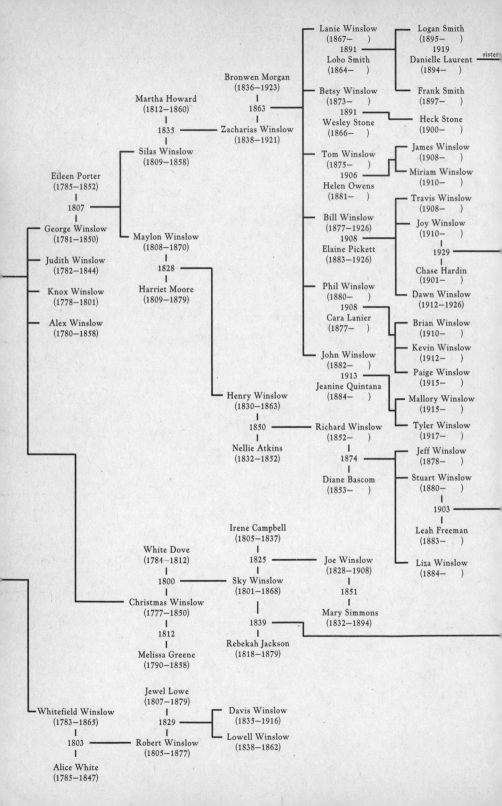

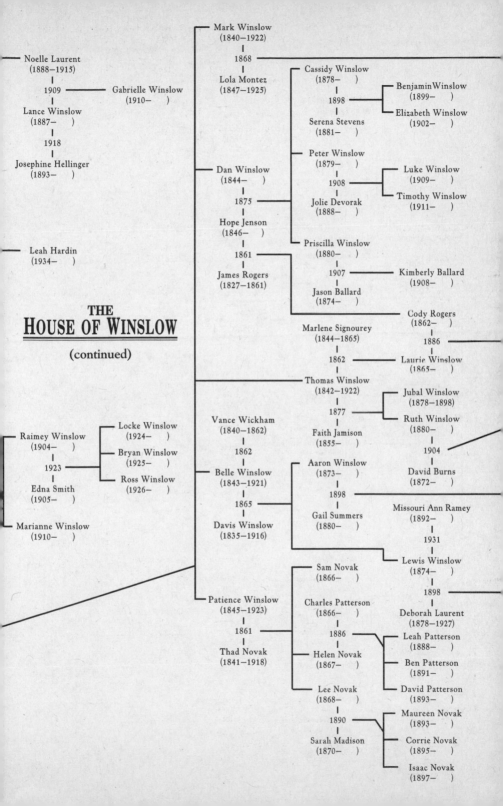

Noelle Laurent
(1888–1915)
|
1909 —————— Gabrielle Winslow
(1910–   )
Lance Winslow
(1887–   )
|
1918
|
Josephine Hellinger
(1893–   )

Leah Hardin
(1934–   )

THE
**HOUSE OF WINSLOW**

(continued)

Raimey Winslow
(1904–   )              Locke Winslow
|                       (1924–   )
1923 ——————            Bryan Winslow
|                       (1925–   )
Edna Smith             Ross Winslow
(1905–   )              (1926–   )

Marianne Winslow
(1910–   )

Mark Winslow
(1840–1922)
|
1868 ————————————————————————————
|
Lola Montez        Cassidy Winslow
(1847–1925)        (1878–   )            Benjamin Winslow
|                   (1899–   )
1898              Elizabeth Winslow
|                   (1902–   )
Serena Stevens
(1881–   )

Peter Winslow
(1879–   )            Luke Winslow
|                   (1909–   )
Dan Winslow        1908              Timothy Winslow
(1844–   )        |                   (1911–   )
|                   Jolie Devorak
1875 ——————       (1888–   )
|
Hope Jenson        Priscilla Winslow
(1846–   )        (1880–   )
|                   |
1861             1907 —————— Kimberly Ballard
|                   (1908–   )
James Rogers       Jason Ballard
(1827–1861)        (1874–   )

Cody Rogers
(1862–   )
Marlene Signourey
(1844–1865)        1886 ——————
|
1862 —————— Laurie Winslow
(1865–   )
Thomas Winslow
(1842–1922)        Jubal Winslow
Vance Wickham      (1878–1898)
(1840–1862)        1877              Ruth Winslow
|                   (1880–   )
1862             Faith Jamison
|                   (1855–   )            1904
Belle Winslow      Aaron Winslow      |
(1843–1921)        (1873–   )        David Burns
|                   |                   (1872–   )
1865 ——————       1898 ——————
|                   |
Davis Winslow      Gail Summers        Missouri Ann Ramey
(1835–1916)        (1880–   )        (1892–   )
|
1931
|
Lewis Winslow
(1874–   )
|
1898 ——————
|
Patience Winslow   Sam Novak          Deborah Laurent
(1845–1923)        (1866–   )        (1878–1927)
|
1861             Charles Patterson  Leah Patterson
|                   (1866–   )        (1888–   )
Thad Novak         1886              Ben Patterson
(1841–1918)        |                   (1891–   )
Helen Novak        David Patterson
(1867–   )        (1893–   )

Lee Novak
(1868–   )        Maureen Novak
|                   (1893–   )
1890              Corrie Novak
|                   (1895–   )
Sarah Madison      Isaac Novak
(1870–   )        (1897–   )

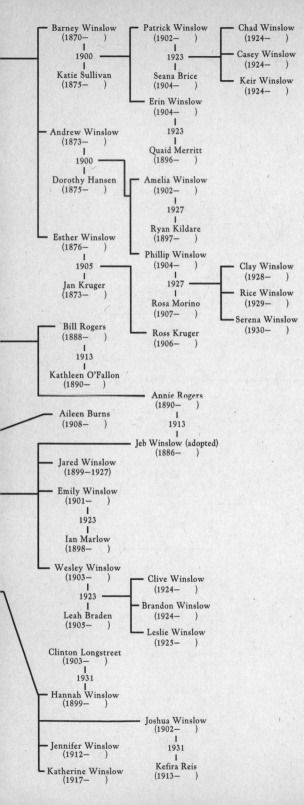

Barney Winslow
(1870–   )
|
1900
|
Katie Sullivan
(1875–   )

Patrick Winslow
(1902–   )
|
1923
|
Seana Brice
(1904–   )

Chad Winslow
(1924–   )

Casey Winslow
(1924–   )

Keir Winslow
(1924–   )

Erin Winslow
(1904–   )
|
1923
|
Quaid Merritt
(1896–   )

Andrew Winslow
(1873–   )
|
1900
|
Dorothy Hansen
(1875–   )

Amelia Winslow
(1902–   )
|
1927
|
Ryan Kildare
(1897–   )

Esther Winslow
(1876–   )
|
1905
|
Jan Kruger
(1873–   )

Phillip Winslow
(1904–   )
|
1927
|
Rosa Morino
(1907–   )

Clay Winslow
(1928–   )

Rice Winslow
(1929–   )

Serena Winslow
(1930–   )

Ross Kruger
(1906–   )

Bill Rogers
(1888–   )
|
1913
|
Kathleen O'Fallon
(1890–   )

Annie Rogers
(1890–   )
|
1913
|
Jeb Winslow (adopted)
(1886–   )

Aileen Burns
(1908–   )

Jared Winslow
(1899–1927)

Emily Winslow
(1901–   )
|
1923
|
Ian Marlow
(1898–   )

Wesley Winslow
(1903–   )
|
1923
|
Leah Braden
(1905–   )

Clive Winslow
(1924–   )

Brandon Winslow
(1924–   )

Leslie Winslow
(1925–   )

Clinton Longstreet
(1903–   )
|
1931
|
Hannah Winslow
(1899–   )

Joshua Winslow
(1902–   )
|
1931
|
Kefira Reis
(1913–   )

Jennifer Winslow
(1912–   )

Katherine Winslow
(1917–   )

# PART ONE

# May–September 1935

★ ★ ★

# CHAPTER ONE

# A Remarkable Graduation Gift

★ ★ ★

Like a giant misshapen elephant, a gray cloud lumbered across the sky, slowly blotting out the brilliant California sunshine. Loren Matthews glanced up at the bulky formation and shuddered at the sudden chill in the air, as if the moment were in some way a warning. Chuckling to himself at such a ridiculous thought, he turned his attention back to the platform on which the 1935 graduating class of Benton Bible College awaited their diplomas. The serious black-robed graduates, patiently waiting in line, reminded him of the penguins he had seen in Antarctica years before on one of his many travel adventures.

A smile curled the corners of his lips at the amusing memory; then he gave his attention to the young woman who was about to receive her diploma from the dean of the college. From his seat in the sixth row, he had an excellent view of Rena Matthews's profile. Auburn ringlets escaped her mortarboard and fell over the back of the graduation gown. She caught his eye, and with a pang of regret he remembered that her blue-gray eyes were the exact color her mother's had been. If only Loretta could have been by his side to witness their daughter's achievement. Rena's heart-shaped face broke into a brilliant smile, and he lifted his program in the air in a proud salute.

While Rena moved forward, Loren's mind was touched by memories of another graduation—Rena's elementary school graduation, when Loretta was still alive. In a vivid flash he could almost feel Loretta squeezing his arm so hard it had hurt when Rena had taken first place in academics. Then another more painful memory touched Matthews— Rena's graduation from high school—painful because Loretta was no longer by his side. Loren had watched alone as his daughter graduated at the top of her class and delivered the valedictorian address.

Loren had never stopped missing his wife. *I wish you could be here, sweetheart. You'd be so proud!*

Suddenly the dean called out, "Rena Gail Matthews"; then, after a slight pause, he pronounced distinctly, "summa cum laude."

Loren wanted to beat his hands together and call out in excitement, but he forced himself to save his outburst for after the ceremony. He watched Rena take her rolled diploma, tied with a scarlet band, and turn to the audience with a triumphant grin.

For Loren Matthews the graduation was over. There were more candidates lined up, but he heard none of their names, for his mind was filled with his daughter, the joy and pride of his life. Like the passing clouds above, another thought passed across his mind to momentarily darken the moment. *I know I've spoiled her. She's had everything I could ever give her. I hope I haven't done her wrong by loving too much.*

Pushing the troubling thought out of his mind, Matthews concentrated on the back of Rena's mortarboard, with its golden tassel dangling over the edge. Soon he heard the dean ask everyone to rise to honor the graduates, and the strains of music filled the late spring air. Watching the graduates process down the aisle, he was able to get a glimpse of Rena's face, and he wondered what this young woman, who had carved out such a place in his heart, would do now. *She'll do fine,* he assured himself. *She can do anything she wants. She's that kind of young woman.*

After the class had filed out, the college chaplain pronounced the benediction, and the hum of conversation filled the air as family and friends spilled out of their seats, anxious to find and congratulate their own graduate. Loren made his way through the crowd until he finally spotted Rena standing beside Dalton Welborne, looking up at him fondly. They were laughing, and another momentary sadness touched Loren. It was the pang that many fathers must feel at seeing a beloved daughter drawn toward another man who will become the center of her existence. Loren had always known this day would come, but it still brought a sharp, poignant grief he had not imagined. The young couple were not engaged, but as Rena put it, they were "promised to be engaged"—whatever that meant.

Loren stopped and waited while Rena and Dalton shook the hands of many who came to congratulate them. Both of them were popular and well known in the college community, leaders academically and socially.

When the crowd finally thinned out around the two, Loren walked forward. Rena's face lit up when she spotted him, and she flew at him with her brilliant, incandescent smile. He braced himself to take the force as she careened into him and threw her arms around his neck. "Congratulations, honey. I'm so proud of you!"

"Dad, wasn't it great?"

"Yes, it was." Loren kept his arm around Rena as he put his other hand out toward the very tall young man. "Congratulations, Dalton."

"Well, sir, your daughter beat me out again."

Welborne had pulled off his mortarboard, and his blond hair showed a hint of red in the sun. His light blue eyes sparkled with excitement, and his open gown blew in the breeze, revealing his athletic body.

"Daddy, can we go out tonight and celebrate?"

"I don't see why not, but I'll have to ask you again, Rena, why didn't you want me to get you a graduation gift?"

Rena smiled. The wind ruffled the edges of her hair, and some private thought danced in her eyes. He watched her face light with pleasure and anticipation and admired the strong set of her shoulders beneath the black gown and the shining auburn hair. Like the breakers of the Pacific Ocean, a wave of warmth rushed over him as he felt the pride a father feels in a favorite child.

"I *do* want a present, Daddy, but I'll have to tell you about it later."

"It must be something big if it takes all this preparation. I hope I can afford it."

Rena stretched up and kissed Loren on the cheek and winked at Dalton. "Oh, you can, Daddy, and it's one present you're going to enjoy giving!"

★  ★  ★

The meal at Francisco's had been excellent, as one would expect of the finest restaurant in San Francisco. But Loren had not fully enjoyed it. Their table overlooked the bay, and now as he gazed at the sun sinking into the ocean, sending its crimson glow over the waters, Loren felt uncomfortable. He had waited for Rena to mention the graduation present, but she had said nothing, and now he wondered with growing apprehension what was going on. He had not missed the furtive glances Rena and Dalton had exchanged, and for the first time, he felt like an outsider in Rena's life. He had always been first with her. Even when she was a child, she had sought him out to share her confidences. Now that day had passed, and his joy in her presence was shadowed by a pensive grief. He decided to come right out with it.

"All right, Rena, what's going on?"

"What's going on? Why, what do you mean, Daddy?"

"You know what I mean, Rena. You've got something in that head of yours. You think I haven't learned to recognize a scheme when you hatch one?"

"I never could fool you, could I?" Rena leaned forward and put her hand on her father's. She squeezed it and said warmly, "I wanted to be sure about everything before I told you."

"That sounds a bit ominous." His worst fears were about to be realized, he decided. This had to do with Dalton, and it could be nothing other than a marriage announcement.

Rena became serious, peering at him with direct blue-gray eyes that seemed bottomless. Her feminine lips, wide and clean edged, were drawn in a way he had learned to recognize. She had prepared this speech for him, he realized, and he waited until she spoke.

"You remember two years ago I told you I believed God was calling me to be a missionary?"

"Yes, I remember that, but you haven't mentioned it since." Loren felt an alarm go off deep inside. "You're not still thinking of that, are you?"

"Yes, I am, Dad."

"But you haven't said a word about it, and that was two years ago."

"I wanted to be sure, and I didn't want to—" Rena broke off suddenly, compassion in her face. "I knew it would be hard for you. You've always planned for me to stay close by, and I didn't want to disappoint you."

This was much worse than Loren had thought! He had been bracing himself for Rena and Dalton to marry, but instead she wanted to go to a foreign country. She would not only leave him but face the dangers of a mission field as well. A nightmarish scenario loomed before him, and it shook him deeply. He reached for his water glass and drank, giving himself time to think. Finally he set the glass down and said, "That's a very serious matter, Rena."

"I know it is, Dad, but I'm sure now that this is what God wants for me. And Dalton has the same calling."

Now Loren felt he was being discharged from his daughter's life completely. He knew she wasn't trying to hurt him intentionally, but she did have an impulsiveness that worried him. He tried to put his concerns into words, speaking carefully, for beneath her bubbling exterior lay a volatile temper. And when she was challenged, she could become stubborn. He knew it all too well because she got it from him.

"Well, you know how I feel about missionaries. I've always supported them, but Rena, it takes a very special person to be a missionary. The life is hard, and most of the missionaries I've known have suffered greatly."

Rena's lips grew firmer, and she sat up straighter. "Are you telling me I'm too soft to be a missionary?"

"Now, Rena, don't get your back up. I just don't want you to make a mistake."

Dalton leaned forward to speak. He had an assurance about him born from achieving success in any endeavor he had ever tried. "We've talked about this, sir," he said. His voice was pleasant, and he kept his eyes fixed firmly on Loren. "Naturally it will be a hard life, but God has called us, and we have to obey that call."

"Don't you see, Daddy? It's not as if we have a choice. We've seen the heavenly vision the apostle Paul saw. You remember in the book of Acts?"

Loren listened as the two spoke earnestly of their faith in God's call on their lives. He was wise enough to know that nothing he could say would change their minds, and he felt as if the earth had opened up beneath him.

The young couple grew silent and waited for his response. Sighing heavily, he said "Well, this comes as quite a surprise."

"You're disappointed, aren't you, Dad?"

"Not disappointed. I'm just . . . well, I'm a little apprehensive, I suppose."

"But you haven't heard what's going to happen." Rena leaned forward, her face glowing as she spoke. She was a self-assured young woman, and everything about her lent itself to this impression. Like Dalton, she had always been the brightest member of any group she'd been a part of, and that had left her idealistic, if not a little spoiled. There was not a trace of doubt in her voice as she said, "Dalton and I have been thinking and praying about this for a long time. We feel that most missionary work is so hard because it isn't planned right and it isn't done right. We're going at this with new methods, and we're not leaving anything to chance."

Dalton spoke up eagerly. "Yes, sir, many missionaries go to the field and come back in a year or two because they didn't know what they were getting into. But we've been studying for well over a year now. Both of us have taken all the courses available on missionary work. We've learned from the history of missions that some tragedies should never have happened. When the first missionaries went to Liberia, for example, over half of them died in the first year. That wasn't necessary. A little proper medical attention would have saved them."

"That's right, Dad," Rena added eagerly, "and we're going to be sure that nothing like that happens to our group."

"Your *group?* Have you already joined a missionary society?"

"Not exactly . . ." Rena hesitated, then took a deep breath. "That's what we want to tell you. We're not joining any society. There are some very wonderful groups, but we need the freedom to do what we think is right."

"I don't like the sound of that," Loren said bluntly. "The missionaries I know talk about the importance of being responsible to a board or a denomination. They all seem to feel they needed to be accountable."

"We'll be accountable to God, Dad."

This did not seem right to Loren, but he put that aside for the moment. "If you aren't joining a missionary society, then what group are you talking about?"

"It's our own group, Dad. And it's all planned out already. There are going to be twelve of us, and we're going to call ourselves 'The Twelve.'"

"And, sir, we definitely feel that our work will be in the South Seas," Dalton added. "We're not sure exactly where, but God will reveal that to us. That's another problem with most missionary societies. *They* decide where the missionaries will go, but we want to find God's will for us by ourselves. That way we'll be sure of exactly where He wants us to go."

Loren listened with growing apprehension and sadness. He saw that the two had made up their minds, and there was little he could do about it. Finally he found the opportunity to ask an important question. "Missionary work takes money. If you're not going to be sponsored by a society, how will you be financed?" He saw something pass across Dalton's face, but the young man remained silent and it was Rena who answered.

"Dad, I've heard you say so many times that God has given you riches so that you can share it with others, and I hope you'll support our group."

Loren had never refused his daughter anything, but now he felt he had lost control of the situation.

Seeing her father's hesitation, Rena said, "I know you love missionaries and their work. This is one time, Dad, I'd like to have your approval. You've asked me what you could give me for graduation. This is what I want. I want you to be one of us. Naturally you can't go, but you can support those that do. It's all I want, Dad."

Rena's proposal had blindsided him, for he had put aside her earlier interest in missionary work as a passing phase. She had committed her life to Christ at the age of fifteen and had lived a life of faith ever since. He had been proud to see her take leadership in their church, but now he felt heavy with doubt. He tried to buy time by saying, "I'll, of course, pray about it."

"I knew you'd say that, Dad." Rena smiled with the self-assurance with which he was so familiar, for both father and daughter shared the trait. He had become a successful businessman starting from nothing, and now he had more money than he could ever use. Giving money for the mission work was not a problem, but worrying about what would happen to his daughter was.

"Are you and Dalton planning to get married?"

"No, sir, not right away," Dalton said quickly. "I'd like to marry her today, but this daughter of yours is headstrong." He winked and said, "I think I know where she gets it from."

"I think getting married would take our minds off our work," Rena explained, "so I've asked Dalton to wait for a time, at least a year. That way we can give all of our energy to the mission."

Rena waited with an expression her father had not seen before. He had always been happy to oblige her requests, always giving her more than she asked for. But she had never before asked for anything so big! Suddenly he had the feeling that things had passed beyond his control.

"I might as well tell you the rest of it, Dad, so you can pray about that too."

Loren was almost afraid to ask. "What's that?"

For the first time Rena showed some apprehension, but nonetheless she faced her father squarely. "I want you to help us get to the mission station in the *Mary Anne*."

Loren Matthews had always loved the sea, and the schooner was the one bit of ostentation that he allowed himself. The *Mary Anne* was a beautiful deep-water sailing yacht. Owning such a ship had been the dream of his life, and from the day he had bought the schooner, he lived for the times he could get away from business and stand at the wheel on the high seas. He had not gone sailing much in the past year, however, for he had developed heart trouble, but the schooner was still his first love after his daughter.

"If I agree," Loren said quietly, "of course we'll get you to the South Seas in the *Mary Anne*, but I'll have to have much time to pray about it."

"Dad, I knew you'd agree, and I know how much the *Mary Anne* means to you."

"Well, we'll leave it at that, then, but if I'm going to be involved in this, I'll have to have some word from God and a peace about it."

"Dad, this time I think you'll have to trust our vision—

Dalton's and mine and the others'. That's the way it was in the book of Acts. You remember how Paul had a vision of a man in Macedonia who said, 'Come over into Macedonia, and help us'? The Bible says they set off straightaway for Macedonia. So it was Paul who had the vision, and the others just had to trust him. Dad, please, I want you to trust me—and Dalton."

Loren understood that if he wanted to keep a firm place in his daughter's heart, he would have to go along with this scheme. He had always been able to make quick decisions in business, and most of the time his instincts were right. As much as this decision hurt him, he somehow felt it might be right.

"All right, daughter, unless I get a direct no from God, I'll stand behind you."

Rena gasped and tears welled in her eyes. "Didn't I tell you, Dalton?" she said. "I told you Dad would be with us." She jumped up, knocking over her glass of water. As Loren got to his feet, she threw herself into his arms. "Thank you, Daddy. I knew you'd understand!"

Loren was not at all sure that he understood, but he knew this was something he had to do. His daughter meant more to him than anything except his loyalty to God, and now he prayed, *Oh, God, I hope I'm doing the right thing. You'll just have to watch over these young people.*

★ ★ ★

"What in the world is this, Rena?" Loren asked less than two weeks later.

Rena, who was working at a desk full of papers, looked up at the newspaper her father held out. "Oh, that's just a story about our work."

Loren read the headline aloud, disgust dripping in his tone. "'Socialite Hits the Glory Trail.' What do you mean by giving out a story like this?"

"I didn't give it out, Dad. I think Dalton talked to a

reporter, and he made all that up—the reporter, I mean."

"It's a terrible story! It trivializes everything your mission stands for."

"Don't worry about it," Rena said. "It'll be good publicity."

Flinging himself into a chair, Loren skimmed the story again, then shook his head with disgust. "It makes you look like a bunch of playboys and social butterflies."

"Nobody believes anything they read in the newspaper."

"I don't like it, Rena."

Rena got up and came around the desk to sit on the arm of her father's chair. She put her arm around his neck and said, "Dad, don't worry about it. Nobody will even remember what it said a week from now."

"Well, I still don't like it."

"You sit right here. I want to show you something."

Rena went quickly to the desk and picked up a paper. "Dalton and I have been very busy making the final selection for the group. I want you to look at them."

Loren took the paper she handed him and glanced at the ten names on it. "Do you know all of these people?"

"Why, of course. Most of them were at college with us. Here, we'll be having them over to dinner tonight, and I want you to study this list and be sure that we agree."

"What if we don't?"

"Oh, Dad, Dalton and I have put in a lot of time on this, but we'd feel better if you'd look at it. Here, let me fill you in on it." She pointed to the first two names and said, "This is Jimmy Townsend and his wife, Abigail."

"You're taking a married couple?"

"Yes—they're newlyweds. They've only been married a month."

"Who are they?"

"Jimmy's father is a successful contractor. He owns a construction business."

"How does he feel about his son becoming a missionary?"

"Well, he's disappointed. He's always wanted Jimmy to

go into the business with him, but Jimmy couldn't see it that way. And Jimmy's wife, Abby, is a dear girl. A bit timid, but she'll get over that when she gets on the field."

"I can't believe a timid woman would be able to face up to some of the things I've heard foreign missionaries have to do."

"She's not too old to change! Jimmy's twenty-five, and she's a year younger. And here's the good thing about it, Dad. Once Jimmy proves himself, his dad has all the money in the world. We can get him involved in the work too. He'll be a great supporter once we sell him on the idea." Rena pointed to the paper again. "There's Karl Benson. He's thirty-two and a very interesting man, and one of the most brilliant I've ever met. He even went through medical school, although he never received his degree."

"Why not?"

"He decided God was calling him to serve on the mission field instead of becoming a doctor."

"It'll certainly be handy to have somebody along with some medical knowledge."

"I don't think Karl does much in the way of medicine."

"Somebody will have to."

"I suppose. But look—here's a real prize. Professor Jan Dekker."

"A professor of what?"

"Of theology. He was our professor, Dalton's and mine, for most of our theology and anthropology courses. He's a brilliant theologian and a great scholar."

"How old is he?"

"Fifty-one." Rena hesitated and then said, "He's a bit liberal. Doesn't quite see the Scriptures the way we do."

"How does he see them?"

"He doesn't believe all of them are inspired."

"Oh? And just how does he decide which are and which aren't? I don't much like that."

"Never mind that, Dad. He's anxious to go to the field. He's never done anything but stay in the classroom, and now he's ready to try out some of his theories for real."

Rena saw that her father was not particularly impressed with Professor Dekker and moved on quickly down the list. "Now, Peter Alford. There's a man you would like very much." She bit her lip and shook her head. "He's a little slow, but he's a very fine young man. Strong too. And his heart's as big as he is. Everybody likes Pete."

Loren fired questions concerning Peter, then finally asked, "What about the women?"

"I've told you about Abby. And you know my best friend, Jeanne Vernay. She's going to be one of The Twelve."

"You two have been in competition for grades and everything else for as long as I can remember."

"Yes, and I think that's good."

"I'm not sure it is. Competing on a mission field might be troublesome."

"Oh, Jeanne and I will be fine."

Loren raised a skeptical brow. "She's a real socialite. I can't imagine her wanting to be a missionary."

"She says she does," Rena said with a shrug. "She hasn't been thinking about it for long, but she's got lots of self-confidence." She moved on quickly. "Here's another one of my classmates, Lanie MacKay. She's very handy at a lot of things."

"Why did you pick her?"

"For one, because she asked to go, and also because she'll be good for doing the practical things. All those day-to-day things missionaries have to do for themselves, you know. As a matter of fact, so will Margaret Smith." Rena bit her lip. "I hesitated about including Margaret. She's overweight, and she may find it all a bit arduous, but she is a fine cook and a great seamstress. She's good at all kinds of practical things, you know, and she loves the Lord too. Her father is a pastor. She's a little shy, but I know I can help her with that."

"What about this Meredith Wynne? That's an odd name."

"I'm not sure about her. Actually, she's the one we'll need to pray about."

"Why? What's wrong with her?"

"Well, she's not very . . ." Rena hesitated. "I don't know. She's brilliant, of course. She's a linguist. That's the reason Dalton and I finally agreed to consider her. We'll need someone to teach us the language, and Meredith can pick up languages as easily as most people pick up a new recipe."

The two continued to go over the list until Rena said, "You'll meet them all at dinner tonight, but what do you think about them so far—just from what I've told you?"

"Truthfully?"

"Of course, Dad."

"I'm a little worried. There's not one person on this list who has actually done any missionary work."

"I know, but we can all learn together. It'll take a little shaking down, but it'll come along all right. I'm sure of it."

"It won't be an easy life, Rena. I know you get tired of my saying this, but it's true."

"We'll hire natives to do the hard physical work, and since you've been so good to let us use the *Mary Anne* and supply us, we won't have to worry about all the details most missionaries do."

Loren laughed. "I think I bought enough supplies to feed a whole village for a year!"

"I know. You've been great about it, Dad."

"But there are only eleven on this list."

Rena nodded. "I know. We're having trouble deciding on the last member. Maybe you can help us select the right one."

"I'd like that."

She jumped up and began to pace the floor, her words tumbling out in her excitement. "It's going to be so wonderful! I'm going to keep careful records so I can show the world what great things can be done on a mission field when it's done right. Of course," she said with a smile, "we couldn't do it without you."

Loren knew this was an honest statement. His daughter did honor him and had made him, as much as she could, a part of the group. He looked down at the list in his hand

and wanted to argue that some of the choices were not the best, but he kept quiet. Rena had the bit in her teeth and was speeding away. Nothing he could say was going to slow her down.

He watched as she flung herself around the room, her eyes brilliant with expectation, and he prayed silently, *Lord, you're going to have to help Rena and the rest of them. They don't know what they're getting into!*

# CHAPTER TWO

# TRAVIS'S MARCHING ORDERS

★ ★ ★

Travis Winslow glanced up at the banner spread out above him proclaiming the Barnum and Bailey Circus. He shook his head, and a slight grin touched his lips as he murmured, "Sis and Chase have sure come up in the world. Not much like the old Carter Brothers Circus. You could have stuck the whole thing in one corner of this one."

The air was rich with circus smells—popcorn, hot dogs, and the acrid aroma of wild animals. No amount of perfume could cover up that! This scene had once been his life, but now as Travis walked along between the sideshows where barkers were shilling the acts, all of that seemed in the very distant past. In fact, it had only been a few years since Travis had been a part of the Carter Brothers Circus, along with his sister, Joy.

When Joy married Chase Hardin, Travis left to enter Bible school with plans to become a minister. The Hardins had since moved on into the world of big-time show business with their now world-famous wild animal act in "The Greatest Show on Earth."

A lion's roar penetrated the sounds of laughter and

shouting from the people in line to purchase tickets. *Must be one of Joy's pets*, Travis thought. *I still can't believe she'd get in the ring with those big cats.*

As Travis edged forward to buy his ticket, his mind replayed memories of how he and Joy ran away from home after their parents had been killed in an automobile accident. Their aunt and uncle took them in, but it was not a happy situation. Travis headed south and eventually got a job on a steamship going to South America. While ashore in Mexico, a man was seriously hurt in a saloon brawl, and Travis was arrested, along with two other Americans, and had to do a year in a Mexican jail. He remembered his shock when he learned that his sister had joined the circus. She eventually became engaged to another animal trainer.

Travis slapped his money on the counter, and a hard-eyed woman with strawlike hair tore off a ticket and handed it to him. "Hope you like it, handsome." She grinned, revealing a missing front tooth.

"I always did." Travis returned her smile. Jostled by the crowd, he moved inside the tent, found his seat, and settled down. While he waited he watched the excited youngsters around him, bright-eyed with anticipation. He noticed a middle-aged woman with three small children who was having a difficult time trying to keep them corralled. "Let me help you with that young'un, ma'am," Travis offered with a smile. He reached out his arms, and the woman gave him a startled look, then laughed. "Don't know if you can or not. He's wild."

"Let me have a try." Travis took the baby and proceeded to make friends at once. The woman was grateful and said, "You must've had some experience with babies."

"I've always liked them but haven't had any of my own yet. This fellow is a fine one."

The two chatted until the lights dimmed and the ringmaster made his entrance. Travis held the baby, asleep now despite the noise, and listened to the ringmaster's grand promises about the most spectacular acts in the world. He felt his mind slipping back to those earlier days. He had good memories of his time with the circus, yet he had no regrets about leaving.

The ringmaster's stentorian voice rang out, "And now, ladies and gentlemen and children of all ages, I introduce to you Captain Chase Hardin and his wife, the courageous and beautiful Joy Hardin. You will see them enter a cage with twenty ferocious lions and tigers. Ladies and gentlemen, the Hardins!"

Suddenly a man and a woman slipped in through a side door of the cage. Travis smiled as he saw them. *My sister is more beautiful than ever,* he thought. Joy Hardin had blond hair and blue eyes, and her trim figure was outlined by the silk blouse and snug-fitting jodhpurs. She wore black boots and held a small whip in her right hand. Her husband was a well-built man with piercing eyes and an engaging smile, but the smile disappeared as the first Bengal tiger entered and circled the cage. One after another the animals emerged from their tunnel, alternating lions and tigers, until all twenty of them were in the ring.

Travis watched with pleasure as the two trainers put the magnificent beasts through their routine. He remembered Joy telling him about her first experiences with the wild animals. She had laughed when she told Travis about tiger cubs, saying, *"They have to be fed just like a baby, and someone has to wipe their bottoms until they learn to do it for themselves!"*

The air crackled with applause, cheers, and gasps as the huge animals performed their incredibly difficult tricks. The largest of the huge tigers walked a tightrope, then jumped through a flaming hoop. When all the other big cats had exited the cage, the huge tiger remained. The audience collectively held its breath as Joy slipped onto his back and rode around the ring as fearlessly as if she were straddling a pony.

"Aren't they wonderful?" the woman said to Travis. "I don't see how they do it."

"They spend lots of time with those animals," he said. "They won't let anybody else feed them. Every night after the circus is over, they go back and feed them by hand."

"How do you know all that?" the woman asked curiously.

"Well, that lady's my sister."

"You don't say! Are you in the circus?"

"No, ma'am, I'm just a poor preacher."

The woman laughed. "Well, I'm glad to hear it. I'm a Christian myself. So is my husband."

"And these children are going to be the same. I can tell."

Travis enjoyed the rest of the spectacle and before he knew it, the final spec, or parade, was winding its way around the Big Top. Joy was riding on the neck of one of the elephants, just as she had done in the old days, while Chase drove a Roman chariot pulled by two snow-white horses. Smiling and waving to the crowd, they passed right by Travis, but neither Joy nor Chase spotted him. He handed the baby back to the woman and said, "Thanks for letting me hold your young'un, ma'am. He's a fine one."

"You're welcome, preacher, and thank *you*. May the Lord bless you real good."

Travis got to his feet and slowly moved toward the exit with the crowd, then made his way around back to where the performers' trailers were parked. He stopped a busy circus hand to ask where Joy and her husband lived.

"That big white one right over there, you see?"

"Thanks, partner."

He went to the trailer, but no one was there.

"Must be feeding the cats, I guess," he said to himself.

He sat down on the front step and waited. It was forty-five minutes later when he finally saw them. Joy was carrying a small child in her arms, and when she saw her brother, she let out a cry.

"Travis!" She shoved the baby toward her husband and ran forward, throwing herself into his arms. "Why didn't you tell us you were coming, you big ape!"

"Don't know. Guess I'm just not very thoughtful." Travis grinned. "You're lookin' fine, Joy, and you too, Chase." He put out his hand and returned Chase's hard grip before exclaiming, "Let me see this here girl child!" He reached for the nine-month-old and held her up. "Why, Leah, you're as good-lookin' as your ma. I was afraid you'd be ugly like your old man."

"So was I," Chase said with a grin. "Travis, it's good to see you. Come on inside."

"Have you eaten yet?" Joy asked.

"You mean lately?"

Joy slapped at him playfully. "Come on in. I'll fix some steaks, and you can tell us what all you've been doing."

Travis sat in the middle of the living room floor playing with Leah while the enticing smells of seared meat and fresh coffee filled the mobile home. He lay back and stood his niece on his stomach, while she gurgled and laughed and jumped. Travis held her chubby arms and glanced over at Chase, who was watching with a smile. "This is some lively girl you've got here. She's gonna run you ragged."

Joy called in from the kitchen, "She already does! And we're expecting another one in a few months. A brother, we hope."

"That means you'll be out of the act."

"Just for a while," Joy said. She was putting plates on the table and added, "I love it too much to quit for good. I always have."

"You're just a showoff, Joy—always were. Have to have that applause and be in the spotlight."

"I just love my work," Joy rejoined. "Now, you come on and eat. Put Leah in her high chair."

Travis chowed down on his steak while he listened to Chase and Joy tell him about their lives.

"People think it's exciting traveling around so much." Chase shrugged as he tore off a piece of bread and stuffed it into his mouth. "But we never see much of the towns we're in. New York, Chicago, San Francisco—they're all about the same. All we see is the inside of the tent. Those cats take more time than babies do."

"But you love it," Joy said, smiling, "and you're the best."

"That's 'cause I've got a good helper." He winked and patted her hand.

Travis was pleased at how close the two still were. Now that they had one baby—and another on the way!—he felt a deep satisfaction in seeing the love that was growing between them.

"You're not married yet, Travis," Chase said. "Why is that?"

"No one'll have me. Too ugly."

"Don't be silly!" Joy exclaimed, looking at Travis with an admiring eye. He was lean and tall and rough-looking, but handsome, nonetheless, with a shock of tawny hair and cobalt blue eyes. A scar on his forehead ran into his right eyebrow, and other vestiges of a hard life marked his features, but no one would accuse him of being ugly.

"Don't you ever want to get married and have a family?" Joy demanded.

"Sure . . . someday . . . when the Lord puts it in my way. I do get lonesome, but I stay busy and don't let that bother me."

"Where are you living now? You move around so much it's hard to keep up with you."

Travis had indeed moved a great deal. He had been in Bible school only a year when God directed him to leave and go to Mexico. He learned to speak Spanish while he worked among the poor, establishing a mission that grew into a church. While some of the local people he had trained took over the church leadership, he moved on to South America.

"Well, I just got back from Guatemala. Been there a little over a year."

"What did you do there? Establish another church?"

"Sure did." Travis nodded, spearing a piece of steak and biting it off the fork. He chewed thoughtfully and said, "I worked with James and Merline Golden, two independent missionaries down there."

"You told us about them in your letter. They must be fine people."

"The best I ever saw. Their whole heart's in preaching the Gospel."

"What sort of work did you do there?"

"Well, Brother James and Sister Merline helped me to do some work with the Indians."

"What kind of Indians?" Joy asked curiously.

"Maya. I never did learn their language like I should have, but some of them spoke Spanish, so we got along fine."

For the rest of the meal, Joy and Chase listened as Travis spoke of his work among the Maya. He made it sound easy, but they knew the work must have been very hard. There were no modern conveniences, and of course, no salary.

Travis stopped his recitation and said, "The offerings you sent down kept me going. I couldn't have stayed if you hadn't helped me."

Joy flushed and shook her head. "It was little enough to do."

"That's right," Chase added quickly. "Did you see many of the natives there get saved?"

"Oh yes—they're receptive to the Gospel, and they make fine Christians too."

"What do they look like?" Joy asked.

"They're very short—short and broad. The men are about your height and the women shorter. I felt like a giant, but they didn't seem to mind. They are fine, fine people."

Leah began to fuss, and Joy left to give her a bath while Chase and Travis continued to talk over dessert and coffee. She came back with Leah in her pajamas, her now-damp blond ringlets clinging to her head. Joy handed the sleepy baby a bottle of warm milk and let her kiss her daddy and uncle good-night, then went to put her down for the night. When she came back she poured herself a cup of coffee and sat down at the table. "What are you going to do now, Travis?"

"Maybe I can help somehow with the act."

"You could go back to your old job"—Chase winked with a grin—"the human cannonball."

"I reckon I'd better not. It didn't seem too hard then, but it's a wonder I didn't break my neck or worse, being shot outta that old cannon." He laughed and shrugged. "People do crazy things when they're young, don't they?"

"It's not like you're an old man!" Joy said, punching her brother's arm.

Travis leaned back in his chair. He looked loose and limber; his physique was the flat, angular shape of a man who made his living with his muscles. The overhead light illuminated his face, making his cobalt blue eyes look darker than ever. He smiled in the self-deprecating way that Joy knew well, his teeth appearing milk white in contrast to his weather-bronzed skin.

"Actually, I don't rightly know what I'll be doing next, but the Lord told me it was time to leave Guatemala."

"I've often wondered how you hear from God," Chase observed. "How do you know where to go next?"

"Don't always know, but if I wait long enough, it sorta swims together in my mind."

Joy laughed, the sound a musical note in the air. "Well, you can stay with us until it all swims together. Oh—I saw an article you might be interested in." Jumping up from her seat, she went into the living room and rifled through the newspapers and magazines stacked on the couch and coffee table. "Here it is," she said, waving a newspaper. She laid it in front of Travis and put her finger on the page. "That story right there."

" 'Going First Class,' " Travis read the headline, then began the article.

> "A new sort of missionary is being birthed in San Francisco. Miss Rena Matthews will lead a group of missionaries, calling themselves 'The Twelve,' to the South Pacific. Unlike typical missionaries, these twelve people are mostly from the upper strata of society, all of them college graduates, and a few among them highly trained scholars. According to Miss Matthews, they are a new and different breed of missionaries. Not content to simply follow in others' footsteps, they plan to forge new paths and lead the

way into a new era of missionary work, work that is well-funded as well as scientifically devised and executed. Missionary Rena Matthews, a bright and attractive woman of twenty-two with a wealth of curly auburn hair, said, 'We're going to use new methods, scientific methods, and all of us are confident that God's going to do great things.'"

Travis looked up, amusement curling his lips into a smile. "A bunch of rich missionaries, huh? Well, that'll be a switch from anything I've ever seen."

He read the rest of the article and shook his head. "Going first class to the South Pacific. I read a book once about the first missionaries who went to the South Seas. Most of them were eaten by cannibals, I think."

"She's pretty, though, isn't she?" Joy said. "Let me see." She pulled the paper over. "She comes from a very wealthy family. Her father is putting up all the money for the mission work and sending them down there in his yacht."

Travis found this doubly amusing. "Well, that's going first class, all right."

"Do you think they'll be successful, Travis?" Chase asked.

"If God's in it, it'll work."

"That's what you always used to say," Joy said, putting her hand affectionately over Travis's. "Now, how about wrestling down another piece of that apple pie?"

"You bet!"

Joy dished up the rest of the homemade pie while the men continued the conversation. When they'd scraped their plates clean, she said, "We have to get up early, Travis. Why don't we read a chapter of the Scriptures together and have a prayer."

"Why sure, sis. I need all the prayin' I can get," Travis said. "Before I went to Guatemala, I had to wait for four months to figure out what God wanted me to do. I hope it won't take so long this time."

★ ★ ★

After a good night's sleep, they all gathered again at the kitchen table. This time Travis was presented with a huge stack of pancakes that completely hid his plate. In the middle of the table was a platter filled with juicy sausage patties. "You remember what I like best, sis."

"I do, indeed. And there's plenty of Vermont maple syrup. The real article."

Chase asked the blessing; then they all tore into their pancakes with healthy appetites. Joy suddenly laughed, looking at the ragged mess she had made of her pancakes, while Travis's plate was neatly arranged with uniform bite-sized pieces. "You still cut up your pancakes like you always did!"

"Reckon it's the only thing I'm neat about," Travis said, smiling back at her. "They taste better if you keep them neat. Look at that mess you've made. It must taste awful!"

"You just eat your pancakes the way you want, and I'll eat mine the way I want."

Chase laughed around a bite of sausage. "You two have argued about how to eat pancakes ever since I've known you."

"Well, Joy just doesn't learn easy. You've probably found that out." Travis winked at Chase, adding, "I knew we'd have trouble with women after we taught 'em to count money and let 'em eat with us at the table."

Reaching over, Joy stabbed Travis in the arm with her fork.

He yelled, "Hey, cut that out, woman! I bleed easily."

After much kidding around, they made it through break-fast and had started to clear the table when Travis said, "Hold on. I have an announcement to make."

Joy and Chase stopped, each with plates in their hands, and waited.

Travis went on. "I'm not going to have to wait four months to find out what God wants me to do. I know already."

"Why, you didn't know last night!" Chase exclaimed. "You mean God spoke to you already?"

"Yep. I was lyin' on that bed almost asleep, and the answer came clear as day. I know what God wants me to do."

"What is it, Travis?" Joy asked. She had always known that her brother heard from God more clearly than most people and took it for granted that if he said he'd heard the voice of God, then he truly had. "What is it? Are you going back to Bible school?"

"Nope. I'm going to the South Seas with those missionaries the paper told about—The Twelve." Travis saw both of them blink with surprise and he grinned. "The answer came right sharp."

"But it's The *Twelve*," Joy said. "The story said they've already got twelve."

Travis Winslow leaned back in his chair and crossed his arms. He looked up at the ceiling for a moment, then shrugged his shoulders. "Well, it may have to be The Thirteen, then."

"But they're all rich society people—socialites. They've got college degrees and money! You wouldn't fit in."

"I don't know about that," Travis said, grinning. But then his expression turned serious. "I do know one thing, though. God himself told me last night I would be a part of that group, and they'll just have to get ready for me, 'cause He's in charge and those are my marching orders!"

# CHAPTER THREE

# A CLASH OF WILLS

★   ★   ★

"Dad, I've got two people I'd like you to talk to."

"You mean candidates for The Twelve?"

"That's right. We have to find one more person. Dalton and I have gone over the whole list, and these are the two I've asked to come for an interview."

"All right. Who are they?"

"One of them is Albert Gibson. He's an excellent scholar. He's just finished his second year of seminary. He's brilliant, Dad. The other one is Sarah Johnson. She's a very capable young woman. She came to speak at our school once, and I was very impressed with her. She's already published two books!"

Loren looked at his daughter doubtfully. "Writing books doesn't necessarily make one a good missionary."

"I know, but just talk to them, will you, Dad? We're scheduled to leave in three days."

"It wouldn't hurt to put off your departure for a few days."

"Yes, I think it would. We've got to stick with our schedule."

"All right. I'll talk to them."

* * *

"Have you lost your mind, Rena?" Loren Matthews said, his face twisted into a scowl. "Either one of those people would wreck your whole mission."

"But, Dad—"

"Just look at them. That young Albert Gibson may be an able scholar, but he's frailer than any girl I ever saw. He wouldn't last a *week* on a mission station."

Rena swallowed hard, for she had almost come to the same conclusion. "I think you may be right about him, Dad, but what about Miss Johnson?"

"She's a loudmouthed, overbearing woman. You'd go crazy in a week."

"Dad, we have to have *someone*."

"Not those two. Either one of them would be nothing but a handicap. You'll have to find someone else."

"All right, Dad. I'll try."

"And you may consider going with only eleven. The number twelve is just an arbitrary number anyhow, a rather foolish idea, I always thought. Now Caleb tells me we should leave soon to take advantage of the good weather. There'll be a chance of some bad storms if we wait too long." Caleb Barkley was the captain of the *Mary Anne*, a man in whom Rena's father had complete confidence.

"All right, Dad, I'll go over my list again," Rena said with resignation in her voice. She turned and left the room, and as she shut the door, she muttered, "I've got to find somebody else. We've *got* to have twelve. That's what we'll be famous as—The Twelve."

* * *

"I just thought I'd see if you were available, Helen. I didn't know you'd already taken a position in Chicago with the Institute."

Rena listened, then said, "We all appreciate your prayers. I wish it would have worked out."

She hung up the phone, and then grimly took a pencil and crossed out Helen Dailey's name from the list. She'd started with a list of eight people to contact and now there were only two, neither of them particularly good choices in Rena's opinion. Getting up from the desk, she paced back and forth, racking her brain for other candidates to consider. She had slept little since beginning her search for the final member of The Twelve. She had called the group together, and they had talked for hours over other possibilities; this list represented their corporate choices. She realized it was too late to be asking people to make such a major life decision, but stubbornly she had kept at it.

Rena moved over to the window and stared out at the emerald lawn. The sprinklers were going, and the dancing sprays made little rainbows in the sunshine. Rather than finding it a cheery sight, Rena sighed disconsolately, her mind filled with worries of how to fill the last vacancy on the team. As she watched, she saw a man walking along the road carrying a suitcase. It was not a widely traveled road, for the houses in their expensive neighborhood were few and far between, and many of them were fenced to keep out intruders and peddlers.

"He must be lost," Rena muttered. She expected him to pass by the house, but instead he turned in to the driveway of crushed oyster shells. *What's he coming here for?* Rena wondered. The housekeeper was off for the day, and Rena considered letting the man think no one was home, but the cars were in the garage, and the garage doors were open, so he could plainly see them. "I'll have to get rid of him. I don't have time for a salesman or whatever he is."

She opened the door after the bell chimed and looked the man over. He was tall and lean and had the bluest eyes she had ever seen. He swept off his hat and nodded pleasantly.

"Hello, miss. Is this the Matthews house?"

"Yes, it is."

"I'd like to see Mr. Matthews, please."

Rena hesitated but decided perhaps her father had sent for the man. He was always hiring people for his business, and this man looked fit and was probably hardworking. "I'll see if my father can see you."

"Thank you very much, miss."

Rena closed the front door, leaving him to wait outside while she left the large foyer, turned right, and walked down to the end of the hall to her father's study. She knocked on the door. "Daddy, are you there?"

"Yes, what is it?"

Rena opened the door and saw her father bending over his account books. "There's a man to see you."

"A man? What man?"

"I don't know, but he asked for you by name."

"Well, bring him in, then."

Rena returned to the waiting man and said, "My father will see you now." When he stepped inside, she said, "You can leave your suitcase there."

"Thanks very much."

"Come this way." Rena led him down the hallway and then nodded at the open door. "He's right in there." She turned around before he could murmur his thanks and returned to the living area. Picking up her list, she stared at it, a frown wrinkling her brow. "One of these will just have to do." She sat down by a small phone table and began to dial a number. It rang three times, and then a man's voice said, "Hello?"

"Hello. Is this Terry?"

"Yes, it is."

"This is Rena Matthews. I hope you remember me. I have something to talk with you about. . . ."

★   ★   ★

"Rena, I wish you'd come in here."

"All right, Dad."

Rena got up, still thinking of the phone calls. She had

called both candidates. Terry McMillan was not available, and she had been unable to reach the other one. She stepped into the study and saw the tall man sitting in one of the leather chairs to the right of her father's desk. He stood as she entered the room.

"This is Travis Winslow, Rena. You met my daughter, did you not, Winslow?"

"Just at the door. I'm glad to know you, Miss Matthews."

Loren was drumming a pencil on his desk and looking at her. "Winslow here feels that God has called him to be a part of The Twelve."

Rena felt her face grow warm. "Well, that's very nice, but I don't think there's any possibility of that."

"Why? Have you already picked someone else from your list?" Loren asked quickly.

"No, Dad—but I still have one more call to make. I feel sure it'll work out."

"I want you to sit down and listen to what Mr. Winslow has to say."

"Dad, we can't—" she gave Winslow a hostile look—"we can't just have people coming in off the streets volunteering. This is a serious matter."

"I think Travis is serious enough," her father replied dryly. "You've had me interview two or three people. Now I'd like to hear you interview him."

"Very well." Rena turned to face Mr. Winslow and said, "Where did you hear about our mission?"

"My sister showed me a story in the newspaper."

"And when was this?"

"Day before yesterday."

Rena could not help smiling. "So you had never heard of us until forty-eight hours ago, but now you think you'd like to go on a trip to the South Seas? Why, I must tell you, Mr. Winslow, that I've had to eliminate a lot of people who thought this would be a pleasure trip. The South Seas are romantic enough, but we're going on serious business—on God's business."

"I'm sure you are, Miss Winslow, and that's why I'd like

to go with you. I'm not interested in vacations."

"But all of us feel that we are called to the mission field."

"I feel the same way. As a matter of fact, I've been on several mission fields for the last four years, almost five."

"What mission fields?"

"Mexico, Ecuador, Guatemala."

For a moment Rena could not take this in. The man did not appear to be old enough to have done all this. "What group sent you out?"

"I guess my committee is the Father, the Son, and the Holy Ghost." He saw her face stiffen. "I'm not being ir-religious, Miss Matthews. That's all I've had. I've never been sponsored by anyone—except my sister and her husband."

"What's your training?"

"Not very impressive. I had a year at the Grace Bible College in Virginia."

"I never heard of it."

"It's just a small school. There were only about fifty stu-dents when I was there."

"And you didn't finish?"

"No, ma'am, I didn't."

"Why not? Did the studies give you difficulty?"

Travis Winslow shifted his weight. "Some of them, but that's not why I left. I would have stayed except I felt God calling me to go to Mexico."

Rena didn't think much of his answer. She had heard of other self-appointed missionaries who simply got on a ship or a plane and went to a country to wait for God's direction, and she took a dim view of such an approach. "I'm afraid we do things a little differently with our group, Mr. Winslow."

"Travis is fine, ma'am. It's what I'm used to. All I can say is that I knew God was telling me to go, so I went."

Rena glanced at her father and saw that he appeared to be impressed. She decided she would have to do something to discredit the man. Winslow seemed able enough, but he would never fit in with the group she had so carefully cho-sen. "Tell me a little about yourself, Mr. Winslow."

"Not much to tell. I was born in Virginia. We moved to North Dakota for a while, and I finally left home and got a job on a steamer making its way to South America. It's kind of a long story, but I was eventually saved in a Mexican prison."

"A prison! You were in a-a *prison?*"

"Yes, ma'am, I was."

"What did you do?"

"The crew of the ship went ashore in Veracruz. Some of us went to a bar, and a fight broke out. A prominent Mexican citizen was badly injured. I had nothing to do with it, but they arrested all of the Americans. Three of us got a year in jail."

Loren spoke up. "It was pretty bad, I suppose?"

"It wasn't pleasant, but I'm glad I went."

"You're *glad* you went?" Rena asked incredulously. "What do you mean by that?"

"I mean I found the Lord Jesus as my Savior while I was there. I might never have been saved if I hadn't wound up in that prison. So I guess the apostle Paul and I have that in common. We've both been in jail."

"It's not a laughing matter," Rena said.

"Why, I wasn't laughing," Travis said, surprise washing across his face. "But I might as well tell you I was in jail in Ecuador too."

"What for?"

"They arrested me for preachin' the Gospel. They let me out after a few days, and then they tried to run me out of the village."

Rena had heard enough. "I'm very sorry, Mr. Winslow, but there's no point in continuing this interview. You see, our group is very special. We're going to be trying some new things that require specialized training. I'm sure that you've done a great deal of good in your own way, but you just don't have the qualifications we're looking for."

Rena expected the man to walk out, but he sat there without moving. "I was visiting with my sister in Los Angeles," he said slowly. "She's with the circus there."

Loren jumped into the conversation. "In a circus? What does she do?"

"She and her husband, a man called Hardin, have an act with wild lions and tigers."

"Why, I saw that act! Chase Hardin, and the young woman he's married to, that's your sister?"

"Yes, sir. You saw the act?"

"They were here last year. I was very impressed."

"It takes a lot of courage to do that. I don't know if I could get in with those big cats, but Joy sure loves it."

Rena felt the situation getting out of hand, with her father showing genuine interest in the man—and now his family. She said briskly, "Well, it was very nice of you to come, Mr. Winslow, but I'm afraid we can't use you."

"But I'm afraid you must, Miss Matthews."

Rena stared at him, thinking she had heard him incorrectly. "What do you mean?"

"God spoke to my heart very clearly. He said I was to be one of The Twelve."

Rena had always had trouble with people who glibly claimed God told them to do this or that. Now she grew angry at the man's arrogance. "Well, I'm sorry to tell you—"

"Just a minute, Rena," her father interjected. "Let's talk this over—just you and me. Travis, would you be so kind as to leave us alone for a moment?"

"Yes, sir, of course."

Rena waited until the door was closed, then turned to meet her father's gray eyes directly. "Father, there is nothing to discuss. He is *impossible!*"

"Why is that?"

"As I told him, he just doesn't fit in. He's not qualified."

"Don't you believe God speaks to people?"

"Daddy, you *know* I do! He called me to go to the South Seas two years ago."

"Then why couldn't He have told Winslow the same thing?"

"He just . . . *wouldn't!* That's all."

"Well, I'm sorry, Rena, but that just doesn't ring true to

me. I like the man. I talked with him for quite a while before I called you in here. He has a real humility and a desire to serve God."

"Dad, there's no point talking about it. He just wouldn't do."

Silence hung over the room, and Rena kept her focus on her father's face. He had not moved, but she saw something change in his features. He put both hands flat on the desk, palms down, and remained in that pose for a moment.

"Did you hear what I said, Dad?"

"I heard what you said, but I don't believe it."

"What do you mean?"

"I mean as I talked to the man, I felt the Lord speaking to me. And what I heard was that this is the man God wants on your team."

"Oh, Daddy, you're too sympathetic."

"I'm not sympathetic at all. I simply believe that God has sent this man to be a part of this mission endeavor."

"I'm sorry, Dad, but—"

"You don't understand what I'm saying, Rena." Usually Loren Matthews's eyes were soft when he looked at his daughter, but now Rena saw what men who had gone up against him in business had found. There was boldness and strength in that look, and it was directed right at her. When he spoke, his voice was calm, but there was no doubt about his sincerity. "I'll have to put it this way, Rena. Either he goes or I withdraw my support."

Rena could not believe what she was hearing. "Why, you can't mean that!"

"I do mean it. You believe that God called you to go; I believe that God has told me this man should go. Are you going to tell me I'm wrong? And just remember that I never questioned your choices."

Rena could not think clearly—a most unusual circumstance for her. Finally she said weakly, "Daddy, we'll have to pray about this."

"I've already prayed. It's not my decision now. It's yours. If God has called you, He'll get you to the South Seas with or without my help. But I feel strongly that I can't be a part of it unless you accept this man."

Rena had never seen this side of her father before. He had always given in to her. She knew she was spoiled, but now she was encountering a different Loren Matthews. Finally she said stiffly, "I'll pray about it and let you know."

"That's fine. I'll just put things on hold until you decide. Go talk to the others and tell Travis to come back in. I'd like to talk with him some more."

"All right, Daddy."

As Rena turned, she felt two emotions. One was fear that the plan would be wrecked and the other was anger. Her anger showed itself as she stepped outside and said, "My father wants to see you."

"Thank you, Miss Rena."

Rena swept by him without another word, furious that this stranger had come and wrecked her well-laid plans. *I've always been able to get Daddy to do things my way. He'll come around—he'll just have to!*

★   ★   ★

" . . . and that's the story. This man Travis Winslow came barging into our house and announced that God had told him he was to join our group."

Professor Jan Dekker lifted his head. "God told him that?" There was a hint of sarcasm in his tone. "Is he another Moses? Was there a burning bush?" Dekker was a small man with brown eyes and gray hair. He took off his thick glasses and polished them. "I believe that God leads people, but not as you have told us."

Pete Alford stood and addressed the professor, his tall, strong frame towering over the diminutive man. "I don't see why you think that, Professor." It was not like Pete to disagree with Dekker. He revered the professor but had never made more than a passing grade in his class. Now he stood tall and declared, "I think we at least ought to listen to the man."

"I think you're right, Pete," Lanie MacKay said, standing by Pete. The very tall redhead gave Rena a nervous glance. "Don't you like him at all, Rena?"

"It's not a matter of whether I like him or not, Lanie. It's just that he's not qualified."

Jimmy and Abby Townsend were sitting holding hands unselfconsciously, like typical newlyweds. "But you say he's done some missionary work?" Jimmy asked.

"He just went down to Mexico on his own, then on to other countries in Central and South America." Rena shook her head in disparagement. "He probably carried nothing with him but a Bible."

"Well, I must say that impresses *me*." The speaker was Meredith Wynne. Her curly black hair framed a narrow face, and her violet eyes shone with startling clarity. Unlike the others in the group, she was almost poorly dressed, not being a socialite or from a wealthy family. She was the only one on the team who had volunteered to come without being invited first, and Rena had willingly accepted her because of her skills as a linguist. Now she defended Travis Winslow, who had also arrived uninvited and volunteered to go. "I think I'd like to hear his testimony."

"Oh, really, Meredith, you can't be serious!" Dalton said, rolling his eyes. "He's some kind of a tramp according to what Rena says."

The argument became heated, and finally Karl Benson broke in. "Do I understand that your father is going to insist on this?"

"Yes, he is, Karl."

"Then I think this meeting is over!" Benson laughed shortly. "We wouldn't get very far without a ship to get us there—or without your father's support."

"But if God wants us to go, we can go without Mr. Matthews's support, can't we?" Maggie Smith spoke up. At the age of twenty-eight, she was the oldest woman in the room, and she spoke confidently now, despite her usual reticence. "We could go on faith."

Professor Dekker laughed. "That went out with the apostles. Part of our mission is to prove that missionaries must be well prepared and well backed financially. It just happens that Mr. Matthews is furnishing all that." He turned to face Rena and said, "I believe we have no choice."

"All right, then. We'll take a vote," Rena said. "All in favor of including Mr. Travis Winslow, raise your hand." The vote was unanimous. Even she had voted yes when she realized the implications of refusing her father. "Let's understand each other," she said. "I'll go tell my father that we've all agreed. It's highly unlikely Mr. Winslow will be able to contribute much. On the other hand, he looks strong and fit, and he'll be a great help in doing the donkey work."

"The what kind of work?" Meredith asked, her eyes intense as she studied Rena.

"Oh, you know, the errands. The manual labor that has to be done. Let's look at it this way," she said with a smile, "we can let Mr. Winslow do the grunt work while we devote ourselves to the *real* ministry."

Meredith gave Rena a curious look, and a smile touched her lips. "I don't think mission teams work that way, Rena."

Pete tried to add a positive note. "He'll be a help to us, I'm sure, and we can use someone with experience on the mission field."

"I don't believe we really need his kind of experience, Pete. He's really a rather arrogant man, talking about God telling him to come with us when he's only just heard of us. But, of course, we'll all have to be nice to him."

Dalton laughed. "Of course we will. What did you think we were going to do—poke our thumbs in his eye?"

Rena stood rigidly, angry to the bone. She could not show her anger to the group, though, and when she spoke again it took considerable effort to keep her voice calm. "We're all agreed, then."

"Don't worry," Dalton said, putting his arm around Rena and smiling at the group. "We'll be sure that he knows his place."

Jeanne Vernay, Rena's best friend, had said nothing, but now she asked, "What does he look like, Rena? I suppose he's pretty shoddy?"

"Oh, he's not bad looking, Jeanne, but he's pretty rough-hewn and dresses like a day laborer." Rena gave her friend a direct look. "We're not taking him because of his looks."

Jeanne laughed aloud and winked at Dalton. "Better check him over, Dalton. He sounds like one of those rugged romantic types. He might try to steal your girl."

"No danger of that." Dalton shrugged nonchalantly, but then he looked at Rena curiously. "I got the idea from what you said that he's a pretty homely fellow."

Jeanne was delighted with his reaction. She and Rena had competed with each other since their childhood. Both were attractive, wealthy, and liked to get their own way. "Tell us more about Travis Winslow, Rena. You've got me curious now."

# CHAPTER FOUR

# THE BLACK SHEEP

★  ★  ★

As Loren Matthews stepped onto the deck of the *Mary Anne,* a strange, unexpected fear sliced through him. Loren loved the sea, but to him it was like a woman who could smile and act charming, but who could also turn cold and cruel without warning. He took in the azure sky. A flight of gulls divided overhead in evanescent shapes, making a kaleidoscopic pattern. The sharp salt smell of the sea surrounded him, and the sun glinted on the small white-crested waves that expanded out into the Pacific. The sun burned a white hole in the sky, and the heat of July was modified by the freshness of the westerly wind. He looked back at the land, and the hazy hills of San Francisco appeared to be brooding over some sullen thought.

"Welcome aboard, Loren."

The speaker was a muscular man of forty, prematurely gray and weathered to a golden tan by years of exposure. His frosty blue eyes were friendly, and when he put out his hand, he almost crushed Loren's with his grip. He was a powerful man in spirit as well as body and a friend as well as employee of Loren Matthews.

"How are you, Caleb?"

"Finer than frog hair! We've got good weather for the trip." Caleb Barkley locked his hands behind his back and studied Loren Matthews. "Wish you were going with us. Sure you won't change your mind?"

"I wouldn't be any good on this trip—much as I'd like to go." Loren suddenly looked embarrassed. "I suppose you think, like everyone else, that I'm a fool for financing this expedition."

"I've never known you to do a fool thing. I don't expect you're starting now."

"Well, Caleb, I've been worried about this trip. They're not exactly a hardened crew."

"They'll make out fine," Barkley said. "It looks like it'll be an easy passage if the weather holds out like this. Smooth sailing all the way."

Continuing their conversation, the two men turned and walked away. As they disappeared down the hatchway, Travis stepped up onto deck, where he was stopped by a massive individual who had planted himself in his way. "What's your business?" the burly man grumbled. "No trespassing on the ship."

Travis studied the man. He had black hair and a pair of intent hazel eyes. His nose looked like it had been broken, and his face bore other marks of past battles. Travis estimated he was in his late twenties and easily weighed more than two hundred pounds. "I'm Travis Winslow. I'm one of the passengers."

"I'm Cerny Novak. I guess you're all right, then."

Two other members of the crew had paused in their deck chores to study the newcomer. "You're one of them preachers, ain't ya?"

"I'm afraid so, but—"

Charlie Day sent a loud laugh through his bad teeth. "Imagine that, Novak. Now we're haulin' preachers for cargo."

The other crew member looked and sounded like a Scandinavian. "I'm Lars Olsen," he said. "You don't look like a preacher."

"I don't expect I do," Travis replied.

"I ain't got no time for preachers," Novak warned. "They just clutter up the earth as far as I'm concerned."

Travis noted the aggressive glare in the big man's eyes. "Well, I don't guess I'm enough of a preacher to make much difference. You might say I'm the black sheep of the whole bunch."

Novak winked at his friends, then stuck out his hand. "Well, welcome aboard, Winslow."

Travis put out his hand, and it was crushed in Novak's grip. He tried not to look too surprised, but he did not miss the amusement of all three of the sailors. He suddenly squeezed his own hand, meeting Novak's grip, and now it was Novak who looked surprised. Travis allowed no sign of strain to show on his face but simply stood there matching the man grip for grip. Novak tilted his head back, and his lips grew thin as he put forth all of his force. He did not prevail over Travis Winslow, however. Travis maintained his grip, giving as good as he got.

Finally Novak released the pressure and pulled his hand back. He stared at his hand for a moment as if it were a traitor, then grinned reluctantly. "Perty good grip you got there. Any other preachers like you in this bunch?"

"Nope, I'm the bottom of the barrel, and I'll tell you right now, I don't know a thing about sailing ships. But if I can help you fellows, I'll be glad to do it."

Novak was amused, yet chagrined. He had rarely been bested in tests of strength, and now he shrugged. "Well, you can help with the loading. See them bags down there? They all gotta come on board."

"Sure," Travis said, nodding and stepping onto the gangplank. The other three followed him, and when they got down to the supplies stacked on the wharf, Travis picked up a hundred-pound bag and put it on his shoulder easily.

The crew introduced him to another sailor who was already helping to load the cargo. "I'm Shep Riggs. I heard you say you don't know much about sailing ships, Mr. Winslow."

"That's right," Travis replied as he headed back up the gangplank. "I've been on several tramp steamers, but this one is different. It's really beautiful."

While Winslow easily navigated the plank back onto the deck, Olsen turned to Novak. "Y'know, he ain't a bad guy— for a preacher."

"If he weren't a preacher, he might be a good guy," Novak muttered, hefting a load onto his shoulder. "But if he tries to preach at me, I'll throw him over the side."

Charlie Day laughed and struggled to get a bag over his shoulder. When it was nestled there, he said, "Before we get halfway to Hawaii, we may throw 'em all overboard!"

★ ★ ★

Rena got out of the car on the dock and approached the ship, but halted when she saw Travis Winslow picking up a bag and lifting it to his shoulder. She rushed up the gangway and demanded, "What are you doing?"

"Why, I'm helping load the ship."

Rena shook her head. "You musn't do that. You have to keep your dignity with outsiders."

"You think loading a ship isn't dignified?"

"I'm not going to argue with you. From now on I want you to keep your distance from the crew." She moved past him and walked on up the gangplank. Travis turned and saw that Charlie Day and Novak were watching him. A crooked grin twisted Winslow's lips. "You fellows keep your distance, now. You heard what the boss said."

Novak laughed aloud. "She's a perty thing but a bit snooty."

"Wait till she gets seasick. That'll take some of the starch out of her," Day said, grinning. "Come on. Let's finish gettin' this stuff loaded. I'm wore out."

★   ★   ★

The sun had dropped from its place in the sky into the sea with a silent splash of light. Travis stood in the bow of the *Mary Anne* listening to the sibilant lapping of the waves on the shore and savoring the aroma of the sea itself. The plan was to get all the supplies loaded and all the passengers aboard so they could sail first thing in the morning after breakfast. Hearing footsteps on the gangplank, he turned to see Meredith Wynne approaching. "Good evening, Miss Wynne."

Meredith stopped abruptly and peered through the gathering darkness. "Oh, it's you, Travis." She came forward to give him her hand. The wind ruffled the edges of her dark hair, and a smile made a small break along her lips. "I'm late," she said, and some private thought amused her, for Travis saw the effect of it dancing in her eyes. "I'm not very punctual, I'm afraid. What have you been doing all afternoon?"

"Helping the crew load the ship."

He saw that his statement surprised her, but she only smiled and said, "I probably should have been here helping to do the same thing."

"What *have* you been doing?"

"I was at the library studying."

"Studying what?"

"I'm a linguist. I study languages."

"What kind of language do they speak where we'll be going?"

"Something like Malay. A little different from anything I've ever handled, but it seems fairly simple."

"I'd like to start learning it as soon as I can."

"Do you know any other language besides English, Mr. Winslow?"

"Spanish pretty well. And a smattering of Maya."

"You know the Mayan language? That's unusual."

"I spent some time down in Central America working with the Maya Indians."

"It sounds like you won't have any trouble learning a new language, then. I can start teaching you as soon as we cast off."

"That sounds good, Miss Wynne. I need a head start over the others. I might be a little slow. I don't have a college degree like everyone else here. They'll probably pick it up quickly when we get to the islands."

"Languages are funny. Some people pick them up very easily. I always did. And some people, no matter how smart they are, can't seem to master them."

"Meredith, come on, and you too, Travis. We're waiting for you."

The pair turned to see an impatient Rena, who had come topside. "Where have you been, Meredith?"

"I forgot myself at the library. Sorry."

"Well, come on down. We need to talk about some things."

Travis followed the two women down the steep flight of stairs and entered the largest room on the *Mary Anne*, the main cabin. It ran the full width of the ship, and portals on both sides admitted light, at least when there was light. Now, however, the electric lights glowed, casting their pale beams over the faces of those who had gathered. Travis moved back against the wall and took his place alongside Pete Alford, who nodded to him, saying, "I should have helped with that loading, I guess."

"There was no need. I just wanted to be doing something."

Captain Barkley got everyone's attention. "Some of you might want to look at this navigational chart." He touched a large map he had pinned to the bulkhead. "In a sailing vessel like the *Mary Anne*, we can't chart our course quite as easily as a steamship can. We go as the wind dictates, so we may take a somewhat circuitous route, but at least you can see where we are now and where we plan to get to."

Travis leaned forward with interest as Captain Barkley put his finger on the spot where the *Mary Anne* was anchored. "We're right here, and we're going all the way across the Pacific to these islands here. But first we'll stop in the Hawaiian Islands at Hilo—here—to take on fresh water and supplies."

Travis listened intently as the captain explained the routine, and when he asked for questions, Professor Dekker spoke up first. "Is there any danger of storms?"

"Always danger of storms at sea, Professor," Barkley replied with a smile on his lips. "It's the nature of the beast. Right now everything looks fine. We'll at least get to Hawaii without any problem."

"How long will the trip take?" Abigail Townsend asked. She was standing beside her husband, Jimmy, and the two looked very young to Travis. He knew they had only been married a couple of months and was pleased to see the obvious affection they had for each other. Now, however, he noticed Abigail nervously reach out and take her husband's hand.

"Impossible to say. With good wind, we'll make it in a few weeks, but we could get becalmed."

"I wonder why your father didn't get a steam yacht," Dalton Welborne asked, turning to Rena. "It would be much more efficient."

"Oh, Dad's such a seaman. He really belongs back in the days when there were only ships with sails," she said with a laugh. "I think he really hates any ship with an engine."

Travis was curious about the young woman. He had seen such contradictory signs in her. Sometimes she seemed hard, but at other times there was a vulnerability about her. Now as he watched her talking, he admired the glow of her eyes and the way her hair shone under the lights. He felt the pull of her presence and was displeased with himself for thinking such things.

After the captain had finished, Rena took over and began to outline the rules. "We will have a prayer time at breakfast every morning. Then in the afternoon we'll have a service for the crew. None of them are believers, are they, Captain Barkley?"

Barkley did not answer for a moment, and Travis saw

that he was irritated. "That's not a requirement for my crew, Miss Rena."

"Well, they need to hear the Gospel," Rena insisted. Changing the subject, she held up a piece of paper and said, "I've been trying to assign the rooms so we'll be most comfortable, but we're one bed short." She turned to Travis and said, "You'll have to find your own place."

Travis felt every eye turn toward him, but he said calmly, "That'll be fine, Miss Matthews. I'll enjoy sleeping on deck."

Captain Barkley stared at Rena and said something to her Travis couldn't hear. After the group broke up, he came by and said, "That was pretty raw, Winslow."

"I'm the low man on the totem pole, Captain, but that's all right."

"Well, I'll find you a bed. Don't worry about it. You won't have to sleep on deck."

★ ★ ★

Lanie MacKay was standing on the deck watching the stars. She saw Pete Alford, who started to pass her by, then hesitated. "Are you excited about leaving, Peter?" she asked.

"Yes, I am." He stood beside her at the rail, and the two gazed out over the sea. The moon was rising, making a V-shaped pattern on the water, narrow on the horizon and widening as it approached the ship. It glittered brightly in the gently rolling waves. "The Vikings called that *the whale's road*," Pete said.

"Did they? I didn't know that."

"I think I read it in a book somewhere. I don't know why I remember unimportant things. Can't get the important things into my mind."

Lanie turned and looked up at Peter. She was five foot eleven and had been embarrassed about her height as long as she could remember. "How tall are you, Pete?" she asked.

"Oh, about six-three."

"It's nice to have to look up at a man. I usually have to look down."

"Being tall is all right . . . but you bang your head a lot," Alford said, grinning. "You don't have a problem with your height, do you?"

Lanie hesitated. She did not know this man very well, and it would not do to start the trip with complaining about things that couldn't be changed. "Oh, I suppose not." She changed the subject. "I thought Rena was pretty mean with Travis earlier."

"I guess she's used to having her own way."

"I suppose so."

"Do you get seasick, Lanie?"

"I have no idea. I've never been on a ship."

"No ship at all?"

"No, not any. Do *you* get sick? At sea, I mean?"

"You bet!" He laughed at his own confession and shrugged. "If you're prone to getting seasick, there's no way to avoid it on a ship at sea."

The two stood there feeling the almost imperceptible motion of the *Mary Anne* beneath their feet, and finally Pete turned to her. "I'm worried about learning the language. I'm so slow. I never was much good at books."

"Don't put yourself down," Lanie said quickly. "I do too much of that myself."

"Don't be silly! You don't need to put yourself down. It's not about being tall, is it?" he asked.

"I . . . I guess it is. The kids at school used to call me Too Tall MacKay."

"Well, I'll tell you what. You and I'll form a club. We'll call it the Poor Me Club. We'll get together every day, and you can say, 'Oh, poor me, I'm too tall.' And then I'll say, 'Oh, poor me, I'm too dumb.' We can cry on each other's shoulders. You can hate short women, and I'll hate all the smart people."

Lanie smiled and looked up into Pete's face. "We'd be the only members, I think."

"I think that's good. We won't take anybody else into our

club. The Poor Me Club, that's what we'll be."

Lanie MacKay was slow to make friends, but somehow she already felt a companionship with this tall man. As they stood talking in the moonlight, she relaxed for the first time since agreeing to this trip, feeling better about herself and about what would happen in the days to come.

# CHAPTER FIVE

# UNDER WAY

★ ★ ★

"I wish I felt better about this mission, but somehow I just can't." Loren Matthews turned from where he leaned on the rail of the *Mary Anne* to face Travis, who stood beside him. Both men had been gazing out past the harbor to the open sea, discussing the challenge that lay before The Twelve. The deep blue sky overhead seemed hard enough to scratch a match on. The water in the harbor was a bit choppy as boats plied their way in and out. The gulls circled, uttering their harsh cries, and as the cook, Oscar Blevins, threw the garbage over the side, they fell on it voraciously. Loren watched this gloomily and shook his salt-and-pepper hair. "I don't know why I should feel so bad. It's a good thing, mission work."

"Yes, it is." Travis was wearing a pair of faded blue jeans and a light blue short-sleeved shirt that exposed the tan of his upper arms. Turning to face the older man, he said, "It'll be all right, Mr. Matthews. I believe God's in it."

"Do you?"

"Why, of course I do. You know that."

"I'm glad you're going," Matthews said. "The rest of the

team seem like a bunch of helpless babies to me."

"They're better than they look, I think."

"I hope so. I've done all I can in the way of getting them ready." Loren Matthews grimaced and shook his head. "It seems like I put enough stores on here to supply the *Queen Mary*."

"We're not going to go hungry, that's for sure. I doubt if many missionary groups go out as well supplied. You've done a wonderful job, sir."

"It's only money."

"Of course it is, but it'll make things easier when we start the work there."

Both men turned to look where several of the passengers had gathered in the bow, talking and laughing as if they hadn't a care in the world. Abby and Jimmy Townsend, as usual, were standing side by side, their arms around each other. "I like to see devotion like that. That couple is going to do fine," Loren remarked. He turned his attention to Dalton and his daughter, standing in the point of the bow across from the Townsends. Rena was laughing up at Dalton, and for a moment the scene brought tears to Loren's eyes. "She's all I've got, Travis." Stifling his emotions, he turned to Travis and said, "I wish you'd keep an eye on my girl."

Travis was surprised at the remark. Loren Matthews was one of the most capable men he had ever met. Starting with a single truck, he had built one of the largest trucking firms in the United States. His lifelong fight against his competitors and the endless government regulations had left its mark on him. But even so, the weariness and apprehension that were apparent just now seemed unusual to Travis. The younger man sought for words to bring some comfort, and finally he said, "She's a strong young lady, Mr. Matthews. She'll be all right. We'll all be all right."

"I'm afraid Rena hasn't been too kind toward you, Travis. I hate to say it, but I believe she's a bit of a snob. I'm glad you're willing to go despite her attitude."

"I'm glad just to be allowed to go," Travis remarked. He

smiled then, and his teeth shone white against the bronze of his face. "But I promise you I'll keep an eye out for her."

"Good. I'd appreciate that."

As the two stood talking Rena left the group in the bow and came toward them with determination. "Travis," she snapped, "go down and help the professor shift his things around. Some of the boxes are pretty heavy."

"Sure, Miss Rena."

Loren watched the lanky young man as he left. "You shouldn't be so curt with him, Rena."

Surprise raised her eyebrows. "Curt? Why, Dad, I was just telling him what to do."

"I don't think you realize how harsh you are sometimes. It's a bad time to be bringing it up, but I wish I'd see a little more gentleness in you, especially toward those who are under your authority now."

Rena stared at her father. "Daddy, I don't know what you're talking about."

"You've always had everything you've wanted, Rena. Maybe I made a mistake doing that. You've got too much pride." He smiled ruefully. "Too late to get into that now when it's time to say good-bye."

Rena was taken aback by her father's declaration. She had always been highly sensitive to anything he said. Since she had lost her mother, she had clung to her father, and now her hurt was apparent as she came closer and rested her hand on his arm. "You think I'm mean and cruel?"

"Of course not! Just—well, a little thoughtless. I guess it comes from having too much money and too much beauty. Maybe you couldn't have been any different with all of that. I couldn't do anything about your beauty, of course, but I suppose I didn't have to give you everything you wanted."

The smile had left Rena's face completely now. She pulled her hand back and tried to speak. Seeing her obvious distress, Loren put his arms around her and drew her close. "Don't pay any attention to me. I'm just an old grouch. You're going to do fine, Rena."

She leaned her head against him and rested there. "I

don't know what I would have done without you, Daddy,"
she said. "You're all I have in the world."

"I haven't been the best father."

"You have too! Don't say such things!"

With no other children, Loren had poured himself into
this young woman, and now as she clung to him, he leaned
down and kissed the top of her head and could think of
nothing to say. She was headed into a world he knew nothing about, and he felt as if a cord were being cut. It brought
him intense sadness—but he knew he could not show it.

"Here, now, this is no way to say good-bye." He grinned
at her. "Come along. I've got to tell Caleb to make you mind
while you're out of my sight."

"You go see him, Daddy. I want to check that everything
is stowed away properly."

Captain Barkley emerged as Rena left. "A good day for
sailing," the captain greeted. "I wish you were going."

"So do I, but this voyage is for young people."

"That Professor Dekker is only a few years younger than
you are, and he's going."

"He may come to regret his decision. I can't do the things
I could do when I was thirty."

"Neither can I," Captain Barkley said, shrugging. "We let
go of things, don't we, as time goes on? There's always the
last of something—the last time we play ball, the last time
we see someone. Life is pretty much a series of endings." He
looked up at the sky and said, "The weather's good. We
ought to make Hawaii with no trouble."

"How long will you stay there, Caleb?"

"Just long enough to take on water and any supplies we
might have forgotten."

The men stood discussing the supplies they would be
needing by that point in the voyage, and finally Caleb said,
"Well, time to set sail."

"Good-bye, Caleb. May God give you a good voyage."

"I'll be careful to get your girl to the islands."

Loren Matthews moved to the gangplank and watched
as the men began to run the sails up. They were good sailors

and he trusted them. He longed to stay on board the *Mary Anne* and forget everything else, but that could not be.

Finally Rena came running to him and threw herself into his arms. "Good-bye, Daddy. Thank you for all you've done. We'll make you proud of us."

"I already am," he said. "God go with you, daughter."

Matthews stepped off the gangplank, and Novak nodded as he undid the mooring lines. "Good-bye, sir."

"Good-bye, Novak. Look out for these people. They'll need your help."

Novak grinned back. "I'll do my best, Mr. Matthews."

Matthews stood on the dock and watched as the *Mary Anne* began to move out slowly at first, almost imperceptibly. The passengers lined the deck to wave good-bye while the crew scampered over the sails and loosed all the mooring lines. The *Mary Anne* turned slowly into the channel, and the breeze caught the sails, puffing them out. Almost like a living thing, the *Mary Anne* surged toward the open sea. Loren looked at Rena, who was in the stern waving. He waved back and cried out, "Good-bye, daughter!"

Her voice came to him clearly, "Good-bye, Daddy—I love you!"

Matthews watched as the *Mary Anne* left the harbor and began to bob gently up and down on the waves. He waited until she was nothing but a dot on the horizon, and then he turned slowly and walked with a heavy step back toward his car.

★　★　★

Rena grasped the rail as the *Mary Anne* lifted and plunged on the open sea. She had only been on her father's yacht once before, and that was only for a short jaunt down the coast. She had felt so queasy on that day trip that she had not wanted to take any longer trips, preferring to take ocean liners, where the floor was almost as steady as at home. As the wind picked up and the motion of the *Mary*

*Anne* increased, Rena suddenly remembered her earlier experience with seasickness. She had forgotten that in all the excitement of planning for the mission. Now the salt water sprinkled her face, and she felt the first pangs of nausea. *Oh no, I'm going to be sick!*

Even as she thought this, she regretted the heavy breakfast she had eaten. Dalton came up to stand beside her, looking aristocratic as always, and untroubled by the movement of the ship. "Well, we're on our way," he said.

"Yes, we are."

"Are you glad? But of course you are." He reached out and took her hand as he gazed at the horizon. "It's a long way in a big ocean." When she did not speak, he turned back and his eyes widened. "You're pale! Are you getting sick?"

"I'm afraid I am, Dalton."

"Well, you'd better go to your cabin and lie down. I hear seasickness is a terrible thing."

Rena licked her lips and then pressed them together. "I got a bit queasy the other time I was on this ship. The motion doesn't bother me on the big steam ships, but this pitching—" Without another word, she left his side and made her way belowdecks. Going to her cabin, she sat down abruptly as the ship began to roll from side to side. The nausea increased, and she rose to get a basin. She did not make it, though, for suddenly she felt sicker than she ever had in her life. She lost her breakfast on the floor, then moaned and fell back on her bunk.

★　★　★

Charlie Day grinned at Novak. "Well, I hear Her Majesty is seasick."

"Yeah, her and that professor both. And the newlyweds too. The wife at least." Novak guffawed loudly. "Ain't they a perty sight? Goin' out to convert the heathen and can't even keep their breakfast down."

Meredith Wynne shared a cabin with Rena. Now she came out and found Travis talking with Shep Riggs, the small, wiry sailor.

"How is Miss Matthews?" Travis asked.

"She's pretty sick, Travis. As a matter of fact, I've got to clean up after her. She threw up on the floor."

"Oh, I'll take care of that," Travis said quickly. He looked at her closely and said, "You don't look too good yourself, lady."

"I think I'll be all right."

"Why don't you go into the big cabin and take it easy? Maybe it'll pass. I'll take care of cleaning up."

Travis went belowdecks and grabbed a pail and towels from a narrow cleaning closet. There were five small cabins, and he knocked on the first one on the right of the short passageway. "Miss Matthews, are you all right?" He waited and heard what could have been a faint answer but could not make out any words. He tried the door, found it open, and said, "May I come in?" Again he got only a faint answer.

Sticking his head inside, he saw that Rena was lying flat on her back. "Meredith tells me you're not feeling well. Let me just do a little cleanup here." When he had cleaned the floor and set the pail outside, he went to the small sink and washed his hands. He got water out of a small reservoir and dampened a cloth with it. "Sometimes it helps to put a cool cloth on your face," he said as he put the cloth on her forehead. "Just close your eyes and try not to pay any attention to the ship. I'll have somebody come by and be sure you're all right. It's good to drink a little water."

"I'd just throw it up." The words were faint, and Rena's lips barely moved. "Just leave me alone."

"All right. I think Meredith will be back to check on you soon."

Leaving Rena's cabin, Travis went to the large cabin used for their meetings and services. He found Meredith sitting there sipping water and nodded with approval. "She's going to be all right, but we need to get her to drink water too, if we can."

"I'm feeling better now. I'll go see to it." Meredith turned and smiled vaguely. "Not a very auspicious beginning for our great missionary jaunt, is it, Travis?"

"We'll be all right. Captain Barkley says we shouldn't hit any rough weather."

"I've got a feeling this is just the beginning, though. We may hit things worse than a little seasickness before this is over."

"Probably will, but God will be with us."

Meredith smiled. "Yes, He will. I'll go check on Rena."

★　★　★

By their third day out, all the passengers had recovered from their seasickness except for Abby Townsend. She kept to her cabin, and Jimmy spent most of his time with her, coming out only for meals. When Travis asked about her, Jimmy bit his lip and said with a worried voice, "She can hardly keep anything down."

Travis tried to encourage Jimmy, but he was afraid that Abby might be one of those people who remain sick for an entire voyage.

As for Rena, she had recovered her strength fully, and on the twenty-fourth of July, a Tuesday, they all met for a prayer breakfast. Oscar Blevins had fixed bacon, eggs, and fresh rolls. After they ate, Rena announced, "I've asked Professor Dekker to lead us this morning. Professor, we're ready if you are."

Dekker rose to his feet and smiled benignly at them. His dark eyes glowed warmly behind his thick glasses. Despite his gray hair and frail appearance, he was mentally acute. He began to expound on a text from the book of Second Samuel.

Travis listened attentively but found himself lost almost at once. The professor quoted liberally from books Travis had never heard of. Often he went into lengthy explanations about the meaning of certain Hebrew words, and he even read aloud a passage in Hebrew, which of course, meant nothing to Travis. He glanced around the room and saw that others were watching with respect, but he himself was disappointed. *I guess I'm just too dumb to know what he's saying*, he thought.

When the professor had finished, he said, "Let us now pray for our mission." His prayer was very much like his lesson—too intellectual for Travis's tastes. He couldn't help thinking irreverently, *I hope God understands him, because I sure don't!* He felt guilty for his attitude, however, and cringed a bit when Rena rose after the service and exclaimed to the professor, "That was very fine!" She glanced overhead and then added, "We'll have the first service for the crew this afternoon. I think the weather is nice enough to have it on the deck, and all of the crew will be required to attend."

"Some of them may not want to come," Jimmy said.

"Some of them aren't exactly devout Christians," another added.

"That's why it's required," Rena said curtly.

Pete Alford stood up, and he had to bend slightly to keep from hitting his head on the low ceiling. "I don't know about that, Rena. I'm not sure that's such a good idea."

"What are you talking about, Pete? We all had required attendance at services at Bible school."

Peter was usually silent in meetings like this. He felt he had not been a good scholar and was rather slow in books, making him feel inadequate. "We were there for such things as chapel and Bible study," he said. "These fellows are just working at their job."

"Don't be foolish, Pete!" Rena said shortly. "It'll be good for them."

Rena turned and looked at Travis as if she expected him to challenge her. When he didn't speak, she said, "I want them all to come. We'll pray that they'll all be converted."

★ ★ ★

Travis spent as much time with the crew as possible. He had learned a great deal in the short time about the sails, the lines, the rigging, and all of the ship's gear. Now as the *Mary Anne* was cleaving her way through the emerald green water, the crew had gathered on the portside for a smoke. Cerny Novak was speaking of the good time they would have in Hawaii; then he winked at Charlie. "Watch out for the preacher here. We don't wanna offend him with stories of what goes on in some of those places. You remember Mama Winnau's place?"

Charlie Day laughed and drew deeply on his cigarette. "I sure do remember it. Especially that one girl named Juanita." He turned and said, "Do you like women, preacher?"

Travis was accustomed to their rough teasing and merely smiled back. "Some of them," he replied.

"You'd like Juanita. I'll introduce you to her. Maybe she could teach you a few things." Laughter went up from the others, but it was good-natured, for they had discovered it was impossible to get Travis's goat.

Lars Olsen looked up at the sky. He had the gift of telling time almost as accurately as a watch. "Almost time for the service."

"I ain't goin' to no service!" Novak growled, his good mood vanishing.

"Me neither," Day said, shaking his head emphatically.

Shep Riggs looked up from his seat on an empty case and shook his head. "You fellows won't have much choice. None of us will."

Novak cursed, but Olsen said, "We'll all have to go, Cerny."

"I'll go if I gotta, but I ain't listenin'."

"I tried to talk her out of this," Oscar Blevins said. "I don't think this meeting's a good idea. What do you think, Travis?" The balding cook was a roly-poly man who had served for years in the marines. He was a crack shot but was retained on the *Mary Anne* for his culinary skills more than for any military training.

"I'd rather it were voluntary," Travis agreed, "but I'm not the boss."

"I don't think you can force people to do things like this," Shep said. "Can't you talk her out of it, Winslow?"

"I'd be the last man who could."

"That's right. You're the low man on the totem pole, ain'tcha?" Novak laughed. "Before this is over you'll be a sailor like the rest of us."

"I wish I had been a sailor. I love the sea, but it's too late now. The Lord's got ahold of me, and I can't get loose."

"Would you want to?" Blevins asked curiously.

"No, the Lord has been good to me. Did I ever tell you fellows I got saved in jail?"

Everybody looked at him in surprise. "In jail! What were you in for?"

"Oh, nothing very serious. It was down in Mexico." Travis began to tell the story of his conversion and noticed that even Novak and Day were interested. He concluded, saying, "A man can find God anywhere."

"Well, I ain't findin' God, and I ain't listenin' to that female. I'll take some wax along and stuff my ears full," Charlie Day muttered. "She can make me come to that dog-gone service, but she ain't convertin' me!"

The service was not much of a success. Travis joined in with the songs and noticed that Shep Riggs had one of the most beautiful tenor voices he had ever heard. Shep also knew most of the hymns. The rest of the crew made no attempt to join in.

Rena had taken it upon herself to preach the sermon. She chose the text from Galatians, "Whatsoever a man soweth, that shall he also reap." She made a pretty enough sight as she stood there facing the passengers and the crew. The captain remained at the wheel, but he could look down through an open window facing the bridge and had a clear view of the group.

Rena's sermon bluntly declared the need of every man to be saved before it was too late. She spoke almost harshly, and when the service was over, the crew shuffled out in silence to resume their duties on deck. Travis approached her with a smile. "That was fine, Miss Matthews."

Rena was perplexed. She had expected more response from the crew, and now she bit her lip thoughtfully. "I guess they're just hardened men, aren't they?"

"Yes, they're pretty tough, all right. They've had difficult lives, most all of them, but Shep there was raised by his uncle and aunt, and his uncle was a preacher."

Surprise washed across Rena's face. "How did you know that?"

"Why, he told me, of course."

"Have you talked to all of them?" she asked, shaking her head. "I'm not sure that's such a good idea."

"Look, Miss Matthews, how are we going to preach the Gospel to people if we don't talk to them? You have to show an interest in their lives first if you want them to listen to you."

"Your ideas are different from mine. First we'll build a church; then they'll come and we'll preach to them."

A protest rose to Travis's lips, but he saw the stubbornness on Rena's face and turned and left the meeting room. Rena watched him go, then found that Lanie and Maggie were waiting for her.

"That was excellent," Lanie said excitedly.

"Yes, it was," Maggie agreed. "Even though they didn't appear to be listening very much—especially Mr. Novak. He just glared at you the whole time."

"He'll come around," Rena insisted. "They just need a firm hand."

★ ★ ★

Later in the week, Cerny Novak was still seething over the required attendance at the services. He had attended three of them, and each time he had sullenly glared at the speaker. He was a moody man, and his discontent centered on Rena.

Rena was well aware of Novak's dislike for her. She did not speak to him personally until one day when she made her way along the deck toward the stern, where she often sat and watched the sunset. She was surprised to see Novak there along the narrow space between the top cabin and the rail. She waited for him to move, but he stayed put, apparently wanting a word with her.

"Yes, what is it, Mr. Novak?" she asked.

"I ain't comin' to no more of your pea-brained services."

It was obvious that Novak was angry to the bone. Rena also suspected he had been drinking. She could not smell it, for the smell of the sea was too strong, but she resented any crew member showing such disrespect. To his rude remark she shot back, "Oh, yes you will—as long as you're a member of the crew. If you don't want to take orders, we'll put you off at Hawaii." She started to pass him and go on her way when, to her shock, he grabbed her arm. He was frightfully strong, and his grip hurt. "Turn me loose!" she cried.

"I oughta throw you overboard for the fish to eat!"

Rena was not afraid of the man, but she tried to jerk her arm free. When she couldn't release his steely grip, she shouted, "Turn me loose, you beast!" and struck him in the face.

Her quick action caught Novak off guard and he snarled, "Why, you little—"

"That'll be enough, Cerny!"

Novak whirled his head about to see who had suddenly appeared behind him. "Turn Miss Matthews loose," Travis told him. "You know better than this."

"What'll you do if I don't?"

"I wish you wouldn't look at it like that. We've got a long way to go, and it's best if we don't have scenes like this."

Novak had indeed been drinking. He was not a heavy drinker, but liquor always made him stubborn and quarrelsome. Now he grinned and kept Rena's arm in his grip.

"Well, I ain't turnin' her loose! Now, you just go about your own business, preacher."

If Captain Barkley had been in the wheelhouse or on deck, he would have quickly squelched Novak, but he was down below taking an early meal, for he had the late watch. Now Travis said calmly, "This is bad, Cerny."

"No, this ain't bad. *This* is bad!"

Releasing Rena so abruptly that she staggered, Novak threw a right fist that caught Travis high on the head. Travis saw the blow coming and tried to dodge, but it scraped along the side of his head and sent tremors through his body. "Cut it out!" he shouted, but he saw that Novak was beyond reason. The big man came at him throwing punches, and Travis fended them off as best he could. He could not block them all, however, and Novak's fist caught him in the mouth. The shock ran down his spine almost to his feet, and he staggered backward. Novak started for him again, but at that instant Captain Barkley's voice cut across the deck.

"Novak, stop that!"

Novak had his fist doubled, ready for another blow. He watched as Travis got up with blood running down from the corner of his mouth.

"What's this all about?" Barkley demanded.

"This man was insolent to me," Rena spoke up, "and Travis was trying to help. I want him discharged as soon as we get to Hawaii."

Captain Barkley turned to face Rena. "No, I won't do that."

Rena stared at him. "Yes, you have to, Captain."

"No I don't. I'm the captain of this ship, not you, Miss Matthews. I'll discipline Novak in my own way, but he's a member of this crew. I guarantee you he won't bother you again, and there will be no more fights. But he stays on."

Rena's face flushed, and her mouth opened. But when she saw the steady eyes of the captain fixed on her, she swallowed hard. "All right," she said resentfully. "See to it, then."

Barkley waited until Rena had left the deck, then turned

and asked, "You all right, Travis?"

"Sure."

Barkley turned to his drunken crew member and demanded, "Novak, what's wrong with you?"

"It's these preachers making me go to those stupid meetings."

"It's just part of the job, Novak. All you have to do is show up at them. But I can't let you off scot-free for your behavior just now. You're way out of line, and you won't get another chance if I catch you drunk again. Now you'll do kitchen duty all the way to Hawaii."

Novak straightened his back and glared at Travis, but he knew his captain well. Barkley was every bit as tough as Novak was, and he was not a man to be trifled with. "All right, Captain. Whatever you say." His tone was resentful, but he shrugged in compliance. "I guess I can stand it. But I'll sure be glad when these no-good preachers are all ashore."

"You keep your mouth shut, Novak, or I'll make you wish you had! Now, get to work!"

As Novak started to leave, he turned to Travis and said, "What'd you have to interfere for?" He waited for Winslow's reply, but Travis merely shook his head and smiled. "You got blood on your face," Novak muttered. "Don't get in my way again."

As soon as Novak was gone, Barkley said, "You got a cut on your mouth?"

"Not bad. I just wish that hadn't happened."

"Novak's a pretty tough customer. You need that kind on a crew sometimes, but if he gives you any more trouble, just let me know."

"Okay, Captain." Travis seemed undisturbed, and he took a handkerchief out and wiped the blood from his face. "You want to show me some more about navigation? I don't think I'll ever get the hang of it, but it's sure interesting."

# CHAPTER SIX

# HALFWAY HOME

★ ★ ★

August came, and the routine of the ship under the firm hand of Captain Barkley did not vary. Prayer breakfasts were held each morning, and Travis found them interesting and even edifying—except when Professor Dekker spoke. He especially enjoyed the morning when Pete Alford spoke. He had grown fond of the tall fellow, and although Pete was no orator and often had to hunt for the word he wanted, there was a glow in his eyes, and he spoke enthusiastically of serving the Lord.

After his brief message, Lanie MacKay smiled warmly at him. "That was really fine, Pete."

Lanie's compliment pleased Pete a great deal. "It wasn't very scholarly, I'm afraid," he said. "I wish I could speak as well as Dalton or Jimmy."

"We all have to do the best we can, and I think you do very well indeed."

When the others had left the room, Pete said, "I think I'll help Oscar clean up."

"I'll give you a hand." The two of them gathered up the dishes and carried them to the small galley, where Oscar had his arms plunged to the elbows in soapy water. He flashed them a grin saying, "Well, preachers are some good after all."

"Some of them are." Pete returned Oscar's smile. He had grown to like the heavyset cook, and he insisted on drying the dishes while Lanie finished cleaning up the dining area.

"That's a right nice lady there, that Miss MacKay, ain't she?" Oscar said.

"Yes, she is."

"Do you like her a lot?"

"Why, sure."

Blevins didn't speak for a time, then he cleared his throat. "I had a wife once. Her name was Lottie—but she died."

"I'm sorry to hear that, Oscar."

"Yeah, she died having our kid." He stared at the floor, then added in a muted voice, "I named the baby Steve, my pa's name."

"How old is he?"

"He's four."

Blevins's tone was spare, revealing nothing, but Pete caught a look on the man's face. "Who takes care of him while you're at sea?"

"My sister-in-law Alice. She was my little brother's wife, but he was killed in an accident before they could have any children. She's real good with the kid." Blevins looked at Pete and cleared his throat. "She's a good woman, Alice is. Don't know what I woulda done without her. She ain't no beauty, but she's good, you know?"

"I'm sure she is."

"Fact is . . . I've thought about maybe askin' her to marry me. Ain't nothing in the Bible says it's wrong to marry your sister-in-law, is there?"

"No, Oscar. I think that would be fine—if she cares for you."

"Well, she does, I reckon. She never said so, you unnerstand, but we always got along real good." Blevins blinked rapidly, then said, "I'd like to see the boy grow up right.

Maybe I could get a regular job so's him and me could do stuff together. Know what I mean?"

Pete dropped his hand to Blevins's shoulder. "I think that sounds very good, Oscar. That way Steve would have a family."

"That's what I been thinkin'." Blevins face broke into a grin. "Well, I gotta start supper. Thanks for listenin' to me run off at the mouth."

"Anytime, Oscar. Anytime at all!"

Lanie had come as far as the door but had stopped and listened as the two men talked. When Pete finally left, she was waiting for him. As they walked through the cabin toward the steps leading up to the upper deck, she said, "I heard some of what you two said, Pete. He's carrying a real heavy weight, isn't he?"

"Yes, he is."

"You gave him good advice."

He shrugged off her praise and then said, "I'm going to have a lesson with Meredith. It's just been me and Travis. Why don't you come along?"

"Where?"

"We thought we'd go up on the fantail."

"I'd like that. I'm anxious to learn the language and would like to get started before we arrive in the islands."

They went up on deck, where they found Travis already listening and writing down words in a notebook while Meredith spoke. Meredith was wearing a light blue dress, and her black hair glistened in the sunlight as she greeted them. "Come to school, have you?"

"Yes, we have. Where's the foot of the class?" Pete grinned. "That's where I always wind up."

"I'd not be too quick to say that. You have a feel for language, Pete."

Pete stared at her. "Me? I never learned a language."

"And I've already found out that you understand the rhythm of it, and you have a quick ear. You can never learn to speak a language unless you have a good ear. I've noticed that musicians usually make good language students."

Pete flushed with pleasure. "That's good to hear. I've never been good at books in any way."

As the four of them sat down on the deck, Meredith laughed and said, "This is the most pleasant school I've ever seen, but I'm afraid it's too pretty. You'll pay more attention to the scenery than to me."

"No, that's not so," Travis rejoined, smiling back. He was leaning against the rail, his feet out straight before him and his notebook on his lap. The wind was blowing his tawny hair, and he brushed it back off his forehead. "You're a good teacher, Meredith."

"I don't see why the rest of them don't join us. They've got to learn the language sometime," Pete said.

To Meredith's chagrin, it was true that except for these three she'd had little response from the others. Abby was still sick most of the time, and Jimmy stayed with her, insisting, "I'll just wait until we get where we're going. I'll pick it up quickly from the people." Karl and Dalton had attended a couple of meetings but then found other activities to occupy their time. As for Rena, she had shown some interest at first, but like most of the others, she'd decided it would be easier to learn it when they got to where the language was spoken. Jeanne Vernay had agreed with her. Margaret Smith had come to some of the meetings.

"Where is Maggie?" Travis now asked Meredith as the *Mary Anne* cleaved its way through the blue-green waters.

"She's sitting with Abigail."

"Abigail's been sick this whole time. Is it usual for seasickness to last this long?" Lanie asked.

"It is for some people," Travis said with a shrug. "I sure wish she could get over it."

They finally settled into their studies until Meredith decided they'd had enough for the day. "Well, class is over for now."

"I guess I can only stuff so much at one time into my thick head," Travis agreed.

"Pete," Lanie said, "would you mind going over the vocabulary with me? I need to catch up!"

"The review would be good for me too," Pete said as the two rose.

Travis watched the two go and said to Meredith, "They're fine people, aren't they?"

"Yes, they are," she agreed, gathering her study materials together.

Travis got to his feet and stretched, and when Meredith started to stand, he reached over and helped her up. "What'll you do now?" he asked.

"I don't have any plans."

He watched her curiously and said, "I don't know much about you. Why don't you tell me a little about yourself."

"There's not much to know."

"Where's your home?"

"I was born in upstate New York, a little town you've never heard of. But I wasn't there long. My parents were anthropologists. They spent most of their time in Egypt and other exotic locations—and they always took me with them."

"That must have been exciting," Travis remarked.

"I suppose it was, but I missed out on so many things."

"What sort of things?"

"Oh, growing up in a small town, knowing everybody. That must be nice."

Travis continued to encourage her, and soon she began to speak freely of her earlier life. She told him how she had been converted when she was fifteen and felt God calling her into mission work a year later, but then something troubling, almost desperate, came into her expression. He watched with astonishment as sorrow pulled her mouth into a tight line, and without warning he saw tears making bright points of light in her eyes. "What is it, Meredith?"

For a moment she did not answer. The pearl-colored air behind her seemed to frame her face, and she turned from him suddenly. He put his hand on her shoulder and turned her halfway around. "Those bad memories pop up unexpectedly sometimes, don't they?" he said quietly.

Meredith found herself looking down at the deck, unable

to meet his gaze. When he did not speak, she looked up and dashed the tears away with her hand. "I'm sorry. I don't mean to be a crybaby. As a matter of fact, I can't remember the last time I cried."

"You had a bad time, I take it?"

"I was supposed to be married." The words seemed stark and hard for her to pronounce. She swallowed and said, "But he died." Then, as if she had said too much, she leaned against the rail and faced out toward the waves. "I had a wedding dress picked out and my bridesmaids were selected. All my life I had looked forward to a big wedding. My folks didn't have much money, but they had saved up for it. And then the week before the wedding, he was killed in a railroad accident."

Meredith paused, and the wind whispered as it swept across the deck. From the bow of the ship Shep Riggs's fine tenor voice rang out as he sang a sailor's ditty. Meredith listened until he stopped, then turned to Travis and said, "I don't know why I'm telling you all this. I've never mentioned it to anyone else, and I'd like you to keep it to yourself as well."

"Of course I will."

Meredith tried to smile, and then she reached out and put her hand on his arm. "Thanks for listening to me."

"Anytime." Travis covered her hand with his. "Dr. Travis Winslow, mender of broken hearts, at your service. We never close."

Hearing footsteps, they both turned quickly to see Rena, who had approached from the bow of the ship. She did not speak, but the look she gave Meredith made her intentions clear. Meredith murmured to Travis, "Guess I'll go below."

When Meredith had disappeared down the hatchway, Rena said, "Travis, I had to speak to you once about improper relationships with the crew. Now I'll have to warn you about the same thing with other members of the team."

"What sort of improper relationship are you talking about? I don't know what that means."

"We can't have romances going on."

Travis looked at her quietly and thought of a retort to her accusation but decided to leave it unsaid. "There's been no romance, Rena."

The sound of her first name on Travis's lips startled Rena. He had always called her Miss Matthews, but now he seemed to have crossed a line with an attitude that startled her. He even appeared bigger to her, and she noted the scar on his temple and the breadth and solid irregularity of his face. His lips made a long, faint smile, and his wistful expression puzzled her. She had never been in close company with a man like this who had bumped up against the raw edges of the world. He stood idly, his large shoulders drooping, and she suddenly wished he didn't know so much more about the world than she did. It made her feel inadequate. Time ran slowly as she waited for him to speak again.

"You have a bad habit of not understanding people," Travis finally said. "You've had an easy life and haven't experienced any trouble yourself, so you can't see how it's come to other people. Take Novak, for example. Do you know that his mother gave him away when he was two years old? He's had to make his own way in a mighty rough world. Not that it makes his attitude right, but you could at least show some understanding."

Rena stood unable to answer, knowing that he spoke the truth. It was one of the few times in her life she found herself absolutely speechless. As he stood with his eyes half hidden behind the droop of his lids, she found a virility in Travis Winslow that intimidated her.

"I'm sorry," she said as sternly as she could, "but I'll have to insist that you keep your distance from the young women of our group."

Travis took a deep breath, held it briefly, then expelled it heavily. "That's what you do, isn't it? Your father's money has built a wall about you. You're an attractive woman, so you can always fall back on your looks. You live behind that nice little wall and never let anyone come through it. They might be a bit dirty or their manners might not please you.

Well, that might work fine for a society lady in San Francisco, but it won't do on the mission field. Until you have a heart for people, you might as well have stayed back in California for all the good you're going to do."

He turned abruptly and walked by her, heading toward the bow of the ship. She watched him, her face pale, and angry words coming to her lips. She saw him sit down beside Shep Riggs and begin a conversation as though nothing had happened. As for her, she found that her hands were shaking, and her knees were not quite steady. She wanted to follow him and continue the argument, but she knew she had nothing to say that could answer the light that glowed from his face. She hastened down to her cabin and shut the door.

★ ★ ★

Maggie Smith came out on deck to flee the galley, where Oscar was letting her try some of his dessert creations. She had always loved to eat, especially desserts, and she had carried on a running battle for years against the accumulating pounds. For a time she had bought clothes much too tight until she discovered that the looser her clothes, the less her overweight figure would be revealed. Now she wore a loose pale gray dress and a light cotton jacket. Her hair was tied back with a ribbon, and she forced the thought of sugary treats out of her mind.

"Hello, Miss Maggie."

Quickly turning, Margaret saw Shep Riggs making his way along the deck carrying a coil of rope in his hand.

"Hello, Shep."

"Enjoying the sunset? We'll get into port by morning." He stopped beside her and pointed ahead. "Hawaii ought to be right over there somewhere."

"Have you been there before?"

"Oh sure. The boss has brought the ship down three times. The crew likes it."

"What about you?" Maggie asked.

"Oh, it's all right."

"Where are you from, Shep? Where's your home?"

"Louisiana. Baton Rouge. Sure do miss that place."

Maggie was interested in Riggs. He was always cheerful, and there was something about him that set him apart from the rest of the crew. He wore no hat, so the wind tumbled his wavy black hair, and there was warmth in his deep-set brown eyes. He was tan like all of the crew, and she admired his tight-fitting white T-shirt. It outlined his muscles, and Maggie couldn't help envying his fit physique. She continued to question him about his past and found out that he was raised by an uncle and aunt in Baton Rouge.

"My uncle was a shrimper, but he was a preacher too. I used to go with him over to New Orleans. He would get out on the street corner right in the French Quarter," Shep said, grinning. "He would just stand there preaching. He wasn't a shouter or a hollerer. He just stood talking as calm as I am to you."

"Did anybody stop and listen?"

"Sometimes they did. I seen one time a . . ." He hesitated and then cast an odd look at her. "I'd seen a woman of the street come outta one of them bad places in the Quarter. She was half drunk, and you could tell she was on the very bottom. I think I must have been no more'n fifteen at the time. She stopped and began to cuss my uncle out. She knew words I'd never heard before." Shep grinned again.

"What happened?"

"Well, Uncle Paul, he just kept on talkin' about Jesus, and the first thing I knew this woman started crying right there in the middle of the street. Just fell all to pieces, and my uncle went over and took her hand and prayed for her right there in the street."

"Do you know what happened to her?"

"Reckon I do. He took her home with us."

"A prostitute! He took her to your home?"

"Sure did, and my aunt Mae, she took her right in. She got cleaned up, was baptized the next Sunday, and never missed a step after that. Married a fine fellow, a plumber. Last I heard they had seven kids—all of 'em on the straight and narrow."

Maggie's eyes were wide. "That's a wonderful story! I've never had anything like that happen to me."

"Well, me neither, but it did to Uncle Paul lots of times. But I guess you bein' a missionary and all, you'll be doin' the same thing."

Maggie shook her head and bit her lip. "I can't imagine doing a thing like that."

"Why not?" Shep asked curiously. "That's what preachers do, isn't it?"

"Some of them just stay in a church, and I'm not even that kind of a minister. I just taught girls Sunday school. That's about all I've ever done."

"Well, there'll be plenty of girls there." Shep studied her for a moment. "I'm surprised you're not married."

Startled, Maggie looked up and saw that he was watching her with an even gaze. At first she thought he was making fun at her, and then the words seemed to just leap out of her. "Men don't want to marry a fat woman."

"Why, I never thought of you as bein' exactly fat," Shep said with surprise. "You're heavier than most women—"

"I'm *fat*, Shep. I eat too much."

Shep Riggs was unable to speak for a moment. He let the rope drop, then coiled it again while he tried to find the right words.

"Well, I don't know about all that. To me it's not what a woman is on the outside, it's what she is on the inside."

"Men want pretty, slender wives, Shep." Maggie tried to look at him but couldn't bear the compassion in his expression. She turned and walked away stiffly, unable to speak another word without bursting into tears.

Riggs watched as she disappeared down the stairs. "She sure is touchy," he muttered. "And she's a right pretty woman too. If she feels so bad about it, I don't see why she don't just lose a few pounds." He struggled with her problem for a moment and then shrugged. "I guess we've all got our problems."

* * *

The *Mary Anne* pulled into the harbor at Hilo on the big island of Hawaii with every passenger and crew member up on deck. Rena caught her breath as she looked up at the soaring volcanic mountains, the highest of which she knew rose to nearly fourteen thousand feet above the sea. As the captain guided the ship into place at the dock and the crew swarmed to tie the craft down, Rena was anxious to get on shore. She turned to Dalton and smiled. "Well, we're half-way home."

Dalton turned and grinned at her. "You're calling the islands *home* already? It'll take me a little longer than that. San Francisco is still home to me."

"Of course. To me too. I'm just trying to get used to the idea. Well, let's get organized here."

Dalton laughed. "You have to organize everything, Rena. I hate to think how you'll organize me after we're married."

"You're organized enough," Rena said, smiling. She called out for everyone to gather around, then told them, "We're all going ashore. I want us to stick together."

Captain Barkley waited until she was through with her instructions, then said, "You'd better get your shopping done quick. I'd like to pull out first thing in the morning."

A mutter of protest went up, and Dalton said, "Look, Captain, we may not have another chance to see Hawaii for a long time. I think we ought to stay here for a few days."

"The weather's pretty iffy, Mr. Welborne. I think we ought to leave as quickly as we can."

Rena interjected, "I do want to stay at least two or three days, Captain. I'm sure the weather will hold out."

Captain Barkley stared at her and appeared almost ready to challenge her but then shrugged. "All right. Two days. Then we have to leave."

Maggie was standing next to Professor Dekker. "Isn't this exciting, Professor?"

"I suppose it is"—he turned and smiled—"for you young folks. Personally, I don't intend to do much shopping."

"Oh, I don't either, but the others probably will."

They were joined then by the Townsends. Abigail still looked pale, and Maggie asked, "How are you feeling, Abby?"

"I'm still feeling sick, but I hope I'll be better when I get on dry land."

The professor lifted one eyebrow. "We still have a long way to go. Maybe we could find a doctor to prescribe something for that seasickness. Benson might be able to suggest something."

"I think I'll go ask him." While the others left to get ready to leave the ship, Abigail went to find Karl Benson and asked, "Karl, is there a drug you could recommend for this seasickness? Maybe we could get a doctor's prescription while we're here."

Karl turned to study Abigail with a critical eye. "I'm not so sure that it *is* seasickness."

"Oh, but it must be. I was all right when I first got on the ship."

"I think you might consider another possibility."

"Another possibility? What do you mean?"

"You may be pregnant."

Abigail stared at Karl, thinking he must not know what he was talking about. "I'm sure you're wrong. I can't be!"

Benson smiled humorously. "You can be if you are," he said. "If I were you, I'd see a doctor while we're here in Hawaii. Have him check you over."

"Couldn't you do that?"

"I've told everybody a hundred times, I'm not in practice and never was. I didn't finish medical school, remember?"

She muttered under her breath and walked away.

Benson stood looking after her, shaking his head at her stubbornness to accept the obvious. He spotted Travis standing at the rail and went over to him. "Shall we go ashore, Winslow?"

"I'm not much on this kind of thing. I saw enough clowns when I was in the circus."

"I suppose that does get boring, but I'd like to see some of the fauna here."

"What's that?"

"The flowers."

"There seem to be plenty of those. Just look at them all over that hillside." Travis hesitated, then asked, "I saw you talking with Mrs. Townsend. Is she all right?"

Everyone on board had been concerned about Abigail being sick for so long, and now Karl said cautiously, "Keep it to yourself, Travis, but I think she's expecting a baby."

"Did you tell her that?"

"Yes, and I told her to go see a doctor."

"But you're as good as one."

Benson laughed harshly. "I know enough to be dangerous, Winslow! As far as you're all concerned, I'm just a missionary. C'mon. Let's go do some exploring."

★  ★  ★

For two days the *Mary Anne* rested quietly in the harbor while the passengers explored the Big Island. Some stayed and rested on the beaches, while the more adventurous hiked up Mauna Loa for magnificent views of the island and ocean. Others kept busy shopping for souvenirs in the port city of Hilo. Most of the crew availed themselves of the local bars and came staggering back each night drunk—all except Riggs. Captain Barkley made no comment on this. He was an exacting commander at sea, but when his crew had shore liberty, he thought what they did with it was their own business.

While in Hawaii Captain Barkley added a member to his crew—a small native named Chipoa. Travis was standing at the rail looking at the shoreline when Barkley came aboard and introduced him. "This is Chipoa, but we call him Chip. He's island born and wants a vacation, so he'll be Oscar's helper. He's a good man with the sails, and he knows the islands like the back of his hand. Chip, this is Mr. Travis Winslow. He's a preacher, so you two should hit it off fine."

"You're a preacher? Fine! You can preach to me." Despite his small size, Chip was lean and well muscled. His skin was golden and his eyes large and alert. "I became a Christian three years ago. Not too good of one, though."

"I'm sure you are, Chip," Travis said, smiling. "I'll want to hear all about how you got saved."

"I'll tell you the short version right now! Jesus God, He came to me in a dream and told me to let Him in. I said, 'Sure, you can come in.'" Chip smiled broadly. "The next Sunday I went and found a church and got baptized. I'm very happy now. I was very bad before. Your turn. Do you want to preach at me now?"

"Don't know about that, but I want some details about how Jesus came to you."

"Chip is a good sailor," Captain Barkley said, "but he gets on the nerves of the crew a little. He made a voyage with me once and tried to get all the crew saved. I had to keep them from chucking him overboard."

"Come with me, Chip," Travis said. "Do you speak Malay?"

"Sure, a little bit."

"Good. We can use another teacher for the language. Come on and I'll introduce you to the others."

"Watch out for him, Travis," Captain Barkley said, grinning. "Don't let Novak or Olsen throw him overboard."

"I'll keep a hold of him, Captain!"

★　★　★

A two-day layover in Hawaii was not enough for Rena. She told the captain in no uncertain terms they would stay at least two more days, and despite Barkley's grim warnings about the weather, she merely laughed. "Look at that sky. It's perfect weather."

On the fourth day Travis, Meredith, Pete, Lanie, Maggie, and Shep decided to stay on the ship to study the language. Shep had taken an interest in the language and had started taking advantage of Meredith's lessons when he wasn't on duty. After they had studied all morning and had lunch, Travis said, "Say, is anyone up for a little fishing?"

"Sounds like fun to me," Shep answered, and the rest of the group agreed. "We'll have to get the captain's permission to use the cutter," Shep added.

Captain Barkley gave his permission gladly, and after putting on their old clothes, they got into the small boat and Shep raised the sail. The small craft spun over the water, and Shep superintended the fishing lines. They had good luck, and soon the bottom of the cutter was filled with exotic fish.

"Mmm—fresh fish tonight!" Shep said.

"I've never caught a fish before," Maggie said, her face glowing with excitement. For once she seemed uninhibited.

"Have you ever cleaned any?" Shep asked with a grin. "Somebody's got to clean all these."

"I can do it," Travis said, and with a wink to Shep he added, "and you all can help me!"

The afternoon passed quickly, and the sun was dropping toward the west when Shep suggested, "Maybe we ought to go along the shore and see if we can pick up anything there."

No one was ready to go back to the ship, so they agreed to Shep's plan. As they were nearing the shore, an unexpected wave caught the cutter and spilled them all out. Travis went under briefly and bobbed up to find that Meredith was still under. The water was not deep and was crystal clear, so he was able to grab her easily and pull her up. "Are you all right?" he asked.

Meredith shoved her hair back and coughed but managed a grin. "I just swallowed a little water is all."

"It won't hurt you," Travis said. He turned and saw that

Pete had rescued Maggie, who had been rolled over by the surf, and pulled her to her feet. He laughed and said, "We're a sorry bunch of fishermen. Shep, you're fired!"

Shep was struggling to get to the boat. He caught it and said, "I'll tell you what. If you like, we can cook the fish here. I brought a frying pan, and it's still here," he said, lifting the pan for all to see, "and there's plenty of driftwood."

"Oh, let's do!" Meredith cried at once. "That would be so much fun."

"It'll be dark soon," Travis said, glancing at the sky.

"We don't have anywhere to go," Maggie said. "I'd love it."

★　★　★

The surf washed a soothing, caressing sound over the four that sat quietly on the beach. Lanie was sitting across the fire from Pete and said, "I never ate so much fish in all my life."

"Nothing like fresh fried fish on a beach in Hawaii!" He looked farther down the shoreline, where Meredith and Travis were walking along in the light of the rising moon.

The two had been silent for some time, but then Meredith began to talk in an animated fashion. She turned to him, and her curly hair had dried out and now made a mass of ringlets around her face. "Most women would give anything to have naturally curly hair like that," Travis said. "It must save a lot of bills at the beauty parlor."

"I thought about trying to straighten it once."

"Why would you want to do that?"

"Oh, I suppose because no one's happy about what they look like."

"Why, I am!"

"Oh, you're so handsome you don't want to change anything?"

Travis laughed. "No, not that. I just don't think about it much."

"Tell me some more about your days with the circus."

"I wish you could meet my sister Joy and her husband." He told Meredith about Joy's career as an animal trainer and said, "I worry about her sometimes. Those big cats can nab you before you know it. Of course she knows that better than anybody. It wasn't all that many years ago that she was attacked by a tiger that got out of its cage."

"That's awful," Meredith expressed. "And she still works with lions and tigers? She must be quite a woman."

They moved on down the beach and heard Shep calling. Travis said, "We'd better get back to the ship. The captain will have my head."

"I suppose you're right," Meredith said. "But it's been fun, Travis."

They rejoined the others and climbed into the cutter. They headed back to the ship, laughing and rehashing their day. Shep held the boat still as they all went up the ladder, and then Travis saw that Dalton was standing waiting for them.

"Where have you been?" Dalton demanded. "We've all been worried sick about you."

"We just went fishing," Maggie said quickly. "We had such fun. Why, we even cooked—"

Rena appeared and interrupted her. "This is pathetic!" she cried. "You've had us all worried sick—and just look at you!"

"The boat overturned," Travis explained. "We got a little wet and wrinkled but no harm done."

Rena shook her head. "You should have had better sense."

"Better sense than what?" Travis asked, his anger stirred. "We went out for a little boat ride and caught a few fish. Have you got a rule against that?"

"Keep your voice down, Winslow," Dalton said. "That's no way to speak to Miss Matthews."

Travis clamped his lips together, resolved to say no more. He listened as Rena delivered a little sermon, forbidding them all to do anything like this again. Travis saw that

Maggie was crying and Pete was downcast. Rena finally dismissed the group.

Travis waited until later that night, knowing that Rena often came up on deck alone. When she arrived with Dalton Welborne, Travis waited nearby until he left. Travis walked up to the woman and said, "Rena, you were wrong to speak to us like that."

Rena had been expecting his reproach. "You can keep your complaints to yourself, Travis," she answered.

"I've told you this before. You need to be more kind. A woman without kindness is no woman at all."

Rena was enraged. "I don't want to hear another word from you, Travis Winslow! You can stay in Hawaii for all I care, and if you can't do any better than you have, I wish you would. Make up your mind before we leave."

Travis stared at her as she walked by him and went down the hatchway. Nothing would have pleased him more at that moment than to leave the ship, but he knew he could not do that. He shifted his focus to the moon, a huge yellow disk in the sky, and knew he would not sleep that night. He was rarely so angry, but he knew that Rena Matthews could make an angel weep!

★　★　★

Rena stared at her best friend in utter disbelief. "You're going to do what?"

Jeanne's face was pale, and she had none of her usual assurance. "I'm not going on to the islands with you, Rena. I know you think I'm foolish, but I just can't."

"What are you talking about? You said all along that God had called you to go to the mission field with us."

"I made a mistake. I got caught up in the excitement of it all, but for some time now I've been having doubts."

"We all have doubts, but we keep on going."

"Not me." Jeanne shook her head and met Rena's gaze. "I know now that I'm not supposed to be a missionary. I'm sorry to disappoint you, but it would be a mistake for me to go on. I'm catching the next ship back to the States."

"But, Jeanne—!"

"There's no use talking about it. I've made up my mind." Jeanne bit her lip. "I'd just be a handicap, Rena. I'll help all I can with money—but I can't go if God isn't calling me."

Rena stood stock-still as Jeanne turned to leave. She felt a flash of anger and cried out, "But we're The *Twelve*!"

But Jeanne was determined, and Rena knew that nothing would change her mind. She stood staring at the door as if she could will Jeanne to come back, but she knew this would not happen. She sat down and began wondering how she would explain Jeanne's decision to the rest of the group. She was accustomed to making plans and carrying them out to the letter, and displeasure scored her face as she sat stiffly thinking of the inconvenience this event would cause. "I'll just have to work harder," she muttered and got up to tell the others what this would mean to them.

# CHAPTER SEVEN

# "WE'RE IN GOD'S HANDS"

★ ★ ★

Karl Benson took his place at the rail in the stern of the *Mary Anne*, staring down at the foaming wake. In the six weeks they'd been at sea, they'd seen nothing so violent. Karl couldn't help but wonder how the women were faring down below. Most of them had been sick back when the seas were calm. Of course that was back when they were all inexperienced seagoers.

After a time he was joined by Professor Dekker, who gripped the rail beside him and stared out over the sea. Finally he said, "You know, Karl, I've never been on a small ship like this at sea. All my experience has been on big liners."

"Are you worried, Professor?"

Dekker lifted his chin. He was not a man to admit a weakness. "Of course not. This is a seaworthy vessel and she has a fine crew."

"Well, I'm glad you're not worried—because I am." Benson paused as the stern dipped down deep into the trough of the gray waters. He waited until the ship dove into another valley. "It's a bit like a carnival ride, isn't it? But more dangerous."

"Don't talk foolishness, Karl," Dekker said hastily. "We're in no danger."

Benson grinned, but there was little humor in his blue eyes. "We're always in danger. I never cease to be amazed at how fragile the human body is. The strongest man can be happy and cheerful and full of life one second and the next crushed by an automobile or a fall from a mountain. A tiny microbe, so small that you can't even see it with a microscope, can destroy an emperor."

"You're sounding a bit cynical, Karl . . . but then you always are, aren't you?"

"I prefer to call myself a realist." Benson looked up at the foaming sea and shook his head. "Those waves look dangerous to me."

The waves looked like enormous rolling hills. They rose to extraordinary heights without breaking; then a line of white would form along the lip and a Niagara of water would burst over the edge, pouring itself down into the trough. Overhead the sky was a dull, leprous gray, and the sun seemed to have died.

Professor Dekker cleared his throat and turned to Karl. "Why did you give up medicine?"

"It wasn't what I wanted to do with the rest of my life." The reply was fair and did not welcome more inquiry, but as much as Professor Jan Dekker knew about books, he knew very little about human beings. "It seems like a waste of time to have quit. It took you years to get as far as you did in your studies, then you simply walked away from it."

"Would you believe me," Benson said, "if I told you that I felt God was calling me into a different life?"

"But you could have used your medical skills so wonderfully well. Medical missionaries are valuable to God."

"All people are valuable to God, don't you agree, Professor?"

"Well, yes, of course. I didn't mean . . ." Dekker hated to be checkmated in an argument, so he changed the subject. "What did you think about Jeanne's decision to go home?"

"I guess I wasn't too surprised."

"Really? Why not?"

"She's never had her heart in this work. I think she probably would have gone home sooner or later."

Professor Dekker nodded slowly. "You may be right. Well, I'm going below. This is too rough for me."

Benson watched the small man leave the deck. He studied the sails overhead, but most of them had been taken down now. He held tightly to the rail as the *Mary Anne* rolled into a trough. He thought about the professor's question. It was one he was often asked and one he was not willing to answer. He made his way along the deck, holding on to the rail, and encountered Lars Olsen struggling to secure one of the yardarms with a length of rope.

"You'd better get off the deck, sir," Olsen said. "It's not safe for you to be out here."

"Not safe for you either, Lars."

Olsen grinned. "I get paid for it. You don't."

Benson nodded but did not go below. He watched the tall blond man struggle with the rope, then turned and studied Captain Barkley through the glass of the pilot house. He was holding on to the wheel firmly with a serious expression. *He's worried*, Benson thought, *and if he's worried, I am too*. He went into the pilot house and stared out the window. "This is pretty bad, isn't it, Captain?"

"I've seen worse."

Benson laughed. "I'm sure you have, but that's not a very comforting reply."

Benson stood silently while Barkley fought to maintain control of the *Mary Anne*, turning the wheel one way or the other, glancing up at the sails from time to time. "If it gets worse," he said finally, "we'll just have to run before the wind."

"I suppose that's the trouble with a sailing ship. You have to go with the wind."

"You can't tack in weather like this." Barkley shrugged. He turned to Benson and asked, "How's everyone taking this?"

"Nobody likes a storm."

Barkley smiled. "I do," he said, "if it's not too bad. There's nothing quite like tearing along under the sky with the waves high, the ship reeling all over the place."

"You have strange sources of pleasure, Captain."

"We all do, don't we?"

"I suppose you're right."

The two men said nothing again, and finally Barkley said soberly, "I've got a bad feeling about this, Mr. Benson."

"What do you mean?"

"This may turn out to be a typhoon. If it is, I'd just as soon be anchored in San Francisco."

"They're bad, are they—typhoons?"

"I think the devil's in every one of them."

★  ★  ★

Abby got up from her bunk and took only two steps before the *Mary Anne* dropped out from beneath her feet. She uttered a shrill cry as she fell headlong on the floor.

"Are you hurt, sweetheart?" Jimmy was by his wife's side immediately, his eyes filled with concern. He waited until the ship righted itself, then helped Abby to her feet. "I've never seen anything like this."

"I'm afraid, Jimmy! I wish we weren't here!"

"It'll be all right," Townsend said, trying to sound reassuring. But he himself had been feeling more than a little fear. The *Mary Anne* was being tossed about like a chip, and he was wishing fervently they had made the trip to the South Pacific in a more durable vessel. "Here, come sit down." Helping Abby to her bunk, he said, "You've eaten hardly anything, and you're pale."

Abby threw her arms around her husband and cried, "We're all going to die! I just know it!"

"Nonsense. Nobody's going to die."

But she shook her head and clung to him fiercely. Jimmy felt again the stirrings of doubt. He had secretly worried for some time that Abby was not nearly tough enough for the life of a missionary in a primitive land, but the idea of joining The Twelve and going out to such a glorious work had seemed so romantic. Now as the ship tossed and dipped and yawed, he felt the first taste of grim reality. He was willing enough to serve God, but he knew that he had led a rather sheltered life. Yet he had been so sure that God was calling him and Abby to spend their lives on the foreign field. Now as the two clung to each other, he tried to pray but found that praying was more difficult in a situation like this than in a nice quiet church in San Francisco!

★ ★ ★

Shep Riggs wiped the seawater from his face and tried to grin at Travis. "Well," he said cheerfully, "it looks like we're in for a bit of a blow."

Travis was soaked to the skin from the waves that were now crashing over the sides of the *Mary Anne* as she dipped, then rose and rolled from side to side. "You call this a bit of a blow? I'd call it a bad storm."

Shep looked at the sky, and doubt tinged his expression. "If it don't get no worse than this, we'll be all right."

"What if it does get worse?"

"Then we'll just have to run it out. We'll put on as little sail as we can—just enough to keep us making headway—and hope this storm runs out of steam. We're way off course now."

"How do you know?"

"Why, can't you tell? We're not on a true course."

"I don't know anything about things like that."

"I'm no navigator, but I know we're miles from where we should be. Of course, as soon as this thing blows out and the sun comes along, the captain will take a bearing and set us right again."

"I'm ready for that right now."

"So am I," Shep said, his voice steady but his face revealing the doubt he felt. "So am I, buddy!"

★ ★ ★

Neither Rena nor Meredith had said anything for ten minutes. Both of them were aware that the storm had increased in velocity, and when they looked out the port-hole, there was nothing to see. Everything was so gray it was impossible to tell the sea from the sky. Finally Rena said in an unnaturally high voice, "Well, we're having a little adventure."

Meredith had been trying to read, but as the ship jerked itself around, it became more and more difficult. Closing the book, she put it down on her bunk and looked over toward Rena. "I suppose we are."

"I think I'll go up and ask the captain how long this is likely to last."

"You'll get soaked," Meredith warned.

"I suppose so, but I'd really like to hear what he thinks."

Leaving the cabin, Rena moved along the corridor. She climbed the ladder that led to the deck, and when she opened the door, she gasped as a torrent of water struck her in the face and soaked every thread of her garments. She gasped and hung on until the ship had rolled so that she could get outside, then shut the door. She made her way into the wheelhouse and saw that Cerny Novak was stand-ing beside Barkley. They could not hear her with the crash-ing waves and whistling wind. But she could just hear Novak shouting, "We're gonna founder if this gets any worse, Captain."

"Take down all topsails. We're going to have to run before the wind."

"Yes, sir."

Novak turned and stopped briefly when he saw Rena. Then he nodded to her without speaking and left the wheel-house. Rena pulled herself forward, hanging on to the side and said, "Captain, how long is this going to last?"

"I have no way of knowing, Miss Rena. But we've got to run before the wind now."

"What does that mean?"

"We take down all except the lower sails and go where the wind is pushing us. We'll be way off course by the time this blow is over, so it'll take longer than we thought to arrive at our destination."

"But we'll be all right, won't we?"

"If it doesn't get any worse."

Rena stared at the captain. "Well . . . what if it *does* get worse?"

Captain Barkley did not answer for a time, then turned his frosty eyes on her. "We'll just have to see what happens." His reply was short, his voice spare.

Rena felt something close around her throat. She did not analyze the sensation enough to know that it was fear, for she had experienced little of that emotion. But as she watched the sailors frantically trimming the sails and saw the captain using brute force to control the wheel, for the first time in her life she felt frail and vulnerable. The *Mary Anne* was a speck, an atom, out on the raging Pacific, caught in the midst of a storm. She had no idea how much punishment the vessel could take. She had always thought of a ship as being like any other vehicle, something you got into, made a pleasant journey, and then stepped off at a safe harbor.

But there was nothing safe about what was going on outside. The horizon was impossible to see, and flashes of lightning broke the darkness of the sky. The wind howled with a demonic screaming as it raced across the sea. Towering waves shattered relentlessly over the *Mary Anne*, one of them catching a sailor—she thought it was Charlie Day— sweeping the small man off his feet and washing him toward the edge. He would have gone overboard if Lars Olsen had not caught him and helped him back to his feet.

Rena shouted to the captain, "It-it'll be all right, won't it? I mean the ship won't sink, will it?"

"I don't mean to frighten you, Miss Rena, but any ship can sink." He turned to her, his face frozen by a terrible sobriety. He was not a man given to fear, Rena knew, but she had never seen this look before. "If I were you," he said evenly, "I'd go down and tell all your friends to start praying. We're going to need God to get us out of this."

The captain's words frightened Rena more than the wind and the waves, and she could not move for a moment. But finally she turned and made her way back belowdecks. She considered doing what the captain had suggested, but she feared the team would panic. She herself was very close to losing control. She was on her way back to her own cabin when Dalton suddenly appeared.

"You've been on the main deck?" he asked.

"Yes."

"What did the captain say?"

"He said . . . that all of us had better pray."

Dalton looked as though he had been struck. He did not move for a moment, then swallowed hard. "I guess he thinks it's pretty serious, then."

"It *is* serious, Dalton. This ship could sink."

Dalton considered this, then said, "I'll go up and talk to him."

"It won't do any good."

"I'll go anyway."

Rena watched him go, then had a thought. She knocked on one of the cabin doors and it opened at once. Lanie stood there, her eyes wide. "What is it? Are we going to sink?"

Maggie was sitting on the bunk, her hands clasped together. She whispered, "What is it, Rena?"

"The ship's in danger. The captain wants us all to pray." She entered, shut the door, and the three women began to pray—that is, Lanie did. The other two appeared to be half paralyzed. Rena was usually the one to lead in prayer, but now her mind seemed frozen. She could no more speak than she could have flown away, and as Lanie prayed, Rena found that the strength had drained out of her. She sank down next to Maggie, and the two women threw their arms around each other as if they were small children afraid of the dark.

★ ★ ★

After twenty-four hours the storm had only increased in velocity. The crew had been living on cold sandwiches, but most of the passengers cared little for food. It was Benson who went around insisting that they all eat. He was now joined by Travis, who was helping Oscar in the galley with the food.

"Have you ever been in a storm like this, Oscar?" Travis asked as he braced himself against the roll of the ship and laid a thick chunk of ham between two slices of bread.

"Once . . . back in twenty-nine. I was on a steamer then. We all thought it was gonna go down."

"But it didn't."

"No, it didn't." Oscar turned to face Travis. "You Christians ain't afraid to die, are you?"

"I'd just as soon not."

"Then you *are* afraid," Oscar said.

Travis knew that Oscar Blevins was a tough man, but he could tell that his self-confidence was shaken now. "I think we're all afraid of anything we've never experienced. Like going down a flight of steps in the dark. You have to feel for the next step because you don't know where it is. It might be gone. That kind of thing makes a fellow a little nervous."

"I'm more than a little nervous," Oscar said evenly.

"You don't know the Lord, do you, Oscar?"

"No."

"It might be a good time to think about it."

"What kind of a man would I be to ignore God all my life and then call on Him just when I'm in trouble?"

"That's the best time," Travis said. He continued to make sandwiches, but he was more interested in Oscar than he was in the food. "Have you ever read the Bible?"

"Not much."

"You ever hear about the thief on the cross when Jesus was dying?"

"Heard a sermon on that once."

"Then you'll remember that the thief had no hope of getting off that cross alive, yet he said, 'Lord, remember me when thou comest into thy kingdom.' And Jesus said, 'Today shalt thou be with me in paradise.'"

Blevins had poised his knife to cut through another slice of the ham, but now he looked at Travis. "You think it's that easy? A man's a sinner all his life and in one second he's not?"

"I think it has to be that way. If it weren't for God's mercy, no man could be good enough to please God. We're all sinners. Every one of us. But Jesus died so we could be fit to meet God."

Both men turned as Chipoa came hurtling through the door. He shut it behind him, muffling the howling of the wind to some degree, then turned to grin at the pair.

"It's a little rough out there," he exclaimed as he pulled his oilskins off and stood beside Oscar. "Not easy to cook with the ship rolling like this."

"You ever been in a blow this bad, Chip?" Blevins asked.

"No. This is the worst."

"You don't seem worried," Travis observed. "I'd say we're in a pretty tight spot."

Chip shrugged and pulled a biscuit out of a sealed box before he answered. "If we go down, we do. If God wants us to live, we will." He appeared calm as always, and as he bit off a chunk of the cold biscuit, he added, "That's one of the good things about being a Christian. No matter what happens, it's from God."

Travis looked skeptical. "Even if it's bad?"

Blevins shook his head. "That don't sound right to me—God sending bad things."

"When that boy of yours gets sick, Oscar, you sometimes have to hold him to make him take the bad-tasting medicine, right?" Chip asked. "But you do it for his good, because you love him."

"I guess . . . but this is different."

"God knew before He made the world that we'd be on this ship," he continued, "and He sent this storm. It's all part of His plan. So I don't worry—whatever happens next, the good Lord planned it all for our good." He turned to Travis, asking, "What's that Scripture you quoted yesterday—about everything being good for believers?"

"'All things work together for good to them that love God, to them who are the called according to his purpose.'"

"So that's all we need to know. This storm will work for our good." He grabbed a Thermos jug and said, "I told Charlie I'd bring him some hot coffee."

As Chip left the cabin, Blevins asked Travis, "You believe all that stuff?"

"Well, it might be a little more complicated than Chip understands, but I do believe that God will take care of me, no matter what." He put his hand on Oscar's shoulder and said quietly, "That's why I'd like to see you safe in Jesus, Oscar. He loves you—and He wants you to be one of His sheep."

As the ship made its way through the mountainous seas, Travis told Oscar about his own experience in finding Christ. He saw that the tough man was listening, and he yearned to see him saved. But finally Oscar said, "I've been pretty sorry, but I'm not going to turn yellow at the last minute. Anyway, I think we'll get out of this all right."

Blevins face appeared to be working through some emotion, but he turned abruptly and left the cabin without a word. Travis stared after him sadly, then said aloud, "Lord, put your hand on Oscar. He needs you!"

Travis went topside, and the screaming wind whipped around him, plastering his clothes to his body. He had long since given up any attempt at staying dry, and now as he held tightly to the rail, he saw that Rena Matthews was there. She was wearing a raincoat and a rain hat, and as he moved closer, he shouted, "You shouldn't be out here alone, Rena!"

Rena turned to face him. Her face was pale, and her eyes were wide with fright. "I can't stay below."

"Well, you're not doing any good here," Travis said. "Come on. Let's go down, and you can put some dry clothes on. Oscar's made some fresh sandwiches."

"Who could eat at a time like this?"

Travis hesitated. Rena was obviously frightened, and he tried to assure her. "I think it'll blow itself out. We're going to be all right."

"What if we don't make it?"

"Well, if we don't, we don't."

Rena lowered her head and remained silent for a long time, and when she did speak, her words were almost inaudible. Travis had to lean forward to catch them over the shrill voice of the wind. "Aren't you afraid, Travis?"

Travis thought of Oscar, a rough fellow if there ever was one, who had just asked the same question. "Anybody would feel fear at a time like this, but I know that Jesus is here. He could speak to these waves, and they would calm down in an instant. He did that once, you remember?"

Rena turned to face him. Water ran down her face, but she paid no heed. "I've read that story so many times. It's . . . it's different when you're actually in a storm like this."

"It'll be all right," he said. "Why, I've had closer calls than this. I had amoebic dysentery down in Guatemala once. I lost fifty pounds, and I thought surely I was going to die."

"Were you afraid?"

"You know, strangely enough, after a while I wasn't. I asked God to give me His peace, and Brother Golden and his wife Merline, the missionaries down there, prayed for me. And it was like God put me in a big bubble. Everything else was outside—all my sickness, all the pain and fear. And inside it was warm—just me and Jesus." He smiled at her. "I never will forget that. I guess that's how I get most of my theology—by just going through things." He hesitated, then said, "I think God's testing us, Rena. There may be harder things than this coming up, and He wants to know if we'll trust Him. So don't look at those waves. Look to Jesus."

Rena did not move. "You're a comfort, Travis," she whispered.

"Go below now and get dried out."

Travis watched as she moved away, feeling a moment of pity for her. *She's never had a tough time before, and she'll have a lot more if we get through this.* He looked up at the sky and lifted one hand while holding on to the railing with the other. "God, I'm just asking you to save our lives. That's all. We have work to do for you, and I believe you're going to get us all out of this. Save every man of us and every woman too!"

★ ★ ★

Rena had managed to go to sleep, but she was awakened when Meredith shook her, saying insistently, "Wake up, Rena!"

"What is it?" Rena asked, yawning as she sat up.

"Travis just came by. He says we're close to an island."

"Then we'll be all right."

"I don't think so. He said Captain Barkley told him he can't control the ship, and we're headed straight for what looks a barrier reef."

"Y-you mean the ship will sink?"

"I don't know, but we've all got to be ready to abandon ship. Put on the warmest clothes you have."

Rena dressed hurriedly, and the two women left the cabin. They found the others all up on the deck, clinging together in the howling wind and holding on to the rails. The ship climbed each precipitous swell, then rushed head-long down into each deep trough. Rena caught at Dalton and screamed into the wind, "What's happening?"

Dalton pointed ahead. "You see those reefs over there? There's no way we can miss them. Look, the sails are almost all gone, and the captain says he can't turn the ship around. We're going to run into the reef, but there's an island there behind it."

Rena strained but could see nothing but a gloomy shadow beyond the reef where the water was breaking with enormous force.

Travis shouted above the din of the raging wind and waves, "We need to go below! When we hit, we could be thrown off the ship."

"What's going to happen?" Rena called out.

"The ship'll break up. But we hope we'll have time to launch the cutter and get to shore. All right, quick. Everybody below."

Numbly Rena obeyed as Travis herded the missionaries down the hatchway.

"Don't go in the cabins," he said. "Just sit on the floor. It'll be a pretty bad bump, I'm afraid."

Abby began to weep, and every face was unnaturally stiff. Travis said, "I think it's going to be all right. We've got a good chance. But it might be a good idea if we just remind the Lord that we're on His business. You want to pray, Rena?"

Rena whispered, "No. You do it, Travis."

Travis lifted his voice and said in an even tone, "Lord, these are your people. I ask that not a man or a woman be lost. We're here on your business, Lord, so save us in the name of Jesus. And we trust ourselves to your everlasting and almighty power."

Travis sat down between Rena and Meredith, bracing his back against the bulkhead. "Shouldn't be long now," he said.

He had no sooner spoken than there came a shout from topside. They couldn't make out what was being said, but a few seconds later there was a crunching, wrenching squeal, and the ship seemed to turn sideways. Although the breaking noise continued, the rocking of the ship suddenly lessened, and Travis jumped up and shouted, "That's it! She's stuck on the rocks. Come on, all of you." He stood at the ladder and urged them all on.

Rena gasped when she stepped outside, for the *Mary Anne* was indeed perched precariously on the rocks that were just breaking the surface of the water. The waves were breaking hard against the boat, and even as Rena watched in horror, Captain Barkley yelled at the crew, "Lower the cutter! We've gotta get off now. She's gonna break up!"

Travis leaped up to help the men struggle to lower the cutter, while the women sat on the deck so as not to lose their balance. The wind was blowing so fiercely it was impossible to speak or hear.

Finally Travis was back, motioning for them all to get into the smaller boat. Rena was frozen in place, so Travis yanked her to her feet.

Putting his lips close to her ear, he said, "Come on, Rena. This is your chance to show what you're made of. Think of what your dad would do."

Rena suddenly pulled herself upright and reached down to take Maggie Smith's arm. "Come on, Maggie. We're going to be all right."

The cutter was pitching, and it was all the crew could do to hold her in place, but finally they were all in. Captain Barkley shouted, "All right, men, into the boat!"

The cutter was packed, and as the sailors scrambled in, taking their place at the oars, the cutter suddenly dipped down and water poured in.

"Shove us off, Travis!" Barkley shouted, and Travis and Novak leaped out of the boat and shoved with all their might to get the boat clear from the side of the *Mary Anne*. The waves caught the cutter, and both men clung to the side.

"Pull them in!" the captain shouted. At once Dalton and Karl were there to haul the two men inside. "We'd better get out of here," Novak shouted, "or we'll break up!"

Rena crouched in the seat between Charlie Day and Lars Olsen. The sailors pulled frantically, but it was the waves that rolled them toward the shore.

After a fearsome ride, Rena felt the prow of the cutter crunch on the sand, and Travis yelled, "Everybody out! Pull the boat in. We'll need it."

Rena almost fell over the side. At Captain Barkley's direction, they all tugged until the boat was out of the reach of the surf.

"We'll have to drag it to those trees or the waves will

take her, Captain," Novak shouted.

It was a titanic struggle, but the sailors attached ropes and winched the boat along painfully until it was up on the line of vegetation.

Rena fell down, panting for breath. She could see the *Mary Anne* out on the reef, being twisted and warped by the waves that struck her broadside. She looked behind her up on the shore. She could see little, for night was almost upon them, but the earth seemed to rise up dark and foreboding. She did not move until Travis came and pulled at her arm. "Come on. Let's get back in the shelter of the trees."

Rena came to her feet and stumbled along with him. She would have fallen more than once if Travis had not helped her, and she noticed that the other men were helping the other women. When they reached the tree line, she took one last look at the wreck of what had once been the pride of her father's life. The trees seemed to close about them, and the wind sounded less shrill. Finally Captain Barkley said, "We can rest here. It'll be safe."

Rena sank to the ground with her back against a palm tree, folded her arms across her knees, and began to tremble. She was cold and weak, and she felt they would never be really safe—not in this awful place! *I wish I'd gone home with Jeanne!* she cried to herself, but then she shoved the thought away and put her head down on her knees and wept silently. She was as miserable as she'd ever been in her life.

PART TWO

# September–December 1935

★ ★ ★

# CHAPTER EIGHT

# THE DARKEST HOUR

★ ★ ★

Rena Matthews had heard the phrase "howling like a banshee" all of her life but had no idea what a banshee howl sounded like. As she crouched with her back against a tree, clutching herself as the driving wind plastered her dress to her body, she felt that she had a pretty good idea. The wind was screaming, and together with the roaring crash of the surf, it made a deafening sound. Dawn had come, but the heavy clouds hung low over the churning sea. As Rena huddled with the others staring out at the waves, she thought she saw faces in their watery depths—terrible, grotesque faces like gargoyles, leering and rushing forward, stopped only by the beach from devouring the survivors.

"What are we going to do?" she whispered.

She was sitting beside Dalton, who seemed to be equally mesmerized by the waves. He turned to her, and she saw that his face was stiff with tension. "I don't know," he muttered. "We've got to do *something*. Surely someone must live on this island."

The words brought little comfort to Rena, and she glanced around in the feeble dawn and noted that everyone was as soaked and miserable as she was. Captain Barkley was standing stiffly, his back as straight as a ramrod, the rain pouring down his hair and face, for he wore no hat. Suddenly he turned and lifted his voice above the din. "Crew members, we've got to go back to the ship."

"Back to the ship?" Jimmy was sitting with his arm around Abby. Both of them looked totally miserable, and Jimmy's voice cracked as he said, "That's impossible, Captain! No one could get back there."

"Somebody had better. We've got to have some supplies." Barkley surveyed the group. "It's gonna take all of us crewmen to fight through that surf. Come on. Waiting isn't going to make it any easier."

Charlie Day whimpered, "But, Captain, I can't swim."

"You might as well drown as starve to death. It'll be quicker that way. Don't argue with me."

"I'll pull an oar, Captain," Pete Alford said as he stood. "I think we can make it."

Travis chimed in, "I'll go too."

"Good. Let's get at it."

Rena watched as the crewmen, along with Pete and Travis, left the shelter of the trees and leaned into the wind, which plastered their clothes to their bodies. She looked beyond them to the raging sea and shook her head. "Dalton, they'll never make it."

"Maybe I ought to go with them."

"No, you stay here. They've got enough men," Rena said quickly. She was ordinarily a strong woman, but all of the sources of her strength had been torn away from her. As she watched Barkley organize the men in the driving rain and push the cutter out into the waves, she thought how she had always leaned on her father. But her father wasn't here now. No one was here, and fear ran along her nerves.

Lanie MacKay was standing close beside her along with Maggie. She said, "This is terrible, Maggie. We'll never get out of here alive."

Maggie did not answer right away but finally said heavily, "We'll just have to pray that God will be with us."

The missionaries all heard this statement, but none of them answered. They were all struck dumb by the violence and suddenness of the catastrophe, and now they could do nothing but watch as the cutter was tossed high by the oncoming waves.

"It's such a little boat," Rena whispered.

"It's little, but it's all we've got," Karl said, his tone resigned and his jaw set. He turned his back and refused to watch the scene. It was as if he knew something terrible were about to happen and could not bear to see it.

Dalton whispered, "We've got to get busy doing something. We can't just stand here."

"What should we do, Dalton?"

"It doesn't matter. Just something to keep busy." He surveyed the area. "We've got to have a fire. Everybody start looking for wood."

"A fire? Why, that's impossible!" Professor Dekker exclaimed. He looked pitifully small as he stood there with water dripping off his hat in a steady stream. "Nobody could start a fire in this downpour."

But Dalton shook his head and said firmly, "We'll have to wait until the wood dries out, but at least we'll have it here ready. Come on, now. Everyone get moving."

Rena felt as hopeless as the professor about starting a fire, but she knew action was better than doing nothing, so she pulled herself to her feet and began to look for suitable wood. "Come on. Things will look better when this rain stops. We'll get a fire started somehow." She headed back into the trees with Dalton and collected branches. Everyone else had also turned to the task as if glad to have something to do. "That was a good idea, Dalton," she said.

"The professor might be right. I don't know how we'll start a fire with this."

★　★　★

"The cutter's coming back!"

Rena was tugging at a branch of a tree that had fallen, trying vainly to break it off, when she heard Maggie's voice. She turned quickly and ran with the others to the beach. Rena grabbed for Maggie's arm as the group watched the small boat head straight for the beach at a terrific speed. The men were rowing for all they were worth, riding the crest of a large wave, and her heart leaped into her throat as she whispered, "Maggie, the boat will be crushed."

"Maybe not. They're good seamen."

They all watched as the cutter was lifted high and then washed up on the beach in a rush. Miraculously it appeared to have been lifted up and placed there safely, as if by a benevolent hand.

"They're all right!" Dalton cried. "Come on. Let's go help unload the supplies."

They all rushed down to the cutter, and as the sailors piled out, Captain Barkley ordered, "Pull it up out of the surf."

Rena took hold of the side of the craft, ignoring the waves that washed up on her ankles, and added her little strength. As the keel of the boat crunched on the rocks, Captain Barkley directed, "Get these supplies out quickly! We've got to go back."

No one needed any urging, for they all realized that any hope of survival lay in the supplies they had brought. Everything was in a jumble—boxes, loose cans, canvas—but no one stopped to sort it out. Men and women alike, except for Abby, worked to empty the vessel. They struggled against the wind, which had not relented in the least, and Captain Barkley instructed them to put the supplies under the shelter of the trees. When they completed the unloading, he shouted, "We've gotta go back. There's plenty of canvas here and there's an ax. Cut some saplings. Rig up some tents for shelter. Come on, you men, we can make it back again."

"It's gettin' worse, Captain," Lars said. "That wind's gettin' higher. If we capsize, we'll all drown. I can't swim a lick."

"Neither can I," Charlie said, his teeth chattering with the cold.

"We're going back and that's it! Come along."

Travis's hands were blistered as he pulled on the oars, and as the cutter rose sharply, he braced himself for the boat to capsize, but miraculously it did not. He swung his head to see that they were approaching the *Mary Anne*, then turned and put his back to the oars. Cerny Novak was sitting beside him, pulling the opposite oar. He handled the oar as if it were a toothpick, the muscles in his frame contracting with little effort. "We've gotta be careful not to crash this cutter against the ship," he shouted.

"I know," Travis shouted back. "We need all the stuff we can get from the *Mary Anne*."

Captain Barkley shouted commands, and when they were close enough, it was Barkley himself who leaped on board and caught the lines that tied the cutter to the ship. "Get all the canvas you can find and any tools."

"Better get the guns too, Captain, don't you think?" Cerny yelled.

"Yes, and all the ammunition you can find. Get with it now!"

For the next thirty minutes the men swarmed over the *Mary Anne*, some dashing below and running into each other in their haste. Travis struggled up the ladder time after time, carrying boxes of canned food, knowing that the food might be the difference between living and dying. He noted each time he emerged from below that the weather was getting worse—if that were possible—and he knew they had to hurry.

Just as he was plunging down for another load, he heard the captain shout, "All right, that's it! Come on! Let's get away from here before this cutter breaks up!"

On impulse, Travis rushed downstairs and grabbed a large canvas laundry bag. He entered the first cabin, which had been occupied by Jimmy and Abby, and scanned the room with a flashlight. He found several books and personal items and stuffed them into the bag. He went into each cabin, as quickly as he could, taking something personal, in most cases notebooks and Bibles. Finally he heard his name being called and rushed back down the passageway, climbed the ladder, and found the others in the cutter waiting for him.

"Where've you been? Get in the boat!" Captain Barkley shouted.

Travis jumped in, falling down and losing his footing. He struck his head on the side, and for a moment the world seemed to be turning, with bright, spinning stars. He felt hands on him straightening him up and looked up to see Pete Alford staring at him strangely. "Where were you?"

"Just getting a few extra things."

"Well, the captain is breathin' fire. We've gotta get out of here."

Indeed, the cutter was now being driven against the side of the *Mary Anne* with frightening force. They all shoved off with their oars, and the heavily laden cutter wallowed, but the men began rowing as hard as they could.

As Travis pulled on his oar, he glanced up and thought he could see a break in the clouds, but the wind howled as fiercely as ever, and the waves were no more gentle. *We've got to get to shore*, he thought. *This cutter won't take much more pounding*.

When they reached the island, the other survivors were waiting to help them, and Travis saw that Dalton and Karl were finishing tying a canvas over a framework to make a shelter. Travis labored with the others to get the supplies under it, and then he realized that he was weak with fatigue. Looking around at the other men trembling, he approached Barkley. "Captain, if we could get a fire started, I think it would help."

"A fire in this downpour?"

"I think that would be wonderful," Meredith said as she joined the two, "but who could start a fire?"

Her eyes looked black in the gloom, and her hair was plastered down. "You think you could do it, Travis?"

"I can try," Travis said. "Of course, it'll be a lot easier if we have a lighter. Anybody got a lighter?" he asked the group.

"I've got one," Charlie announced, "but it's awful wet."

Professor Dekker snorted, "Impossible in this weather! We'll have to wait until the sun comes out and dries the wood."

"I don't want to wait. In Guatemala I made a fire under some pretty bad conditions. Not this bad, but I think I can do it."

Travis looked around and saw the fear and fatigue that was reflected on every face. He grinned suddenly. "An old Boy Scout like me can always make a fire. Let's go find some punk."

"Punk? What's that?" Shep Riggs demanded. "I've known some punks in my day, but that's not what you mean, is it?"

"No, come on. I'll show you. Some of you break up the smallest pieces of wood you can find. Just very small twigs."

Leaving the shelter of the tarpaulin with oilcloth and ax in hand, Travis plunged out into the rain, accompanied by Pete and Shep.

"I don't know what punk is either," Pete said. "What is it, Travis?"

"It's this." Travis stopped beside a fallen tree and spread the oilcloth on the ground. "See this tree? We've got to get into the middle of it. It's been down a long time and it's rotten, but inside you'll find some punk."

Travis used the ax to break through the bark. Soon he had cleared away enough to get his hand inside. "You see this stuff? It's dry, and it burns better than anything."

"I gotcha," Shep said, and he and Pete began hacking away at the tree. They worked hard, and it did not take long for them to fill up the oilcloth.

Pete wrapped it up and asked, "Will this be enough?"

"I think so. Come on. Let's get back and try it."

The three made their way back to the tarpaulin, where they found that Rena had led the search for tiny branches. "Will this be enough, Travis?" she said, waving at a pile.

"It'll be enough to get us started, but keep breaking off some more." Travis knelt down squarely under the center of the tarpaulin and looked up. "We'll have to be careful not to burn that. Let's have some of that punk."

Pete laid the oilcloth down. Travis began to make a small pile of the punk, adding some of the smallest of the twigs. The twigs were wet, but the punk was bone dry. "Alright, Charlie, let's have that light."

Charlie plunged his hand into his pocket. "Like I said, it's gotten pretty wet."

Travis took the lighter and gave it a try. Nothing happened. He tried three times.

Charlie groaned, "It ain't gonna work!"

Even as Day spoke, the lighter caught, and quickly Travis touched the tiny flame to the punk. He held it steady, and the punk caught almost at once. "Let's have a few more pieces of punk." He began crumbling it up, and soon the twigs, wet as they were, began to catch.

"That's beautiful, Travis!" Maggie exclaimed. "I never thought a fire could look so good."

"Little things make a difference," Travis said. He continued to add small twigs, and soon the fire was dancing wildly in the wind. "Make a circle around it and cut off the wind."

"Gladly," Oscar Blevins said. "If we can keep that fire going, we can make something to eat."

"That's a great idea, Cook," Captain Barkley said. He knew the value of food for hungry, tired, wet people. "We'll fix us a meal and dry our clothes out. This weather has to clear off some time or other."

"Look, I found this coffee," Lanie said. "You think we could find something to brew it in?"

The search began, and soon stew pans and a coffeepot appeared. At Travis's direction, enough stones were brought in to make a makeshift stove on which the coffee could be boiled.

They all watched as Oscar made the coffee and Novak searched through the paraphernalia to find enough cups. Oscar boiled coffee in the stew pans as well as the coffeepot while Travis tended the fire, making sure it was spread out over a wider area rather than lumped in one large flame. Lanie smiled at him as she helped. "That coffee smells better than anything I've ever smelled in my life."

"Nothing like good coffee, Miss MacKay."

"Just call me Lanie, Travis. I don't see much use for formality in this place." She stretched her fingers out toward the fire. "It's amazing how much difference a fire and the aroma of coffee make."

"Hope feeds on very small things." Travis smiled. He studied her for a moment and then said, "We're going to have some hard times, Lanie. You're strong enough to help the others."

"What makes you say that?"

"Oh, I'm an expert on women."

Lanie laughed. "Good to have one expert on this island."

Finally the coffee was ready, and while no one got a large amount, they all had at least one cup. As they enjoyed their coffee, Rena asked, "Captain, how long do you think it'll be before a ship comes by?"

Everyone turned to face Barkley. He took another sip of the coffee and then shook his head. "We've got to be honest about this. We were blown off course hundreds of miles. I don't think we're on any of the main shipping lanes now, and I doubt that we're close to any of the mainlands."

"But ships do come by, don't they?" Abby said nervously. Her eyes were wide, and she was obviously much the worse for fear.

"I don't want to be unrealistic, Miss Townsend, but there's always hope. Most of these islands are uninhabited. Ships have no reason to go near them. But we're lucky about one thing."

"What's that, Captain?" Dalton asked. "I don't see we've had much luck."

"Some of these islands are pretty flat and some are hilly or mountainous. The ones with some elevation are the best if you've got to be marooned."

"Why's that?" Dalton asked.

"Because the flat ones get practically cleared off every time a storm comes along. But if you can get up the mountain away from the surf, you'll have a better chance. There's more wildlife. If we have to live on what we can kill, this looks like a fairly good place."

"But we won't be here that long, will we?" Maggie said, fear in her voice. She had downed her coffee quickly and now stood with her shoulders drooping, a pathetic figure in the weak light that filtered through the heavy clouds.

"No one knows. But like I say," Captain Barkley said with a shrug, "we can always hope."

The captain's words cast a gloom on the group, and they gazed dejectedly into the fire.

"You know," Pete said, "I think we should have a thanksgiving service to mark this day."

"What have we got to be thankful for?" Cerny Novak snapped.

Travis turned and said, "You're not feeding the sharks, for one."

"That's right," Barkley said. "I think a service would be a good idea. Oscar, do you think you can put a meal together?"

"Yes, sir."

"You do it, then, and afterward you folks can have your service." He turned to face the crew. "I guess if you've got to be marooned on a desert island, it's a good thing to have a bunch of missionaries along." He laughed loudly. "You'll have a built-in congregation of sinners that can't run away. Come on, Oscar, fix that meal!"

★　★　★

Travis sat down with the tin plate in his hand that contained a slice of ham, some canned green beans, and a biscuit. The sailors and missionaries had all more or less dried out huddling around the fire, and now they enjoyed the meal. As soon as Travis took a bite he found that he was ravenous. He ate slowly, chewing the food thoroughly, and noted that most of the sailors had bolted their portions.

Meredith was sitting on Travis's right, with Pete on her other side. Meredith looked at Pete's plate and said, "Pete, it's not fair that you get the same size as I do. You're twice as big. Here, have some of mine."

"No, Meredith, that wouldn't be right," Pete said, then called out, "Hey, Shep, why don't you sing a hymn for us?"

"You know hymns, Shep?" Karl asked. "I thought you were just a rough, tough sailor."

"I wasn't always a sailor. I was raised by a preacher, and I've got a good memory for hymns," Shep said.

"Well, let's have one, then," Rena put in.

"Yes, and make it a cheerful one," Dalton added. He licked his fingers after eating the last of his food and asked, "What kind of hymns do you know?"

"Oh, my uncle wasn't any regular brand of preacher," Shep said, grinning. He was sitting beside Maggie and turned to wink at her. "I guess I know two kinds of songs. One's hymns and the other's rowdy sailor songs."

"Do you know 'It Is Well With My Soul,' Shep?" Travis asked.

"Sure, I know that one." Shep, without embarrassment, lifted his head and began to sing. He had a beautifully clear tenor voice, and the melodious sound of it filled the surroundings in a mysterious way.

"When peace, like a river, attendeth my way,
When sorrows like sea billows roll;
Whatever my lot, Thou hast taught me say,
'It is well, it is well with my soul.'

"It is well, with my soul,
It is well, with my soul,
It is well, it is well with my soul.

"Though Satan should buffet, though trials should come,
Let this blest assurance control,
That Christ has regarded my helpless estate,
And hath shed His own blood for my soul.

"My sin, oh, the bliss of this glorious thought!
My sin, not in part but the whole,
Is nailed to the cross, and I bear it no more,
Praise the Lord, praise the Lord, O my soul!

"And, Lord, haste the day when my faith shall be sight,
The clouds be rolled back as a scroll;
The trump shall resound, and the Lord shall descend,
Even so, it is well with my soul."

"That's kind of a mournful song," Novak said.

"It's a good one, though," Travis said. "I read the story of how that hymn came to be. It was written by a man named Horatio Spafford. He was a Chicago businessman who lost just about everything in the Great Chicago Fire. They had also lost a young son the previous year. He and his wife decided to go to England on vacation as well as to help their friend Dwight L. Moody with his evangelistic tour. Spafford was delayed by business and sent his wife and four daughters ahead on a ship called the *SS Ville de Havre*, and he planned to follow them in a few days."

Travis reached out and picked up a twig. He held it in the fire until it caught and then stared at it as if it had great meaning. Silence had fallen around the small shelter. The wind had died down some, though it still moaned far out over the sea, and the crash of the waves was audible. Travis continued, "The ship hit another ship and it went down within twelve minutes. Two hundred twenty-six lives were lost—including the Spaffords' four daughters."

"How terrible!" Rena whispered, her eyes fixed on Travis.

"Mrs. Spafford was saved, and when she got ashore in England, she sent a two-word telegram to her husband: 'Saved alone.' Mr. Spafford took the next ship across the Atlantic to join his wife and asked the captain to awaken him at the place where the *Ville de Havre* had gone down. As he looked out over the waters, God spoke to him, and he went to his cabin and wrote that song."

Travis seemed lost in thought, and then he said, "I've always loved those words. 'Whatever my lot, Thou has taught me to say, "It is well, it is well with my soul."'"

"That's a beautiful story," Lanie said softly.

"Yes, it is," Maggie said. "It's hard to realize that it is

well when you're in trouble like this."

Dalton spoke up. "Maybe we should have a sermon."

"Yes, you preach a good one, Dalton," Rena said.

"Not me. Professor, you give us a message."

Professor Jan Dekker was huddled with his back to a stack of supplies. "I don't feel much like a sermon." His tone was mournful, and he shivered. "Maybe some other time."

"Why don't you give us a sermon, Rena?" Maggie suggested. "You've always got a good one."

Rena swallowed hard and said, "I guess I'm like the professor. I don't think I have a sermon in me just now."

"Well, I do." Everyone turned toward Jimmy Townsend, sitting with his arm around his wife, looking at them in a strange way. "My sermon is this," he said. "Jesus said, 'I will never leave thee, nor forsake thee,' so that means He's right here around this fire with us. That's my sermon."

"Best sermon I ever heard," Travis called out. "Short and sweet and theologically sound."

Cerny Novak joined in the laughter. "That's the kind of sermons I like too."

"Well, I've got a surprise for you." Travis got to his feet, and picked up the canvas bag. He reached into it, saying, "On my last trip to the *Mary Anne* I went down to the cabins and grabbed whatever was on top of the furniture—mostly Bibles and books." He picked one out and handed it to Dekker. "I believe this is your Bible, Professor."

Professor Dekker jumped up. "Did you get any of my other books?"

"I got this notebook."

Dekker's eyes gleamed, and for the first time since the wreck, he seemed alive. "My notebook! It is irreplaceable. Thank you, Travis."

Travis pulled out other books, and everyone exclaimed over them.

"This is a funny one I got out of your cabin, Rena. *Robinson Crusoe*."

Rena laughed. "I don't know why I brought that book, but it's a good one to have in our condition." She went over and took the book. "Crusoe was just like us—tossed onto a desert island—but he never stopped trusting God."

"Did he ever get off that island, miss?" Novak demanded.

"After a long time he did. I think it was something like twenty years. I haven't finished it yet," Rena said.

"Well, I hope we don't have to stay twenty years in this place!" Dalton exclaimed. "That would be terrible."

Pete was running his hand over the Bible that Travis had salvaged from his cabin. "My mother gave me this. She's gone now, but it's filled with notes from her. I thank you, Travis. This means a lot to me."

Everyone joined in Pete's sentiments, and finally Travis said, "Well, I think what we'd better do now is try to get up some individual tents. One for the ladies and one for the men."

"Yes, the rain has slowed down. We could probably do that now," Captain Barkley said.

They all went to work, and by the time it started to get dark, a camp had been arranged with three tents—one for the men, one for the women, and one to store the supplies and keep them dry.

Oscar cooked another meal for supper, and later they sat around the fire long after dark, no one wanting to go to bed. Rena sat beside Dalton, staring at the fire. She was weary and tired, as they all were, and her spirit seemed to sink. Outside of the little ring of fire that they kept going constantly, there was nothing but darkness and mystery and the sound of the surf. She looked up at Dalton, who sat silently, and asked, "We'll be all right, won't we, Dalton?"

"We've got to be," he said grimly.

"This is the darkest hour. It'll be better when the weather clears. And a ship will come. I know it will." Even as she spoke these words Rena felt a twinge of doubt. She did not really believe what she was saying. She said it again as if repeating it would make it so. "A ship will come," she said confidently. "We won't be here long. . . ."

# CHAPTER NINE

# FOREVER IS A LONG TIME

★ ★ ★

The sun was a bright yellow wafer pasted in the blue sky overhead. The heat of the sun warmed Rena's face, and as she rode down in a semicircular direction, she screamed and leaned over toward the big man beside her. She was actually afraid of heights, but as his arm enveloped her and his voice rang out over the laughter of the crowds filling the fairground, Rena felt safe and secure.

The Ferris wheel rolled past the earth, then rose back up, sailing high in the air. Rena lifted her head to watch but still clung to her father as the world fell away and they reached the dizzying apex. She delighted in looking way down at the people milling about like ants, then far off to the rising hills of the countryside.

Down and then up in a huge circle like a giant swing. She looked up and said, "Daddy, this is the most fun I've ever had."

"Is it, sweetheart? Then we'll have to come to the fair every day as long as it's here."

"Can we really?"

Rena's father laughed. "Why, sure we can. What else

would be more important to me than taking you for Ferris wheel rides?"

Happiness filled Rena, and she clung to her father's arm, safe and—

Rena abruptly awoke and quickly realized that the sunshine was a mere dream, as was her father's presence. She stiffened as she lay in the darkness, filled with fear, for something had just scampered across the blanket that covered her. Shep had warned them that land crabs might crawl over them as they slept on the ground, but he had assured them they were harmless.

That assurance did not ease her panic, and she shook the blanket violently—the action bringing a protest from Lanie, who lay on her right.

The tent was dark and the ground unbearably hard. The oilcloth under them gave some protection from the dampness but no cushioning. The blankets had dried out enough for each of them to have one. She was thankful for the efforts of Travis and Dalton to provide this much shelter, but it was nothing like the comfortable bunk of the *Mary Anne* or her own bedroom at home. Rena's eyes were open wide, but it was as dark as if they were closed. For a time she lay listening to sounds she could not identify except for one, the exotic cry of a bird. Finally she became aware that light was creeping through the walls of the tent and through the gaps where the flap covered the entrance. Throwing the blanket back, she rose and moved carefully across the tent. Abby, Meredith, Maggie, and Lanie all shared it with her, and she did not want to step on any of them.

As she emerged, she saw that the east was touched with a pale milky light, and the first rays of the sun were filtering through the towering trees. She saw the fire was kindled under the cooking canopy, and two figures were vaguely distinguishable. She moved closer and shivered in the cool morning air. The surf was still crashing, and the wind was brisk, though not as severe as it had been during the storm. As she moved closer, she could make out Travis and the stocky form of Oscar. The two men were talking in subdued voices.

"Good morning," Rena greeted.

"You're up early," Travis said. "You should have slept later."

Rena did not want to admit she couldn't get back to sleep with crabs scuttling across her body, so she simply asked, "What are you doing?"

"We got a prize here, Miss Rena," Oscar said. He motioned down at his feet, and Rena leaned forward to see a huge creature. "A fine turtle. We'll be havin' turtle soup for lunch today. Better than you could get at the Waldorf."

Rena peered at the sea turtle. "It must have taken both of you to carry him here."

"It did. We were lucky to run him down," Travis said. "We were walking at the water's edge when I spotted him heading for the ocean. Got to him just before he hit the surf. Saw some other turtles too, so that's a good sign. We won't starve to death as long as fellows like this are around."

Oscar said, "How about some coffee?"

"We'd better go easy on that," Travis warned. "We can't run down to the grocery store and get a fresh supply."

Oscar chuckled. "Yeah, you're right. Maybe we can find some kind of edible root to make tea with. I had a friend once that dug sassafras root down south somewhere."

"I used to dig 'em myself," Travis said. "Makes a pretty good tea. There should be something like that on this island."

Rena stared at the two men in disbelief. They were speaking as if they planned to stay on the island forever. The thought disturbed her, and she quickly changed the subject. "Is Dalton up yet?"

"All of the men got up early. The captain took a crew down along the beach that way. Dalton and three of the sailors went the other way. They want to see what kind of a place this is."

"I wish I'd known. I would have gone with them."

"They left about an hour ago," Oscar said.

Travis nodded. "I plan to be back sometime before noon, but don't worry about me if I'm a little late, Oscar."

"Where are you going, Travis?"

"I thought I'd go exploring inland and see if I can figure out how big the island is."

"I'll go with you," Rena said impulsively.

"Oh, I don't know, Rena. It'll be rough. We'll have to tramp through bushes and up steep hills."

"I don't mind. I won't hold you back."

For a moment Travis hesitated, and Rena grew agitated. "I'm going, Travis!"

Travis lifted his eyebrow and turned his head away. Rena thought he winked at Oscar, but she could not be sure.

"Be glad to have you," he conceded. "We'd better eat something first, or maybe carry some food along."

"We've got some canned soup here. I can heat it up in a jiffy," Oscar offered.

At the mention of food, Rena realized she was ravenous and said, "Yes, let's have that."

Fifteen minutes later they had eaten the warmed soup. Travis took one of the rifles and put several extra cartridges in his pocket. "I guess we're ready," he said and, without waiting, turned and walked directly into the trees that towered behind their small camp.

Rena hurried to keep up with him, and for thirty minutes they walked steadily. She was wearing a thin dress and was glad she still had her sturdy walking shoes. Travis wore a pair of wrinkled khaki trousers and a tan shirt open at the neck. He held the rifle loosely at his side. He did not speak for so long that Rena wondered if he was irritated at her insistence on coming. "How big do you think this place is?" Rena asked.

"We'll find out something about that today. I hope it's big."

"Why is that?"

"The bigger it is, the more life it'll have on it, and the more chance that some ship might see it. It looks favorable.

Look at those peaks up ahead, and the land's rising already. Can you tell?"

Indeed, Rena had been aware that they were walking up a gradual hill. The sun was climbing, and the sound of the surf had faded now, but the wind was still brisk. The forest seemed to be growing denser, however. Travis paused to point out a brilliant-colored bird with a long tail.

"It looks like a parrot," Rena said.

"Yes, I believe it is. They're all over the Pacific islands, I understand."

Travis moved easily, and Rena was aware of his keen strength. He wore no cap, and his tawny hair was tousled. She noticed it was growing long on the neck, and she wondered if the men had managed to salvage a razor and shears. She hated the thought of them looking like a bunch of savages, like the hero in the book she was reading. Robinson Crusoe had hacked his own hair off but had let his beard grow long. She remembered what a struggle the marooned man had just simply existing. "Maybe if we get up on those peaks, we'll be able to see smoke from a village."

"I hope so, but Captain Barkley doesn't think this is a very big island. He knows about things like that, I suppose, and Shep said the same thing."

"How can they tell?" she asked.

"Well, Shep's been around a lot of islands. He knows the feel of them, and the same is true for the captain." He paused and gave her a sideways glimpse. "Are you getting tired?"

"No, I'm fine."

"We're going to try to make it as far as we can," he said.

His words seemed like a rebuke to Rena. She had always prided herself on her strength. "Then let's go faster," she said. "You don't have to slow down for me." She deliberately threw herself into a fast walk but soon realized that his legs were so long he could easily beat her at this game.

They walked steadily, stopping once at a small spring. "This is great!" he said. "I've been worried about fresh water. I've been thinking about rigging up something so we could store rainwater."

Rena was thirsty indeed, and she leaned over and drank from the trickle emerging from a rock wall. It was a minuscule stream, but the water was cold and delicious.

"Probably runs year-round. Shep said there'd be springs like this. Wish I'd brought something to carry water in. We'll have to mark this spot."

"How will we mark it?"

"I'll tie my handkerchief up here, and we'll try to remember the way we came. Do you see that huge tree over there? It's much bigger than the rest. We ought to be able to spot it on the way back. Then, if we need to, we can come back here and get water for camp."

"It would be a long walk."

"We might want to move the camp here. Fresh water is essential."

★ ★ ★

After three hours of hard walking, Rena found herself panting for breath.

"We'll take a rest here," Travis told her. "And look, there's some kind of berries over there. I hope they're not poisonous."

Rena was alarmed. "You're not going to eat them, are you, without knowing?"

"I'll tell you what," Travis said and went to the bush to pull off some dark purple berries. "You eat one, and if you don't die, I'll know they're safe."

Rena glared at him indignantly and then saw his eyes were dancing with good humor. "I don't see how you can be so cheerful."

"Why not? We're alive, and we've just found lunch, I think." Travis put one of the berries in his mouth and chewed it thoughtfully. "Good," he said. "Real sweet. I was afraid they might be bitter. Here, have some."

Rena watched as Travis moved around the clump of bushes, pulling off berries, and she finally joined him. She found they tasted stronger than blackberries with a tangy essence. "These are good!"

"We'll have to remember this spot too. I wonder if you could dry these things and eat 'em like raisins."

The two ate their fill of berries, then found themselves thirsty again. "We'll watch for another spring or maybe even a stream."

Rena sat down and rested against a huge tree trunk. She ran her eyes around the surroundings and said, "This looks like a picture from *National Geographic*."

"It does at that," Travis agreed. He sat down across from her at another tree, laying the rifle down and stretching his legs out. He rolled his head around as if easing his neck muscles. "We could have had things a lot worse. Shep says some of these islands are nothing but coral. We'd have had no chance of survival on one of those."

"I think we'll be off of here soon enough," she said.

"I hope so."

"You don't sound very optimistic, Travis."

"I just don't know, Rena. We're way off the shipping lanes, but a ship might come by tomorrow. That's another thing. We've got to build up a huge supply of wood for signal fires. Three of them so that a ship will recognize it's not natural and that somebody is signaling." He rolled his head around again. "Why don't you take a little nap? I'd like to go farther if you can make it. But you need to rest first."

"I'm fine." Rena surveyed the rising terrain before them. The trees here were not as tall as those along the shore, and she noticed they had straight trunks. "Travis, would it be possible to build a raft with these?"

"Float ourselves back to civilization?" Travis shrugged. "I couldn't do it. But the captain and the sailors might know how to do it. It would be hard. You'd have to carry lots of water, and we don't have anything to carry it in."

"Robinson Crusoe made himself a boat, didn't he? How'd he carry water?"

"He grew gourds, I think, then dried them out to make containers."

"Well, it'd be nice to have some gourd seed. I doubt if there's anything like that on this island."

The sun had climbed high in the sky by now, and for the first time since the wreck, Rena found herself growing warm. This did not make her any more comfortable, however, for she ached in places she had never ached before, and her arms, legs, and face stung from the numerous scratches she'd acquired on their hike through the dense foliage. Their clothes were stiff and crusty with salt, and for a moment she wondered how they would wash out the salt without moving closer to a source of fresh water. She leaned back against the tree and closed her eyes, trying not to think of their plight, but that was impossible. Finally she opened her eyes and saw that Travis was still leaning on his tree, resting.

"We could build a ship, though, couldn't we?" she asked.

"I wouldn't count on it," Travis murmured, not opening his eyes. "We might stay here the rest of our lives."

"You give up too easily. Come on. Let's go."

Travis grinned as he got to his feet. He picked up his rifle, and they started west toward the high mountains ahead of them. They hiked steadily for almost an hour without speaking, and suddenly Travis threw his arm up. Rena whispered, "What is it?"

"Look over there."

Rena followed the direction of his gesture. At first she saw nothing, and then something moved. She strained to see what it was. "It's a goat," she whispered.

"That's right. A wild goat."

"Could you shoot it from here?"

"I doubt it."

"Maybe you can sneak up on it."

"It'd be too far to carry it back to camp. But it's good news. It proves there's water here. See, there are more. There's a whole bunch of them."

The two stood and watched, and Rena felt better. If there were animals, there was food.

"We'd better keep moving," Travis said, "but those goats make me feel better. You know, we could capture a male and a female and raise our own herd."

"That's what Robinson Crusoe did. He had milk and cheese too."

"Say, that's right."

After watching the goats for a few minutes, Travis decided they'd better get back to the others.

"You don't have to turn back on my account," Rena said.

"I'm already hungry, and we'll be plenty more hungry by the time we get back. That turtle soup sounds better all the time."

"All right. I'm getting thirsty again too."

The two turned and hiked back in the same general direction they had come. Rena was troubled that they had seen no sign whatsoever of human life. No smoke from a village, no well-traveled paths, no other sign.

As if reading her mind, Travis said, "There could still be people here."

"We don't know how big this island is, Travis. It might be twenty miles or more to the other side. If there are people over there, it could take us a while to find them."

"We'll never know unless we try."

The two scrambled back down the hill, and when the trees began to grow thicker, he said, "Look. There's that big tree where the spring is."

"I could use a drink of that water."

"It's odd how little things become so important in a situation like this," Travis remarked as they moved quickly toward the big tree.

"What do you mean?"

"I mean like fresh water. We always took it for granted at home, and now I'm looking forward to a cool drink like my life depends on it and thanking God that there's a spring here! Maybe many of them. We've got a lot to be thankful for, haven't we?"

"Yes," Rena said reluctantly, "but I'd be more thankful to see a ship anchored off shore when we get back."

"I doubt that will happen, Rena, but it would be a good thing to pray for."

Rena sighed disconsolately and shook her head. It was true she had been glad to find fresh water and goats, which meant a prolonged existence on the island would be possible. But how long could she endure that kind of existence? Who would want to live like Robinson Crusoe for the rest of their lives? She said nothing as the two hurried now, both anxious to reach the spring for a refreshing drink.

★  ★  ★

Maggie was sitting on the beach looking out at the wreck of the *Mary Anne*. It swayed slightly each time the waves broke against it, but it had not completely broken apart. She wondered if the men could go back and get more things. She had slept poorly all night and felt dirty and gritty. Hearing a voice, she turned and saw that Shep was coming along the beach carrying something slung over his back. Getting to her feet, she felt a moment's gladness. Shep always made her feel better. "What have you got, Shep?"

"Coconuts. How 'bout some nice fresh coconut milk?"

"Oooh, that sounds good!" Maggie watched as Shep undid the rope net. "Where'd you get the net?"

Looking at her with surprise, Shep grinned, "I made it, of course."

"All those little knots? I couldn't do that."

"You're not a sailor like I am. Sailors do know how to tie knots. Here, I'll get you a drink." He pulled a huge knife from his back pocket and used it to hack away at the coconut until he had worn away a jagged hole. "Try this."

Maggie raised the coconut and took several swallows of the liquid on the inside. "My, that's good!"

"Well, we won't starve, anyway. We may just have to live on coconut pie and coconut soup for the rest of our lives."

"Did you find any sign of life that way along the beach?"

Shep was hacking away at another coconut. "Not a thing," he said. "Captain didn't say it, but I don't think he expects to find anything. Not people anyway."

Shep's word disappointed Maggie. She lifted the coconut again and drained the last of the fluid. "I'm frightened, Shep."

Surprise flared in the sailor's eyes. "Well, there's nothin' to be afraid of. I don't think there's any wild animals here, and we're not gonna starve."

"But to think of staying here forever . . ."

"Well, maybe a ship will come along sooner or later."

"Do you really think so?"

"Sure. Why not?" He took a drink of coconut milk himself. "What have you been doing all morning?"

"Nothing really."

"I've got a job you can help me with."

"What can I do?"

"I don't really like sleeping on the ground. Too many land crabs."

Maggie shivered. "They give me the creeps," she said. "But what can we do about it?"

"We can make cots to get ourselves off the ground. We get one of the axes and go out and cut some saplings. We've got enough heavy cord and rope to make a framework, and then we'll take a canvas and sew it together and stuff it with leaves or moss or whatever we can find for a mattress."

"Oh, that sounds wonderful! I'll help, but you'll have to show me how."

"No problem."

Maggie felt better as Shep walked beside her, the load of coconuts slung over his shoulder. She looked down and a troubling thought came to her. "I wish I weren't—"

Maggie broke off suddenly, and Shep looked at her. "You wish you weren't what?"

"I wish I weren't so fat."

He laughed. "You don't have to worry about that now. You won't be fat for long!"

"What do you mean?"

"I mean this kind of living will wear us all down. In a few weeks you'll be wishing you had some of those pounds back again."

"Never! I've always hated being fat, yet I never manage to stop eating so much."

"Well, just trust Dr. Shep Riggs on this one. I guarantee you in two weeks you'll have to take that dress in because you'll be lost in it."

Maggie laughed too. "I've tried all my life to lose weight and never could. If I could just be like other women, I wouldn't care if I *was* on a desert island."

Shep hoisted the coconuts off his back and put the bundle by the other supplies. He turned to face Maggie. "Why, you're a fine-looking lady, and like I say, before long you won't have to worry about extra pounds. You'll be able to eat all you want."

"All the coconuts anyway. Shep, you make me feel better."

Shep was embarrassed. He had been intimidated by this group of highly educated missionaries, but he saw now that this woman was just a person after all. She was frightened, just like most of the others were. Shep was a simple enough man that he thought mostly of survival for one day at a time. He had lived that way his whole life, and now it gave him pleasure to realize that he would be able to help this woman who was so much above him in other ways. "C'mon. We'll make *your* cot first. You'll sleep like a baby tonight."

★ ★ ★

As Rena and Travis arrived back at camp, Dalton met them, his mouth drawn tight in an expression she had learned to recognize. "Where have you been, Rena?"

"Travis and I wanted to see what was inland."

"You shouldn't have gone," Dalton said angrily. "It's dangerous."

Travis was watching Dalton carefully. "Nothing more dangerous than getting tired, but we did find a spring of fresh water and some wild goats. So that's good news."

Dalton did not relax, however, and as soon as Travis was out of earshot, he said to Rena, "That wasn't thoughtful of you."

"What wasn't?"

"Going off like that without telling anyone."

Rena looked up quickly. "You mean without telling *you*. What's wrong, Dalton? You're not really angry, are you?"

"I was worried. Don't do that again."

Suddenly Rena grinned. "Why, Dalton Welborne, I believe you are jealous."

"Of Travis? Don't be ridiculous! I know you'd never have anything to do with a roughneck like that."

The words struck Rena as being wrong, although she herself had had exactly the same thought. Not wanting to quarrel with Dalton, however, she quickly apologized. "I'm sorry. I didn't mean to trouble you. But it is good news about the water and the goats, isn't it?"

"Yes, it is," he conceded.

"Did you find anything farther down the beach?"

"Not a thing. We ran into a promontory that we couldn't walk around. The plan now is to row around it in the cutter, but we're all pretty well agreed that it's a small island."

The two made their way over to the cooking tent, where an enormous pot of turtle soup was waiting for them. Oscar said, "If I had some herbs, it would taste better, but I done the best I could. Here, somebody help me dish it out."

"I'll do that," Meredith offered. She took the ladle and filled the bowls as the others gathered around. "We're lucky to have bowls and spoons and knives," she said. "Who'll ask the blessing?"

"You do it, Meredith," the professor said.

She bowed her head, and the others followed suit. Even the crew did the same. "Lord, we thank you for this food and for this provision. We recognize that as a maiden looks to the hand of her mistress, so we look to your hand for everything we have. Never before have we realized, Lord, how dependent we are on you. So we thank you for this meal and ask you to provide others. We ask this in the name of Jesus."

*Amen*s went around from the missionaries, and they all found some place to sit.

"This is really delicious!" Meredith said. "It couldn't be any better."

"That's right," Benson agreed with a nod. He took another spoonful of the soup and blew on it before sipping it. "As long as the turtles hold out, we'll eat well."

"Maybe some of you didn't hear," Rena said, "but Travis and I found some wild goats."

"I love roast goat," Shep said. "How far away were they?"

"About five or six miles, I'd guess. There's a good spring too."

"We found some breadfruit trees down along the shore," Shep said, stripping off his shirt. The wind ruffled his black hair, and his warm brown eyes sparkled as he smiled cheerfully. "When you roast it, it tastes a lot like bread."

A murmur went around, and the conversation turned to different kinds of food. Finally Captain Barkley said, "We've got to go slowly on the food supplies we brought from off the ship. We need to live off the land as much as possible. That means we'll have to hunt and fish, and Chip here can help us identify the edible plants."

"We found some delicious berries," Rena said. A pixyish notion came to her. "Travis found a way to decide whether or not they were poisonous."

"How was that?" Dalton asked.

"He told me to eat one, and if I dropped over dead, he'd know."

Dalton's jaw tightened. "That wasn't very funny, Travis."

"Oh, he was only teasing, and he ate the first ones," Rena assured him.

Travis saw that Dalton was staring at him with disdain. He had never crossed the tall man, but he knew that Dalton felt superior to him.

"Is there any hope of building a ship, Captain?" Lanie asked.

"I don't think so," he responded. "A raft maybe, but we couldn't all go. We'd have to just send one person with supplies and hope they hit land and could send back help. It would be a dangerous undertaking."

"Then we'll just have to wait for a ship." Lanie shrugged.

The captain began to outline the work that needed to be done, and after the meal he assigned most of the crew to cutting firewood for signal fires. He agreed with Travis's idea about having three, and they talked about keeping the wood as dry as possible to start the fires with.

The work parties broke up, and Charlie Day moved out with Lars Olsen. "We ain't never gonna get off this island!" he growled.

"We might someday," Lars said. "Ships go everywhere. You know that, Charlie."

"Yeah, but chances are a thousand to one! This is a little bitty speck."

"Well, we gotta mind the captain, so let's get started on that firewood."

Charlie turned and faced Lars. "Who says we gotta mind the captain? We ain't on no ship now."

"What do you mean by that?"

"I mean the captain ain't got no authority over us here. It was only on the ship."

"But he's the captain," Lars said. "We gotta do what he says."

Day stared at the tall, angular Swede and shook his head. "No we don't. If we stick together, we can do what we please."

Olsen dismissed the idea at once. He shouldered the ax and repeated, "He's the captain. C'mon, let's go cut wood."

# CHAPTER TEN

# "You Must Help Her!"

★ ★ ★

As Travis moved up toward higher ground, he glanced back and could see the bare summits of the ridges through which he, Pete, and Shep had come. He could even see the faint smudge that marked the three signal fires at the camp far behind him. This was virgin forest, and the silver foliage of a clump of trees he could not identify contrasted with the dark green of the bush. They had passed the coconut palms, which grew near the sea, and now the foliage of the trees was a variegated green, restful to the eye.

"Mighty pretty weather." Shep turned and waited until the two larger men caught up with him. The wiry man was much faster on his feet than either Travis or Pete, and now his eyes danced as he waited for the two. "You fellows better hurry up," he said. "You're mighty slow."

"I never thought a runt like you could outclimb me," Pete said. His blond hair was ruffled by the breeze, and his blue eyes matched the sky above as he grinned at the smaller man. "I think you must be part mountain goat."

Pete and Shep had become good friends, though they were rather strangely matched. At six-three, Pete towered over Shep, yet he felt inferior to the smaller man. Travis, following behind them, listened to their conversation, pleased that they had found some common ground on which to form a friendship. *I wish everyone got along as well as those two.*

They had been on the island for eight days now, enough time for Travis to identify the group's weaknesses. Although they had worked furiously to create a world for themselves, it was obvious to Travis that trouble lay ahead if they were not rescued soon. He said nothing about it to anyone else, however.

"Where were these here goats you've been telling us about, Travis?" Shep asked. He searched the wilderness ahead, shielding his eyes from the sun with his hand.

"Not too far away."

"How do you propose to catch 'em?"

"Well, I'm not sure. We could shoot 'em, of course, but I'd rather capture several females and a male, and then we can breed 'em."

"That wouldn't be bad," Pete murmured. "Then we could have milk and cheese anytime we wanted—not to mention the occasional roast goat sandwich! But I imagine they're pretty wild."

"I hope we can rope 'em, but I'm not much of a cowboy."

"I am," Pete piped up. "I grew up on a ranch in Montana."

"Is that what you brought that rope for?"

"Yup. Out here, you'd better make yourself useful."

As the three men forged steadily upward into the clean, pure air and the bright sunlight, they finally crested a ridge and then started down. They kept a hard pace until the land began to level off. "See that valley over there?" Travis asked. "That's where Rena and I saw them."

"I see 'em now," Shep announced.

"Can you see that far?" Pete asked enviously. "How many are there?"

"About twenty it looks like," Shep said, "but I don't see

how anybody could rope 'em. You can't run as fast as a goat, can you, Pete?"

"I think there's a better way than that," Travis said. "Shep, you and I are going to split here. We'll get around on the flanks of those goats and try to run 'em through that gap. See it, Pete, right over there? It's like a little door to that valley."

"Yeah, I see it. So I drop a rope over one of them when they come through."

"*If* they come through," Shep said dubiously. "Some of them goats have got a pretty good set of horns. A poor sailor like me don't need to be beat up by a goat."

"Shep, you go that way, and I'll take the right here. Pete, you get down to that gap."

"Right."

Pete watched the two as they divided and disappeared to his right and to his left into the underbrush. He made his way forward, fingering the rope, and when he reached the gap that Travis had pointed out, he stationed himself behind an outcropping of rock covered with moss. There was nothing else he could do. He could not see the animals through the gap, so he waited for what seemed like a long time.

"There they come, I think," he muttered as the miniature thunder of the hooves came closer. He made his loop and held it loosely in his right hand with the rest of the rope in his left. He risked a quick look around to see the animals as they were herded toward the gap.

"Shouldn't be too hard." He put his arm back and started swinging the rope when three of the animals burst through. He dropped the rope over the head of the leader, a big male, and threw his weight backward. "Gotcha!" he yelled as the animal cartwheeled over when he came to the end of the rope. Pete ran forward as the animal was getting up and starting to run away. Pete threw himself forward and wrestled the animal to the ground. Pete ignored the other goats passing by and quickly pulled out his pocketknife, sliced off the free end of the rope, and tied three of the goat's legs together just above the hoof. He heard Travis yelling, and grabbing up the rope, he formed his loop again.

A large white nanny was charging along, followed by a kid. She tried to dodge, but expertly Pete dropped the rope over her neck, and when he hauled her to a stop, the kid ran by but stopped a short distance ahead.

"Come on back, baby goat," Pete said. The nanny was bucking and trying to get away, but Pete overhanded the line until he brought her up. She tried to butt at him, but he put his free hand on her forehead, holding the rope with his left.

"You got two of 'em. That's great!" Travis exclaimed, running over to look down at the bound goat that was struggling to get up. "How'd you know how to do this?"

"Used to rodeo a bit. That's the way we bulldog yearlings. You tie 'em up like that. Never tried it with a goat, though."

Shep ran over and stopped to admire the nanny. "That's a fine-looking goat. Look, she's got fresh milk too, for the kid. I might sample a little of that."

"Can you milk her?" Pete asked with a grin.

"No, can you?"

"Sure I can. You think a Montana boy wouldn't know how to milk an animal?"

Travis was excited over the ease of the capture. "We can come again tomorrow and get some more. Maybe bring some of the other guys with us."

"We'd better see if we can get these home first," Shep said, stroking his chin thoughtfully with a cautious eye on the big male. "That fellow there doesn't look like he's gonna be led too easy."

Indeed, that proved to be the case. The big male was strong, and he proved to be practically impossible to lead. He darted off in all directions, hauling Travis with him. He seemed tireless.

The female was almost as bad, and when they had covered less than a quarter of the way, they finally put two leads on the big male. Travis and Pete each took one and found they could control him that way. Shep led the nanny, who by now was more placable, and the kid followed along, bleating pitifully at times.

When they were close to home, Travis shook his head. "This is a hard way to serve the Lord."

"Sure is," Pete panted, struggling with the goat, which never seemed to give up. "Come on, you ornery critter. If you don't behave yourself, we'll have barbecued goat for supper!"

★  ★  ★

Rena submerged herself in the stream and came up gasping, for in contrast with the heat of the sun, the water felt colder than it really was. She tried to wash herself, but without soap it seemed rather fruitless. She ducked her head under again, then came up and tried to comb her hair out with her fingers, but it simply stuck together. "Oh, just think of all the soap I've thrown away!" she whispered. Her voice sounded loud in the glade, and she looked around quickly to be sure she was alone. She and the other women had made this their bathing station, but it was close to camp. So close, in fact, that once she thought she could hear the faint voices of two of the men arguing over something.

Finally she waded out of the stream and attempted to dry off with a piece of canvas she had brought for a towel. An image of hot water, fragrant soap, and fluffy washcloths and towels filled her mind, but she shook her head of such thoughts and got dressed. She looked at her thin dress and wondered, *What will we do when our clothes wear out?* Looking down at her feet, she thought with anguish that it would be even worse when her shoes wore out. Then she noticed that her calves were tanning and her arms also. She had fashioned a bonnet of sorts out of a piece of the ship's canvas. It looked ridiculous, she knew, but it kept her face from burning under the tropical sun.

As she walked back toward the camp, she was met by Meredith, who was on her way for her own bath. "You'd better hurry and settle the argument," she said, shaking her head in disgust.

"What argument?"

"It's Dalton and Jimmy. Jimmy took a can of meat from the storage tent, and Dalton's giving him grief for it. They're like children. I give up on them."

"I'll see what I can do," Rena said. She walked quickly into the camp, catching the ever-present smell of the wood-smoke, and found Dalton and Jimmy glaring at each other and talking heatedly. Dalton's face was blistered red with sunburn and his nose was peeling, for he had ignored Karl Benson's advice to take the sun in small doses. As Rena hurried up to the pair, she heard Dalton say, "I'm telling you, Jimmy, you can't go eating food from our stores. It's not fair for the rest of us."

"What's going on?" Rena asked quickly. She put a smile on her face and took her stand beside the two men. "What are you two fussing about?"

"All I did was take one little can of meat from the stock-pile. Abby hasn't been able to eat the fish we've caught, or anything else, for that matter."

"Well, she's just going to have to eat like the rest of us!" Dalton flared. His face was fixed in a frown, with lines of stubbornness around the edges of his mouth that Rena had learned to recognize. He was usually a smiling man, but she had discovered that he could turn angry quickly if crossed. Now she put her hand on his arm and said, "What harm would there be in letting Abby have just one can, Dalton?"

"We can't make exceptions, Rena."

"Come along. I need to talk to you."

Dalton hesitated, then shrugged. "You mind what I said, Jimmy."

Dalton allowed himself to be led away, and when they were out of earshot of the others, Rena reached up and touched his face. "Your poor face. You burn so terribly."

"Doesn't matter."

"I know it must be painful. Your skin is peeling off in strips."

"Jimmy's spoiled. He and his wife have to take their lumps just like the rest of us."

"I think we have to be careful, especially about Abby. She hasn't been well the whole trip—even before the wreck."

Dalton gave her a cynical sneer. "If you'd discovered the theft instead of me, you would have been peeling their hides the same way I was. You're bossier than I am."

"I guess you're right," Rena agreed. She put her hand on his arm and said, "I know it's harder on Abby."

"No harder than on the rest of us."

"I really think it is." Rena sobered and shook her head. "She's been babied all her life. You know how her mother and father took care of her. Why, they practically didn't let her feet touch the ground until she was six years old. Carried her all the time. And then Jimmy. He's much the same way. Abby's not as tough as you are. You have to be gentle."

"I guess so, but it's going to be tough making it out here."

Rena started to answer when she heard a shout, and both turned quickly. "Look," she said, "Travis is back with the others. C'mon. Let's see what they've caught."

She ran back toward camp, where she and Dalton saw the three men dragging the two goats and the kid.

"You got them!" Maggie was saying. "How'd you do it?"

"It was Pete here mostly. He's a cowboy—well, a goat boy, I guess you'd say now," Travis said, grinning. "We drove 'em into a valley, and he just dropped a rope over them. But they're the stubbornest critters I ever saw."

"How are you gonna keep 'em here?" Captain Barkley asked as the crew gathered around the goats.

Oscar Blevins knelt down and picked up the kid, which struggled to get away for a moment, then looked into Oscar's face and bleated piteously. "You're all right, little fella," he said.

"I expect we'll have to make a pen of some kind, but it's too late today," Travis said. "Why don't we just keep 'em tied up for now?"

"Now we can have milk in our coffee!" Karl Benson exclaimed. "It's almost like being civilized."

"As long as the coffee holds out," Professor Dekker grunted.

Meredith was trying to pet the nanny. "Here," she said with a laugh, "I think I'll call you Eve, and we can call the male Adam."

"Who is the kid? Cain or Abel?" Maggie asked with a smirk.

"Call 'em anything you want," Shep said. "There's plenty more where these came from. We can get quite a herd." Shep smiled around at the group. "It'll be good to have food we can count on."

★ ★ ★

Building the pen for the goats the next day was fairly simple. The men all joined in, cutting saplings and weaving them together with wire they had salvaged from the ship. It was a small pen, so during the day they staked the goats out where they could graze. It had provided a break from the monotony of their lives and given them a bit of hope. They had all sampled the milk and decided they needed more females, so a new expedition was planned after a bigger holding pen had been constructed. Most of the ship's crew were working on the construction, and even Karl Benson joined in, while Professor Dekker stood and watched, offering his advice.

Rena had been happy with their progress, but her contentment was shattered when Jimmy Townsend came to her at the end of the week with disturbing news. He found her late one afternoon standing on the beach, staring out over the water.

"Rena, I've got to talk to you."

Rena could tell from his tone that something was wrong. "What's the matter?"

"It's Abby." Jimmy's usually carefree boyish face looked

troubled. He stared at the ground for a moment, and when he lifted his eyes, Rena saw the anxiety there. "She's going to have a baby," he said.

"Oh, Jimmy! Are you certain?"

"Yes, it's true. She's waited long enough to know, but I'd feel better if Karl examined her just to make sure she's healthy and the baby's okay."

"When do you think the baby is due?"

"Abby says maybe the middle or end of March."

"Everything's going to be fine, Jimmy. We'll be rescued long before then, and you and Abby can go back to the States."

"But what if you're wrong and we're still here? She can't have a baby out here. She's not as tough as you are, Rena."

"We'll all take care of her, and you'll have a healthy child."

"Abby's scared witless about having the baby and what'll happen afterward."

"It'll be all right," Rena assured him. "Let me talk to Karl. I'll have him look at her."

She went off to talk to Karl, who was on the other end of the beach, squatting on a weed-covered rock beside a shallow pool. He had baited his hook with a bit of meat, weighted it with a bolt, and thrown it out into the deep water on the other side of the rock.

"I've got to talk to you, Karl," she said as she approached him.

"What is it?" Benson asked. He was a lonely man, tall with very light blue eyes and a crop of tawny hair. He had always reminded Rena of the paintings of Vikings she had seen, and at one time she had fancied herself attracted to him. That had passed, however, for he kept himself shut off from others almost as if he had posted a big sign on his chest that read KEEP OUT.

"It's about Abby. Jimmy says she's pregnant."

"I was pretty sure she was," he murmured.

"You'll have to help her, Karl."

"How many times do I have to tell you people? I'm not a doctor."

"But you were going to be."

"Yes, but it's not the same thing."

Rena tried to persuade him, but as Karl continued stubbornly to resist, she grew angry. "What kind of a man are you, Karl? You call yourself a Christian, don't you? And here is one of your own in trouble. You have more medical knowledge than any of us. You have to help her."

Benson stared at her with an unreadable expression. Finally he felt a tug on the line and turned back to pull in what he'd caught. She watched him pull in a fish almost a foot long, and then she repeated, "You must help her, Karl, you *must!*"

"I'm not a doctor," Benson repeated. "*You* help her. It's a woman's business."

Rena stared at Benson, unable to believe what she was hearing. "You're a sorry excuse for a man, Karl Benson!" she exclaimed. She turned around and walked back down the beach, her back stiff and disappointment filling her.

Benson stared at her for a long time, then removed the fish, tossed it back in, and began walking the other direction down the lonely beach.

# CHAPTER ELEVEN

# A LESSON IN HUMILITY

★ ★ ★

Chipoa, who was never called anything but Chip by the castaways, had become the most valuable member of the party. He was good at finding food and could point out which roots were safe and which ones were poisonous. Travis had gone fishing with him and caught an odd-looking fish about a foot long with a small mouth and a strange square body. Travis looked at the odd black-and-white checkered fish. "What's this, Chip?"

"A *huehue*," Chip said. "There's poison in them."

"Poison!" Travis started to throw the fish back, but Chip stopped him.

"Don't throw it back. The flesh is sweet and wholesome if the gallbladder is removed. The gall's without color and has no strong taste, but a few drops of it will kill a man."

Travis shook his head. "I don't think we want to fool with that," he said.

But Chip insisted that he would gladly eat it, so the two brought their catch back to the camp. Chip told the group he was going to go looking for eggs out on the cliff over to the east.

"Eggs? That sounds good," Meredith said. "Can I go along?"

"It's pretty dangerous up there," Chip said, "but I guess you could come if you think you're up to it."

"I want to go too," Rena was quick to put in. She had become quite jealous of Meredith, for the other woman had adjusted more easily to the hardships of island life and had often gone out on expeditions with the men.

Travis looked up from where he was laying the checkered fish out to be cleaned. "Why don't we all go?" he said. "It'll be kind of like an Easter egg hunt."

Chip laughed, his white teeth gleaming against his olive skin. "I don't think it'll be quite that much fun," he said. "And like I said, it's dangerous."

He could not have said anything that would have challenged Rena more, and soon the four of them headed for the cliffs, having turned the checkered fish over to Oscar, who had received very specific instructions from Chip on how to clean it. They each carried a canvas bag tied with a cord.

The sun was high in the sky as the four went along, Chip leading the way with Meredith and followed by Rena and Travis. They first made their way up the hill behind their camp, then walked eastward, where they could approach the cliffs from the top. When they reached the high cliffs that plunged straight down to the beach, Chip walked right over to the edge and looked down. "Lots of eggs," he announced. "Not so easy to get."

"That's quite a drop," Meredith said. "Where are the birds?"

"The wind and water make holes in the cliffs. The birds nest in them," Chip said.

Travis and Rena joined them. "Wow," Travis said, "that *is* a drop! How do you get down?"

"Oh, it's not as steep as it looks," Chip said, shrugging his shoulders indifferently. "Come along. I'll show you." He looped his bag around his neck and started to climb down. He had gone about ten feet when he said, "Here, these will be good."

Travis was still peering over the edge, but Meredith eagerly followed, with a sack tied around her own neck, and soon she and Chip were moving along the face of the cliff. They both were laughing and seemed to have developed a contest as to who could get the most eggs.

Rena came to the cliff edge very cautiously, standing as far away as she could, and leaned over. She did not want to admit it to Travis, but she was uncomfortable in high places. At least, that was what she called it—"uncomfortable." In fact, she was terrified.

"Look at Meredith sticking to that cliff," Travis said with admiration. "She's like a fly on the wall."

Rena looked at him. "Meredith has a lot of talents, doesn't she?"

Travis was surprised and turned to face her. "Why, yes, I guess she does. She's one of the smartest women I'll ever know."

"And attractive too."

"Well," Travis said with a shrug, "yes, she is, but I wasn't thinking about that. I was thinking about how few women would go down a cliff like that. I'm not too good at heights myself."

Rena was a proud young woman who felt that she needed to excel in everything. She stood looking down, then forced her fears away and said, "I think I'll go help them. It looks like fun."

Travis, however, had noticed that Rena was a bit pale. "I don't think it's a good idea. Let them do the egg gathering. You and I can go fishing."

"You think I'm afraid?"

"I didn't say that."

"You didn't say it, but you thought it. I'm going down."

Taking a deep breath, Rena forced herself to climb down onto the cliff face. She kept her eye on the ledge beneath her, with her face turned toward the cliff so she would not have to look down at the water. She never removed her hands from the wall, and soon she had descended about twenty feet. She took a different direction from the other two, and when she found a hole she was afraid to put her hand in it, although she could see the eggs inside. *What if there's a spider in there or a centipede?* The thought frightened her, but she looked up and saw Travis watching her, a worried expression on his face. "I found some," she said cheerily. She made herself reach inside, snatched the three eggs out quickly, and put them in her bag. "There's nothing to it," she called back up to Travis.

"It looks like that ledge you're on ends just over there, Rena. You'd better come back and at least let me tie a line about you."

Rena stubbornly refused. "No, I see another hole. I'm going to get what's in there." She ignored Travis's calls and started back along the face of the cliff. The ledge she was on started to narrow, and she made the mistake of looking down at the water. The whole world started to spin, and she flattened herself against the cliff face and tried to dig her fingers into the rock. She felt her fingernails scraping the edge, and she heard Travis cry out, "What's the matter, Rena?"

"I . . . I think I'm going to fall."

"Hang on. I'll be right there."

Rena closed her eyes and hugged the wall, trying to press her body into the side of the cliff. She could feel the empty space and was acutely aware of the sound of the surf far, far below. A fear greater than anything she had ever known caused her stomach to churn, and she thought she might faint.

She felt a hand take her arm. "Come along. We'll go back. Don't be afraid."

Rena kept her eyes closed. She felt Travis's hands go behind her back and pull her along the narrow ledge. She found breathing a difficult chore, and she fought the urge to simply collapse.

"Here, the ledge gets wider. Come along."

Rena had lost control of her will, and she allowed Travis to pull her along, guiding her every step. Finally she felt herself being pulled upward and she gasped, "Don't let me fall!"

"Here. It's all right," Travis said. "You're safe now."

For a moment Rena could not speak and still found it difficult to breathe. She felt Travis pulling her farther away from the edge, and then he stopped. "It's all right," he repeated. "We're on solid ground."

Rena opened her eyes to see Travis smiling at her. He gently took one of her hands and held it palm up. "You cut your hand on that rock." He pulled out a handkerchief and dabbed at her hand.

Rena had had dreams of falling before, plunging through space and awakening with a sharp cry just before she hit the bottom. Something like that happened now. She felt any strength she had left flow out from her legs, and she started slumping. Instantly Travis's arms went around her, and he held her.

"Come along," he said. "We'll move farther away from the cliff." He led her several yards farther back but did not remove his arm. "It grabs you like that sometimes."

Rena put her head against his shoulder and began to tremble. She could not speak but felt there was safety in Travis's embrace. She felt the strength of his body as he held her, and she suddenly experienced a strange sensation of complete and absolute trust. She also was aware of how masculine he was, and when she opened her eyes and looked up at him, something passed between the two of them.

At that close range she was intensely aware of the sunlight touching Travis's forehead. She noted that his skin made a tight fit across his high cheekbones, turned a ruddy bronze by sun and wind, and the freshness of his complexion made his blue eyes a shade darker than they really were. A warmth passed between them, strong and unsettling but not unpleasant. She felt his hands tighten on her back, drawing her closer until she pressed against him. She saw him lower his head, waiting for her to protest, but she did not.

Rena had been kissed before, but now she felt stirred in a way that shocked her. She sensed his desires too, which revealed themselves in the strength of his arms, and when his lips touched hers, a thrill passed through them both. It almost frightened her that she had the power to stir him so. She too was giving in to feelings she didn't want to identify. Finally she put her hands on his chest and stepped back. "You shouldn't have done that."

Travis said a very strange thing then, something she did not understand, nor could she forget. "Don't be afraid of life, Rena."

"I'm not afraid. I just don't want you mauling me." Turning quickly, she moved away, furious with herself. She was aware that he had stepped beside her, and she turned and said almost bitterly, "You'd take advantage of a woman, wouldn't you?"

"Rena, don't be afraid to open your mind. Stretching it would do you good."

"I don't know what you're talking about, but I'm telling you now not to touch me again."

"I probably will."

"I thought you were at least a gentleman."

"No, you knew I wasn't a gentleman."

"And I was right."

He stepped closer to her and took her arm. "Come along. I'll take you back to the camp."

But fear got the better of her, and she yanked her arm away. "No, I'll wait here until they get back."

"All right. You want to sit down?"

"No."

Rena whirled away from him and walked back to the cliff. She did not go to the edge, however, but waited at a safe distance, listening to the two far below laughing as they collected the eggs. Hearing Travis walk up behind her, she said, "I could have gotten back up myself."

"Maybe."

Rena did not know how to talk to such a man. He was different from Dalton. He was different from any man she had ever known, and finally she changed the subject and began speaking about the food situation, about building another shelter, about anything. She was desperate to keep the conversation going so there would be no more awkward moments of silence between them. "I've noticed that the crew is getting a little out of hand."

"Yes, things are a bit different."

"They need to show more respect."

"I think in a place like this we'll have to do more to get their respect."

Rena pursed her lips. "What are you talking about?"

"Your dad paid them before. They *had* to show respect. They were like the serf tugging his forelock when the mistress of the manor came before them. But that won't work anymore."

"I don't know what you're talking about, Travis. You're not making any sense."

Travis frowned. "Rena, have you ever read the part of the Bible that talks about being submissive when serving others?"

"Of course I have."

"Well, have you ever read about Jesus washing the dirty feet of His disciples? Does that mean anything to you?"

Rena fell back on the theology she had learned from the professor about this matter. "It was different in that day. It was a custom."

"That may have been, but it wasn't a custom of the master to wash the feet of the servants, and that's exactly what Jesus did. He washed their dirty feet. And I think He did it for a purpose."

Rena wanted to change the subject, but she was caught by his words. She looked at him and demanded, "What are you talking about?"

For a moment Travis did not answer, and Rena was conscious only of the sound of the wind as it whipped along the top of the cliff and of the faint voices far below. She did not want to continue the conversation with Travis, but she could not help it.

"When I was in Guatemala," he finally went on, "I worked with some Indians called the Maya."

"I know who the Maya are."

"They didn't believe in Christianity, but the old chief listened to me try to preach. I didn't think I was doing much good, but he was listening more than I thought. Then he put me to a test."

"What kind of a test?"

"I read to them from the Bible about Jesus washing the feet of the disciples. The chief came to me one day and said, 'Are you like Jesus?'"

"'I try to be,' I told him."

"'Good, then you come with me.' He led me to a hut, and I smelled the filth before I got there. When I stepped inside it was dark, but I could see a sick man, almost a skeleton. And he was filthy, Rena. I don't think anyone had made any attempt to clean him up. I knew what the chief was going to say, and he did."

"What did he say?"

"He said, 'You wash his feet.'"

Travis stared off into the distance.

Finally Rena asked, "What did you do?"

"What do you think? I knew I had to show the chief that I believed what Jesus said. I didn't have any choice. So I got some water and soap, and I bathed him, put fresh clothes on him."

"Did the chief get converted?"

"No, he didn't, but the sick man did."

Rena stared at Travis for a moment, then said, "I think you're trying to tell me something here."

"I'm only trying to say that most of us have a problem with pride, Rena. Pride was the sin that led to the devil's downfall, and think it's at the root of most of our problems."

Rena felt a surge of resentment, but she could not answer, for she knew that Travis had touched on a painful area of her life. She turned away from him and said, "I'm going back to the camp."

"Do you want me to go with you?"

"No, I'll go alone."

Travis watched her go. *She's got so much going for her,* he thought sadly, *but she'll have to suffer much hardship before she finds out what God's looking for.*

★  ★  ★

Oscar prepared a fine meal that night. In addition to the tropical fish, Dalton had prepared a goat to roast. And there were plenty of the bird eggs that Chip and Meredith had gathered.

Rena looked around at the others as they were eating and felt a twinge of remorse. Travis had said no more to her after he had returned from the cliff, but she found herself remembering his embrace and the kiss. She was angered by it and knew that she would have to blot it out of her mind, but that was proving to be difficult.

She sat beside Abby and noticed that the woman ate almost nothing. When the meal was finished, Abby rose without a word and started toward the shelter. Jimmy started to rise too, but Rena said, "Let me talk to her, Jimmy."

Rena could see that the tender young man was torn by his wife's attitude. "You talk to her, then. She won't listen to me."

Rena went to the women's tent, where she found Abby sitting alone, bent over with sorrow in every line of her body. Sitting down beside her, Rena put her arm around the woman and said, "I hate to see you like this, Abby."

Abby lifted her head, and Rena saw the absolute misery in her face. "I never should have come, Rena. I should have gone back home with Jeanne while I had the chance!"

"Don't say that."

"I don't think God ever called me to be a missionary. I think I just got caught up in it all. It sounded so exciting, and now it's just awful."

"We all get discouraged at times."

"But not all of you are going to have a baby out in this place with no doctor, no medicine. There's no hospital. I'll die, Rena! I'll die!" she declared and dissolved into tears.

"No, you won't. We'll take care of you." *Karl has got to help*, Rena thought. *He's the only one who can*. Rena sat beside the weeping woman and found that, although she had always been able to speak freely in any situation, she could think of nothing to say to Abigail Townsend.

★　★　★

Lanie and Pete volunteered to do the cleaning up after dinner. They carefully preserved everything that was left over to save for another meal. Pete was not usually very talkative, but he found it easy to talk to Lanie. As he scoured the pots and dishes with sand, he watched her as she worked beside him, admiring her red hair and long limbs. He noted that the hardships here had not discouraged her as they had some of the others. Turning, she found him looking at her, and she grinned at him. "What are you looking at me for?"

"Sorry," Pete said, embarrassed. "I didn't mean to stare."

A smile touched the corners of her lips. Pete noticed that she had a long, composed mouth, and her throat looked like ivory, with a summer darkness laying smooth over her skin.

Lanie said, "You know why I like you, Pete?"

Pete was startled. "I didn't know you did."

"Couldn't you tell?"

"Well, not really."

"I like you because you're so tall. Well, I guess that's not the only reason, but it's one of the reasons."

Pete laughed. "So if I were short, you wouldn't like me at all?"

"Sure I would, but all my life I've hated being so tall. I shot up like a weed when I was in my teens. When I went to dancing school, none of the boys wanted to dance with me because they had to look up at me." She put one of the knives down and picked up another and began rubbing it with a piece of worn canvas they used for a cloth. "I guess I let it get to me."

"You seem just right to me."

Lanie gave him a surprised look. "That's because you're tall."

"I guess so. But, anyway, I know how you feel."

"I don't think you do."

"Yes, I do. I always hated being so dumb."

"You're not dumb, Pete."

"I'm pretty slow."

Lanie shrugged. "I think that's not bad all the time. People who do things quickly sometimes do them badly."

"I always thought I'd marry a smart woman," Pete mused. "She'd be smart and I'd be dumb, so between us we'd average out."

The remark amused Lanie, and she shook her head as she smiled at him. "You know between us, we're just right. Just the right height, and I guess our IQ would be average."

The conversation turned to life on the island. "Do you worry about getting off this island?" Lanie asked.

"I try not to, but I think about it, of course."

"Travis is the only one who seems to be content—and Chip, of course. But those two would be happy anywhere, I think. I envy them."

"We just have to trust God," Pete said simply.

Lanie felt a sudden wave of affection for this tall man. He was not the smartest man she had ever met, but he certainly was kind, and she felt secure with him. "That's right," she said quietly. "We have to trust God."

# CHAPTER TWELVE

# A Bar of Soap

★ ★ ★

"I wish we'd been able to get some soap off of the ship before it washed away."

Rena pulled her fingers through her hair, and a grimace marred her face. "I never knew how much I loved soap until I had to do without it."

Captain Barkley had been whittling some pegs out of hardwood when Rena burst out with this. He leaned back and said, "It's not as easy as running down to the store, is it? Or having a servant do it for you."

Rena looked at the captain. He was wearing only a pair of trousers, and his upper body and face had been turned a ruddy bronze by the tropical sun. They had been on the island since early September, and their notches in the tree they used for a calendar indicated that it was now early December.

"I wasn't complaining, Captain. I was just making an observation. I never thought I'd see the day when soap would be so important."

"Why don't you pray for some?" A whimsical expression crossed the captain's face. "Doesn't that Bible you read say you can ask for anything you want?"

Rena knew the captain was not a Christian, but he had never made fun of anyone's religion that she knew of. Still she answered with some asperity. "I don't think it means exactly that, Captain."

"Why doesn't it say what it means, then? That's one thing that's always troubled me about the Bible. I just never understood it. Now, you take navigation. Numbers mean something, and they can't mean anything else. But what little I've studied of the Bible makes me wonder how anybody ever could get any sense out of it."

"A soul isn't exactly the same thing as a navigational chart."

"You've got that right, Rena. Don't pay any attention to me. I guess I'm just getting crabby." He pulled his fingers through the whiskers that had not been cut since he last shaved. "I always said I'd never wear a beard, but that razor of mine's getting dull, and I don't like pulling whiskers out with pliers."

They were interrupted when Travis came up carrying a load of breadfruit in a net. The captain said, "It looks like you got a good harvest there, Travis."

"We're not going to starve," Travis said cheerfully.

As Travis hung the breadfruit on a limb of the tree that Rena and the captain were sitting under, Barkley grinned and said, "We're having a theological discussion here."

"Is that right? What's the topic? Are you trying to figure out what the gray beard of Daniel's billy goat stands for?"

"Nothin' that important. Rena here was just wishing for soap when I told her that the Good Book says, if I remember rightly, all she has to do is pray for some."

Travis's eyes grew smaller, and wrinkles appeared out at the corners, as they always did, when he grinned. "What did you tell him about that, Rena?"

"I told him it doesn't mean that exactly."

"And I was tryin' to figure out why Jesus didn't say exactly what He meant."

Travis laughed. "I've often wondered that myself."

"Don't encourage him, Travis," Rena said. "He's making fun of what we believe in."

"No, I'm not," Barkley said, shaking his head, "but I've really wondered why the Bible's so hard to understand."

Travis sat down at the base of the tree and looked at Rena. "I think sometimes we'd be better off if we did just take the Bible for what it says."

"You mean like praying for soap?" Rena said. "I don't think so."

"Well, if God can make the world, He can give us a little bit of soap, I would think. Although personally, I can think of some things I'd rather have than soap."

"That's because you're not a woman and don't have to put up with this long, gritty hair." Rena grabbed her hair and ran her hand through it again. "Oh, I'd give anything for just one bar of good, sweet-smelling soap!"

"Well, I don't see why we don't just ask the Lord for soap," Travis remarked.

Rena stared at him. "That would be frivolous. God's not interested in frivolous prayers."

"I don't think it's frivolous if you need it. He told us to pray for daily bread because we need it. Obviously soap is a good thing." He leaned forward and said, "Tell you what. Tonight when you're praying, just throw in a little prayer there for soap."

Rena laughed. It was the first time she had shown any pleasure at all in Travis's presence since the time he had kissed her when they were on the brink of the cliff. "All right," she said, "I will. I'll leave you two to study theology." She got up and left, and when she was out of hearing distance, Barkley said, "That girl's got a lot of spunk. She's takin' this better than I thought she would."

"You've known her a long time, haven't you, Captain?"

"Since she was ten years old. That's when I started working for her father." He leaned back and fingered one of the pegs he had been working on. "I hate to think about what her dad's going through. He's bound to be going crazy. That girl was the light of his life."

"We'll get out of this all right."

"You guarantee that?" Barkley said, his eyes glinting. "We might be like that Robinson Crusoe fellow that Rena keeps talking about. He was on that island of his for thirty years or something like that. A long time."

"God can get us off anytime He wants to. He knows we're here, and He knows why we're here. I don't understand it, Captain, but He does. Here we had this nice little plan all made out. Go to the South Sea islands and form a mission there and preach to the natives, and here we are instead."

"Nobody to preach to but each other. Things have gone a bit wrong, I'd say."

Travis leaned back against the tree and studied Captain Barkley. He admired the man greatly and had prayed for him almost every day since they had first met. He knew better than to attack Barkley head-on with an evangelical barrage, but he never let an opportunity pass to talk to him about God and what Christ meant in his own life. Now he said, "You know God said that He works in ways that are kind of like a river. Jesus said that when a man obeys Him, rivers of living water would flow out of him. That means, I think, that His life through that person is like a river."

Travis leaned over and picked up one of the long shavings that had fallen from the captain's knife. He stretched it out, let it curl up again, and then continued speaking slowly, his brow furrowed with thought. "You know, if I wanted to get water from one place to another across land, I'd dig a canal just as straight as I could from point A to point B."

"That's the way to do it, all right."

"But a river doesn't go straight. You know that. It meanders like a snake. I've seen the Mississippi. It crawls all over the place and even cuts back on itself. Nothing straight about it. I think that's the way God works in our lives."

A puzzled frown came to Captain Barkley's face. "I don't see what you mean, Travis."

"I simply mean that God is always doing things in our lives, but He doesn't guide us from point A to point B in a straight line. He nudges us in directions we'd never think of going. Think of Joseph, for instance. You know the story?"

"Sure. Think I'm an illiterate?"

Travis grinned and shook his head. "Not at all. Well, God was going to use Joseph in great ways. So what did He do? First He had him thrown into a pit by his brothers, then sold into slavery. Then He had him locked up in a prison in Egypt. Nothing good, it seemed, ever happened to that man. There's a verse in the Psalms that says of Joseph, 'Until the time that his word came, the word of the Lord tried him.' God took Joseph down some mighty strange paths, but when He was through with him, He had a man He could use."

"Oh, come on, Travis. You don't think God put all of us out here on this island to make better people out of us, do you?"

"I think that might be true."

"That's foolishness!"

"Let me ask you something, Captain. Have you thought about God more or less since we've been marooned here?"

A scowl crossed the big captain's face. "More, I guess," he confessed.

"Sure, all of us have. He's got our attention."

Captain Barkley got up and gathered his pegs. He paused and wheeled around. "You're preachin' at me, boy."

"Sure I am. Next thing you know I'll be taking up a collection."

"Don't quit," he said gruffly. "Just keep on preachin'." He turned and walked away, a big form burned by the sun, as tough as boot leather.

Travis watched him go and then whispered under his breath, "I won't quit. You can bet on that, Captain Barkley!"

★ ★ ★

Rena forgot the conversation she'd had with Barkley and Travis about soap. But on the very last day of 1935, early in the morning, Travis stopped her as she was preparing to go down to the beach to catch crabs. They had discovered that ugly as the creatures were, Oscar had a way of cooking them that made them delicious.

"Hey, Rena, you ready to see your prayer answered?"

Rena turned. "What prayer are you talking about?" She had not forgotten Travis's embrace on the top of the cliff and had resisted his efforts at friendliness since then. She wasn't sure if she was afraid of him, but she certainly knew she was afraid of herself around him. She was determined never to let such a thing happen again.

"Do you remember what you talked about with Captain Barkley a few weeks back?"

"I don't know what you're talking about."

"He told you to pray for soap."

"Oh, that!" Rena waved her hand in disdain. "I remember it now."

"Did you pray for it?"

"Why, I think I did that night, but I felt silly doing it. Why?"

"Because you're going to have soap today," Travis said with a light of humor dancing in his eyes. "We can't let the captain think our God's not able to give us a little soap."

Rena stared at Travis. "What are you talking about? Did you find soap washed in from the wreck?"

"Nope, didn't come that easy, but I've got everything we need now." He laughed at her disbelieving expression. "We're going to make soap!"

Rena's astonishment was evident. "You're kidding me."

"No. Took a while to get the materials ready, but I thought you might like to help me."

"If you mean it, I'll do anything. How in the world do you make soap?"

"Come along. I'll show you." Rena followed Travis until he stopped beside a strange-looking contraption set up under a tree. The wooden device resembled a barrel set in a frame more than anything else she could think of. It was about a foot and a half high, and the top was about eighteen inches square. It tapered down smaller at the bottom, and there was a bucket sitting under it. Another bucket was suspended from a tree branch directly above the device.

"This is what you call a *hopper*," Travis said as he pointed to the funnel-shaped barrel.

Rena examined the affair from all sides. "You make soap with this?"

"Sure do," Travis said breezily. He was enjoying himself and laughed at her confusion. "And here are the ingredients." He pointed to a small pile of sticks and a large pile of ashes. Travis picked up some sticks and arranged them in the bottom of the hopper. Then he scooped up a double handful of ashes. "Help me fill it up."

"But . . . but these are *ashes*! You can't make soap out of ashes."

"Don't take any bets on that. We're gonna fill it plumb to the top."

Rena was afraid Travis was playing a joke on her, but she helped him anyway as he filled up the hopper. "Now we pour water through it." He removed a small stick that she now noticed had been plugging a small hole in the bucket. Water began dribbling out. "All we have to do for this first step is to just let the water filter down through the ashes. It'll come out here, and we'll catch it in this other pail. It'll take a while for those ashes to soak up the water."

Rena was staring at the device in disbelief. She shook her head and said, "This doesn't make any sense."

"You'd better watch close, preacher lady. You're about to see a miracle."

★   ★   ★

Rena watched as Travis took the brown water that had been filtered through the ashes. Rena stuck out her hand, intending to touch it.

"Don't do that. It wouldn't be good for your finger." He

laughed at Rena's expression. "What you have here is a form of lye."

"Lye? That's the way you make lye?"

"It's one way of making it. I expect there are better ways, but this is the only way I could think of here with the materials we have. Now we're ready for step two." He had already made a fire, and she watched as he put a large deep pan on it and then poured the brown lye water into it. "Now," he said, "we need one more thing, and I've got it right here." He pushed another pan over toward her. "There's the basis of your soap."

"What is it?"

"It's fat—animal fat. It took a long time to get it, but every time we ate meat, I went around and saved all the fat. There's not much fat on those wild goats, so this won't make much. I think if we could find something besides animal fat, we could make lots of soap." He poured the fat into the pan with the water and then picked up a primitive spoon he had carved out of wood. "I boiled this fat yesterday to get it ready."

"Is that what smelled so awful yesterday? I wondered what you were up to."

"Yep. It sure stinks up a place. Now, we just stir it up and let it boil for hours."

Rena was fascinated. She sat down and watched as the mixture boiled.

After a while, Travis remarked, "It's beginning to get thick now. It looks a little like chicken gravy, doesn't it? Well, there's one more thing to put in it. Chip made this donation." He produced a small canvas sack. "Smell this," he said.

"Why, it smells wonderful!"

"It's some kind of flower that Chip found. You want to put it in?"

Rena took the bag and began to put the small leaves into the pot. When they were all in, Travis said, "I'll give it a good stir, and then we can just come back once in a while and make sure the fire's still going fine."

Early that evening Rena and Travis checked on the soap and determined that it was ready. Travis went to the supply tent and came back with a large, deep, flat pan. "I'm glad we managed to salvage all these pans. Don't know what we would have done without them. Okay, we're ready for the soap now." He carefully lifted the pan from the fire and poured the mixture into the flat pan. Then he sat back and said, "Now we let it sit until it cools."

An hour later they returned to check the soap. Rena could hardly wait, and she talked excitedly as she knelt in front of Travis, staring into the pan. She did not know what an attractive picture she made to Travis. He couldn't help but notice the clean-running physical lines she had. Her thin dress had been softened by many washings, and the light that filtered through the trees showed the full, soft lines of her body, the womanliness of her form. Her face was a mirror that changed as her feelings changed, and as always, he noticed that she had a beautifully fashioned face, with generous features capable of robust emotions. He saw also the hint of her will and the pride in the corners of her eyes and lips. Finally she looked up, her face bright, and said, "Is it ready now?"

"It should be. Here." He opened up his knife and handed it to her. "Just cut it into squares like it's fudge."

Rena took the knife and sliced the mixture into small squares. She carefully lifted one out and sniffed it. "Travis, it smells heavenly!"

"Better go try some of it. Share it among the ladies."

"I will right now. Oh, thank you, Travis!" She got up and started away more excited than he had ever seen her, then she stopped suddenly and turned around. A look came over her face that Travis could not explain. He had watched her for these months and had seen very little gentleness. Indeed, he had seen some bitterness over the way they'd been forced to live, but now there was a softness and even a hint of vulnerability. Through soft lips she said firmly, "I'll tell Captain Barkley about how God sent soap in answer to my prayer."

"I think that would be good. He's a man who needs to find God. Go wash your hair now."

★  ★  ★

Rena took all of the women down to the stream to bathe. She shared the soap with them, warning them not to use any more than they had to. The soap worked well to remove the grime from their bodies and the stickiness from their hair. When they dressed, Rena flipped her clean hair around and held it to her face. "Oh, it smells so good!"

Meredith Wynne had enjoyed the bath and the smell of clean, fresh hair as much as Rena. "I think it's so wonderful the way Travis made this soap," Meredith exclaimed. She ran her hand over her hair and laughed aloud with sheer delight. "I think I could just kiss Travis for this!"

Startled, Rena looked at Meredith. She had noticed more than once that Meredith and Travis spent a great deal of time together. Meredith was an attractive woman, but it had never occurred to Rena that she might be attracted to Travis. Back in her world that would have been impossible, but in this world perhaps it was not. "Yes, it was thoughtful of him," Rena said quietly.

Meredith stared at Rena and then laughed. "He's an attractive man, and our options out here are pretty limited. None of us is going to marry a millionaire or a duke—not as long as we're on this island." As the others turned to look at her, Meredith continued, "As a matter of fact, he's a prime candidate in this world."

"Don't be foolish! We'll be off of this island one day," Rena said.

"I don't think so," Meredith said. "I have a feeling about this. I don't think we'll ever get off this island. So we'd better make the best of it."

"Don't talk like that," Abigail said quickly. "We'll get off."

"Sure we will," Maggie put in. "We're going to make it

fine. If God can give us soap, He can get us off this island. Now, don't talk like that anymore."

"I know He *can* get us off this island," Meredith said with a smile, "but if He *doesn't*, Travis is my pick for a husband."

★　★　★

The men were working on a more permanent storage place for food and water at Chip's insistence. "When another big storm comes along," Chip had informed them, "the water might not be drinkable for a while—even from the spring. We'd better have some stored along with the food. We need to build something well off the ground to keep it protected." The men worked hard cutting timbers with the hatchets and forming a framework.

The story of the soap making had got around, of course. As they cut timbers they talked about the women's excitement over the soap. Charlie Day couldn't understand what all the fuss was about. He huffed, "If you wanna make somethin', Travis, make a still. I'm dyin' for a drink."

"I wouldn't mind a drink myself," Oscar Blevins said. "Just somethin' to warm me up on these cool mornings."

The day was blistering, and Day's remark earned approval from Cerny Novak. "That's right," he said. "It should be as easy to make whiskey as it is to make soap."

"I don't think we need anything like that," Captain Barkley said.

"I ran a still once," Lars Olsen put in. "It wasn't too hard." The big Swede was leaning back against one of the timbers that supported the platform. "Of course you've got to have copper tubing."

Cerny Novak stopped working. "You know how to make a still?"

"Sure I do," Lars said.

"We won't have any stills," the captain said in a flat voice.

Novak turned to the captain. "If we wanna make a still, and we know how, we'll make one, Barkley!"

Everyone grew still. It was the first time any of the crew had ever left off the captain's title. Now suddenly, out of the quietness of the afternoon, a crisis had erupted. To Travis it was almost as if a bomb had gone off. He tried to ease the tension by saying, "Well, there's no point in arguing about that. There's no copper tubing here."

"If I find a way, I'll make it," Novak growled. He made a threatening figure, big and strong and dangerous. "Let's get one thing straight right now. Back when we were on the ship, you were the captain and we were the crew. But we're no longer under sail. Nobody's paying anybody else."

"Somebody has to be in charge," Captain Barkley said.

"Who said it had to be you?"

"I see you think you could do a better job."

"It's kind of like in the old days. The best man runs the show. I think I'm a better man than you are, Caleb. I always thought so. You might be able to navigate better than I can, but that don't mean a thing out here."

"Wait a minute," Travis said quickly.

"No, *you* wait a minute," Cerny snapped. "Who said we have to be democratic here?" A grin creased his meaty lips. "Maybe there'll just be a king. Whichever man is the strongest, eh?"

"I hope it doesn't come to that, Cerny," Travis said.

"You think you can take me?"

"I think all of us together could."

"That's right," Pete Alford said. He came to stand beside the captain and Travis. The three of them, all strong men, stared at Novak. "We don't need to fight about this thing."

"Yes," the professor said. He had been of little use on the structure, for he was not good with his hands, but now he did not like what was happening. "Nobody wants to lord over anyone, but we have to have a leader."

Cerny Novak was no fool. He saw that the tide was against him and laughed shortly. "All right, I guess you're still the boss, Captain." He sneered as he used the word *cap-*

*tain,* and then he turned and walked out into the woods.

Charlie Day called out, "Wait a minute, Novak!" Charlie took off after Novak.

When he was gone, Captain Barkley said, "That could have been a bad scene."

"Yes, it could." The professor gnawed his lip. "I'm glad you two stood by the captain. I'm afraid Novak could be a very violent fellow."

"He would be if he had a chance," Dalton said. He had taken no part in this conversation until now. "But there's one more thing. We do need to be sure that we have some sort of democratic system here."

"Do you want to be the leader, Dalton?" the captain asked.

Dalton flushed. "I didn't say I wanted to be the leader, but I think it's important that we don't get divided."

"I think it'll be all right," Travis said. "Everyone knows that the captain is used to leading men."

Dalton started to respond, then shook his head. "All right, we'll have to keep an eye on those two. Now, let's get this platform built."

# PART THREE

# February–March 1936

★ ★ ★

# CHAPTER THIRTEEN

# CLOTHES MAKE THE WOMAN

★ ★ ★

Feeling a slight pull on the string she had tied around her index finger, Rena quickly reeled it in. Skillfully she plucked the soft-shell crab off of the end, where he clung tightly. She had mastered this rather simple art of catching crabs, having learned from Chip that all you needed was a piece of meat on the end of a string. The crab clung to the morsel of meat.

"You're a pretty silly fellow," Rena said under her breath. "All you had to do was to turn loose of that bait, and you could go on about your business. Now you'll wind up in a stew tonight."

The sound of her own voice disturbed Rena, and she shook her head as she plucked the stubborn crab loose and tossed him into the canvas bag by her side. She never used to speak aloud to herself and knew that this was just another result of the life she had been living for the past five months. She tossed the bait back into the pool, then leaned back and looked up at the sky. She had learned to judge the weather with a little help from Chip, who seemed to be a reliable weather prophet. She knew there would be rain later on, and this again caused her to think. Before they had landed on this island, Rena had hardly ever paused to even look up into the sky, but now she was a part of nature in a way she never had been before.

Her thoughts were cut short when she heard a voice calling her name and looked up to see Chip walking toward her. He wore only a pair of shorts, as was his custom, on his lean, tan body. "Having any luck?" he called out cheerily as he approached.

"Yes, I think I have about enough for supper. What have you been doing?"

"Gathering some herbs," Chip said. He opened the small canvas bag he was carrying to let Rena look inside.

Rena plucked out a broad-leafed plant with orange in its center.

"It's good for killing pain."

"Really? What do you do with it—just chew on it?"

"Chew on it or soak the leaves in water and let them boil. When I was a little boy I had a toothache, and my mother used to dope me up with this stuff." He grinned at her. "I learned how to do it by watching my mom, and one time I decided to dope myself up. I made up a bunch of it, and my tooth was hurting real bad, so I drank it all." He laughed, his white teeth flashing. "I nearly killed myself. I think it slows the heart down or something like that."

"That could come in handy."

Chip sat down beside her, and the two talked freely as the sun climbed higher into the sky. The Hawaii native had become a good friend to Rena, and she had been shocked to realize what a wealth of knowledge he possessed. Before being cut off from her own world, she had been quite a snob, though she had not been conscious of it. It would never have occurred to her then that someone as uneducated as this man could have far more knowledge than she had. She listened as he told about a plan he had devised to build a better shelter, and she realized that he was worth far more to the group than she herself was.

The subject progressed to the meeting they'd had the

night before. "That was a fine sermon you preached last night. I love good preaching like that."

"I wasn't too happy with it," Rena said. "How did you become a Christian?"

"I was just a wild young fellow, seventeen, but I had been to a mission school, and I'd heard all about Jesus. Made no impression on me, though," he said with a sigh. "I wasted a lot of years."

"But how were you converted?"

"I got with a bunch of no-good friends, and we all wound up drunk and in jail. The jailer there was a Christian man. He could barely read, but he knew his Bible. I woke up with my head splitting and feeling miserable. It was a dirty and awful place, that jail. The jailer—his name was Lewis Simpson—he began to tell me how wonderful it was to be a Christian. I'd heard it all before, but somehow the Lord touched my heart there. I looked at my life and saw what a mess it was, and after Lewis shared the Gospel with me and asked if he could pray with me, I said he could. While he was praying, it was like the Lord himself spoke to me, and I began to cry. I called out and asked Him to save me." Chip smiled, and she saw tears in his eyes. "Life's been different since that day, Miss Rena."

"That's a wonderful testimony, Chip."

"Well, I wish I could get all the other members of the crew to believe it, but some of them are pretty hard cases."

Chip rose and said, "I guess I'll go try to find something nice to put in the stew for lunch. I just wanted to tell you that was a good sermon you preached. It helped me a lot."

After Chip left, Rena stayed for another half hour, caught a few more crabs, then decided to go back and help Oscar prepare lunch. She had become a fair cook under his training. As she started back for the camp, she made a little detour to go by the stream where they had put in some fish traps. She found Travis emptying one of them. "Anything big enough to eat?" she called out.

"Most of them are pretty small," he said. The fish traps were simple enough, put together with wire from the wreck.

Chip had taught them how to make the traps, so they now had fish as a regular part of their diet.

Travis replaced the bait in one of the traps and put it back into the water. When he reached the bank he glanced at her bag. "What have you got?"

"Soft-shell crabs."

"I always enjoy those. I'll walk back with you if you're through."

"Yes, I want to help Oscar cook the meal."

The two walked alongside the stream, then veered off on the path they had made, which wound its way back to camp. They had not gone more than two hundred yards when suddenly Travis stepped to one side. He plucked something from a branch and extended his hand to Rena. "A flower for you."

Rena reached out and took the beautiful flower. It was an exquisite light lavender with a dark purple center. "It's an orchid," she said. She lifted it to her nose. "If we were home, this would probably cost a lot of money, and here they're free."

Travis smiled. "The best things in life are free, I guess, as the old saying goes."

"I never really believed that before."

"Before we came here?"

"Yes. I can look back now and see that I missed out on so many things."

"I guess most of us feel like that." He watched her lips make a small change at the corners, and she lifted her shoulders in a little gesture that somehow seemed filled with grace. She wasn't really smiling, but there was the hint of a smile at the corners of her mouth and in the tilt of her head.

"Things have changed for us, haven't they, Rena?"

Looking up quickly, she tried to see if there was anything behind the casual words. "What do you mean by that?"

"Well, I mean we've had to give up a lot of things we thought were important, and maybe we found a few things we never expected to. At least I have."

"I see what you mean," she said thoughtfully.

His voice changed abruptly. "Aren't you ever going to forgive me, Rena?"

She knew what he meant. Ever since he had kissed her, she had kept her distance from Travis. They had spoken politely, but she had never relaxed and let her defenses down. Now she suddenly realized she had been foolish. "It was my fault as much as yours, Travis. I'm sorry I've been such a sorehead."

"That's good to hear."

An awkward moment quickly passed, and he laughed. "I never was much good at apologies, but I'm having to learn."

"I was never any good at it either," she confessed. "Why is it so hard just to say those two words 'I'm sorry'?"

"I think it's a matter of pride," he said. "We don't want to admit to being wrong, but I'll say it now. I'm sorry if I offended you. It wasn't intentional."

"You're forgiven." He stepped back onto the path. "You ready to go?"

As the two made their way back to the camp, Rena reflected on their encounter. She had hardened herself against any overt move he might make, but now as he spoke quietly, she found herself thinking what a good man he was. Over the months she had watched him without comment as he constantly put himself out for others, and now she realized she had been foolish to judge him so harshly. She was glad that the wall between them was now down.

★　★　★

The meal that night was especially good. The crabs were succulent; the white meat of the fresh fish peeled off in flaky layers. The breadfruit had been roasted in an oven that the men had built out of stone. All of it was excellent. Chip had shown them how to make a delicious coconut sauce, which he served over a pudding made of taro root, coconut, and honey.

Everyone was tired, but there was a peace about the meal that Rena was happy to see. She took the time to scrutinize the group. She had a mind that organized things methodically. This sometimes went against the streak of deep romanticism in her that she tried to ignore. It was a strange mixture. Now the mathematical, orderly part of her mind observed the group, and she organized them, almost as if writing it down on a blackboard, into Men, Women, and Crew.

The men all wore full beards now, having long ago agreed that there was no reason to bother trying to keep a razor sharp. Rena looked at Dalton, and a frown creased her brow. He was not the same man she had known back in San Francisco. The months on the island had not improved his character. He had grown quarrelsome and surly, and no matter how Rena tried, she could not get through to the man she had thought she had known. She felt herself frown as the question formed in her mind, *Was I really in love with him—or am I now? He's not the same as he was.*

Quickly she put this question behind her, for it was not something she cared to think about. She looked at Professor Dekker and felt a tinge of worry. Dekker had become withdrawn. He was not suited for a rough life. He had known only the ease of civilization in its highest form, and now he would speak only when spoken to. He missed his books, his libraries, his scholarly friends. Rena knew he was miserable.

Karl Benson was speaking quietly with Jimmy Townsend. The two men were quite a contrast. Jimmy was a cheerful, smiling, good-natured man with very little self-confidence. He was, of course, worried sick about his wife, who was now approaching the time that the baby would have to be brought into the world. Rena could not hear their conversation, but she guessed that Jimmy was trying to pry some answers loose from Karl about the medical side of pregnancy and childbirth. Karl was listening, but there was something in his face that resisted Jimmy's earnest pleas. He was a man of science like the professor, and he had never yet revealed himself fully to any of the group. Something set him off from the others—some sort of secret, Rena thought, but she did not know what it was.

Rena's mind went to the next category: Women. She looked at Abby, who was sitting next to Jimmy and eating slowly. She had changed greatly, of course, her body now swollen with the child that was soon to come. She was a pretty woman, but fear had drawn lines in her face that had not been there before. She was the most vulnerable of all the women, Rena thought.

Meredith Wynne was speaking to Travis. The two of them spent a great deal of time together, and for an instant Rena felt a tug of jealousy. *They look like man and wife sitting there smiling and talking.*

The thought disturbed her, but she didn't know if anything would come of their relationship.

Rena surveyed the other three women. Maggie Smith was no longer the overweight young woman who had staggered ashore. She was now very shapely, and there was a liveliness about her. *A hard way to lose weight,* Rena thought. She saw that Maggie's eyes often went to Shep Riggs, and she wondered if there was an attraction there.

Lanie MacKay was sitting close to Pete Alford. These two made quite an impressive pair, both of them being so tall. Lanie seemed to have found a peace with herself.

Next Rena looked at the crew. Captain Barkley, as always, was a tower of strength. When he caught her gaze, he winked at her and grinned, his frosty blue eyes twinkling. He was a good man, and he had done a good job of keeping things together.

Cerny Novak and Charlie Day, as usual, were sitting together. The big bulk of Novak seemed to dwarf Day, and the two of them whispered, having little to say to anyone else. Lars Olsen, Shep Riggs, and Oscar Blevins sat together, laughing as Blevins told them a story of his early days. Chip was also in this group, and he glanced around often as he watched the others carefully.

After she finished eating, Rena got up and went over to sit beside Abigail. She touched the young woman's arm and said, "How do you feel, Abby?"

"Not very well." Abby turned, her eyes filled with misery. When she could no longer fit into the dress she had come onto the island with, Maggie had offered to trade with her. Since Maggie had lost so much weight, her own dress made a suitable maternity outfit for Abby. But even that was getting tight now. "Even this dress doesn't stretch around me anymore," Abby said sadly.

Rena looked down at the thin, worn dress, which could no longer be buttoned over Abby's belly. Jimmy had fashioned an apron of sorts out of palm leaves to tie around her middle for the sake of modesty, but it wasn't very comfortable. She shook her head. "I wish I could find something better to wear."

"We're all in the same boat," Lanie said as she joined them. She looked down at her own dress, washed thin by many washings and from being dried in the hot sun. "Maybe we could learn to weave clothes out of leaves or something," she suggested. "Maybe we could make ourselves skirts out of those palm leaves like the hula dancers!"

Suddenly Rena had an idea. "I know! Ladies, we're all going to have new dresses."

Her voice carried enough so that everyone turned to look at her.

"Are you going to go down to the store and buy them?" Dalton said, his voice dripping with sarcasm. "If you do, buy me some more clothes too, would you? I could use 'em."

"Be quiet, Dalton. I'm not talking to you." Then turning her back to Dalton, she spoke to the women. "I know what we can do. I don't know why we didn't think of it before." As she began to explain, an excitement ran through the women. "Why, of course," Meredith exclaimed. "We've got plenty of material!"

"Material? What are you talking about?" Abby wailed. "We don't have *any* material."

"Yes, we do. We've got plenty of canvas."

"You can't make dresses out of sails," Abby said with a sour expression on her face.

"Some of the sails we kept are made from very thin canvas," Meredith said.

"But we don't have any needles or thread," Abby objected.

"We've got plenty of twine, though," Rena put in, "and Shep knows how to patch sails. So we'll just *make* us some new outfits."

The women perked up at once, and Rena was glad to see it. "I guess you'll be in charge, Meredith. You know how to sew, but I've never made anything in my life."

"All right," Meredith said, excited. "Let's start now." Meredith was usually a calm woman, but there was a Welsh strain in her background and a passion that lay deep. She ran over to Shep Riggs. "Shep," she said, "we're going to make some new clothes out of that thin sail canvas. Will you help?"

Shep just laughed, amused by it all. "Well, I never thought I'd be a ladies' dressmaker, but I'll do what I can."

★   ★   ★

The dressmaking proved to be an exciting affair, providing some diversion from their everyday activities. With Shep's assistance, Meredith chose the lightest-weight sail, some of it very worn, but it would do for their purposes. "We're going to make a maternity dress first, Shep."

Shep laughed. "All right. Let's get at it."

The small group gathered around Abigail, who stood with her arms straight out while Meredith took her rough measurements. Shep was there with a pair of scissors, and soon he had cut out the pattern indicated by Meredith. He left and came back with an awl and some twine and showed them how to piece the various parts together.

It was an amazingly short process, and when it was done, Meredith took Abigail off to her tent. When the two women returned, Abby was actually smiling. "It feels so good," she said. "I can actually move around."

The dress was rough, but it was loose fitting, and Abigail found it a great relief over what she'd had before. She actually got interested in helping with the others, and for the next two days the women made dresses, all the while ignoring the men.

Finally all of the women had new attire.

Meredith had made her own dress, and now she came to show it to Travis. She had nipped it in at the waist, and despite the stiff cloth, it still revealed her trim figure. She spun around, saying, "How do you like it?"

"Fine. It was a great idea. I hope the canvas holds out."

"If we had sheep, we could gather wool and make a spinning wheel."

"Do you know how to spin wool?" Travis asked, surprised.

"I used to help my grandmother back in Wales."

"Maybe we could use goat hair instead."

As the two stood there talking, Travis found himself liking this woman a great deal.

"Next, you men are going to have some new shorts."

"It wouldn't hurt," Travis said, smiling.

"C'mon. I'll take your measurements. I've never made a pair of shorts before, but I believe I can do it."

Ten minutes later the two were laughing as Meredith measured Travis as best she could.

The two were unaware that Rena was scrutinizing them as she boiled water over the fire. She was shocked when a voice beside her said, "They make a good-looking couple, don't they?"

She turned to see Captain Barkley standing beside her, a slight grin on his face. "She's quite a woman, that Meredith," the captain said.

Rena could not answer for a moment. Finally she said, "Captain, what would happen if a man and a woman fell in love in this place?"

"I expect they'd get married," he said, looking at her

curiously. A grin broke across his lips. "And live happily ever after, just like in the stories."

"But how could they get married?"

"Easy enough. We have a whole island full of preachers here and one ship captain. Why? Are you and Dalton ready to get married?"

"I wasn't thinking of myself," she said quickly. "But sooner or later it's going to come up."

"Well, I wouldn't be surprised. It's natural enough for you young people to be drawn to one another."

Rena took one more glance at Travis and Meredith and then turned away, saying, "Let's hope it doesn't come to that."

# CHAPTER FOURTEEN

# DESPAIR SETS IN

★ ★ ★

The excitement over their new clothes lasted only until a week of heavy rain and strong winds devastated their camp and their spirits. It took days to clean up the mess and rebuild their shelters. Their new canvas clothes did not dry quickly, so when they gathered for their regular Sunday morning service after the week of bad weather, it was with sodden clothes and heavy hearts. They had thought their fortunes on the island were improving, but this seemed like a titanic setback, and it was hard to be thankful to God.

The service proved to be a grim affair. The missionaries were all there, but the only crew members attending were Shep and Chip. The group sang a few songs, and when Rena stood up to preach, she realized she had absolutely nothing to say. Every word felt as though it had to be dredged out of her. In desperation she finally asked, "Does anyone have a testimony to share?"

No one said a word, and Rena saw weariness and fatigue on every face.

Finally Maggie spoke up. "I think sometimes we give up on God too soon." When everyone looked at her, she seemed embarrassed.

"What do you mean by that?" asked Travis, who was sitting beside Shep.

"Well, I mean . . ." She hesitated. "Well, with all of our problems, you might think it strange that I should think of this. But, you know, I spent most of my life ashamed of being overweight. I don't know how many times I prayed and how many diets I tried, but nothing ever worked."

"I don't think being overweight is an earthshaking problem," Dalton said. "We're stuck out on this island, and apparently God has forgotten about us. Being overweight is not a big thing compared to that."

"Well, it was for me," Maggie said. She gave Dalton a long, level look, then she glanced at Shep, who was grinning at her. They had talked about this many times, but she had never spoken of it to the group.

"I don't think anything's too small for God to pay attention to. It never ceases to amaze me that God knows all of my thoughts. And He knows the thoughts of everyone here—and everyone all over the world at the same time. And He knows every problem and He cares."

"If He cared about us, He'd get us off this island. I hardly think He cares that you've lost weight here!" Dalton said stubbornly. He picked up a stick and began to dig in the ground with it aimlessly. "I've come to the point where I don't think God cares about little things."

"Well, I disagree," Maggie said quietly. "I've asked God so many times to let me lose weight, and now He's done it."

"It's hardly worth the hardship the rest of us have had to endure!" Dalton said in a biting tone. "I can't believe you're saying this."

The group fell silent. Finally Travis, who usually sat quietly at their meetings, spoke up. "I've got a word I'd like to share." Everyone turned his attention to him. "We're going to get off of this island. I believe that with all my heart." He looked at Dalton, whose face revealed utter disbelief. "I know it doesn't look very good, but I was reading just this morning in the book of Acts, and it seemed like God put that story in there just for us." He opened his Bible. "You remember the story where Paul was a prisoner on his way to Rome with some Roman soldiers? When they got on the ship, they ran into a storm, and it even had a name. Here in Acts twenty-seven, verse fourteen, it says the storm's name was *Euroclydon*. It's a funny thing for a storm to have a name, so it must have been a dandy. Anyway, when everybody had given up hope, Paul stood up and spoke. I'd like to read for you what Paul said." He began to read in a steady tone.

"Sirs, ye should have hearkened unto me, and not have loosed from Crete, and to have gained this harm and loss. And now I exhort you to be of good cheer: for there shall be no loss of any man's life among you, but of the ship. For there stood by me this night the angel of God, whose I am, and whom I serve, Saying, Fear not, Paul; thou must be brought before Caesar: and, lo, God hath given thee all them that sail with thee. Wherefore, sirs, be of good cheer: for I believe God, that it shall be even as it was told me."

He closed the Bible and said softly, "You know, sometimes God puts us in a place where our only hope is in Him, and that's a good place to be." He smiled and lifted the Bible high. "When we're flat on our back, there's no way to look but up, and when we look up, there's the Lord Jesus."

As Travis continued to speak words of encouragement, Rena felt a weight descend upon her. She felt totally helpless; all that she had valued in life seemed to have turned to dust and ashes. She was astonished to find tears filling her eyes, and she bowed her head and brushed them away before the others could see. She kept her head bowed and listened. Travis spoke with such hope and confidence that she felt ashamed at her lack of faith. Finally Travis closed the service with a prayer full of such hope and cheer that Rena could only feel astonishment that he could keep up his spirits after so many months of such misery.

After the service was over, Rena walked quickly away. Dalton joined her, and the two walked silently down to the water's edge. When they reached it, they stood looking out over the sea. It was a beautiful sight, yet Rena hated it. "I feel so trapped here, Dalton," she murmured, despair in her voice.

"You are trapped. We all are." He stared moodily out at the waves that came in relentlessly, filling their ears day and night with noise like thunder. "We were fools to even think about becoming missionaries."

Rena had had such thoughts herself, but she had never expressed them. Now she turned to him and said, "We mustn't give up hope."

Dalton turned and put his arms around her. He kissed her, his lips hard and demanding.

She struggled against his embrace, for he was no longer the man she had felt she was in love with.

"Don't do this, Dalton," she begged.

"Why not? We might as well do as we please. We love each other, and we should take whatever pleasure we can."

He pulled her close again, and he ran his hands over her in a way she could not permit. Wrenching herself away, she said, "I'm going back to camp."

Dalton called after her. "We might as well take what we can get, Rena. It's all we're going to have in this cursed place!"

★   ★   ★

Lanie pulled up a root and laughed. "Well, I found another one."

Pete took the root from her hand. "That's a nice one." He hesitated, then said, "You know, I never thought about living like this, Lanie."

"I didn't either. It's changed everything."

The two had come out to dig taro roots, and both of them had been silent for a while. They too had struggled with feelings of depression, but lately they had been encouraged by Travis's optimism and encouraging words.

Pete's feelings for Lanie had grown during the time

they'd been on the island. Now as he knelt beside her, he dropped the root he was holding and reached for her hands. She set down the butcher knife she had been using for digging, her face full of astonishment. "I've tried to keep quiet about the way I feel, Lanie, but I can't anymore."

Lanie grew still. She was a highly intelligent woman but a very lonely one. Her parents had died of disease while missionaries in China, and she missed them a great deal. She was also embarrassed about her height and felt that men were not attracted to her. Now as she stared at Pete, who was trying to put words together, she saw something in his face she had longed to see in a man but had never dreamed she would. She knew that Pete Alford was basically shy, and when he seemed unable to speak, she asked quietly, "Do you care for me, Pete?"

Pete's eyes widened, and he nodded, then said huskily, "Yes, I love you, Lanie."

Lanie was hungry for such words. She knew this man would never be eloquent, but he was honest to the bone—a good man and strong—and he cared for her! She got to her feet, and when he arose with her, she put her arms around his neck and pulled his head down to kiss him on the lips. As their kiss lingered she felt his arms go around her, almost crushing her with his strong embrace.

When he lifted his head, he said, "I've never loved another woman."

Lanie smiled, and a tear trailed down her cheek. "One's enough."

Still holding her, Pete said, "I don't know what to do next, but I want to marry you."

"Do you, Pete?"

"Yes. Do . . . do you feel that way about me?"

Lanie MacKay smiled fully and freely, feeling as if she had come home after a long, hard journey. "Yes, I do feel that way." He swung her around as if she were a child, and the laughter she had kept bottled up for years spilled out joyously as she clung to him.

★ ★ ★

"You and Pete want to get married?" Rena stared at Lanie, who had drawn her aside to tell her what had happened. Rena had never seen Lanie like this. Her eyes were dancing and her smile was brilliant, revealing a buoyant spirit that Rena had never seen. "But that's impossible."

"No, it's not," Lanie said.

"But what if we get rescued?"

"If we do, that's fine. We'll still be man and wife, but we're going to get married, Rena."

Rena tried desperately to think of reasons to deter her, but nothing came. Finally she said, "If you'll just wait—" An urgent cry broke into her words, and both women turned to see Dalton and Cerny Novak coming out of the woods carrying a limp form. The rest of the crew was huddled about them.

Rena cried out, "What is it, Dalton?"

"It's Captain Barkley. We were chopping down trees, and a big one fell on him and crushed his leg."

Rena saw that the captain's face was pale, his teeth clenched in a grimace. She looked down at his left leg, which was twisted into an abnormal position. The sight sickened her, and she could not think for a moment.

"We've got to help him," Travis said. "Where's Karl? He'll know what to do."

"He went hunting over to those ridges in the east," Shep said. "I'll go get him."

"Bring him back as quick as you can," Travis directed, his face drawn. He leaned over the captain as Shep raced away, saying, "You'll be okay, Captain. We'll make it right."

But Caleb Barkley gave a sharp cry and suddenly went limp as they started to move toward his shelter.

"That leg looks bad," Novak said. "It may have to come off. I've seen breaks like this before," he added tautly. "This ain't no simple break, and nobody here can help him." He locked eyes with Rena. "You believe in prayer, you say? I think it's a good time to start."

★ ★ ★

Karl Benson kept his emotions out of his face as he examined the captain's leg. The man was conscious again and let out a moan each time Benson touched a sensitive area.

Travis pulled him out of the tent and asked, "What do you think?"

"That's a compound fracture. There's nothing I can do here on this island with no surgical supplies and no anesthetic. They'd have trouble helping him even in a hospital. If we were near a hospital, the doctors would take that leg off."

"You've got to help him, Karl!" Travis insisted. "You're the only one here with any medical background at all."

Rena came up in time to hear the last words. "Yes, Karl. What can we do to help? Just tell us."

"I'm not a doctor! Can't you understand that?" Benson asked, sounding frantic. "I can't do it."

"You've got to do it, man!" Travis said, his voice harsh. He grabbed Benson's arm. "You can't let our captain suffer like that!"

"You don't understand, Winslow."

"You're right; I don't understand. I don't understand why you refuse to help when you're needed. We're going to trust in God, and you're the man God has sent!" Travis said, his voice sharp.

Karl Benson looked from Travis to Rena. "If I tried to put that leg back together without an anesthetic, he couldn't stand it."

"Wait a minute," Rena said. "Chip knows about a plant that's a painkiller. He said he made himself unconscious with it one time."

"What kind of plant was it?" Benson asked.

"I'll go find Chip and ask him."

Rena dashed off calling for Chip, and Travis put his arm

around Benson's shoulder. "I don't know what's the matter, Karl, and I know this is hard on you. But you're a man of God, and you and I are going to pray that you have the wisdom to do what needs to be done and that the captain will be all right. That he won't lose that leg."

Travis was aware that Karl was struggling with some deep pain that he hadn't shared with the others. Finally Travis whispered, "Jesus is the great physician, but He uses people. He wants to use you now, Karl, to help the captain. Will you do it?"

Karl's hands were shaking as he pushed them through his thick blond hair. A storm seemed to sweep over him, but finally he half whispered, "I'll try, but it'll take God to bring him through it!"

★ ★ ★

Rena and Travis collapsed onto the ground after Karl set the captain's leg. "You should lie down," Travis told Rena. "You look like you're about to faint."

"That was terrible, Travis. I felt strong and capable while we were in there, but now that it's over I don't feel so great." Rena shut her eyes. They had both been present when Karl had set the captain's leg. The narcotic Chip had brewed had helped a great deal, but Karl had been afraid to administer too much—afraid that it would kill him, he had said.

Karl had been gray with strain, but he had worked on the captain's leg while the strongest men available—Travis, Dalton, Pete, and Cerny—had held the captain still. Rena had acted as an assistant, helping as Karl instructed. The captain had cried out in agony despite himself, and the procedure had taken a long time. Now the two sat there completely drained. "I hope we never have to go through anything like that again," Rena said hoarsely. "I don't think I could stand it. It was terrible."

"I thank God for that narcotic Chip found and that Karl was with us. What would we have done if he hadn't been?"

"I don't know, but I do thank the Lord that he was here."

"Karl told me that if the shock of this didn't kill the captain, he's optimistic that the leg will heal. He'll probably limp for the rest of his life."

"But he's alive, and he can keep his leg."

"Come on," Travis said. "You need to lie down." He rose and pulled her to her shaky feet. He kept his arm around her, and they walked toward the shelter that Rena shared with Maggie, Meredith, and Lanie. When they reached it, he turned her around and looked into her eyes. "Lie down and try to sleep."

"I will," she said. "I'm just beginning to find out how weak we all are. I thought I was a strong woman, Travis, but I'm not."

"Only God is strong," Travis said. "The quicker we realize that, the better." He put his hand on her cheek. She covered it with her own, and he smiled at her. "You did fine, Rena. Now go rest."

Travis removed his hand and walked away. She watched him go, then went in and lay down on her cot. She felt the tension begin to dissolve in her. She prayed as she had when she was a little child, a simple prayer, straight and direct. "Lord Jesus, let the captain keep his leg, and keep us all safe. In Jesus' name . . ."

# CHAPTER FIFTEEN

# A NEW REGIME

★ ★ ★

Karl leaned over the next morning and examined the captain's leg as the man lay prone on a cot. Karl's face was intent, and as Meredith watched near the entryway, she thought, *He looks like a doctor!* She had come with him to see how Captain Barkley was doing, and now she stepped up to the cot. The captain was still rather pale, and she knew that setting the leg had been a grueling experience. She put her hand on the captain's forehead and smiled. "I hope you're not going to be as bad a patient as most men are."

A grin came to the captain's lips. "I expect I will be. I haven't had much experience being a patient." His eyes went to Benson's face, and he asked quietly, "How does it look, Doc?"

"Better than it might have been." Benson's words were spare, and there were lines of weariness and fatigue on his face. He hadn't slept well the night before, for he had been concerned that infection might set in. Setting the compound fracture had proved to be a terrifying experience, and the lines of his face showed it. "I think you're going to be all right, Captain," he said finally, summoning up a smile. "I'd rather you were in a good hospital in San Francisco. We're not exactly equipped to take care of cases like this."

"If you hadn't been here, Doc, I don't know what I would have done. Lost a leg for sure. Maybe the whole thing."

"I'm glad I was here."

Meredith was proud of Benson. She knew he had abandoned his medical studies to become a missionary for a reason. But it was a mystery to her, as it was to everyone else. It would have made sense to all of them for him to have gotten his degree and become a medical missionary. But he was strangely silent on the subject, refusing to discuss it.

"I know you're in a great deal of pain," Karl said to the captain. "We'll give you some more of this drug that Chip made up for you."

"It's pretty strange stuff. You know what's in it?" the captain asked curiously, watching as Karl poured a brown liquid into a cup.

"Some kind of opium, he says. I'm just glad Chip knew about this folk remedy. Drink it down, Captain."

Barkley downed the cupful of liquid, then shuddered and bared his teeth. "That is the worst stuff I've ever tasted!"

"But it works, doesn't it? You relax now. You'll go to sleep pretty soon."

Caleb Barkley stuck out his hand. "Thanks a lot, Doc. I'm awful glad you're here."

Meredith watched as Benson took the captain's hand. "Glad I was able to help," he said with a shrug. "Get some sleep now."

Meredith followed Benson outside the shelter, and when they were twenty feet away, she said, "Do you really think he's going to be all right?"

"As far as I can tell, but you never know about things like this. We don't have any kind of antiseptic here except that small stock of whiskey the sailors brought ashore."

"You did wonderfully well, Karl," Meredith said, smiling. She reached out and squeezed his arm. "I thank the

Lord that you are with us. The captain might have died if you hadn't been."

Benson shrugged his shoulders. There was an obvious heaviness in him that Meredith wished she had the power to drive away. But she soon found herself asking about Abigail. "Have you had any experience delivering babies?"

"Not much."

"I guess we're all worried about Abigail."

"She doesn't have the right temperament for a rough birth, as this is sure to be. No hospital, no clean sheets, no equipment or medical team—just a medical school dropout, a flunky."

"Don't call yourself that!" Meredith admonished.

"It's true enough."

"Why do you put yourself down so much, Karl?"

"Because I know myself."

Meredith was at a loss for words.

"I think I'll go try to find some more of this narcotic herb," Karl said.

"Mind if I come with you?"

"No, come along."

Karl picked up a canvas bag, and they spent the next hour foraging through the woods. Chip had taught Karl how to recognize the plant, and Karl and Meredith managed to gather a fairly good supply.

Finally he dusted off his hands and said, "This should be enough for now. We'll have to go chop it up and soak it in water."

"It's not as easy as going to a pharmacy, is it?"

Karl grinned at her. It made him look much too young to have nearly finished medical school. "Not quite as easy." As they started back toward camp, he suddenly asked, "Why haven't you ever married, Meredith?"

The question caught her off guard, and when she finally spoke, her answer was guarded and careful. "Why, because I never met a man I loved."

Karl shifted the bag to his shoulder. "I always thought

marriage was just about finding someone you can feel comfortable with."

Meredith laughed. "I felt comfortable with my eighty-two-year-old Greek teacher, but I didn't think that was enough to make a marriage. What about you? How old are you, Karl?"

"I'm thirty-three."

"And you were never in love?"

For a brief moment she saw something flicker in Benson's eyes. "I guess not," he said. "Come along. Let's get this stuff ground up."

★   ★   ★

"Abigail, you've got to eat something," Jimmy implored.

"I'm just not hungry."

"But you haven't eaten anything all day. Oscar made this especially for you." He picked up the plate and held it in front of her. The two were sitting on her cot, where Jimmy had come to bring the lunch Oscar had taken such pains with. "Just have a few bites of it."

Abigail took the plate and managed to eat several bites, then she shivered. "I'm afraid," she whispered as she put the plate down and leaned against his shoulder.

He pulled her close and whispered, "Don't be. We're going to get through this just fine, and then we'll be a real family."

"But I'm so scared."

She straightened up, and Jimmy saw the tears running down her face. She stared into the plate blankly, and he could not think of a single comforting thing to say. In all truth, he was terrified of what lay ahead of them. He had always wanted children, but out here in this primitive place with no medicine, no nurses, and only Karl to help, he knew exactly how she felt. "We'll be all right," he said as he pulled her into another embrace.

"Jimmy, I've been thinking," Abigail said, pulling away

again, her voice tightly in control. "Ever since all this happened, since the wreck, I've been thinking how shallow my Christian life has been."

"Why, you've always been a fine Christian!"

"No I haven't. I learned how to talk like one and say the right things, but it's almost like I'm playing a role. I've always envied people who had a real experience with God."

Jimmy became very still and did not speak for a time. Then finally his voice came out in a low whisper. "I know what you mean, Abby. I love the Lord, and I know you do too, but this business of being out here cut off from everything has not been easy."

The two sat there miserable, unable to comfort each other, when suddenly Maggie Smith came through the entryway. "What are you two doing huddled up in here?" Maggie said cheerfully. "Come on out in the sun. It's a gorgeous day."

"I don't think so, Maggie," Abby answered. "I'm tired. I think I'll just lie down."

Maggie took in the tense expressions on both of their faces. *They've been quarreling,* she thought. "Well, I'll tell you what I'm going to do. Shep and I are going to go to the cliff and get a bunch of eggs. When I get back, I'm going to make you the best omelet you've ever tasted. I may not be much of a cook, but it's hard to go wrong with eggs fresh from the nest."

"I'm really not hungry, Maggie," Abby said.

"You just lie down and rest," Maggie replied. "When you get one whiff of my omelet, you'll sit up and take notice." She left the shelter and joined Shep, who was waiting for her. "Let's go, Shep."

He grinned and said, "Kind of like an Easter egg hunt, ain't it, Maggie?"

"Did you go on those when you were a child?"

"Me? No, my uncle and aunt weren't much on playing games on Easter."

They made their way to the cliff, and for a moment they stood looking down at the incredible view. "You ain't afraid of heights, are you?" Shep asked.

"No, not a bit. I've been afraid of other things but never that."

Shep felt strange in this woman's presence. She was so far above him in so many ways. He was raised by a shrimper who doubled as a street preacher, and she was educated and cultured, from an altogether different world. But the two of them somehow felt right together. They stood there enjoying the breeze and the hypnotic motion of the green water that washed onto the white sand below, the harsh cries of sea birds in their ears. "I noticed that most of your preacher friends have been pretty down," Shep remarked. "All except you and Travis. You seem to have survived this pretty well."

Maggie shook her head and defended her friends. "It's been hard on some of us. We're a spoiled bunch, Shep. We've always had everything we needed or wanted, and when that's stripped away from you, it takes a little adjusting."

Shep stooped down to pick up a stone and threw it over the cliff. He watched it fall before answering her. "But it ain't bothered you much. You're always smiling."

"Well, I guess that's because I got what I've always wanted."

"And what was that?"

"All my life I wanted to be slender like other women that I looked at."

"Well, you got that." Shep grinned. "Pretty hard way to lose weight, though."

Maggie laughed. "It is, isn't it?"

"Did it really mean that much to you? I mean, after all, there are lots of happy people that weigh a little too much."

"I know that. I guess I was a little obsessed about my weight. You know, Shep," Maggie said slowly, "it's the oddest thing. No matter how much I weighed, I always felt skinny. Inside, I mean. But then I'd look in the mirror and see this overweight girl. I felt like I was trapped in a body that belonged to someone else."

"It seems that some people are just naturally heavy."

"You're right, they are," Maggie said. "But I wasn't one of them. I was overweight for one reason. I was a glutton, Shep. I was an unhappy girl and then grew up to be an unhappy woman. And when I got unhappy, I would eat." She turned to face him and laughed. "Now I don't have to worry about overeating, or if I do, I work it off. Come on. Let's go get some eggs."

The two made their way down the face of the cliff, and from time to time, Shep would toss her an egg, which she would catch adroitly and put into the bag she wore around her neck. Laughing, she suddenly was aware that she was truly happy. Here in this primitive place with a man she hadn't even known for a year on the face of a cliff, she was happy. Marooned and with only the barest necessities, when before she had had it all. But now she felt a contentment she could not explain, but could only delight in.

★ ★ ★

Charlie Day and Lars Olsen came up to stand beside Cerny Novak as he stared out at the sea, his face fixed grimly.

Charlie searched the endless sea for ships. "I wish we was off this blasted island."

"It don't do any good to talk about it," Novak grunted, "so shut your face."

Day was accustomed to Novak's moods, and he saw that the big man was obviously in a bad one. "I been thinkin'," he said finally. "I'm about ready to get in the cutter, rig it with a sail, and try to get off this place."

Lars laughed mirthlessly. "You wouldn't do it," he said in disgust. "You'd be afraid to, and so would I."

Novak gave Olsen a quick look. "I don't know, Lars. We might make it."

"We might . . . and we might not."

Novak kicked a shell at his feet and said harshly, "I'm

tired of lettin' those preachers tell me what to do."

"So am I," Day agreed. "They ain't got no authority over us."

Olsen stared at the two and then finally fixed his eyes on Novak's face. "What are you thinkin', Cerny?"

"I'm thinkin' I'm through waitin' on them. That's what! And the next time one of them gives me an order, I'll show you. There's going to be a new order around here."

Charlie Day laughed. "That's the way to talk," he said. He grinned and added, "Maybe we'll all just call you Captain now."

The three made their way back to camp. As they approached the clearing, Professor Dekker left the fire, where Rena was poking at it with a stick, and approached Novak, saying with some irritation, "We need more firewood, Novak."

Something snapped inside Cerny Novak. "You need more firewood? Go cut it yourself."

Lanie MacKay, who was cutting up some breadfruit beside Pete and Karl at their crude table, looked up with anger. "Don't speak to the professor that way, Novak!"

"Don't tell me what to do!"

He turned abruptly when he heard Maggie and Shep laughing as they returned with two canvas bags bulging with eggs. Maggie did not catch the tension that had suddenly risen, and she held up her bag and said, "Look, we've got lots of eggs. I'm going to make one of my famous omelets for Abby."

Novak had always hated to take orders, and now with the captain laid up, he realized there was no one to curb his rebellious streak. "You make *me* an omelet, Maggie!" he ordered.

Maggie looked up at the big man in shock. He had never been very approachable, but he had always been more or less respectful up to now. "I'm Miss Smith to you," she said with asperity.

"No you ain't. You're Maggie, and I'm telling you to make me an omelet with about a dozen of them eggs!"

Lanie stepped toward the two anxiously. "You mind your manners, Novak."

"And you shut your mouth!" Novak said, whirling to face her.

"Let's not make an issue of this," Pete said reasonably.

"I'll make any kind of issue I want, Alford." Novak yanked a knife out of his belt and grinned at the tall, raw-boned man. "You wanna argue about it?"

Fearful at what was happening, Lanie quickly offered, "I'll make you an omelet, Novak. We don't need any trouble."

Novak was still staring at Pete, but when the tall man did not speak, he said, "There's gonna be some changes around here." He lifted his voice, aware that the two men who might have challenged him, Travis and Dalton, had gone to catch another female goat to add to the herd. If those two had been there, he would have been slower to act. "Things are gonna be different from here on out." With a laughing sneer, he ordered, "Now, let's have that omelet."

Maggie quickly said, "I'll make the omelet." She glanced at Benson, who was glaring intently at Novak. Seeing the possibility for violence, she whispered, "It's all right, Karl."

"No, it's not all right," he whispered under his breath. "You give a man like that an inch, he'll take a mile." He shook his head. "You'll see," he promised grimly.

# CHAPTER SIXTEEN

# BRUTE FORCE

★ ★ ★

As soon as Travis caught a glimpse of Rena's face, he knew something had happened. Her lips were pulled into a straight line, her face filled with either fear or anger.

"What's wrong, Rena?"

She stood in front of Travis, not speaking at first. Then the words spilled out in a hurry. "It's been terrible, Travis." Dalton, who had been trailing them, came up to join the two. "Oh, Dalton, I'm glad you're back," Rena said. "We've got a problem."

"A problem? What kind of a problem?"

"It's Cerny Novak. He's pushing his weight around and acting like he's the boss around here."

Dalton was not a patient man. He was angry to begin with that Rena and Travis were talking, and now he drew himself up straighter and said, "What's he done? Has he insulted you?"

"It's worse than that, I'm afraid." Rena told the story quickly, her focus shifting from one man to the other. She finished with, "They've got the three guns now, and they claim they're going to be in charge of things."

"We'll see about that," Dalton huffed. He started off but Travis stopped him.

"Wait a minute, Dalton. We need to be careful about this."

"Careful! I don't need to be careful when I'm handling a bunch of roughnecks. If they want trouble, they can have it!" He spun and marched away, anger evident in his posture.

"Travis, Dalton doesn't understand how bad this is." Rena shook her head. "I'm afraid of Novak."

"He's a dangerous man. C'mon. We need to stop Dalton."

Dalton was in no mood to listen, however, and shook them off. When he reached the camp, with Rena and Travis close behind, he saw Novak leaning against a tree holding the rifle loosely in one hand, eating a mango with the other. Day and Olsen were on either side of him, both with revolvers stuck in their belts.

"All right, Novak, I hear you've been making some wild talk."

Novak took a bite of the mango and smiled a wolfish grin. He made a dangerous-looking figure, and if Dalton weren't so angry, he would have seen it.

"What's the trouble, preacher? You sore 'cause someone else is gonna be the boss around here?"

Dalton was ordinarily careful enough, but he hated to be crossed. Ignoring the sinister light that flickered in the eyes of the bulky Novak, he approached him and held out his hand. "I'll take that rifle."

Novak laughed. "You will, eh? All right. Take it, preacher."

Novak moved so swiftly that Dalton had no time to react. In one motion he dropped the mango, flipped the rifle up butt first, and drove the butt into Dalton's forehead. The blow made a meaty sound, and Dalton fell backward full-length. He lay there, his legs twitching, his eyes rolled up into his head.

Novak reversed the rifle and turned to Travis. "You wanna try your luck, Winslow?"

"There was no call for that, Cerny," Travis reprimanded.

Rena had never seen explosive violence like this. A cold chill ran up her back at the cruelty gleaming in Cerny Novak's eyes. She ran to kneel beside Dalton and gingerly touched the huge bump that was emerging over his left eye. She turned and yelled, "Karl, he's hurt!"

Karl Benson, who had been watching this along with the others, joined her at Dalton's side. He pulled Dalton's eyelid back and peered at the pupil, then took his pulse. "He has a good, strong pulse," he said. He turned to Novak. "But a man can be killed with a blow like that."

"I don't think the preacher there will be needing any more. He's a pretty smart fellow. One knock in the head is prob'ly enough for him."

Charlie Day exposed his yellow teeth. "Any of the rest of you want a dose of the same, we can take care of you." He pulled the pistol from his waist and swung it around. "Any takers?"

The group was silent.

Professor Dekker cleared his throat and attempted to speak. He coughed and tried again. "There's no call for violence, Novak."

"There won't be any as long as you folks stay in line," Novak shot back. He fixed his eyes on Travis. He was well aware that Winslow was the one who was most likely to give him trouble. He stepped forward, holding the rifle loosely pointed in Winslow's direction. "Travis, you're the best of these sorry hymn singers. You come over to our side. That's where you belong."

Every eye went to Travis. "There shouldn't be any *sides* among us, Cerny," Travis asserted. "We're all in the same boat here."

"Not exactly. You preachers have been treating us like slaves. Well, when we were on the ship I was willing to take Captain Barkley's orders, but this is another kind of ship— this here island—and if there are any orders to give, I'll give 'em."

Rena saw that three of the crew, Shep, Oscar, and Chip,

were doing their best to stay out of the confrontation. There were only three weapons on this island, and they were in the hands of Novak, Day, and Olsen. Rena looked at Travis, who was studying Cerny intently.

"I'm not on anyone's side," Travis asserted. "We all need each other."

Cerny studied the tall figure of Travis Winslow, then expelled his breath. He grinned. "You stay out of it, Travis, and you'll be all right." He turned to face the others. "You can sing all the hymns and play church all you want, but from now on I'll give the orders." Cerny snorted a half laugh, and then turned to Day and Olsen and said, "C'mon, guys. Let's go fishin'. When we get back we'll talk about this some more." The men collected their fishing gear and headed toward the cutter.

Captain Barkley made his way slowly out of his shelter and leaned up against a tree, easing his leg and holding his makeshift crutches in position. The pain from the leg was severe at times, but he hated to keep taking the narcotic that Chip and Karl had distilled from the plant. It made him half sick and dizzy. True, it did dull the pain, and enough of it would put him under, but he hated the way it made him feel out of control.

He had heard the confrontation from inside his shelter and now watched as the missionaries gathered in small groups to figure out what actions they might take in reaction to Novak's challenge. They were all frightened, he could see, except for Travis. He listened as they spoke among themselves, knowing that they were out of their element. Meredith turned from the professor, who she had been sitting with, to the captain. "What do you think, Captain Barkley? Can't you reason with these men?"

Barkley shook his head. "I can try, but you have to realize that the only thing these men fear is force."

"If they were that kind of men," Professor Dekker asked, "why did you have them on your crew?" Dekker's hands were unsteady. He, more than anyone, had been upset by the violence. He had led a sheltered life in his world of books and classes, and now the violence of the real world had shaken him. "Can't you threaten them somehow?"

"Threaten them? How? If I didn't have a broken leg, I might. But the only thing these fellows understand is brute force."

The other missionaries stopped talking amongst themselves to hear what the captain had to say. Pete looked up from the piece of wood he was whittling. "There are more of us than there are of them," he commented. "Maybe we could gang up on them."

"But they've got the guns." Captain Barkley shrugged. "That pretty much settles the argument."

Rena was sitting beside Dalton, who was half lying against a tree. He'd regained consciousness, but the bump on his head had grown. Rena leaned over and whispered, "Are you all right, Dalton?"

"Of course I'm all right," he spewed with sullenness and anger in his voice. "If I could get that gun away from Novak, I'd give him a lesson."

"But, Dalton, we can't use force."

"Of course we can. That's the only thing those bullies understand."

Rena felt helpless against Dalton's anger. She called across the clearing to Travis, who was talking quietly with Karl. "Travis, what do you think we should do?"

Everyone's attention turned to Travis, and Rena realized, with surprise, that he had become the natural leader of the group. This came to her as a shock, for she remembered that all of them had at first looked down on the tall, rangy man who had volunteered to join them. Now she saw that he had a strength in him that the rest of them lacked. *I'm so glad he's here*, she thought. She addressed him again, "Travis, you must have some idea."

"I don't think we ought to do anything rash," Travis said slowly. His eyes went around the group, and he added, "Cerny's a rough fellow and has had a hard life, but I don't think he's as bad as some of you do."

"Not as bad!" Dalton burst out. "Why, he's a bully!"

"I guess all of us have a little of that in us." Travis shrugged. "But I think if we handle the situation carefully, he'll come around. You know," he said, "the hardest thing in the Scriptures is the commandment Jesus gave to love our enemies. Right now it's pretty hard to love Novak."

"Love him? I can't love a man like that!" Dalton exclaimed.

"Neither can I with my own heart," Travis replied, "but I've discovered that if someone mistreats me and I give myself over to God and ask Christ for His spirit, then I can love that person in a way that's not my own. Jesus can love our enemies through us."

"I think you're right about that," Lanie agreed. She was sitting next to Pete, her face intent. "My parents were missionaries in China, as you know. Some of their fellow missionaries were killed by the Boxers. My parents told me many times how they hated the Boxers. They also said their lives as missionaries were finished until they learned to let Jesus control their emotions. I think that's the secret of it."

"I think you're exactly right, Lanie," Travis said. He smiled and shook his head. "They'll be waiting for us to make a break—which will be an excuse for them. Let's not give it to them. You know the Scriptures say that if a man takes away your coat, give him your cloak also. I think what we should do now is show love. It's the only way.

"I'm going to go check the fish traps. But before I go, let's pray that God will perform a miracle in the hearts of these men."

They all bowed their heads, and Travis prayed a short prayer for the three men. "Lord, you know the hearts of these men, and you love their souls. We know that Jesus died for them, so give us your spirit that we might love them through your power."

When Travis left, Rena turned to Dalton and saw the dissatisfaction in his face. "I know it's going to be hard, Dalton, but I think Travis is right."

"No, he's wrong. They'll make slaves out of us. You just watch."

★  ★  ★

Rena took one look at Meredith as she came into their shelter and asked, "What's the matter?" Meredith was the most stable of all of the women on the island, but now she looked disturbed.

"It's that man Charlie Day. He . . . he put his hands on me, Rena."

"He attacked you?"

"Didn't go quite that far, but it was close. I was walking along the stream when he came up to me. I didn't say a word to him, but he began walking beside me. He was trying to tell me . . . well, how pretty I was. I told him I didn't want to hear that, and he grabbed me. He's small but he's strong." Meredith's face wrinkled with the taste of the memory. "I fought him off, but he laughed. He said he'd have me sooner or later."

Rena was frightened. "We have no defense against these men."

"I know, but I think we'd better tell someone. Maybe the captain."

"He can't do anything—not with that leg of his."

"But he can talk to Novak and ask him to keep those men in line. Anyway, I'm going to see what he has to say."

"I'll go with you."

The two women left the shelter and found Captain Barkley talking to Pete. The captain struggled to his feet on the crutches Shep had made for him as the two women approached. Seeing their faces, he asked, "What's wrong?" He listened as Meredith repeated her story and finally said, "Captain, you've got to talk to Novak."

"I'll do what I can," Barkley said.

They waited until Novak came in from fishing a while later, carrying a young sea turtle in one hand, the ever-present rifle in the other. He put the turtle down in the clearing. "There's supper tonight. Nothin' like turtle soup." He glanced at the captain and said, "What's wrong, Cap?"

"It's about Day."

"Me!" Charlie emerged from his shelter when he heard his name. "I ain't done nothin'!" Day stood defiantly, glaring at the captain. "You never liked me."

"What's he done?" Novak growled.

"He's forced his attentions on one of the women."

"Which one?" Novak grinned.

"It was me," Meredith said, facing Novak squarely. "I want you to tell him to leave me alone."

"Why don't you tell him yourself, missy?" Novak's grin remained.

"Cerny, we've known each other a long time," the captain said. "This situation has gotten out of hand. I want you to tell Charlie here to leave this woman alone."

"Cap, I've always respected you. But now it's a different day."

Pete Alford joined the discussion. "Look, Novak, we all know you have the guns, but there's such a thing as being right and being wrong."

"Up to now, Preacher, you folks have decided what's right and what's wrong, but now I'll do the decidin'. If you don't like the way we act, it's up to you to change us." Novak knew that next to Travis, Pete was probably the one who could give him the most trouble. "Just settle down, Alford. Nothing's happened to the woman."

Charlie Day laughed. "Not yet anyway." He pulled the revolver out and waved it in the general direction of the group that had gathered to listen. "You've always treated us like dirt. Well, we ain't dirt, and it's about time we started doing things our way around here."

★  ★  ★

When Travis returned from checking all the traps, Rena repeated the story. "You've got to do something, Travis."

"Do what, Rena?"

She stared at him. "I don't know, but something terrible

is going to happen if those men aren't stopped."

He said quietly, "Rena, would you have me start a war?"

"Are you afraid of Novak?" she challenged. She had not intended to say this, but it came out before she could stop it. "I didn't mean to say that. Of course anybody's afraid of men with guns."

"I think this is a challenge for us, Rena. Maybe this is the challenge God has put us here to face. We were all so busy rushing to the islands to be missionaries that we forgot there are men like Novak and Day. They're the object of Christ's quest just as much as the islanders we were going to."

"I can't grasp what you're trying to tell me. They're the enemy."

"Christ died for them, Rena. You can't deny that."

Stubbornly she stood her ground. She knew he was speaking the truth, but part of her refused to accept it. "I'm disappointed in you, Travis. I thought you were more of a man." She whirled and walked blindly away. Even as she walked, she knew she was being unfair, and she almost turned back to tell him she was wrong. But admitting mistakes had never been one of her virtues, and now she knew she had slammed a door in Travis's face.

She found she could not pray, could not even think straight, so she just walked for a long time alone. When she finally stopped, she looked up at the sky, her heart heavy. She cried out in her spirit, "Lord, what's wrong with me? Don't I have any faith at all in you?" She waited, but there was no answer, and heavily she turned and trudged back toward the camp, not knowing what the future would bring.

# CHAPTER SEVENTEEN

# SURVIVAL OF THE FITTEST

★ ★ ★

"Take it easy now, Cap," Shep said. He was standing off to one side watching as Captain Barkley carefully navigated over the tree roots sticking out of the sand using his crutches. His face was pale with strain, Shep noticed, and he urged him, "You'd better just take it a little at a time."

"A man can't sit around all day doing nothing," Barkley said irritably. His lips were set in a straight line, and it was obvious that the pain was having its way with him. He swung himself carefully forward, putting his weight on his good leg and holding the other awkwardly off the ground. He made a rather circuitous route and then came back to stand before Shep. "You did a good job on these crutches, Riggs. Couldn't have asked for better."

Shrugging his shoulders, Shep smiled deprecatingly. "Not much of a job to make those. I wish I could make us a ship big enough to get us off this place."

"Maybe you should give it a try."

"I think I could do it, Cap, given long enough. We don't have the best tools in the world. But we got plenty of time."

Easing himself down onto the chair Shep had fashioned

for him, Barkley ran his hands over the crutches, his face studious. "I been thinkin' a lot about that. We could be out here for the rest of our lives if we don't do something."

"Aw, Cap, sooner or later a ship'll come by."

"Maybe. Maybe not. One might come by in the night or on the other side of the island and we won't even see it. And even if they were on this side, there's no saying they'd stop. And it's a real pain keeping those signal fires going all the time. I don't know how much longer we can keep at it."

The two men continued discussing the issue for a while, and finally Shep shifted his weight nervously. "What are you gonna do about Novak and the others?"

Barkley looked up. "If this blasted leg wasn't broken, I'd do something in a hurry."

"This mutiny probably wouldn't have happened if you hadn't been hurt, Cap, but now it's lookin' worse all the time."

"It's just the three of them, Shep," Barkley said. He thought for a moment, then scratched his beard. "Oscar and Chip wouldn't give anyone any trouble."

"And Lars isn't a bad fellow either, but he's easily led."

"We may have to wait until I get on my two pins again. Until then, we'll just have to make the best of it."

Shep picked up a stick and examined it as if it had some meaning. When he looked up, his countenance was troubled. "I don't know, Cap. Cerny and Charlie have been acting pretty bad toward the women."

"I know, but I can't do anything about it in my condition. Maybe if I could just get one of those guns—"

"I'm afraid they'd shoot you down if you tried."

Captain Barkley groaned. He was not accustomed to being in situations he couldn't handle, and the gloom he felt was etched across his heavy features. His eyes were fixed on the distance, where he could hear the voices of Novak and the other members of the crew. "We'll have to wait until I'm strong enough," he murmured. "Then we'll see."

★　★　★

Chip had taught the women that the soap they made with such an arduous method was not the only way of washing clothes. He had introduced them to pumice, an extremely lightweight stone that was readily available on the island. "All of my womenfolk back home use it when they run out of soap. It's almost as good," Chip had told them. "And what's more, you'll never run out of it."

Rena had gathered a bagful of clothes and gone to the stream with it. She had been doing Abigail's washing as well as her own, and for half an hour she had been scrubbing, thinking with some concern of Abigail's approaching labor. Karl was still not willing to help with the birth, and when asked for advice, he said little. She couldn't understand his attitude, and it troubled her.

When she finished the washing, she wrung out the clothes as well as she could, then started back toward the camp to hang them on ropes to dry. She had come close enough to camp to hear muted voices, when Cerny Novak appeared from around the bend in the trail. She stopped abruptly. Nodding curtly, she said, "Hello, Novak."

"Been doing washing, have you?"

"Yes."

"Here, lemme help you carry that." Novak reached to take the bundle of wet clothes.

"That's all right. I can handle it." Rena noticed that one of the pistols was in the belt holding up his faded jeans. With no shirt, his powerful build was obvious, and his hair was now long enough to hang down over his back. Rena started to hurry by, but he grabbed her by the arm.

"What's your hurry?"

"Let me go, please."

"Well, ain't you got fine manners." Novak grinned but did not release her arm. "Look here. There's no sense in being so standoffish. I'm a perty nice guy when you get to know me."

Novak's grip was like steel. Rena felt a touch of fear, even though she was within calling distance of the camp. Determined to appear fearless to Novak, she said quietly, "Let me go, please. I need to get these clothes hung up."

"Plenty of time for that. Look, things are a little different now. There was a time when you was the queen of Sheba and I was just one of the slaves." Novak pulled her closer. "A little different now, ain't it?"

Rena was shocked that he would be so overt in his approach. She knew he had watched her, as he had watched the other women. There was a wolfish air about the man, and now it occurred to her that he considered her his prey. He suddenly snatched the clothes from her grip, and she tried to break away, but he was too quick for her. He threw the clothes on the ground and grabbed her by both arms, yanking her forward. She was powerless in his grip, but she managed to turn her face away as he tried to kiss her. "Let me go!" she cried, struggling valiantly to free herself. "Help!" she screamed. "Somebody help me!"

"Who you think's gonna help you, sweetheart?" Novak leered. "What you been needin' is a real man instead of that punk you got."

"Let her go, Cerny."

Novak whirled, keeping Rena's arm gripped with one hand as he faced Travis, who had come up behind them. "You don't want to do this, Cerny."

"Butt out, Winslow!"

"I can't do that. Let her go and things will be all right."

Travis was no more than three feet away, his gaze fixed on Cerny. He stood in his usual relaxed manner, Rena noticed, yet there was an alertness about him. He seemed dangerous in a way he never had before.

"I'm tellin' you to stay out of this," Cerny muttered with quiet menace in his voice.

Travis saw a flicker in Novak's eyes, and as the burly sailor's hand dropped to the pistol in his belt, Travis sprang forward, throwing a powerful punch that caught Novak high on the cheek and drove him backward. Travis made a wild stab for the pistol but missed and caught Novak's wrist instead. He tried to twist it, but the man was too strong.

As the two fell to the ground struggling, Rena rolled out of Novak's grip. Novak's fist caught Travis high on the forehead. Travis avoided the knee that was aimed at his groin and managed to jam his elbow at Novak's mouth. The impact was solid and brought a gasp from the burly sailor. The two men struggled over the pistol, rolling on the sandy ground and striking blows where they could with their free arms.

Novak staggered to his feet, dragging Travis with him. Both had bloody faces now and were driving in blow after blow, some of them awkward but all of them doing damage, for they were both strong men.

Travis was holding his own for the moment but knew he couldn't win against Novak's superior strength. A hard jab landed on Travis's shoulder, and then as Novak pulled back for another strike, Travis grabbed his right wrist. With a twist he lifted the arm and stepped under it, using a trick he had learned from a wrestling champion, and Novak spun in the air and went crashing down. Travis jerked the pistol from his hand, but even as he did a voice rang out.

"All right, Winslow, drop the gun!"

Travis turned to see Charlie Day standing not ten feet away with the rifle aimed directly at him. He had no chance at all, so he tossed the gun onto the ground. "All right, Charlie," he said.

"Get away from him." Day moved over to stand beside Novak, who was getting to his feet.

Novak wiped the blood from his face, eyeing Travis with an odd expression. He picked the gun up, and for a moment Travis thought he would shoot him.

But Novak laughed instead. "Well, you're the first man that ever put me on my back like that, Winslow."

"Let me shoot him, Novak!"

"Shut up, Charlie. You're not shooting nobody." Novak held the pistol easily in his hand and became aware that the others had gathered and were watching. He studied the group, noting the fear in their eyes, and then he turned his attention back to the tall man in front of him. "Travis, it was a fair fight, but there won't be no more of it. I'll kill you if you step out of line again."

"I believe you would."

"You know I would. Now, all of you watch what you're doin' or you'll be sorry."

Novak and Day turned and left. The others gathered around Travis, with everyone talking at once.

"Your face is all cut," Rena said to Travis.

"I've had worse."

"Come on. I'll clean you up."

The two went back to the camp, where Rena got a dish of water and a clean cloth. She began to dab away at the cuts. "I wish we had some kind of antiseptic."

"Doesn't amount to anything. I'll be fine."

Rena stopped her nursing, suddenly frightened over what could have happened. "You know, I've never had a problem like this."

"I have." He grinned wryly. "I've been in lots of fights."

"You must be careful, Travis. He's got a wicked streak in him. He'll shoot you if you give him an excuse."

"I don't think so. I think he's a better man than the one we see."

She shook her head. "I don't believe that's true." She was quiet for a moment, then said, "You know, Travis, I've always been able to solve my own problems. If I couldn't, I would take them to Dad. I used to have enough self-confidence for ten women, but I don't have it anymore."

"That may be a good thing."

"What do you mean?"

"I mean I think God builds our faith by putting us into situations we can't handle. That's the way I've learned what little I know about the Lord. Maybe God's getting you ready for something that calls for great faith."

Rena's shoulders sagged. "I'm so tired, Travis. I just don't know anymore. I think the whole thing was a mistake coming out here, bringing these amateurs." Her voice was bitter, and her hopelessness was evident. She was not the same woman, Travis knew, who had left the States months earlier. He took her hand and held it for a moment, smiling. She met his gaze and noticed how his skin was deeply tanned and without a wrinkle, and his full beard made him look ruggedly handsome. She also saw in his face an approval of her, and more than that, she thought she saw a clear, bold expression of warmth. This brought a flush to her face.

Travis said gently, "You're growing in grace, I think."

Rena did not know what to say to this, but the intimacy of the moment was interrupted when she heard Jimmy Townsend calling. She turned and saw the young man running toward them, his face pale.

"What's wrong, Jimmy?"

"It's . . . it's Abigail. She's having her baby."

"Are you sure?"

"Yes, it's happening now. Where's Karl?"

"He went fishing. I'll go get him," Travis said. Without another word, he turned and plunged off down the beach.

"Come along. You don't want to leave her alone, Jimmy."

"No, but Karl's got to help. He just has to!"

"He will," Rena said soothingly. "Come on, now. Let's go see to her."

★　★　★

To Jimmy the minutes crawled by like hours. Karl had come back from the beach and had gone to see Abigail, but the sight of her wan face and her agonizing cries practically destroyed him.

"Can't you give her some of that dope Chip found, Karl?"

"It wouldn't be good at this stage, Jimmy. She has to help push."

"Oh, I wish we'd never come to this place!" Jimmy muttered under his breath. "What's going to happen?" he asked Meredith and Rena, who were comforting Abby. "I don't know anything about having babies. Back home they just take care of it at a hospital and come out and tell the husband when it's over."

"Come outside, Jimmy," Karl instructed.

Something in Karl's voice startled Jimmy. As they stepped

outside, he said, "What's the matter? Is something wrong?"

"Yes, there's something wrong," Karl said as they moved further from the shelter. "The baby is turned the wrong way."

"What does that mean?" he whispered.

"I'm not an expert, as you know. As a medical student I observed several deliveries and all of them went well, but this one . . ." Benson swallowed hard and ran his hand nervously across his forehead. "I'm no good for this, Jimmy."

Jimmy grabbed Karl's arms and practically shouted, "You've got to be, Karl. Nobody else around here has even observed a delivery!"

Karl pushed Jimmy's hands away. "You can't ask me to do something I can't do!" he wailed, his voice on the verge of panic. He turned and walked away blindly. Jimmy stood there as helpless and frightened as he'd ever been in his life. He heard a voice and felt a touch and turned to see Pete standing there beside Lanie.

"What's wrong with Karl?" Pete asked.

"He . . . he says he can't do it. He can't help Abigail."

"But he's got to!" Pete exclaimed.

"Let me go talk to him," Lanie said.

"Come along, you'd better go back and be with your wife," Pete said, taking Jimmy by the arm.

Jimmy was trembling. He loved his wife with all of his heart, and now he feared that he was about to lose her. "She can't die, Pete. She just can't!"

★ ★ ★

Abby's screams drove some of the group far from the camp. Among the crew, only Chip and Oscar were able to bear it. They sat silently by the fire, exchanging haunted glances. Even the tough-minded Oscar said, "I've never heard such screams. My wife never carried on like this when she had our son."

Chip agreed. "Yeah, it's bad. How long can a woman go on like that?"

For the others, the time dragged by. Karl had disappeared, and no one knew where he was. Meredith and Rena stayed with Abby, trying to comfort her but not really knowing what to do.

Finally Rena, her face drenched with sweat, said, "I've got to go find Karl. You stay here, Meredith."

Rena ran out of the shelter and quickly found Travis. "You've got to help me, Travis," she cried. "I don't know what's wrong with Karl, but he's got to do something!"

"You're right." Travis agreed. "Whatever his problems are, they can't be as bad as what Abby's going through. Nothing's more important right now than Abby and that baby."

They hurried out together in search of Karl and found him five minutes later. He was sitting in the woods, his face pale and covered with sweat. When they approached him, he couldn't meet their eyes.

Travis grabbed him by the arm. "Karl, I don't know what's wrong with you, but I'll tell you this. You're going to come back with us and do whatever you can to help Abby. If she dies, she's going to die with you looking right at her."

"I can't go back. I just can't."

"What's wrong with you? You're the one most fitted to help," Rena cried. "Don't you care?"

"Don't I care? Yes, I care! I care too much."

"What does that mean?" Travis asked in exasperation. "The woman is dying!"

"You think I don't know that?"

"Then why won't you help her?"

Karl tried to turn away, but Travis kept a firm grip on his arm. His eyes looked haunted and his lips seemed paralyzed.

"You've all wondered why I gave up on my dreams of becoming a doctor. All right, I'll tell you. I had a problem with alcohol, and I let it get in the way of my work. In a drunken state one day, I ordered the wrong medication for a woman who was in labor. She died because of my carelessness—and her baby too. I can never forgive myself as long as I live!"

Rena saw the torture in Benson's face. "That's in the past, Karl. Now you've got a chance to make up for it."

"I can't, I've told you! Do you know what's going to have to happen for her to live?" Benson asked slowly, his voice unsteady. "She'll have to have a caesarean. That baby will never be born normally. If she doesn't have an operation, they'll both die."

Travis said, "Then you've got nothing to lose, Karl. She'll die if you don't do a caesarean, and maybe she'll live if you give it a try. Come on. You have no choice."

"Are you crazy, Travis? A caesarean? Out here? I've got no anesthetic, no surgical tools, no nothing!"

"Listen," Travis said. "You know we have a good assortment of knives, and we've got a few supplies in the first-aid kit. Besides that, we have Chip's anesthetic. I know it's not what you'd have in a hospital, but it's better than nothing." Travis took a deep breath and put his hand on Karl's shoulder. "We're all believers. We know that God can help. We're going to pray right now that God will help you to do what needs to be done."

Karl stared at Travis for a long time, and then a tear trickled down and into his beard. "It will have to be God who does it."

"We'll pray," Rena encouraged, "and God will give us a victory. You'll see."

The three bowed their heads, and Travis and Rena held on to Karl. They prayed fervently, and when they lifted their heads, Karl was a changed man, glowing with optimism. "All right," he said. "I can guarantee nothing, but I'll do my best."

"And God will do His best." Travis smiled. "Come on. Let's go."

# CHAPTER EIGHTEEN

# NEW LIFE

★ ★ ★

All three returned to the camp, where the air of tension was almost unbearable. The missionaries had returned in groups of two or three, hating the screams but wanting to be nearby if they could be of any assistance. Karl said to them all, "God will have to do a miracle here."

He started giving orders as authoritatively as any head surgeon. "Pete, I need you to get our best fillet knife and get it as sharp as you can. Lanie, bring me the first-aid kit and make sure the stitching supplies are ready to go." He turned to Rena and Meredith and said sternly, "You two will help."

It was not a request, and Rena cringed at the task that lay ahead. She saw that Meredith was also stunned, but she said, "We'll have to do it, Meredith."

The two women went into the shelter with Karl while Pete and Lanie ran off on their assignments. Travis joined the others around the fire. He noted that of the various reactions of the group, Professor Dekker seemed the most bothered. His eyes, behind his thick glasses, were puzzled, and he said, "Travis, I don't have any experience in this. I guess I've lived too long away from real life."

Travis laid his hand on the professor's shoulder. "Well, you're getting a dose of real life now."

"Do you think Karl can help her?"

"I think God can help her, and He'll use Karl. Don't you believe that?"

Professor Dekker had lived most of his life alone, never having married, and had devoted himself to the world of scholarship. He had been prepared to lead the missionaries, teaching them daily from his deep understanding of the Scriptures. Now he realized that his world had been turned upside down. "I'll have to find God in some new way, Travis," he whispered. "It's not enough to know the Book about God. We must know God himself."

Travis smiled. "I think you're right about that." He left the professor to his thoughts and went to talk to Oscar, who was cleaning fish. "Need some help, Oscar?"

"No, I could do this in my sleep." He looked up and said, "I hope the little lady's all right."

"I believe with God's help, she'll be all right."

"Look, Travis, I hope you know that me and Chip and Shep, we ain't in this thing with Cerny. He's wrong."

"I knew you weren't in on it, Oscar, but I appreciate you coming right out and saying it."

★　★　★

Abby's screams finally quieted and were replaced with the squeal of a newborn. After a moment the baby stopped crying as well. Karl stepped out of the shelter and walked quickly over to Jimmy, who was speaking quietly with Travis.

"How is she, Karl?" Abby's husband asked.

"She's going to be all right," Karl assured him.

"Thank God."

Travis's arm went around Jimmy, for it was obvious he was so shaken he could barely stand up.

"Thank you for what you've done, Karl. I am so grateful."

Everyone gathered around Karl, and as Travis saw the new confidence in the man's face, he realized he had passed some sort of test within himself. *He's going to be a better man because of this*, Travis thought.

"Can I see her, Doc?" Jimmy said.

"Yes, of course. Go on in. And congratulations! You have a fine baby boy."

Meredith came up to Karl and said, "You did a wonderful job, Karl."

"And so did you," he replied, "but you know, it was really God who did it."

"Yes, I'll say amen to that."

Travis saw that the group was relieved and a sense of well-being enveloped them. The crisis had almost destroyed them, but now they were rejoicing together in God's goodness. Travis breathed a prayer of thanks for the outcome, then went to see about Novak. On his way, he ran across Lars Olsen, who looked at him cautiously.

"How's the lady?" Lars asked.

"She's doing fine. Where's Cerny?"

"What do you want with him, Travis?"

"Just to talk."

"All right, but he's pretty sore. He's down the beach a ways. Try not to stir him up."

Travis nodded, then walked on quickly down the shore until he reached Novak. The sailor was sitting on a rock staring moodily out at the sea. When Travis came closer, he called out the man's name and sat down next to him.

"Abigail's all right," Travis began, "and the baby too. It's a boy. Just thought you'd like to know."

"That's good," he grunted. His face was battered, and there was a look that Travis could not identify in his eyes. "You cut me up pretty bad, Winslow."

"Sorry about that. You and I shouldn't fight."

"I meant what I said," Novak came back. "Don't challenge me, and don't come at me again."

"I'll do what I have to do to keep peace on this island. We all have to live together."

"Sure we do, and someone's gotta make the rules. I've been bossed around all my life, Winslow, but I'm better fitted for living in this place than any of those weakling preachers."

"Physically you're the strongest, Cerny, but there's more to life than that."

"Not to me there ain't."

Travis had prayed much for this big man. He was a rough individual on the surface, but there had to be more to him than met the eye. Travis hesitated, then said, "One of these days, Cerny, you're going to be old, and you'll lose your strength. You won't be the strongest anymore."

"I don't think about things like getting old."

"No, we never do. But we should. The time's going to come when you're going to need more than the strength of your arms."

Cerny smiled, his battered lips twisting cynically. "You gonna preach to me?"

"No—no preaching. I just want you to know that if it weren't for Jesus, I'd probably be dead."

"Save the sermon."

"Sorry, I can't do that."

Cerny stood up. "I don't want to hear no more about God." He stalked off down the beach, not giving Travis a chance to answer.

Travis watched as the figure of the bulky man grew small. "Lord," he said, "I pray you'll bring that stubborn man to his knees—whatever it takes."

★　★　★

It was close to the end of March, two weeks after the birth of the baby, whom the parents had named Michael. All the missionaries helped with the newcomer in whatever way they could while Abigail recovered from the traumatic birth. Despite the severity of her experience, she did recover quickly. She was able to nurse the baby without any problem and was tremendously proud of her son. Jimmy was as proud as a man could be, and neither of them could let Karl pass without giving him a word of thanks and praise.

Karl repeatedly said to Travis, "I wish they'd be quiet about it."

"I don't think they can," Travis always responded with a smile. "It meant so much to all of us. You've become a better man, and I'm proud of you too."

Travis himself had been drained by the crisis. He was thankful that Cerny had kept to himself lately, not offering any more insults. But Travis continued to pray for him and sought others to join with him. Early one morning he got up, ate breakfast, and prepared to leave camp.

Rena was up early too and asked him where he was going.

"I just need to get away for a while."

"Let me go with you," she said.

Travis shrugged. "Sure. Come along."

The two left, carrying enough food with them for the day. Travis set out at a good pace, and he was pleased to see that Rena kept up with him. They hardly spoke to each other until they stopped to eat an early lunch. Then he found himself telling Rena about his difficult childhood. She listened patiently and with interest until finally he stopped and said, "I shouldn't be burdening you with all this."

"You had a hard time of it, Travis."

"Not as hard as some."

"My childhood was easy," Rena admitted. She leaned back against a tree trunk and watched a group of gulls fly over. When they disappeared, she turned to him and shook her head. "I've been so rotten all my life."

"I don't know why you'd say that."

"Because it's true," she said, a tinge of bitterness in her voice. "I was spoiled rotten. I thought I knew everything. I was smarter than most of the people I knew and had more money, and somehow I let that blind me to many of their good qualities."

It was Travis's turn to listen, and he did not attempt to stop her. As he watched her talk, he saw a teasing expression suddenly come across her face, a provocative challenge. She laughed, and color ran freshly across her cheeks. "I never talked so much like this to anyone in my whole life." She got to her feet and turned away from him. He rose and came to stand at her side. He touched her arm, and she turned around. "We're friends, aren't we, Travis?"

"Of course we are, Rena."

"We weren't at first, though. I was so beastly to you."

"That's in the past. I've learned to bury those things. I used to worry about all the sins I committed, but an old missionary once told me that Jesus takes all of our sins out, dumps them in the deepest part of the sea, and then puts a No Fishing sign out. We shouldn't be dredging them up again."

She looked up at him and smiled. "You're good for me. Let's start all over right now."

"Sure," he said. A light danced in his eyes, and he said, "Don't you think friends should express themselves with some sort of symbolic gesture?"

Rena laughed. "Is that your way of asking if you can kiss me?"

"I guess it is."

"You kissed me once and it frightened me, but I could never be afraid of you now, Travis."

He lowered his head and kissed her, and an unexpected wave of emotion flowed through her. She stepped back, feeling heat rise in her cheeks.

"You're a woman to be desired and to be loved," Travis said simply.

The words stirred her, and she could not answer for a moment. Finally she said, "I . . . I think we'd better go."

He did not argue with her, but simply helped her gather up the remains of their meal and put them into the sack. "Say," he said, "would you like to see one of my favorite spots on this island? We're not far from it now."

"Sure. No one's expecting us back soon anyway."

They headed for the far side of the island, directly across from the camp. Both remained silent as they walked, thinking of what had passed between them.

Before long, Travis said, "I can hear the ocean. We're almost there."

They were approaching the top of a cliff. Travis had sat there on other occasions, scouring the horizon for ships. They reached the edge of the cliff and looked down, shocked at what they saw.

"Look at that," Rena whispered.

"I can't believe it."

Neither of them could say another word. There beneath them on the beach, a large vessel built like a catamaran was pulled up on the sand, and a group of people were cooking around a fire. Rena broke the silence between them. "We're not alone, Travis."

"No, we're certainly not. That's a strange-looking vessel. I wonder how far they've come in it. There must be another island close by—one that's inhabited!"

She took a deep breath. "Come on," she said with excitement. "Let's go down."

"Wait," he cautioned, taking her arm. "They might be cannibals or headhunters."

Rena had been so excited at seeing other people she had not thought of the potential danger. "What do you think we should do?"

"Let's go back to the camp and tell the others. We'll have to decide as a body."

"But they might leave before we can return."

"I don't think so. It looks like they're settling down. They'll still be here if we hurry. It won't take us nearly as long to get back as it did to get here, since we weren't taking a straight path this morning."

"Let's go quickly, then."

Travis led the way, quickening the pace to a jog. As they excitedly made their way back to camp, Travis said, "I hope either Chip or Meredith can speak their language!"

# PART FOUR

# March–September 1936

★ ★ ★

# CHAPTER NINETEEN

# A GROUP DECISION

★ ★ ★

Oscar Blevins looked up from the coconut he was chopping to the nearby shelter, his brow furrowed. "What's all that racket about? Why are them women being so noisy in there?"

Shep Riggs, who was relaxing against a tree, said, "Sound happy, don't they?"

"What are they so doggone happy about?" Oscar said gloomily.

"It's that baby."

"What's to be happy about? A baby is nothin' but a bunch of trouble. That's what babies are."

"But you got a kid yourself, ain't you, Oscar?"

"Yeah, I do." He looked down at his hands and then shook his head. "I think about him all the time, how he's doin' now. I hope my sister-in-law is takin' good care of him."

Shep asked curiously, "Kind of like to be around him, wouldn't you?"

"I ain't been the best dad in the world." Oscar started to say more, but the laughter of the women floated across the clearing. "I don't reckon I'll ever see him again."

"Don't say that. Maggie says we're gonna get off of this island."

"Well, what in blazes does *she* know about it?"

Shep didn't answer for a moment. "It's a funny thing," he said finally. "That woman knows God. If I had met her when I was a mite younger, I would have stayed out of all the trouble I got into."

"Some women get men into trouble."

"Sure, some do. But this one don't."

Oscar laughed, his eyes almost disappearing into his cheeks. "You're gone on her, ain't you, Shep?"

"I reckon I am a little bit, Oscar, but nothin' will ever come of it."

"Why not?"

"Oh, you know how it is. She's a refined lady, and I'm just a roustabout."

"That was back in the other world. Out here in this place what matters is what a man can do with his hands. Look at the professor. What good does all his diplomas do him out here? Why, he can't even cook a meal or drive a nail. He's the most helpless feller I ever saw."

Shep did not answer. He was thinking about Maggie. He had felt an attraction toward Maggie even back when they were on the ship. But he was a realistic young fellow and had grown accustomed to his place in society. At first, he and Maggie didn't seem to have much in common, but the months on the island were changing her. She had trimmed down and become physically strong, and somehow her weight loss had changed her personality. She had a glow about her, and she laughed a great deal. And the rules of society didn't seem to matter much anymore.

Another peal of laughter burst from the shelter, and Shep grinned. "They're sure enjoyin' that young'un," he murmured.

The two men continued talking, for they had always been good friends. Suddenly Shep looked up. "Somebody's comin' in a hurry."

"You got ears like a fox," Oscar said, shrugging his beefy shoulders. "I don't hear nothin'." He turned, however, and looked in the direction Shep gestured. "You're right. Somebody's comin' on the run."

"It's Travis," Shep said, getting to his feet. "And Miss Rena's with him."

"Must be trouble for them to come that fast." Oscar tossed the knife aside, and the two men met the runners at the edge of the clearing. "What is it, Travis?"

"Go round everybody up," Travis ordered. "I want everyone to hear this at once."

"Must be important," Shep said. "I'll go fetch 'em, but it may take a little while."

★   ★   ★

Travis looked around the group and saw the curiosity on every face. Rena was standing beside him, and he caught her eye. She smiled encouragingly, and he announced, "Exciting news, everyone. We've got company!"

"Company!" A babble of voices broke out, and Novak, who stood slightly back beside Day and Olsen, said, "What do you mean 'company'?"

"A boat has landed down on the opposite side of the island. About twenty people are on the shore; they look like island natives to me."

The onlookers began to fire questions, but Travis raised his hand. "It looked like there were about sixteen men and five women. That's really all we know."

"Did you speak to them?" Meredith asked, her eyes wide.

"No, we were up on the cliff above them, Rena and I, and we decided not to go down and meet them right now. We couldn't be sure if they were dangerous or not."

"Were they carryin' weapons?" Novak demanded. "Did they look like fighters?"

"I don't really know. We didn't see any weapons, but we

both were so shocked we couldn't pay much attention to details."

"I wanted to go down and meet them," Rena said, "but Travis thought it would be better if we came back here and make a decision all together about what to do."

"Good thinking," Karl said. He slammed his fist into his palm. "This is great news! That means there must be another island close enough for them to touch on this one."

"That's right," the professor said. "The islanders aren't great travelers. They know little about navigation."

"So maybe they're from really close by," Maggie said. "Maybe from an island where ships land!"

The babble of voices rose again, with many of them striving to be heard. Finally Dalton's voice rose above the others, "Look, we've got to go back and make contact with them. They might sail away and leave us here."

"I think you're right, Dalton," Rena said. "But I wanted us all to be in on the decision."

Dalton said impatiently, "Rena, there's no decision to be made. We've got to go!"

Charlie Day pulled the pistol out of his belt and barked, "Right, we can take over that bunch and make 'em sail us back to the other island."

"Don't be foolish, Charlie!" Rena said. "We can't use force on them."

"Sure we can," Cerny countered. He lifted the rifle in his hand. "This rifle holds ten shells. That's half of 'em. With the pistols, it could take care of the rest."

"You'd kill them all?" Travis said quietly. The air bristled with the tension between the two men. "You'd just shoot them down, Cerny?"

"If we had to," Cerny answered, "but we prob'ly won't. I've been on these islands before. Most of these natives are pretty friendly to white people. I'm just sayin' if they ain't friendly—if they're headhunters or cannibals—we can take care of ourselves."

Lanie touched Pete's arm and whispered, "We can't let that man go. There's no telling what he'll do."

"I think you're right," Pete answered quietly. He spoke up. "Novak, we've got to be sensible about this. I think maybe God has sent these people to us. We can't go down there threatening them with guns."

"You don't know some of these natives, Alford," Lars said slowly. "I've seen 'em do bad things. They ain't all of them gentle."

The debate went on for ten minutes, and finally Travis said, "We can't discuss this all day. We've got to go back. I'd hate for them to sail off without making contact. Chip, you'll have to go, and you, Meredith. The two of you might be able to speak to them. Do you think you'll know their language, Meredith?"

"I won't know until I hear them. It's more likely that Chip will be able to communicate."

Every eye went to Chip, and he shrugged, saying, "Maybe. I'm willing to try."

"All right. We'll go, then."

"All of us?" Jimmy Townsend said.

"No, Jimmy, you stay here with Abby and the baby and the captain. I think you should stay too, Cerny."

"I'm not stayin'," Novak said bluntly.

"Well, all right," Travis said. "But will you agree to keep those weapons out of it—and not use any of them?"

"I'll keep the weapons out of it, but I'm going," Novak stated flatly, his eyes narrow. "We'll try it your way first, but they'd better watch what they're doing. We don't know if they can be trusted."

Travis smiled. "We don't need guns, Cerny. We need prayer." He ignored the hard look on the big man's face and turned to face the others. "Let's ask God to show us the way to be a blessing to these people." He bowed his head and began to pray, and the missionaries all followed suit. Cerny Novak drew his lips together in a tight line, and he held the rifle tightly in his hands.

After the prayer Jimmy and Abby watched as the others made their preparations to leave. Jimmy said, "Why don't you take some of those trinkets we salvaged off the ship?"

"That's a good idea," Rena said brightly and went to fish out some beads and bracelets.

"Take some of those good knives too," Karl suggested. "Most natives don't have steel knives."

Shep and Oscar chose to stay behind with the Townsends and the captain, and as they watched the party leave, Oscar shook his head. "I hope they don't run into trouble."

"They will if Novak has his way about it," Shep said. He watched as the last of the party disappeared into the tree line and sighed heavily. "Well, we'll know soon."

★ ★ ★

Novak held back his pace, allowing twenty yards between the missionaries and his crew. Charlie stayed by his side, while the big, rawboned Olsen kept close behind. None of them spoke until they had traveled for an hour. Finally Charlie turned and grinned at Novak. "You hear what them two said about the natives?"

"What about 'em?" Novak grunted, not turning to face his smaller companion.

"He said there was some women with 'em. That's what I'm lookin' for!"

Olsen laughed. "You'd better watch out for their menfolk. They'll put a spear right through you, Charlie."

"Not while I got this." Charlie pulled the pistol out and waved it in the air. "We got the bulge on 'em, ain't we, Novak?"

"We'll wait and see."

The three forged steadily ahead, but Charlie could not stop talking. He got close enough to dig into Cerny with his elbow. "You remember that time when we stopped off in Samoa? You remember them gorgeous black-eyed women?"

"I remember."

"They were really somethin', and they knew how to make a man happy. And that whiskey! I don't know how they made it, but it had a kick like a mule. I betcha this bunch knows how to make somethin' like that too."

"Yeah, they probably do," Lars said. "Everywhere we ever been there was people who could make whiskey."

Charlie had been a failure at most things in life. He was a drunk and a womanizer and had done time in jail for minor offenses. Now his voice was shrill with excitement as he continued to talk about the possibilities that lay before them. "Lookee here, you guys! What we gotta do is go back with these here natives. We could be kings there! We could have anything we want. All the liquor and women, and we'd never have to do a lick o' work."

"They might be cannibals," Novak said. "We don't know what they are."

"I bet they ain't!" Charlie exclaimed. "Wherever they come from, it can't be too far away, and maybe a ship will stop by there."

"That's right," Lars said. "And like Charlie says, if there ain't no other white men there, they'd take us for gods or something. And if they try to fool with us, we've got the guns to show 'em who's boss."

"Shut up, both of you! I've gotta think," Novak blustered. He looked ahead and said, "When we get close, we'll stay back. If these natives are bad news, it'll be those preachers up there that'll find out about it first." He grinned sourly. "Better them than us, I say."

★　★　★

"What do you think we'll find, Pete?" Lanie asked. She and Pete were walking side by side, for the trees had thinned out somewhat. They were headed uphill now and climbing steadily. Lanie was delighted that she was not even breathing hard. She expanded her lungs and took a deep breath. "Do you think they'll be peaceful?"

"I hope so. I feel a bit shaky about it. I wish you had stayed back at camp until we found out."

"We're all in this together, Pete."

The two kept close together as they wound their way toward the crest of the mountain. The way grew steeper, and finally Lanie asked, "What would you do, Pete, if they were able to take us to wherever they come from and a ship came by?"

"You mean would I go back to the U.S.?"

"Yes, and what would you do there? Would you still feel that God wants you to be a missionary?"

After thinking about his answer for a minute, he grinned. "Yes, I know God still wants me to be a missionary." He reached over and took her hand.

Lanie felt the strength of his grip and the power in this quiet man whom she had come to love and admire.

"I don't much care what I do as long as I do it with you, Lanie."

"I feel exactly the same way, Pete. I love you."

"I love you too. I've never felt this way about anyone else before. It's you or nobody for me, Lanie."

★   ★   ★

"There's the cliff right ahead," Travis said quietly. He turned to Rena, who was beside him. "Are you scared?"

"A little. Are you?"

"You know it's odd, but I'm not. I believe God is in all of this."

"I wish I had your faith, Travis, but I don't."

"Well, I've had a lot more experience than you have being around natives, but I just know in my spirit that God is doing something great. I don't know what it is yet, though."

As they approached the edge of the cliff, Rena said, "I've changed so much since I've been here, Travis. I'm ashamed to think of what I was when I first met you."

Travis smiled. "God's done a work in you, I can see that."

"All right, then. Let's go see what God has for us from here on."

# CHAPTER TWENTY

# FIRST ENCOUNTER

★ ★ ★

As Rena stepped outside the tree line onto the broad beach, she felt weak and knew that if she tried to speak, her voice would not be steady. Down the way along the white sands, the brown-skinned newcomers were sharing a meal together. The smoke from their fire rose into the air, a steady column at first, then broken up by the sea breeze into a filmy gray haze. She was aware of the harsh squawking of the sea gulls and the rush of the waves onto the shore. The sound they made would ordinarily be pleasing, but now she could think only of the moment that lay just ahead.

*I'm scared to death,* she thought. Her life before the shipwreck had been sheltered; her father had protected her from anything harmful. Now, however, as she felt the sand give under her feet, she knew there would be no protection if these natives proved to be deadly. Glancing to her right, she saw that Travis was focusing on the group down the beach. She could see no trace of fear in him and envied his presence of mind. She was very, very glad that he was there beside her. She longed to reach out and take his hand, for she needed his encouragement and strength, but she did not do so.

A shout came from one of the group, and Travis murmured, "We've been spotted." He raised his voice and said to the others following them, "Everyone hold steady, now. We'll wait right here. They've seen us."

Rena stood absolutely still and watched as the natives down the beach all leaped up and came running. She had time to see their faces more clearly as they ran, and she had one clear thought: *They're such a handsome people!*

Indeed, they were an attractive group, but they all bore weapons in their hands—some had either smooth-shafted spears or crooked daggers, while others carried what looked like axes.

The leader gave a shout and lifted the long daggerlike weapon in his hand, and Rena understood that it was not a peaceful cry. The group broke apart like waves bursting on a rock and surrounded the little group of missionaries. They all lifted their weapons high, their eyes glittering with excitement. She saw that the men were short and the women even more so, and they all had black hair. The leader was taller than any of the others, and he positioned himself in front of Travis and Rena and spoke a few words that neither of them understood.

Travis lifted his hands into the air, palms up. "Everyone hold your hands up like this," he instructed. "Chip or Meredith, can either of you understand what they're saying?"

"I can't," Meredith said. "It sounds a little familiar, but I can't make anything of it."

Chip said, "I'm catching most of it. He told his warriors to kill us if we move."

"Can you tell him we're friends?"

"I'll try," Chip said. "Their language is similar to one I learned when I was a kid. Some of the words are pronounced a little differently."

Chip began speaking in a halting voice, and Rena felt a rush of relief, for the chieftain before them half lowered the weapon in his hands. He listened and then spoke rapidly.

"He wants to know who we are," Chip said.

"Tell him that we are friends and that we mean them no harm."

As Chip translated the words as best he could, the chief kept his gaze fixed on Rena and Travis.

The man spoke again, this time a longer sentence.

"Best I can make out he wants to know who we are, how we got here, how long we've been here, and where we're from."

Travis said, "Ask if we can go to their camp and have a meeting with them. Tell them we have some gifts for them."

Chip interpreted this, and for a moment Rena did not think the chief was convinced. But then she saw his eyes change. He spoke a word to his followers, then turned and started back toward the campfire.

Rena and the others followed, and Lanie whispered to Pete, "They don't look like cannibals, do they?"

"I don't know what a cannibal looks like," Pete answered, keeping his voice low.

One of the women surrounding the missionaries as they walked along reached out and plucked at Lanie's canvas dress. She said something that neither of them could understand.

"I think she likes your dress. Smile at her."

Lanie smiled and spoke. "My name is Lanie. What is yours?"

She was greeted with a tumble of words, and the woman lifted her voice and called out something to the leader, who ignored her.

It was only about a hundred yards to their camp, and when they got there, Rena saw that they were roasting a goat. The meat had been skewered on sharp pointed sticks, and the aroma of cooking meat was in the air.

Travis looked back down the beach, searching it, and said, "I hope Novak keeps his head." He had no time to say more when the chief turned to him, and the natives all circled around.

Rena noticed that they kept their weapons in their hands, and she said, "I hope they're friendly."

Chip had come to stand beside Travis to serve as interpreter. "Tell him we mean no harm. That we have no weapons," Travis directed.

Rena listened to the language she couldn't understand,
grateful that Chip was with them.

When Chip had finished, the chief struck himself on the
chest, and she heard the word *Lomu.*

"That's his name—Lomu," Chip explained.

"Tell him my name," Travis said. And when Chip had
done this, he went on, "Ask the chief if he will sit down and
talk with us."

As Chip spoke, Lomu listened and watched Travis, but
finally the man nodded.

"Everybody sit down and smile," Travis said, "especially
you ladies. We want to look friendly."

Rena forced a smile to her face and joined the others as
they sat down on the sand.

The chief spoke, and three of the women came and
pulled some of the meat off of the fire. One of them offered
it to Travis, who tore off a chunk and said, "Everybody take
some of the meat and eat it." They all followed suit, and
Travis said, "Give the chief our thanks, Chip, and ask him if
he will receive our gifts."

Lomu listened as Chip spoke. He said nothing, but Chip
said, "He'll take our gifts, Travis."

"Karl, let's have that bag," Travis instructed.

Benson, who had been bearing a large bag, as had Pete
Alford, opened his, and Travis said, "Everyone come and
get a gift. Mostly give them beads and this junk jewelry we
bought in Hawaii."

Rena reached in and got a bracelet made of sparkly red
stone. It was not expensive, she knew, and she approached
one of the young women who had brought them the meat.
She smiled as she held up the bracelet. The woman stared at
her. She was short but well shaped, and her skin was an
almond brown, rather golden in texture. Her hair fell down
her back and was as glossy as a crow's wing. She reached
out and took the bracelet, saying something Rena could not

understand. She assumed the girl was asking what to do with it, and she smiled even more brilliantly and said, "You wear it on your wrist like this." She slipped the bracelet onto the woman's wrist and was rewarded by a giggle. The woman held her wrist up, speaking rapidly to the others.

The other women were receiving similar gifts, and while the jewelry was being passed out, Travis unfastened the sheath from his belt and pulled out the knife he always carried at his side. It was a fine blade, and he always kept it spotlessly clean and as sharp as a razor. He approached Chief Lomu, bowed slightly, and smiled. Holding the knife out, he said, "This is my gift to you, Chief Lomu."

Lomu stared at Travis, not moving. Travis thought the chief meant to reject the gift, so Travis held out his left arm and with a single stroke, shaved the hair off his arm. He looked up to see Lomu's eyes turn bright with interest. The chief said something, then took the proffered knife. He tried the edge of it, and a pleased expression crossed his face. Travis said quietly, "We're going to have to bring the other sailors in. If they find out we're hiding people, we could have trouble."

"I'm not sure that's a good idea," Karl Benson said. "You know what they're like."

"We'll have to caution them to behave themselves, but we have to be honest with these people." Turning to Chip, he said, "Tell Chief Lomu that there are some others of our party that stayed behind farther down the beach. Ask if we can invite them to the meal."

Travis listened as Chip spoke to the chief and saw a slight hesitation on Lomu's part. Chip said, "He wants to know how many."

"Tell him there are three."

Lomu received this and nodded.

"Run down the beach, if you will, Dalton, and tell the others to join us calmly and peacefully."

★　★　★

They all watched as Dalton ran down the beach in search of the crew members who had hung back. When he got close to the edge of the tree line he called out, and the three men emerged.

They followed Dalton back to the gathering of natives and missionaries, and as they came closer, Travis called out, "Keep those guns in your pockets. They probably don't know what they are, but they're friendly, and we don't want to harm them."

Cerny held the rifle lightly in his left hand. He came forward and said, "They seem friendly enough."

"Just don't make any sudden moves," Travis said, noticing that the native men were tense, their weapons ready. "Tell the chief we'd like to sit down and talk," Travis said.

Lomu listened to Chip as he spoke and then nodded. They all sat down, but most of the natives kept to their feet. They were watching their visitors with avid curiosity.

The chief spoke a word, and two of the young men ran to the large catamaran. They came back, bearing vessels of some kind. "The chief wants us to drink with him. The peace drink, he calls it," Chip said and smiled. "It's going to be all right. When they offer to drink with you, they're not going to cut your throat."

The drink was offered to them in hollowed-out gourds. When Rena tasted it, it burned her throat. "I think this is whiskey," she complained.

"Everybody take some of it anyway. It'd be impolite not to," Travis directed.

Rena smiled as the jugs went around. She noticed that Novak, Day, and Olsen drank deeply from the vessels, and she whispered, "It was good we've been away from whiskey."

"I'd just as soon they hadn't offered this," Travis said calmly, keeping a smile on his face but concerned about how the whiskey would affect the crew. "We'll have to watch them."

One of the native women offered Dalton a drink. He looked down at her, tasted it, and smiled. She reached up and put her hand on his face. Dalton was taken aback, but he did not remove her hand. She called out something to the other women, and they all laughed. Even the men smiled.

"What did she say, Chip?" Rena asked.

"She says she likes him. She wants to have him for her man."

Dalton flushed, but then he laughed. "She's got good taste. I'll say that much for her." The woman said something else to him and handed him the jug again.

He took another drink, upon which Rena said, "Dalton, be careful. We don't know what that is."

"I'm all right," he said. The young woman was now stroking his arm as she smiled up at him with her beautiful white teeth and bright eyes.

Disturbed by this, Travis said, "Dalton, watch what you're doing." Then he turned to the chief, who came and sat down in front of him. "Chip, tell him how we came to be on this island and how long we've been here."

As Chip haltingly spoke to the chief, Rena noticed that the crew were taken with the women. She knew enough about men to know that there was real danger here. She looked over at Dalton again. The young woman standing beside him continued to smile. Rena saw her take Dalton's hand and put it on her cheek. She also saw that Dalton seemed fascinated by the woman, and she wanted to cry out a warning but did not.

When Chip had finished, Lomu began to speak. Chip listened, then interpreted. "He says his grandfather saw white people once, but he did not believe they existed."

"That means ships have never come to his island or he would have seen white people," Maggie said.

"Not necessarily," Meredith spoke up. "There could have been Chinese ships. They sail these waters too."

Lomu spoke again, and Chip asked questions as prompted by Travis. It appeared that their home was two days' voyage away. Their tribe was not large. He had not seen any ship with white people on it.

The conversation was slow because Chip was awkward

with the language. At one point Meredith said, "I could learn this language. It's a little bit like Malay. I think it has the same kind of structure, and that's about half the battle."

"That would be good. I'm glad Chip's with us. We'd be in trouble if he weren't," Rena said.

"Ask the chief if he'll come to our settlement and honor us with a visit. Tell him that we have a few more people there. We'd like to offer him our hospitality."

Chip put the question to the chief, who seemed to like the idea. He inquired as to how far it was, and then he began giving orders. He told Chip that they would go, but they would have to beach their craft.

The native men began to pull their catamaran up high on the beach, and they devised an anchor by driving stakes into the sand and tying the catamaran to it. That was apparently all the preparation they needed, for Lomu spoke again, and Chip translated. "He said let's go. He will walk with you, Travis." Chip grinned. "He thinks you're the chief."

"He'll find out better than that soon enough."

Lomu called his people, and Travis said, "Walk with us, Chief, and tell us about your people. Chip, you'll have to interpret."

They left the beach with Travis, Rena, and Chief Lomu speaking through Chip. Rena had time to notice that the crewmen were all watching the young woman who was interested in Dalton. She also noticed with some displeasure another factor. "They're bringing that liquor with them. I wish they wouldn't do that."

"So do I," Travis said, "but it's their say." He smiled and said, "We're still alive. That's the important thing."

"Yes, God was with us, wasn't He?"

"He always is." Travis smiled and turned to question Chief Lomu.

★ ★ ★

When they were almost back to their own camp, Travis noticed that the young woman was still clinging to Dalton, even more obviously now. "Chip, ask the chief who that woman is."

Chip spoke, and when Lomu answered, he said, "Her name is Tabita."

"I don't know how to ask this, Chip, but find out why she's hanging on to Dalton the way she does."

Chip put forth the question, and when he received an answer, he said, "The chief says she lost her mate a while back." He smiled briefly and said, "He says she's been trying out men."

"Trying out men!" Rena exclaimed. "What does that mean?"

"I reckon it means about what you think it means, Miss Rena," Chip said. He shook his head sadly. "Not much morality among these people. If they're like most of the tribes, women do about as they please in that respect."

"Don't they have any rules against . . . well, against adultery?"

"I don't think so, miss."

"Ask the chief about it. Be as tactful as you can," Travis said.

The conversation went on for some time until they were almost in view of their camp. Finally Chip turned to them and said, "It's about like I thought. Women are very lax. No rules like we've got. As a matter of fact, Lomu can't even understand the question. When a man and a woman get married they're monogamous, but if a woman has no mate, she's pretty free to do what she pleases."

Meredith, who was right behind Chip, said, "That's terrible. It must be an awful thing for them."

"Why, it's all they know," Chip said with a shrug.

Rena became more and more agitated. She fell back and walked beside Dalton, saying, "Dalton, you've got to be more careful."

"Careful about what?" he asked.

"About, well—about showing any affection for these women."

"They seem very friendly. Especially this one. I'm just being friendly back."

Rena did not know how to express herself. She finally said bluntly, "This woman lost her husband. Among these people, when that happens, a single woman can . . . well, try out men."

"You mean sleep with them?" Dalton said with some surprise. "Is that what you're talking about?"

"Well . . . yes."

Dalton laughed. "My, my, that's something, isn't it?"

"It's serious, Dalton!"

"Look, Rena, it's been pretty clear for some time what's happening to you."

"What are you talking about?"

"You're in love with Travis. Whatever you and I had, it's over."

At that instant Rena knew this was the truth. She said quietly, "I think you're right about us, but we must be very careful with these people."

"Don't worry about it," Dalton said. There was a hard edge to his voice, and he turned and smiled at Tabita, who laughed and said something to him.

Rena was shocked by Dalton's attitude. They were coming into the camp now, and the ones who had stayed behind came to meet them. She went to Travis and said, "You'll have to speak to Dalton, Travis."

"About the woman?"

"Yes. I . . . I don't know what to say. He's changed."

"Men do that sometimes. Bad things can happen in situations like this. I'll talk to him."

As the tribe was introduced to the other members of their party, she could not help noticing the hungry look of the three sailors she did not trust. She realized for the first time, perhaps, what bringing a new set of values could do to a people such as this. She found herself praying, "God, don't let us hurt these people. We came to help them."

# CHAPTER TWENTY-ONE

# VISITORS TO THE CAMP

★ ★ ★

Those who had remained at camp were apprehensive, especially Oscar Blevins. He had frozen up when he saw the natives coming, and only after Travis assured them that the natives were friendly did he relax.

"Oscar, I think we need to fix the best meal we can for our new friends here."

Glad to have something to do, Blevins threw himself into the work of fixing a feast. He butchered a fat goat and filleted the fish that had been captured in the traps earlier that day.

As for the natives, they appeared perfectly at home. They laid their weapons aside and ran around like children, fascinated by simple things. Lomu's sharp eyes were everywhere, and Travis made certain to stay close beside him, along with Chip to do the translating. Lomu was very interested in the construction of the shelters and he also seemed curious about the tools. He held a double-bitted ax in his hand and obviously was much taken with it. He said to Travis through Chip, "This is a good thing. Two sides."

"Yes, when one side gets dull you can use the other side."

Lomu ran his thumb along the edge and smiled with approval. "Very sharp."

"Accept it as a gift, Chief Lomu," Travis said. Fortunately they had four of these axes, and he saw a chance here for winning the friendship of the chief.

"It is a great gift," Lomu said. "Travis is a generous chief."

"I'm no chief," Travis said. "Tell him, Chip, that we don't really have a chief here."

This concept proved to be rather difficult for Lomu to grasp. "Someone has to be the head man. How would you decide if there was a disagreement?"

"Sometimes we take a vote, but come to think of it, we do have one man who's the chief. Come, and I will introduce you to him." Lomu was introduced to Captain Barkley, and it seemed to reassure the native that there was a leader.

He kept looking back and forth between Travis and Barkley, and Chip said, "He can't understand why you're not the chief, Travis. You are obviously in charge. It's got him bothered."

"Tell him the captain was hurt, and I'm just filling in."

This seemed to satisfy Lomu, and Travis left the two of them to talk with Captain Barkley while he helped Oscar with the feast. The women were helping too, and the meal was soon ready. The natives waited until Lomu gave the sign, and then as the missionaries passed the meat out, they fell on it like hungry wolves.

"They act like they haven't had a bite to eat in days," Karl murmured.

"I don't suppose they've had much except maybe fish," Professor Dekker said. "They didn't get a chance to eat the goat they were cooking on the other beach." He was watching the natives with great interest, for he was an anthropologist as well as a theologian. "They're fine-looking people," he said. "Primitive, of course."

"That might not be the worst thing in the world, Professor."

"What do you mean, Karl?"

"I mean when I look at some of the terrible things that go on in civilization, like the Great War, there's something to be said for the placid life these islanders live."

"That's not exactly accurate. Pacific islanders have wars among themselves, and they can be as vicious as the American Indians were when their territory was invaded."

The two men talked quietly, and finally they all sat down. Lomu made a short speech, which Chip interpreted. "We thank you for the food. You are good people and wise too." His speech went on for some time, but to everyone's relief he finally sat down.

Rena said quickly, "You'll have to respond to that speech, Travis."

"Captain, why don't you do it?" Travis said. "You're the leader."

"No, Lomu's got it right. Since I've been holed up, you're chief now, Travis."

As Rena surveyed the group she saw Dalton sitting with the woman called Tabita beside him. Dalton was looking at Travis with dislike, and she knew there was something in his heart that was wrong.

Travis shrugged. "Well, I'll do the best I can." He stood up and spoke with lengthy pauses, allowing Chip time to interpret. "Chief Lomu, we are believers in the one God. Our God has sent us here to the islands to tell those that we meet about Him."

"What is your God's name?" Chief Lomu interrupted. "We do not tell others about our God. We do not even say his name among ourselves."

Travis knew this was not uncommon with some native peoples. He smiled and said, "Our God is called Jesus. It means 'One who saves His people.'"

"That is good." Lomu nodded with appreciation. "Do you make sacrifices to your God?"

Travis hesitated. "There was a time when the followers of our God killed animals, but now He asks that we sing to Him and honor Him in other ways."

"I would like to hear such singing."

Travis was caught off guard, and it was Pete Alford who lifted his voice and began singing "The Old Rugged Cross." It was his favorite, and all of the missionaries joined in, as well as Shep and Oscar and Chip.

The natives applauded and cried out with pleasure, smiles on their faces.

"My people like to sing too," Lomu said. "Tell us more about your God."

As Travis continued he kept his words as simple as possible. He spoke of God the Father, who had made all things and who kept all things in order. He indicated the sun and said, "Our God makes the sun to send its beams upon us all. He made the stars to give us light at night. He gives us rain and He blesses the earth with fruit. The animals He gave us for food."

The natives sat listening avidly as Chip interpreted Travis's words. Finally Travis said, "I hope you will all come to love Jesus."

Lomu shook his head. "We have our own god."

"Do you love him, Chief Lomu?"

"Love him!" Lomu exclaimed. "No, I fear him!"

"We serve the God of love," Travis went on. "That's what He wants from us—love. He loved us before we even loved Him." For some moments he continued speaking, and then he said quietly, "I hope in the days to come you will allow us to tell you more about Jesus, this God that we love."

"We will hear more of this Jesus God," Lomu said.

When Travis sat down Rena reached out and squeezed his arm. "That was wonderful, Travis. Just exactly right. The Lord was with you."

Travis's face was wreathed in smiles. "I believe we've found our mission field," he whispered. "He's a good God, isn't He, Rena?"

★　★　★

"I'm surprised the natives have stayed four days," Lanie said. She and Pete were dressing fish for the evening meal.

"It's just a big vacation for them, isn't it?"

Pete cut the head off of a fish and tossed it into the pile. "It sure is. And they sure eat a lot!" He grinned. "I guess it's just rest and recreation for them."

"It's marvelous, isn't it, that God has given us this opportunity to share the Gospel?"

"Yes, it is." Pete shook his head with wonder. "They listen to the Gospel so readily."

"I wish I could speak their language."

"Well, Meredith is making progress. She's learned to say some sentences. She can teach the rest of us what she's learned."

As the two continued to clean the fish, Lanie smiled at him and said, "I like doing everyday things with you. It's good to have a man."

Pete smiled. "It's good to have a woman. That's what the Bible says. You know the first thing God said to Adam was, 'Son, you need help.'"

"And I'm your help."

"Yes, and I'm yours."

Another conversation was going on at this same time among Day and Novak and Olsen. The three had imbibed freely of the alcoholic drink the natives had brought. Apparently they had transported a good supply. All three men were now half drunk. Day leered at the native woman who stood before them holding the jug. "They ain't bad-lookin' women," he said.

"You'd better watch out. If you touch one of 'em, their men might cut your head off. I ain't sure they're not headhunters anyway," Olsen grunted. Two days earlier he had started to touch one of the young women and had been challenged by one of the natives, a strong-looking young man who had drawn a jagged-looking knife and was stopped only by Lomu's quick action.

"There's ways of gettin' around that," Day said.

Novak had said little, but he had been watching. Now he sipped at the drink the young woman offered him, coughed, and handed it back. "We don't need to get drunk. Somehow we're gonna get off this crazy island. I don't care what these preachers do."

"Chip said the island they live on is only two days' sail away," Day said. "Why don't we go back with 'em?"

"In the first place, they might not wanna take us," Novak said.

"But we got the guns."

"Use your head, Charlie, if you have one. What are we gonna do—shoot 'em all? How will we find the island? No, we've gotta find a way to persuade 'em to take us with 'em."

"We could have a good life there if the preachers weren't there. They've already started preachin' at 'em," Day complained.

"We'll find a way," Novak said. "Don't worry about it."

★ ★ ★

Novak was not the only one thinking about a way to get off of their island. Captain Barkley set up a meeting with Travis and Pete to discuss it, and when the rest of the missionaries heard about it they all decided they should be in on it.

Pete opened the conversation by saying, "Captain, why can't we go to the island they live on?"

"We don't know that their island's any better than this one—as far as getting rescued is concerned," the professor observed. "It's all a gamble."

"I'm more interested in the people there than I am in getting a ship," Travis said. "I think God sent us out here for a purpose, and if we were on that island, we could work with the people there, bringing them the Gospel."

"I think that's right," Rena said quickly. "God's put us here, and we need to serve Him while we can."

Dalton lifted his head. He had been a disappointment to everyone. To their dismay, he had not discouraged the attentions of the young native woman. He had also been drinking too much of the liquor that the natives had brought. "I don't think God brought us here at all," he said. "I think it was all an accident."

Rena's heart sank. "You don't really believe that, Dalton."

Dalton glared at her. He got up and left the group without looking back.

"Dalton's in a bad way," Benson said. "He's going downhill quickly."

"We've got to pray for him," Abby said. She was holding Michael in her arms, cuddling him. "But I do think we need to do all we can to visit that island. Will they take us, do you think?"

"I've been talking to Lomu about it, and he hasn't said one way or another," Travis said. "I think he's afraid we'll try to take over."

"He's not far wrong about that when you think about Novak," Captain Barkley said. "I wish they didn't have those confounded guns. I've been trying to think of a way to take them away from them."

"I'd like to do the same thing," Pete said, "but it would be tough."

They talked for a long time and finally concluded that they would try to persuade Lomu to take at least some of them back to the island.

"I think it might be good," the captain said, "if they would take some of us there and teach us how to build a boat like the one they've got. Then we could come back for the others."

"Put it to him like that, Captain," Travis said. "I think he'll listen to reason."

★   ★   ★

The morning after the missionaries had their meeting, Rena was awakened by the sound of angry voices. She sprang from her cot in one bound and tore outside. She saw a great number of natives speaking in angry voices, but she could not make out what they were saying. She found Travis and asked, "What's going on, Travis?"

"It's Dalton. Not good news, Rena."

"What is it? What's happened?"

"One of the young men of the tribe caught him with Tabita. The man wants her for his wife, and when he caught the two together, he jumped on Dalton and cut him pretty badly."

"Is he . . . is he okay?"

"I'm not sure. Karl's working on him now, but the whole situation put us in a pretty bad light." Travis nodded over toward Lomu, who was watching them. "I've been trying to explain to him, but he's unhappy about it."

"I don't blame him," Rena said.

"Come on. Let's go try again. Maybe he'll listen to you."

Rena shrank from going, but she accompanied Travis. Chip was standing near the chief, shaking his head.

"The chief is very mad," Chip told them. "The girl is his relative, a cousin of some sort."

Rena stepped forward. "Chief," she said quietly, "I'm so sorry. You must understand that what the man has done was his own idea. The rest of us, all of us, are against things like that. We want to honor you and your people. He's done a bad thing, but our God teaches us to forgive our enemies."

Lomu blinked with surprise after Chip had translated. The chief stared at her and said a few words.

Chip said, "He doesn't understand that. He doesn't believe in forgiving enemies."

"It's what Jesus did," Rena explained. "He was being put to death because He loved all of His people, and as He was dying, one of the last things He did was to give forgiveness to those who were hurting Him. That's the kind of people we're all trying to be, and I ask you to show mercy to this man who has offended you."

That was not the end of it. Lomu listened but was still angry. All day long Rena and the others waited, and more than one of them went to plead for Dalton.

As for Dalton, he had been badly slashed by the knife, but Karl had been able to staunch the flow of blood and stitch the worst of the cuts. "He'll be all right eventually," Karl told Rena and Travis grimly. "But he's a fool. I thought better of him."

★  ★  ★

After supper, Chief Lomu sat for a long time with two men who were evidently his advisors. They spoke intently and finally they stood up. The chief said through Chip, "We will not kill the man."

Travis responded, "We are very grateful to you. You are a great chief, Lomu."

"You do not understand our ways."

"It is hard for two peoples to come together. I know some of our ways are displeasing to you, but we want to do you good." Travis hesitated, then said, "Chief Lomu, we think it would be good if you would take some of us back with you to your home, where we might meet your people and learn your ways. Perhaps there will be something we can do to help you."

Lomu stared at the sky for a long time, and both Travis and Rena thought he would say no. Instead, he said, "We will do that. Six of you can come in our ship. We will leave in the morning."

Travis and Rena immediately left to have a private discussion. "We've got to decide which six are going and who will stay," Rena said.

"I know three who will go right now," Travis said grimly. "Novak and his friends; they'll insist on it."

"Our strongest people will have to go to try to keep them from harming Chief Lomu's people," she said.

"We'll have a meeting," he said. "We'll have to decide. Come along. Let's get the word out."

# CHAPTER TWENTY-TWO

# "I'M GONNA LET YOU PRAY FOR ME"

★ ★ ★

"Lomu says they can only take six of us." Travis ran his hand through his hair and looked at the group that had gathered around him. All of the missionaries were there, as well as Captain Barkley. They had drawn apart from the natives, and now many of them had confusion written across their features.

"Why can't they take us all?" Meredith asked. "Isn't their boat big enough?"

"I don't think it is, Meredith," Travis said. "And I think he has other reasons besides, but I don't know what they are."

"Do you think they're afraid of us or don't like us?" Abby asked. She was holding Michael tightly to her breast, and her face was filled with apprehension. "I don't understand why we can't all stay together."

Professor Dekker said, "I think it has something to do with their religion, but I'm not sure." He scratched his grizzled beard and then put his hands out in a gesture of helplessness. "Who knows what's going on in a primitive mind?"

"Well, whatever it is," Pete put in, "we're going to have to decide which six of us are going."

"There won't be six of us going."

"What do you mean by that, Travis?" Rena asked. "I thought you said six would go."

"I did, but you can rule three out because Novak, Day, and Olsen have already invited themselves to the party." His lips drew tight. "They've got the guns, and they want to go."

"You know why, don't you, Travis?" Lanie said. "They want to go because of that liquor the natives have learned how to make."

"Yes, and because of the women they think they'll find willing," Maggie said.

"I think you're right, but there's nothing we can do about it unless we get those guns away from them, and they've been pretty careful about that," Karl said. He stood for a moment with his head bowed, then looked up. "So that means only three of us can go."

"It looks that way," Travis said. "Captain Barkley, what do you think?"

Barkley was leaning against a tree. His leg was much better now, and he had learned to maneuver quite easily on the crutches Shep had made for him. It had been a hard time for the captain. He was accustomed to being in command, and his injury had removed him from that post. Now, however, he thought hard about the matter and said, "I think we ought to take a vote. It wouldn't do me any good to go, so I'll take my name off the list."

Rena saw the wisdom of his suggestion. "Let's do this," she said. "Let's have a prayer and ask God to choose whom He wants to go. With those three awful men going, God will need some voices on the other island to speak for Him."

Travis suddenly felt a warm admiration for Rena. Even in the fading light he was reminded of how she combined beauty and strength. He put his hand on her shoulder and smiled. "I think you're becoming a real missionary, Rena."

Rena flushed, embarrassed by the praise. "It just came to me," she said, "that when the apostles decided to elect another to take the place of Judas, they cast lots."

"I think it's a good idea," Meredith said warmly.

Travis and the others agreed. "Let's pray first for God's guidance," Travis suggested.

They all bowed their heads and remained silent for a few minutes. From time to time someone would pray fervently. As Travis sought God, he was aware of the changes that had been wrought in this group. They had been a proud company when they had left the States, but time and circumstance and hardship had broken and molded them.

Finally Travis closed the prayer and took a deep breath. "Well, how shall we do this, Professor?"

Professor Dekker reached into his pocket and took out a sheet of folded paper. "One side of this is covered with my notes, but the other side is blank, so we can use it for ballots." He tore the paper into strips and handed a strip to each one. "Do any of you have pencils?"

None of them did, so the professor wrote quickly with the stub he had and then handed the pencil to Travis. Travis wrote down a name and handed the pencil on to Rena. All of them waited their turn, and finally when all of the slips had been signed, Pete took off his hat and went around collecting them in his hat. "Who wants to draw?" he said with a smile.

"Let me do it," Lanie offered. She pulled out the first slip of paper. "*Travis*, it says."

"One vote for Travis. Take the next one," the professor instructed.

The next vote was also for Travis, and when all of the votes had been taken, there were seven votes for Travis and five for Rena.

"I'd say that's pretty conclusive," Captain Barkley said.

But Rena was confused. She had not expected to be chosen. She looked at Travis, and he smiled at her, giving her confidence. "But that's only two of us."

"The other one will have to be Chip," Travis said. "He's the only one who can speak the language."

"I never even thought of that," Rena said. She looked around and asked, "Is that all right with everyone?"

"I think the Lord has just spoken to us," Lanie said warmly. She came over and put her arms around Rena and kissed her cheeks. "Go with God. We'll wait here while you go speak for God there." She went then to Travis and touched his cheek. "Take care of her and of yourself. I know God has put you in this place."

One by one they all gathered around and wished the two Godspeed.

"You'd better take everything you can think of that will help you, especially Bibles and books."

"Yes, we'll definitely need our Bibles," Travis said.

The last one to come speak to the two was Dalton Welborne. He had said nothing as the discussion went on around him. He was in a great deal of pain from his numerous cuts but was on his way to recovery. His face was filled with shame as he finally addressed Travis and Rena. "I've been wrong," he said. "I found a weakness in myself I didn't know was there."

"You're going to be fine, Dalton," Travis responded. "We all get off on the wrong foot every now and then."

"Good of you to say that, Travis." Dalton shook Travis's hand and then put out his hand to Rena. "This is good-bye in more ways than one, but I know it's the right thing for us."

Rena took his hand, and in her heart she said good-bye to this man who had once meant so much to her. She smiled at him and said, "Get well quickly, Dalton."

The two turned and walked over to where Lomu was watching the proceedings with a careful eye. "The two of us are going, along with Chip," Travis said.

The chief smiled and responded, and Chip, who was never far from the chief, said, "He thinks it's good for you two to come."

The next morning everybody was up with the sun. After

a quick breakfast they gathered their supplies, said their good-byes, and started their hike for the other side of the island.

Everybody helped load the catamaran with the supplies and then pushed it into the choppy waves. It was crowded, and Rena stood close to Travis as the paddlers propelled the vessel into the endless water.

Rena said, "It makes me sad to leave like this, Travis. I've almost come to think of this island as home."

"We'll be back before long, I hope."

★ ★ ★

"I don't like the look of that sky," Cerny Novak said to Travis early that afternoon as they stood in the bow of the catamaran looking up. The paddles of the natives made a regular cadence as they drove themselves tirelessly. "I'm afraid we're in for a blow."

"Do you think it'll be bad?"

"It won't be good. I sure wish we were there already."

"We'll make it," Travis said. "God isn't going to let us down now."

The two men had taken their turns at the oars, as had Chip, Day, and Olsen. It was hard work, but there were enough natives that some could rest while the others rowed. The catamaran was rising now to meet a rolling swell. The ocean waves were like moving hills, rolling and swelling, and the catamaran rose and fell with them. There was an oily look to the water that made Novak nervous.

"I've seen seas like this before," Novak said. "If we get caught between islands in a hurricane, we're goners."

Travis did not know the sea as Novak did, but the sky and the sea did look ominous. He glanced back and saw Rena talking with Chip and the chief. He wondered what they were talking about, and then his mind came back to the darkening clouds.

"I don't much like this," Novak grumbled. "Maybe we oughta turn back."

"Chief Lomu doesn't look worried, so I guess I'm not gonna worry either. He gives the orders around here."

The two men surveyed the turbulent seas in silence. Travis finally said, "Do you have a family anywhere, Cerny?"

"You mean a wife? No. What would I be doing with a wife?"

"Well, you might have children."

Cerny laughed. He stroked his crooked nose with his forefinger and looked at Travis as if he had said something amusing. "What would a rough like me be doing with a wife and kids?"

"Lots of men have them."

"I guess maybe you're planning on something like that."

"I've always liked children."

"You've got your sights on Rena, don'tcha? That's easy to see."

"She's a fine woman," Travis said. "She's changed a lot since we landed on the island."

"You got that right," Cerny said. "She was proud as a peacock when we left. Didn't care a whit for nobody 'cept her own kind. She's changed, though," he said thoughtfully. He balanced himself against the boat as it lifted then ran down the slope of gray water. "I have to say I've changed my ideas about preachers a bit—mostly about you and her. But the others ain't bad either, most of 'em."

"Cerny, you're a smart guy. You must have thought about what happens when you die."

"I try not to."

"I can understand that. I did the same thing before I knew the Lord. But now we could all die in this storm that's blowing up. I'd hate to see you go out to meet God without hope."

Cerny didn't answer. Travis knew that at one time he would have sharply rejected any talk of religion. Travis had tried before to speak with him about Jesus, but Novak had simply ignored him or walked away. Now he saw that Novak had placed the rifle down. It was wrapped in oilcloth to keep it dry, and he knew that this marked a change in Novak's thinking. Always before he had kept it in his hand and ready to use anytime he was close. Travis put that thought aside and said, "You know, you're the kind of man Jesus could use."

Astonishment swept across Novak's face. "Me?" He laughed and shook his head. "I can barely read, and I ain't led a good life. You know that, Travis."

"You remind me of the apostle Peter. He was a fisherman, a sailor like you. A big, rough fellow, apparently, always talking when he should be quiet. But when Jesus came along, it changed him. He became a great man of God."

"That's him, and I'm me."

Travis continued to share Bible stores and Scripture and was aware again that something had happened to Cerny Novak. Perhaps it was the fear of the storm that he was afraid to show, but he knew that every man and every woman had thoughts about what would happen after death. He did not press the big man, but he simply gave his own testimony and talked about how he had come to know Jesus.

Cerny listened, his eyes sometimes on the sea, sometimes coming to rest on Travis, and finally he said, "You're a right guy, Travis. You and me have been crossways, but that's been my fault."

"I think we're really alike in more ways than you think. Neither of us has any polish. The only difference is that I've let the Lord come into my life. I'd like to see you do the same thing, Cerny."

"Too late for me," Cerny said with a tone that seemed to shut the door to further discussion. "That's for better guys than me."

He turned and moved away from Travis, going to one of the natives and reaching out his hand for the paddle. He sat down and concentrated on propelling the craft through the rolling sea.

★ ★ ★

Rena was soaking wet. The catamaran was lifting now in two directions. The bow would rise and fall, but at the same time one of the hulls would dip. At times she was terrified, thinking the vessel was going over for certain, but it never did. The wind and rain had arrived viciously, and the craft was tossed about like a chip. She was holding tightly on to the gunwale when Travis came over and sat down beside her. He put his arm around her, and she turned to him, grateful for the assurance she saw in his face. Although it was only midafternoon, it was almost as dark as twilight.

"I don't mind telling you, Travis," Rena said, wiping her face with her hand, "I'd just as soon not be here."

"Me either, but we'll be all right."

At that moment the ship was wrenched forward and cast to the left. Travis was nearly thrown overboard. Rena grabbed at him, and he managed to hang on to the side of the vessel. Others were scrambling to stay in, and it was a miracle no one was thrown out. The craft righted itself, and Lomu was shouting orders at the rowers, who were paddling furiously. "I'd better go help paddle," Travis said.

"Don't . . . don't get lost overboard."

"I'll try not to. You know what this reminds me of?"

The rain had plastered Rena's hair down and was running down her face. Her clothes were soaked, and her hands ached from holding on to the leaping, plunging craft. "It reminds me of the book of Acts, the part where Paul is on the ship and they're in a bad storm. You remember what he said? He said, 'I believe God.' Well, that's what I do. I believe God put us here to witness to Lomu and his people, as well as the sailors who came with us. And if that's what's on God's mind, He'll get us there."

Rena reached up and pulled Travis close, putting her lips

to his ear. "You're a comfort, Travis Winslow." She kissed his cheek, and when he drew back, he had a surprised grin on his face. "You're getting to be right forward, woman!"

Despite the dangers of the moment, Rena found that the fear had left her. "I guess you're right about that. We'll talk about it later."

Travis realized at the moment that Rena was now a woman of real faith, and she had taken on a new humility.

★　★　★

"Doesn't look like there was ever a storm, does it, Rena?" Travis was pulling rhythmically at one of the oars, and Rena was beside him. The sea had calmed overnight and was now almost as still as a tabletop. The catamaran sliced its way through the sparkling green waters, and ahead of them a long line of beach was marked with people singing and crying out.

"It's amazing how quiet the ocean is," Rena said. "I believe our fellow passengers got a bad scare yesterday."

Indeed, it was true. At the worst of the storm, all three of the veteran sailors had been sure they were all going to die. Now that the danger was over, it appeared to Rena that Olsen and Day had put the storm and their fear out of their minds. But she kept watching Novak, who seemed more contemplative than he had in the past.

"You've been talking to Novak a lot," Rena said.

"God's given me a promise that he's going to get saved," Travis said. "He's a tough nut, but the hound of heaven is on his trail."

They had no time to continue their conversation, for the catamaran had reached the sandy shore. Many native men plunged in to grab the vessel and drag it ashore. Rena and Travis both stood up and leaped out into the water. "They seem glad to see us, don't they?" Travis said as they waded to shore and were quickly surrounded by curious natives chattering at the top of their lungs.

"I wish I could understand them," Travis said.

"We'll learn," Rena said.

Chief Lomu was smiling as his people gathered around the white visitors. They all wanted to touch them, and many were crying out in wonder. Finally Lomu raised his hand, and silence came over the group. He began to speak, and Chip, who was standing close to Rena and Travis, whispered, "He's telling them that we're visitors. That we've come to tell them about a new God who made all things."

"Well, that's a good thing for missionaries to have the king of the island on their side."

Lomu finished his speech and came over and spoke to them briefly.

"The chief says we are going to stay at his house."

"Tell him we're very grateful," Travis said.

Rena asked, "Is his house big enough?"

"I have no idea," Chip said with a grin. "But I always wanted to stay at a palace."

★ ★ ★

The "palace" was not exactly what Chip had envisioned. It was an expansive open shed supported by round beams cut from trees. The roof was made of saplings tied together with vines, and the whole thing was thatched with long leaves.

"But it doesn't have any walls!" Rena exclaimed as they moved through the house.

"I guess you get to know people pretty quickly," Travis with a laugh. "Not much for modesty, though."

Indeed, there was not much use for modesty. Travis and Rena soon discovered that the king had many sons and daughters and most of them lived at the so-called palace, sleeping on simple pads stuffed with dry grass. Rena was assigned to a corner with the king's oldest daughter. She was given a pad to sleep on, and that was it.

Before they even got a tour of the island, the king's

daughter, Lomishu, made it quite clear that Rena would not be idle while they were there. Lomishu took Rena by the arm and pulled her to a large area of the palace that was obviously used for cooking and food storage. The dark woman handed Rena a large empty vessel and took one for herself, and then pulled her out of the palace and down a trail.

Even with no words passing between them, Rena understood that they were going to get water. Rena smiled to herself, thinking back to how she would have reacted to a similar situation only a year ago. She understood that her role here was to be a servant, much as Christ was a servant when He came to earth.

After they had filled their vessels in the stream and returned to the palace, Lomishu told Rena, through Chip, that she could investigate the island with her friends.

The rest of the evening was given to walking around, investigating the new environment, but the islanders were so curious they could not get far without attracting a crowd. Both Travis and Rena had picked up a few sentences from Chip, and when they spoke to the islanders, the people were ecstatic. More than once the women gathered around Rena, chattering and giggling, wanting to touch her auburn hair or her white skin.

"You're quite a curiosity to them," Travis commented with a grin.

Chip nodded. "They've never seen white people before." One young woman came and stood before Rena, touching her arm and obviously asking a question.

"What does she want to know?" Rena asked curiously.

"She wants to know," Chip said with a shy grin, "if you're white all over or just on your arms and face."

Rena flushed and said, "Tell her that I am."

Travis tried not to laugh but couldn't help it. "They seem like nice folks."

"I think so too."

Novak, Day, and Olsen were staying with other families. They were still carrying their guns, and Travis said, "I hope they don't use those things. That would be tragic."

"Surely they won't," Rena said hopefully.

Lomishu approached the group and said something to Rena as she took her by the hand. "My father needs us," Chip translated as Lomishu led Rena toward the palace.

For the next few days Travis and Rena watched carefully to see what the sailors would do. They were not terribly surprised when Day and Olsen got access to some liquor and became so drunk they passed out.

"There's nothing we can do about that, I'm afraid," Travis said grimly. "I noticed that Novak drank a little, but he didn't get drunk. Maybe he can handle those two."

"I wish he'd take those guns away from them."

"Maybe we can talk him into that. He knows they're not the steadiest men in the world. They could cause real trouble."

★　★　★

The days passed quickly for Rena. She spent a fair amount of time with Lomishu and her mother, Lomu's wife, learning how to cook Lomu's favorite foods and attending to Lomu's every wish. At one point it occurred to Rena that she might be called a royal handmaid. But somehow the title sounded more romantic than it actually was.

Rena and Travis spent an enormous amount of time studying the language. They had plenty of tutors. Chip, of course, was their main teacher, but the natives were fascinated by the white people's attempts to learn. "They never saw anyone who couldn't speak their language," Chip explained, "and now it tickles them that you can't."

"I get so angry with myself," Rena said. "I want to speak to them so badly."

"You're doing good, Miss Rena."

"Better than I am," Travis said ruefully.

"Well, we're both making a lot of mistakes."

"You're right about that," Travis said with a laugh. "I

tried to say, 'That's a beautiful baby you have,' to one woman, and they all started laughing at me."

"You know why, don't you?" Chip asked.

"Not really."

"You didn't say the baby was beautiful. You said the snake ate the baby."

Rena burst into a good, hearty laugh and shook her head. "There's no telling what I've said to some of these people."

"I've been thinking we should have some kind of a service," Travis said. "I asked Lomu about it, and he's willing enough."

"You know, I have no idea what day of the week it is."

"All I know is it's somewhere in mid-April, but I've lost count too. So let's just say tomorrow's Sunday, and we'll have a service."

★　★　★

The crowd for the service was large, for everything the white people did was a source of interest to the natives. Chip served as the interpreter, as usual, and Rena insisted that Travis speak.

"You sing and then I'll speak," he said.

"All right," Rena agreed, smiling.

The sun was already a quarter of the way up the sky, and the morning breezes were cool.

Rena stood up and waited while the group settled down. She started singing in her clear contralto voice, and the natives, who had discovered little about music except for some very somber chant, were transfixed by her voice as it rose. They did not understand the words, of course, but as she sang, Chip would translate them from time to time. She sang her favorite hymns, and when she finally smiled and sat down, the natives began waving their hands in the air.

"They like it," Travis said. "I hope they like what I've got to say." He stood up and began his sermon, speaking a sentence or two at a time and then waiting for the translation.

Chip, he felt, must be very good at this, for he saw that no matter what he said or how he said it, the islanders showed the same kind of emotion he wanted to convey. When he lifted his voice, Chip's voice lifted also. When he spoke quietly, Chip modified his speech.

"We've come to speak of the God who made the sky and all the stars and who made the earth."

Rena sat off to one side, her focus fixed on Travis. He spoke simply, slowly, and eloquently. He did it so well that she hardly noticed Chip's voice as he translated the words. As Travis spoke of the goodness of God and the strength of God, she scanned the congregation of dark-skinned faces. Some were no darker than a white person who had spent much time in the sun. They all had dark liquid eyes and dark hair, and they listened with a reverence and an attention she had rarely seen in a crowd in the States.

"This great God who made us all and who loved us all," Travis was saying, "knew that all men and all women have wrong in them. And because they have wrong in them, they have to pay for this wrong, but this great God did not want people to perish. So he had His own son come to be born on the earth. His name was Jesus, and that name means 'One who saves His people from their sins.'"

He went on to briefly describe the life of Jesus, and then when he spoke of His death on the cross, to her amazement Rena saw many villagers wiping tears from their cheeks. These were a compassionate people, tenderhearted, she saw, and her own eyes began to grow wet with tears.

"So we have come to tell you about this Son of God—Jesus—who is alive today in the heavens with His father. But we can all know Him, and when we die, we can go live forever with the one who has loved us so much."

Travis closed his sermon with a prayer and then asked Rena to sing again. She stood up and began to sing "The Old Rugged Cross," looking at each individual in attendance as she worked her way through the verses. At the edge of the crowd, to her surprise, she saw Cerny Novak. As soon as she met his gaze, however, he dropped his head and turned and went away.

After the service was over, many came around asking questions about Jesus. Travis sat beside Rena, and with Chip by their side to translate, the two of them answered every question as well as they could.

Finally they left the gathering place and went down to the beach to talk about the service. "That was a wonderful service, Travis. We're going to see God do great things here."

"Your singing moved them, Rena. That's going to be a real tool for evangelism as soon as you learn the language."

"I'm going to ask Chip to help me learn the words to some of the old hymns so I can sing in their own language."

"That's an excellent idea," he said, gladness in his voice.

Rena picked up a beautiful shell and examined it. "Did you see Novak?" she asked. "He was at the edge of the crowd."

"I saw him. I was glad he came. The other two didn't show up, though. I think they were drunk again."

They continued walking along and finally stopped and faced the sea. The sun was high in the sky now, and the ocean was beautiful—emerald green with tiny whitecaps breaking and gentle waves rolling in. "I feel like God has put us in this place," Travis said simply. He turned to her and asked, "How do you feel about it, Rena?"

Rena could not speak for a moment. "I feel like life is just beginning for me, but God can do all things. He's changed my heart so much." She turned to him and put her hand on his arm. "And He's used you to make me into a different person."

"I like the person you've become, Rena." He put his hand on her cheek and held it there for a moment. She looked up at him, and the two smiled. "Come on. Let's get back."

★ ★ ★

For a month Cerny Novak had watched Lars and Charlie turn themselves into drunkards. The native men simply would not refrain from giving them liquor, and the native women apparently had different standards for morality, so the two of them had become womanizers from the very beginning.

Novak himself had tried the drink and several times had drunk himself into insensibility, but always when he awoke, there was something gnawing at him. Finally he realized he could not go on like he was. He had kept mostly to himself and had also kept close watch on his two friends. When he had found them drunk one day, he had taken the pistols away from them, afraid they would shoot themselves, or worse, one of the natives.

He had attended the weekly services and had soaked up Travis's preaching and Rena's singing. He could not understand what was happening to him, but he knew he was miserable and unhappy.

"I've gotta get off this place," he finally muttered to himself, as a scheme began to form in his mind.

It was several days after this that he went to Travis and said, "I've gotta get off this island. A ship's never gonna come by here."

"That might be true, Cerny. You never know."

"No, and I can't wait." Novak stood there, a big burly man full of determination. "This situation is fine for you and Rena. You're doing what you think is right, but I'm leaving, and I'm taking Charlie and Lars with me."

Travis blinked with surprise. "What are you talking about?"

"There's bound to be civilization not too far from here. All we have to do is build a boat big enough to carry food and water, put a good sail on it, and let the prevailing trade winds carry us right into it."

"Cerny, you don't even know where we are. It's too dangerous. You don't even know what direction to head."

"Sure I do. If we go west, we're bound to hit either Australia or New Guinea. If we miss that, we'll hit Borneo, but

I don't think it'll come to that. The Pacific is full of islands, and sooner or later we'll hit one where the traders stop. I've gotta do it, Travis."

"Do you realize how big of a boat you'll have to build to hold the three of you plus enough food and water for an indefinite period of time?" Travis asked. "And it'll have to be stable enough to weather storms."

"I know the danger, Travis. I've just gotta get out of here."

"You may not make it."

"Maybe not, but I'm gonna get out of this place one way or another."

★   ★   ★

When Cerny Novak spoke to the chief through Chip, he found that the chief was astonished that he wanted to leave, but he offered to help him make his boat. The chief and his sons spent the next two weeks helping Cerny build a small catamaran, and Cerny rigged a sail out of some canvas they had brought with them. Water was stored in empty coconuts that were stopped with wooden plugs, and the villagers were generous with their food. Dried meat and fruits and root vegetables were stored carefully.

Novak had tried to talk Charlie and Lars into going with him, but both men steadfastly refused.

"I ain't goin' nowhere. This is a great life," Charlie said.

"All the women and all the liquor we want," Lars added. "I'm stayin' here!"

By late May, Cerny was ready to shove off. He stood beside the new boat as it bobbed with the tide. A large number of the natives had come to see him off, in awe that a man would try such a thing on his own.

Travis made one last attempt to stop him. "Don't do it, Cerny. I feel like we're friends, and I hate to see a friend throw his life away."

Novak's eyes were sober, but then he grinned. "That's all

right. I've decided to let you do something for me."

"Decided to let me do what?" Travis asked.

"Why, I'm gonna let you pray for me." Cerny laughed, adding, "Ain't that square of me?"

Travis put his hand out, and when Cerny took it, he said quietly, "I haven't waited for permission, Cerny."

"That's okay, then."

Cerny turned to Rena. "You're a fine lady, Miss Rena. You can pray for me too, if ya want."

"I will, Cerny."

Novak turned and climbed into the craft. He quickly ran up the sail, and the wind puffed it full. The villagers pushed the catamaran away from shore, and then they stood in the surf calling out as they waved good-bye.

Cerny returned their waves, and then when he was about fifty yards out, he called out, "Hey, Travis, I'll remember what you said about Jesus."

The villagers waded back to the beach, but Travis and Rena watched until the craft was a mere dot. She turned to him then, with tears in her eyes. "I wish he hadn't gone," she whispered.

"So do I, but God can take care of him." He looked back at the tiny dot. "He'll have to, I think. But He's a big God, and He's on Cerny Novak's trail."

# CHAPTER TWENTY-THREE

# A NEW DAY

★  ★  ★

"Shep, when do you suppose Travis and Rena will come back?" Maggie asked. "They've been gone an awfully long time."

Shep looked up from the fish he was cleaning. "Gosh, I don't know. I thought they'd be back by now." As he looked at Maggie, he thought again about how much she had changed since he first met her. His mind went back to the first day on the ship when she had come aboard. He remembered her as an overweight woman who seemed shyer than anyone he had ever known. Since her loss of weight, the bony structure of her face made definite strong and pleasing contours. Finally he shook his head. "You know, Maggie, you've changed so much nobody would recognize you for the same woman."

Maggie smiled, and a small dimple appeared at the left side of her mouth and a light danced in her eyes.

"Well, I lost the woman you saw. You know, Shep, it was like there were two of me. I was so overweight I couldn't bear to look at myself in the mirror, but in my mind that heavy woman wasn't me."

"What do you mean, Maggie?"

"I mean I thought of myself as being slender or, perhaps *dreamed* might be a better way to put it. Under all that excess weight there was another woman who always wanted to get out, but couldn't. Every morning I'd wake up thinking I'm going to lose weight today, I'm not going to eat so much, but I was never able to keep it up."

Shep filleted the fish with quick motions of his razor-sharp knife and laid the fillet in a bowl that sat on a simple table he had made. He picked up another fish but did not begin to work on it for a moment. "Well," he said with a quick grin, "you turned out fine."

Maggie flushed at the compliment. "Thank you, Shep. You've been a big help to me. You know," she said, "you're the first man who ever seemed to like me in spite of how much I weighed."

"Why, sure I did! I really didn't notice your size."

"That's a rare gift you have, Shep. You see past the skin and into people's souls."

"I don't know about that, but I'll say one thing. You sure have become a good-looking woman." He tilted his head to the side. "You know, you and me never could have become friends if we hadn't gotten shipwrecked."

"That's true enough. It's a shame that there are barriers between people."

"Well, there still are. I mean you're a fine lady, and I'm just a rough sailor."

"Oh, Shep, don't be foolish! Those differences that matter so much in the world don't matter here at all." She put her hand on Shep's arm. "You've made me feel like a woman for the first time in my life, Shep."

He looked down at her hand on his arm. Her hand was tan now and strong, and her arm was firm but slender. The thin canvas she had fashioned into a garment revealed the strong figure of a woman who wasn't afraid of hard work. He swallowed hard and said, "I guess I never was much of a ladies' man, Maggie, but I gotta tell you . . . I never knew a woman any sweeter or any finer than you."

Her eyes misted over at his compliment, and she whispered, "It's so good to hear that."

Shep laughed and said, "Look at us out here talking like a couple of teenagers."

"We're not so far off, are we? How old are you, Shep?"

"I'm twenty-eight."

"Well, then you'll have to be more respectful to me."

"More respectful? Why?"

"Because I'm twenty-nine, and you're supposed to be respectful to your elders."

Shep dropped the knife and grabbed her by the arms. His eyes were dancing, and he said, "You talk to me like that and I'll turn my elder right over my knee and spank her."

Maggie began laughing, and she pretended to struggle, but Shep held on to her. He leaned forward and kissed her on the lips. As he pulled back, she put her hands behind his neck and pulled him forward for another kiss. "There," she said, "let that be a lesson. You start chasing an old maid and you're liable to get into trouble."

"I'm in trouble, all right. I guess we'd better get these fish cleaned," he said, but he didn't move. They held each other for a moment, and then he released her and picked up the knife.

He began cleaning the fish, and Maggie saw something was troubling him. "What's wrong, Shep? Did I do something wrong?"

"You? Why, you can't do nothin' wrong, Maggie. It's just that, well . . . I might as well tell you I've had feelings for you, but—"

"What is it?"

He lifted his rich brown eyes, and the breeze was ruffling his wavy black hair.

"I mean you're educated and a fine lady, and I'm just a sailor."

Maggie touched his cheek and said, "That doesn't matter, Shep, especially out here."

"Don't it, now?"

Maggie Smith had been lonely all her life, and this man

had come to her bringing life, telling her she was attractive, and she could see the love he had for her. "No, it doesn't."

"But if we got serious about each other and then we got rescued off this island and went back to the States, that would be different."

"I'll never go back to the States. I'm going to stay in the islands. Even if we get off this one."

The words seemed to sink in to Shep, and for a moment he could not speak. Then he grinned broadly and said, "Well, in that case, you can look for me to come courtin'."

"And you may look for me to welcome you."

Maggie watched as he picked up his knife and started on the next fish. "I'm still thinking about Rena and Travis and Chip over on that island with Chief Lomu."

"I know. I can't believe they've been gone for four months." His brow furrowed. "To tell the truth, I've been gettin' a little worried about them."

"So have I. Anything could have happened."

"I miss them. I think everybody's worried," he said. "Nobody talks about it much, but they coulda been wrecked in the storm that hit the day they left."

"Somehow I just don't think so. I think God is in all of this. I think He was in our being shipwrecked here, and it may have been for the purpose of getting the Gospel to Chief Lomu's people."

"I hope you're right."

Maggie watched as he finished the last fish and said, "Let's go back. It looks like you filleted plenty for a nice meal."

"You know what I miss? T-bone steaks," he said wistfully. "That's my favorite meal."

"Well, maybe we can get a T-bone, of sorts, out of one of the goats."

Shep shook his head and grinned woefully. "It ain't the same thing, Maggie. It just ain't the same thing."

★　★　★

Two days after this conversation, Maggie was sitting in front of her shelter sewing a bit of canvas into a bodice. She was sleepy, for it was a warm afternoon, and she had stayed awake the night before. Oscar had cooked a big meal and afterward they had sat up talking about the Scriptures. The professor had come to know the Lord better in his heart during their year on the island. He had spoken enthusiastically about his favorite subject, which was faith, and the rest of them had listened and then had a talk fest. Maggie and Shep had sat together, aware that the others were curious about the subtle change in their relationship, and afterward they had gone down to the beach and sat watching the moon make its way across the sky. Now she closed her eyes for a moment, leaned back, and dozed off.

A sharp cry brought her out of her sleep, and she looked up to see Pete Alford emerging from the woods, running and shouting. She could not make out his words, but she immediately feared that something must be wrong. Jumping up, she ran over with the others who were converging on Pete.

"They're here!" Pete shouted. "They're here!"

"Who's here?" Jimmy Townsend asked. "What are you talking about?"

"It's Lomu's ship—only this time there are two of them!"

"Travis and Rena and the others must be with them," Meredith said, her face alight.

"They're landing farther down the beach. Come on, everybody."

The entire group hurried toward the landing site, and when they arrived, Maggie cried out, "Look, it's Travis and Rena! They're in that first boat. And so are Chip and Chief Lomu."

Indeed, the two catamarans were being steered into the beach. It was low tide, and there was not much surf. Maggie cried out, "Travis—Rena!" and ran to meet them. She was followed by all of the others, and when the first craft nosed into shore, both Rena and Travis leaped out and came running forward. Maggie grabbed Rena, and the two women hugged, and Pete did the same with Travis.

There were several native men on the other boat. She did not see the other crew members who had left, however, and knew that something had happened.

"Welcome home," Karl Benson cried out. He gripped Travis's hand warmly and then went to Rena. "You look well," he said.

Indeed, Travis and Rena both looked well. They were obviously strong and fit.

Travis said, "It's good to see all of you. I can't tell you how we've missed you."

"Why did you wait so long to return?" Professor Dekker asked. "We've all been worried sick about you."

"That's right," Dalton added. "We thought maybe the storm on that first day might have gotten you."

"It almost did, Dalton," Chip said.

"But the Lord brought us through it," Rena chimed in. She turned and spoke to Chief Lomu, who was standing off to one side. She spoke in the native's language, and he came forward at once.

"You've learned to speak their language," Meredith said. "How wonderful!"

"It's not hard," Travis said, grinning. "If a dummy like me can learn it, anybody can."

Chief Lomu spoke, and Travis interpreted. "He says he's got a surprise for you."

Chief Lomu spoke at Travis's nod, and it was Rena who interpreted. "I have come to invite my brothers and sisters to my home. I am now a believer in Jesus. You must come and help us learn the ways of the Father above."

For a moment the only sound was the wash of the waves and the cry of the gulls overhead. Then the professor went forward and took the chief's hand. His eyes were glistening. "I am so happy for you, my dear brother."

Others crowded around the chief, and finally Rena said, "I hope you are all ready to move."

"Are we really going to the other island?" Maggie said.

"Yes. It's much larger than this, and we brought two

boats so that we can take everything we want to carry back with us."

"That's right. We need every hand now. We're going to build a church."

"Tell us all about this, Travis," Karl said. "It's the most wonderful thing I've ever heard."

"Well, one thing hasn't changed. No ship has ever come to the chief's island, but there is plenty of missionary work to be done right there."

"What about Novak and the other sailors?" Shep asked.

"Novak built a boat of his own and decided to try to get back to civilization. He left more than two months ago. We haven't heard anything, of course."

Oscar said, "What about Charlie and Lars?"

"Not very good news there. Charlie got into a fight with a native over a woman. Charlie shot the man and killed him, and the man's brother cut Charlie's throat. Lars is still on the island."

"I think he's beginning to listen to the Gospel," Rena added. "There's still hope for him."

Rena went over to where Abigail was standing. "Look at that baby!" she said. "Isn't he beautiful! And he's getting so big!" She took Michael and hugged him and kissed his fat cheek, and he gurgled with happiness. "You'll have lots of other babies to play with and grow up with there."

"That's wonderful," Abigail said. "It'll be so nice to have some other children around. He'll be needing playmates before we know it."

"Well, we'll have plenty of company where we're going," Rena said with a smile. "Now it's time to start packing."

★　★　★

The rhythm of the paddles as they struck the water punctuated the sound of the wind as it pushed at the two catamarans. Pete and Lanie were sitting together, Pete resting from his turn at the oars. Both craft were laden with materials and animals that they were taking with them. Lanie shook her head. "We had to leave so much behind."

"We can come back for it," Pete said. He put his arm around Lanie and asked, "Are you happy?"

Lanie took his hand and held it in both of hers. "Yes, I am."

"Not as happy as you *will* be."

Lanie turned to Pete and saw that he was smiling at her. "What do you mean?"

"Well, after you're married to me, you'll be happier than you can dream." A mischievous look came over his face, and he said, "An old fortune teller once told me that the woman I married would be the happiest woman in all the world."

Lanie laughed aloud. Pete was not a great talker, but she had found out that he had a dry wit that delighted her.

She said, "I know what. Let's make our announcement right now."

All the missionaries were in the same boat, as well as the sailors. The natives and Chief Lomu were in the other boat. "You want me to tell everyone?"

"I expect they already know, Pete. I told Rena a long time ago, and I imagine word has gotten around."

"Well, we'll make it official." He stood up in the boat and called out loudly, "Attention, everyone! I have an announcement to make."

Those who could turned his way, although the paddling did not stop and the rhythm remained the same.

"I wish to announce the engagement of Miss Lanie MacKay to Peter Alford."

Happy cries went up as the missionaries dropped their oars and began to applaud. It broke the rhythm of the boat, which fell back, but no one seemed to care.

After a round of congratulations, Maggie piped up, "I have an announcement too." She looked across at Shep, who was staring at her. She stepped over to him and said, "I wish to announce that Miss Margaret Smith is engaged to Mr. Shepard Riggs. All are invited to the wedding." Shep's jaw dropped. "Now you can't get out of it, Shep."

Shep suddenly laughed. He stood up and took Maggie in his arms. "Who wants to get out of it?"

Travis looked at Rena, and he saw her happiness. Something passed between them, but neither spoke.

Oscar Blevins left his post to shake Shep's hand. "You got a fine woman there, Shep. Be good to her."

"I will, Oscar. You better know it."

"All right. Let's get these oars going," Barkley said loudly. "This ain't a ship we're on, it's a doggone matrimonial bureau! Get cracking, now! Let's see a little life in you lovers."

The oars picked up the beat, and Shep whispered to Maggie, "I didn't even ask you."

"You never would have, Shep."

"I wouldn't have had the nerve."

"You're not sorry, are you?"

"Not a bit of it." He squeezed her hand and said, "I got a lot to learn about bein' a good husband."

"We'll teach each other," Maggie said, a contented smile flowing from her. She looked out at the water and said, "I'll be so glad when we get to our new home."

# CHAPTER TWENTY-FOUR

# HEAVEN'S MYSTERIES

★ ★ ★

Travis sat beside Rena cross-legged, and she had her feet tucked in under her. He had to lean forward to speak to her to be heard over the babble of voices. "Some wedding, huh?" he said. "I don't believe there was ever a noisier one."

"The people are so happy." Rena leaned closer to him, her shoulder pressed against his. "And the brides are both so beautiful."

The two were sitting in the midst of a large open space. The ground was covered with mats that were loaded with food of all kinds, some of which Travis and Rena did not recognize.

"These folks really know how to cook up a feast. I think Oscar's in heaven learning all these new dishes."

Rena, however, was focused on Maggie and Lanie. They were standing off to one side, surrounded by a group of young native girls who were chattering at them like magpies. "They're so radiant, aren't they, Travis?"

"Yes, they are, and the grooms look almost as happy." He turned his head to take a look at Shep and Pete. Pete towered over Shep, and both were surrounded by the young men of the island.

In the month since the missionaries had all settled in to the island, there had been other trips to bring the rest of the animals, tools, and supplies. The marriage celebration had been a week in preparation.

"You know, you'd think the brides would be nervous, but I believe Shep and Pete have got them beat."

"Oh, they're all so happy! Isn't it wonderful, Travis?"

Rena's eyes glowed, and a smile turned her lips up at the corners. Her skin was tanned golden by the tropical sun, and Travis could see a faint trace of freckles across the bridge of her nose. "Did you know you have freckles?" he said as he tapped her nose.

"Do I? I know I had them when I was just a little girl. They horrified me. I tried to wash them off. Nearly scrubbed my face raw."

"Well, don't do that. They look fine."

Travis looked up. "I think the wedding is about to begin."

Captain Barkley was able to walk now with a cane, and he smiled as he limped to the front of the crowd and held up his hand for silence. "I think it's time to get these young people married up," he announced. He looked over and said, "Travis, you and Rena come get this ceremony under way."

Travis rose and helped Rena to her feet. They went to stand beside the captain, and Rena sang two songs, each one twice—once in English and once in the language of the islanders. The natives loved her singing, and after each song there was tremendous applause.

When the applause died down, Travis said quietly, "It's always a holy moment when a man and a woman come before God to join themselves together." Travis interpreted for himself, speaking first in English and then putting his words as best he could into the language of the dark-skinned people who listened to him. "Our God has told us that a marriage is something that lasts as long as they both shall live. It is said that the woman should obey the man exactly as a man should obey God, and it is said that a man should love his wife as Christ loved the church and gave himself for it."

Travis paused and smiled at the two brides and two grooms standing before him. "There are very few things that last a lifetime in this world. Most things get old or broken or worn out and cast away, but God has given us this one thing that's meant to last a lifetime. As long as you two are faithful, you will be one flesh."

Rena was absolutely still, drinking in Travis's words. She felt a tug in her heart as he spoke of marriage and love in such gentle tones. She had never known a man who spoke so reverently about marriage.

Finally Travis said, "Shepard and Lanie, Margaret and Peter, I want you to hold hands as you kneel down and commit yourselves to each other. Before the captain asks you to say your vows, we're going to pray that God will keep you in a state of holy love for one another."

The two couples knelt down, and Travis prayed a beautiful prayer. When it was ended, he said, "All right, Captain. Come and tie the knot."

Captain Barkley had agreed to officiate at the marriage ceremony, although he had warned them he had never married anyone before. But all the women had attended enough weddings that they knew all the words to the ceremony. They had written them out, and Travis had seen to it that the captain had memorized them.

Now Captain Barkley said, "We are gathered together in the sight of God and in the face of this company to join this man and this woman in holy matrimony. . . ."

The captain performed magnificently, and he concluded, "I now pronounce you, Shepard and Margaret, husband and wife. And I pronounce you, Peter and Lanie, husband and wife—" He laughed aloud and said, "You may kiss the brides."

Both men put their arms around their new wives and kissed them thoroughly, to the pleased applause and shouts of the crowd. Then Travis and Rena went toward them, followed by the others, and soon the couples were being hugged and kissed and congratulated in two languages.

"There's going to be a lot of eating and, I'm afraid, drinking going on now," Travis whispered to Rena. "Let's go down to the beach."

"All right, Travis."

The two left the celebrants and walked through the underbrush on the narrow beaten path down to the beach. The sea was calm and as still as they had ever seen it, and they began walking slowly along the sand. From time to time crabs would scurry in front of them, and birds hopped along seeking food. Overhead the gulls, as always, uttered their harsh cries and swooped down toward them.

"That was a beautiful wedding, wasn't it, Travis?"

"Yes, it was."

Rena was strangely silent. Travis stopped and picked up a smooth rock and skipped it into the ocean.

As he picked up another, Rena said, "You believe very strongly in marriage."

"Why, of course. Don't you?"

"Oh yes. I just never heard anyone put it so clearly as you did."

"I guess I'm pretty set in my ways."

"Did you mean what you said about a man and a woman being joined together as long as they live?"

Travis looked at her with surprise. "Of course."

"Not everybody agrees with that."

"But you do, don't you?"

Rena smiled and shook her hair back in a graceful motion. "Yes, I do," she said quietly.

Travis was quiet for so long that Rena finally asked, "What are you thinking about, Travis?"

"About marriage. It's one of those things that no one can know what it's like until they're actually in it. At times I've thought that it must be like becoming a Christian. You can tell people what it's like in your own experience, but they won't really know for themselves until they trust in Christ and begin to walk in the Spirit. Marriage is a walk of faith."

"I never thought of it like that, but I believe you're right."

"It's easy enough to get married," Travis said with a grin. "I could become a husband in just a few minutes. But I'm afraid it would take me a lifetime to learn how to be the husband God would want me to become."

"That's true, isn't it? My father and mother had a beautiful marriage, but Dad told me one time he had to unlearn a lot of habits. He said he was selfish, and finally he learned the way to be happy was to make Mother happy. So that's what he did."

"That makes sense." He turned to her and said, "I guess you know how I feel about you, Rena."

She stood very still, looking up at him with trembling lips. "How *do* you feel, Travis? A woman needs to hear it said out loud."

"Why, I love you. I have for a long time."

"Not at first you didn't." She smiled at the memory. "Who could love a spoiled brat like I was?"

"Well, that's all in the past. The woman I love now is a royal handmaid," Travis said with a grin. Travis reached out and took her by the shoulders, his face turning serious. "I want you to marry me. I want us to be man and wife, and I promise that I'll love you as Christ loved the church and gave himself for it. No matter what happens, I'll love you, even if you get sick. When you get wrinkles in that beautiful face of yours, I'll love you then. No matter what, I'll always love you."

Tears flooded Rena's eyes as the simplicity of his declaration went straight to her heart. With no hesitation, she reached up and put her arms around him, her expression sweet. She had known for some time that she loved him.

Travis drew her close and lowered his lips to hers. Her kiss stirred him as he had never known a woman could stir him. She was like the sweetest fragrance or the most moving melody imaginable. It was like falling into softness. "Let's love each other all of our days," he whispered after he pulled away.

"All of our days."

Rena laid her head against his chest, and he held her tightly. She knew that this love was something she had been searching for all of her life. Finally she lifted her head and said, "Let's never lose each other, Travis."

"We never will."

The two of them turned and began to walk along the shore. They remained silent for several minutes, too full of emotion for speech. "Shall we tell the others?" she asked.

"Whatever you want."

★　★　★

By late afternoon the wedding feast had broken up as people went back to their everyday affairs. Travis and Rena had returned to the village but now found themselves rest-less. "Let's go back to the beach," she suggested.

"You just want more kisses and more sweet talk, don't you?" Travis said with a grin.

Rena smiled at his teasing. "That's right. I will require a great deal of that."

"You should marry a poet, then."

"I can teach you," Rena quipped.

The two left hand in hand and went back to the beach. The sun was beginning to sink into the west, illuminating the sky and water with its usual tropical brilliance. Even though they had enjoyed the sight many times now, its beauty and splendor still took their breath away.

The two of them walked along, Rena stopping from time to time to pick up a shell. She found herself talking nonstop and finally said, "I'm babbling like a crazy woman."

"I guess I'll have to put up with it for the next fifty years or so."

"Yes, you will. I want something put in the wedding cer-emony when the captain marries us."

"What?"

"I want him to put a promise in there that you'll tell me

you love me every day, even when we're fighting."

"Fighting! We'll never fight."

"That's what you think!" Rena laughed shortly. "We'll have some hard times."

"I guess you're right. You're pretty cantankerous. Okay, I'll ask the captain to put that in the vows. Does that only work one way?"

"What do you mean?"

"I mean, do you have to tell me you love me every day too?"

"Of course. And let's agree never to go to sleep mad at each other."

He laughed. "What do you mean by that, Rena? What if a fuss lasts two or three days?"

"Then we don't sleep. We stay awake until we both say we're sorry and make up."

Travis rubbed his beard and grinned. "A fella could miss a lot of sleep like that."

"Will you do it?"

"Oh, we don't have to put it in the wedding vows. Let's just promise each other now."

"All right."

Rena laughed again. "We're making up all sorts of rules for ourselves, aren't we?"

"Not a bad idea."

"I'm not sure it always works that way. People can make lots of plans, but then they don't always work out like they want."

Travis seized her and spun her around. "*You're* what I want! God has given me two great gifts. One is salvation in Jesus and the other is a woman to love for the rest of my life. That's all a man needs, Rena, and I've got them both."

He kissed her then, and she clung to him. Finally she pushed him away breathlessly. "That's enough of that. Come along. Let's walk some more."

They walked for no more than ten minutes when suddenly Travis halted. "Do you hear something?"

Rena looked at him with surprise. "No . . . what do you hear?"

"I don't know."

The two stood absolutely still, straining to hear, and suddenly Travis whirled and pointed out toward the ocean. He yelled, "Look!" And when Rena's eyes turned to follow his gesture, she saw a dot in the sky and heard a faint buzzing. She grabbed Travis's arm with both hands and held on to him.

"Travis," she whispered, "it's a plane!"

"Yes, it is!" He pulled away from her and began dancing around, waving his arms. "Here we are!" he yelled. "Look, here we are!"

Rena laughed. "They can't hear you." But she could not resist joining in and began waving her arms and crying out too.

The dot became larger, and suddenly the plane dipped and banked to one side.

"They've seen us!" Travis yelled. "Look, they've seen us!"

"What kind of an airplane is that? I've never seen one like it," Rena said.

"Why, it looks like a catamaran with an airplane on top of it. Look, Rena, they're landing!"

The plane swooped down for a landing. It touched the water, bounced once, and then settled onto the ocean, taking a long distance to stop. Travis and Rena watched speechless, holding each other.

"We're saved, sweetheart!" Travis said.

"It's a miracle!"

"I've been praying for a miracle to drop out of heaven, and one literally did. Look, they're putting a boat out."

The plane had come to rest about a hundred yards from shore. A door opened, and a small rubber boat was released. Two people got in it and began to paddle. "I can't believe it," he whispered. "You see who that is?"

Rena shaded her eyes and suddenly gasped. "It's my dad!" she cried.

"And do you see who the other one is? It's Cerny Novak."

The two stood at the edge of the water, and as soon as the small boat was close, they began calling out. Rena ran into the water, and Loren Matthews jumped out of the boat, crying, "Rena—Rena!"

Rena ran to meet him as fast as she could in the water. He grabbed her and held her so tightly she could barely breathe. "I found you, Rena! I found you!"

By now Travis was by their side too, and Cerny Novak leaped out of the boat to pull it onto the beach. As Travis grabbed the boat to help him, he was grinning broadly. "You son of a gun, you did it!"

"I reckon those prayers of yours must have done some good," Cerny said as he put out his hand to Travis. "You're not going to believe this, but I'm on the glory road now." He laughed aloud. "I thought I was a goner, but God put me in the right place at the right time."

By this time the shore was filled with people, natives and missionaries alike, all hurrying and shouting and babbling. "Dad, come on."

She pulled him onto the shore, and he was met by Captain Barkley, who was smiling broadly. "Well, you took long enough to get here, Loren."

"Sorry about that, Caleb."

Rena would not let go of her father. She clung to his arm as he greeted the others, and Novak was greeted as well, especially by Shep and Oscar and Chip.

Oscar shook his head. "Never thought I'd see you again, Cerny."

"Well, I was about ready to die, but God had other ideas. Wait'll you hear what happened."

The group started moving inland, and Loren said, "Cerny, will you go back and tell Captain Williams and the copilot we need to pull the plane in? We're going to be here for a while. I imagine we can get something to eat and maybe a dry place to spend the night."

"Right, Captain," Cerny said.

The group moved as a mass, everyone talking at once, but Travis stopped Loren by saying, "Mr. Matthews, let's get one thing straight right now."

Surprised, Loren turned and said, "What's that, Travis?"

"I want permission to court your daughter."

Loren's eyes opened wide, and he turned to face Rena, who was still holding on to his arm. "Is that the way it is, Rena?"

"Yes, it is, Dad. I love him with all my heart. He's the best man I've ever known."

Loren kissed his daughter and hugged her firmly. He put his hand out to Travis. "All right, son, you come courting. And I'll dance at your wedding."

The crowd pulled Loren away, and Travis took Rena's hand, holding her back. They lingered behind until the voices grew faint; then he turned to her and said, "You know how God has promised in the book of Romans that He will turn any situation to good?"

She smiled up at him. "How many times have we quoted that verse to each other this past year? 'And we know that all things work together for good to them that love God, to them who are the called according to his purpose.'"

"Do you believe that, Rena?"

"How could I not, when I look at all the tragedy and heartache we've suffered together and how such joy and happiness have come out of it? Who could have done this other than God?"

"One could almost believe that He made this all happen on purpose—just to bring the two of us together."

Rena touched his cheek tenderly and said, "You're right. I could almost believe it."

Travis wrapped his arms around her and held her close. "It is a great mystery to me how God could have done this thing. And whether He meant for it all to happen exactly this way, we'll never know. But I do know this—nothing happens in our lives that is out of His control. He has brought you into my life for a purpose. We would never have known each other without all this hardship, but I believe He means for us to be together now."

Rena laughed and squeezed him tightly. "I think you're right," she said. "Marriages *are* made in heaven."

Travis lowered his head and kissed her, and then the two turned and made their way to where the joyous sounds of laughter filled the air.

# HISTORICAL FICTION
# READERS WILL TREASURE!

## You'll Love This Heroine With a Heart for Justice

Following fast on the beloved SHANNON SAGA, Kit Shannon returns for more dramatic law cases, more romance, and more 1900s Los Angeles history. Engaged to a man who may be more than he appears and faced with some of the toughest cases in her life, Kit now must struggle to preserve her fight for justice against those who would stop her.

THE TRIALS OF KIT SHANNON by James Scott Bell
*A Greater Glory • A Higher Justice • A Certain Truth*

## Return to Lowell With Tracie Peterson and Judith Miller

A Southern belle's journey north opens her eyes to illusions of her genteel life and puts her heart into danger when a ruthless cad sees an opportunity to use her trust as a pawn for his own gain. Forced to rely on her own strengths, Jasmine Wainwright finds unknown courage and faith in this wonderful opening novel in Tracie Peterson and Judith Miller's new LIGHTS OF LOWELL saga.

*A Tapestry of Hope*